His Lordship's Wayward Wife: A Kinky Historical Romance
Written by Jolynn Raymond

Jolynn Raymond's Websites

My Books on Amazon:
http://www.amazon.com/Jolynn-Raymond

Jolynn Raymond's Dark Obsessions:
http://jolynnraymond.com

Dark Obsessions is an informational/educational BDSM Forum. Feel free to comment and write me. Email me at: jolynnraymond@gmail.com

My fan page on Facebook:
https://www.facebook.com/JolynnRaymond

Follow me on Twitter:
https://twitter.com/JolynnRaymond

Prologue

England 1802

The library of the manor house held something far more alluring than books on the damp autumn afternoon. A fire blazed in a hearth crowned by a magnificent oil portrait of the Lord of the manor, chasing away the chill of the day. Blue white pipe smoke drifted through the air creating a richly scented haze that reflected off the glow of the lamps throughout, to provide ample light for each man there to see the others and their lovely playthings.

The men, fifteen in all, were seated in large, exquisitely carved chairs arranged in a circle, and the women, fifteen as well knelt nude at their feet. Some were being absently stroked or played with, some simply stayed frozen in place at the side of their husbands. A number of women had nipples that were clamped, while others bore the marks of ownership left by their master upon their skin. One unfortunate woman knelt with her bottom thrust into the air, hands holding her cheeks wide open to expose a crinkled hole that was red and inflamed from torment, for those in the library to see.

All wore collars and leads as if they were dogs, and all were silent, even the one whose husband was twisting and tugging at her nipples in a manner that had to be painful, and the one who wept silently from shame. They were the wives of the Order of Exalted Blackguards, and their purpose in life was to see to the every need of the man they had wed, be it sexual, sadistic, or lewd, and though the discussion that was taking place concerned their daughters, none would dare utter a sound.

A gentleman in their midst, Gabriel, was speaking in an effort to convince the others that a motion that had been purposed was sheer folly. He was adamant in his stance, and was, therefore, taking it upon himself to lead the discussion. One of the men in their Order had put forth the suggestion that their daughters be raised in a manner that would allow them to see what life would bring them from the start. Not that they should be trained or touched, but that they bear witness to the everyday lives their mothers lived. He felt a level of complete submission could be obtained more readily if they were aware of how their mothers were kept nude, well disciplined, and concerned only with pleasing their husbands. Gabriel disagreed, and despite his best efforts to keep the conversation focused, it was straying into talk of training methods and new debauchery, as often was the case when the fifteen of them met. He knew he needed to bring them back to the point at hand, so Gabriel cleared his throat and raised his voice over the din.

"Gentlemen. Gentlemen. It isn't our wives we've come here to discuss. While I enjoy hearing fresh ideas, our daughters are what we need to agree upon here and now. They are the topic at hand."

The other men in the room nodded their agreement with Gabriel's words, settling back into silence. Gabriel reached over and stroked his wife's bowed head, the show of affection one might expect to be given to one's dog, but it was received with a small shiver of pleasure nonetheless. The woman remained silent, hands out before her, palms up, the end of her leash lying across them, stock-still. She would remain so until given the command that would allow her to move once more.

Another in the group removed his pipe from his mouth and shook his head as blue-white smoke puffed from his mouth. "There are some who would feel it was their business to interfere if word got out, be it our daughters or our wives they heard whispered about. The church elders in all their piety would call me a heathen or worse because of the sex acts Mildred performs as well as taking offense to the fact that she goes about unclothed for all to see."

Gabriel spoke up again, seizing the opportunity to close the conversation once and for all with a vote that favored his opinion. "We all know the church would proclaim us sinners for our way of life. It's for that very reason we keep our activities a secret. The question before us concerns our girl children. In my opinion, it has only one possible conclusion, still, I must ask you to decide if we should raise them unaware, or condition them from the start. My own are kept in the nursery wing and only brought forth when requested. I allow Abigail to visit of course. It's one of the few times she is allowed to dress. I know most of your households are run the same. No one takes an active hand in the raising of children; therefore, secrecy is easily maintained. The question is, should it be?"

Heads nodded in agreement so Gabriel pushed on, knowing actions could speak louder than words. He stood, snapping his fingers as he did so, causing his wife to scramble before him and unlace his breeches post haste. She took his cock in her mouth and began to suck in earnest as Gabriel's eyes met each of the men's in the room.

"Is this what we want to have revealed? Do we want condemnation because of this? My wife sucks my cock like a well-trained whore, and in my mind, that is as it should be. Do any of you disagree?"

Not a man could say yes as Gabriel grasped his wife's head by tangling his fingers in her hair and held her still as he pumped his cock in and out of her mouth, his member sliding effortlessly down her throat without gagging her. When his member was ridged and pulsing, he moved his hand to her cheek and stroked once. She again became stone still, her mouth open, Gabriel's cock resting on her tongue, shiny with spittle, the head red; the shaft marbled with blue veins. He drew his attention back to the men in the room before continuing, certain that his wife wouldn't move and inch.

"The girls are best kept unaware. While they have little contact with outsiders, our families are all subject to the whims of the crown. If summoned to court, we must go. A young lady who is well aware that her fate is one that involves lewd sex acts and strict chastisement is apt to let something slip if she finds herself among the gentry in London. Girls have loose tongues. Though kept under a vigilant eye, we would be unable to watch over them if the king decided one of our daughters was to become a handmaiden to the queen."

His hand once again moved to stroke his wife's cheek, this time doing so twice. The woman kneeling before him with hands clasped behind her back moved only her tongue at the silent command. She lifted and lowered it with Gabriel's hard cock still upon it, doing so repeatedly, waiting for another command. The other men watched with approval at the show of submission and the strength of the woman's tongue. All of their wives were trained in such a manner, their first obligation being to please their husbands sexually. The ability to suck and pleasure their master's cocks vitally important be it with their bums, mouths, or sexes.

After a full minute of making her husband's cock bob up and down with only her tongue, Gabriel stroked her cheek once in another silent signal. The woman immediately became motionless her mouth open Gabriel's cock resting on her tongue as drool dribbled down her chin.

"It is for this reason that I urge you to vote no. Keep them unaware until it's time for them to marry. Any of our sons will have the skill needed to tame his wife, especially if she has no hope of receiving help from her family. My Catherine will be kept ignorant of her fate until she is of age. I will then put her up before you, a maid in need of marrying and teaching."

Tired of waiting for his pleasure, Gabriel took his wife's hair in his hand and then gritted his teeth as his hips rocked faster, pumping into his wife's mouth as her cheeks sucked inward, and her bottom jiggled from the force of his actions. All at once he stopped, thrusting forward one last time as she began to slurp wildly. She hollowed her cheeks, milking the last drops of her husband's cum from his cock, and then cradled it in her hands as it softened, bathing it with her little pink tongue, cleaning him and paying homage to the man who was her master.

Across the room, the pipe smoker emitted a loud burst of laughter. Gabriel had proven his point most admirably. No one would wish to change their way of life or put how they chose to live in jeopardy. It was best the girls be kept ignorant. A girl should be trained when she was old enough to stand before the eligible men on her bargaining day and receive her first taste of what her life would be like. The methods they employed were very persuasive. She conformed and became the whore her husband wished, or her body was punished in any way he saw fit. Whether given to the best bidder like a slave or passed privately to her new husband when her father and the man in question came to an agreement. None had ever won her bid for freedom, none had been able to resist the life that was chosen her, and none were within earshot of those who would frown on their way of life without staying at her husband's side for strict supervision.

"All who agree with Gabriel say aye." The room echoed with the sound of all fifteen men proclaiming the word. The nude women were put into positions where they could either suck or be taken, as a gavel pounded announcing the official end of the meeting. The Order of Exultant Blackguards was in full agreement, there was nothing more to be said. It was time to take their pleasure.

Abingdon, England 1890

Chapter One

Claudia Rose Stafford picked at the roasted pheasant on her plate, one hand pushing the food about with her fork as the other gripped the linen napkin in her lap. She was struggling to remain silent and to sit up straight as her parents carried on yet another dull conversation. The meal was just like all the other boring dinners Claudia had sat through at their country manor in Abingdon, which was miles away from their townhome in London, where Claudia desperately longed to be.

Claudia was doing her best to remain attentive and act ladylike. She was well aware of the stern glances her father gave her every few minutes, and she didn't want to anger him. He'd been away on business in India for the last year, and a half and Claudia had taken full advantage of that fact, but now he was home, and her days of freedom had come to an end. Her mother had told him of her exploits and immoral behavior, and to say that he was angry was an understatement.

While her father was gone, her mother and her governess had lacked the ability to control her. She'd always been strong willed and became even more so after she discovered the power her body had over men. At first her father had been home to keep her new-found capability in check. Her father was keen to see a change in her almost at once, and took a strap to her the first time he caught her using her womanly wiles to outwit one of the stable boys, but once he had gone there had been no one strong enough to put a stop to her wild behavior.

Claudia had been a tall and gangly girl who was all legs, and had lacked any coordination or social grace. Her dark hair had always been a mess; her clothes more often than not dirty or torn from running about outside, catching frogs, climbing trees or engaging in other activities that always brought a scolding. She'd had no interest in needlepoint or playing the piano like young ladies were supposed to, and though her nurse reprimanded her, her parents hadn't forced her to change while she was still a young girl. It hadn't truly mattered before she was of the age where one was expected to act properly.

She'd been uncomfortable with her new curves and budding breasts when they first began to develop. Her changing body embarrassed her, and she was appalled when her mother declared it was high time she put away her childish pinafores and tomboy ways and begin wearing stays and mounds of skirts like the women of high society did.

Claudia had hated the contraption. It squeezed her waist and made her breasts more prominent in the ridiculous gowns she had to wear. All her objections fell silent when she began to notice the men and boys around her were looking at her in a whole new way.

The stable hands who had teased her and compared her to a clumsy newborn foal looked at her with desire and became tongue-tied. She caught the butler looking at her breasts when he brought her a post, his hand shaking as he held the tray, and Henry, a boy from the estate next to theirs, stopped tussling and climbing trees with her, and instead started calling her Miss. It had annoyed her until she saw how he would look her body up and down with yearning and agree to anything she asked.

All of them were suddenly eager to please and quick to do what she wanted, and Claudia found she liked her new ability very much. If they refused at first, she would touch their arm and smile oh, so pretty until the odd bulge appeared in their trousers. She'd been bold enough to ask her nurse about it, but the woman blushed five shades of scarlet and told her ladies didn't discuss such things. Her nurse had been replaced by a strict governess shortly after, but though the new woman tried; Claudia refused to be tamed.

It had been a glorious year and a half while her father was overseas. He was out of sight and therefore out of mind. She'd come out at last season's Debutant Ball at the age of seventeen and had very much enjoyed the social life in London, blissfully unaware of what her future truly held. It had been a wonderful time, going to the parties, the opera, and grand balls. The men told her she was beautiful and fell over themselves for a chance to dance with her or sit beside her and do their best to make her laugh with witty conversation.

She'd shunned the young men her mother invited over for dinner, not caring a wit that these were the men she was supposed to enchant because they were suitable marriage prospects. She deliberately behaved without any social graces and left them running for the door. She also made it a habit to sneak off without a chaperone with those men whom her mother deemed as unsuitable or dangerous. Claudia found these men much more fun than those who were perfect gentlemen. Their kisses were exciting. She simply smiled at her mother when she went on a tirade about the scandal Claudia had caused.

When the season was over, they came back to their country home in Abingdon and her fun came to a halt. While it was true, she could flirt with the stable hand or any one of the men who served them, it simply wasn't the same. She'd survived though, and was looking forward to this year's social season and being able to return to London, but that was before her father came home.

He'd been livid, and had taken a strap to her, lecturing her on how a proper lady was to behave, and that he simply refused to have a daughter who behaved in such a way. He'd punished her and asked over and over if she were still a virgin until finally accepting her repeated cries of yes. Her bottom had been sore and welted for days after, and she remembered the punishment each time she sat down.

Her mother was full of joy with her father being home. She doted on him made sure each detail of their home and meals met his demanding standards. Claudia had walked in on them in her father's study when her mother had been kneeling at her father's feet. It was bad enough that her mother was in such a position, but matters were made worse by the fact that her mother hadn't risen when caught in such a subservient pose. On the contrary, she bowed her head so her father could stroke her hair like a dog, and then bent low to kiss his feet. Claudia couldn't hide her sneer of disgust. That attitude had earned her another strapping, and after that she'd done her best to steer clear of her parents except for when she had to make an appearance at the table.

Now Claudia was sitting here, pushing her food about with her stomach in knots. The social season was beginning soon, and her father had made no mention of when they were going back to London. Claudia was dying to get away from this place where there was nothing to do and out from under her father's ever present eyes. True he'd be there in London to monitor her behavior, but his business kept him from attending all the events. She had received a post from her dearest friend and partner in crime, Marie, and knew she simply had to work up the nerve to ask when exactly her father intended for them to make the trip.

Her parents had just finished a discussion about replacing one of the maids, and, in the ensuing silence, Claudia finally saw her chance to tell her father of the post she'd received. Marie had written to inform Claudia that her family was already in London and that her father was holding a dinner party a week from Saturday. Claudia was certain their family's formal invitation which would have been addressed to her father, must have arrived, as well. It would be the perfect way to ask when they were finally going to go back to London.

"Father, I received a post from Marie today. She was wondering when we were going to arrive back in London."

"Are you looking forward to our return to the city?" Her father's gaze was steely as he asked the question.

"Yes Sir, very much. Marie's parents are hosting a dinner. I'm sure our family's invitation arrived along with my letter from her. Have you had a chance to see it, Father?"

"Yes, Claudia, I've seen it. I've replied that your mother and I will be in attendance."

Claudia blinked as she looked at her father. He must have simply omitted her name because she would go where her parents went.

"I see you are looking a bit perplexed my dear. Is there something wrong?" Now the steeliness had been replaced by a look of amusement.

"No Sir, I mean, well... You... You didn't say my name."

"Claudia it is unseemly to stammer, you know I expect you to behave like a lady."

"Yes, Sir, I apologize."

She didn't ask about attending the dinner again. There was something strange going on, but she didn't know what it was. She had an inkling it wasn't going to be to her liking though. Claudia very much disliked being in a position where she wasn't in charge, and the baiting by her father was maddening. That and the fact that her mother was staring at her with a smugly satisfied look on her face was very unnerving.

"Claudia, your time of rebellion has come to an end. I have been a permissive father while you were just a child, but I would be very negligent in my duties if I allowed you to continue with your scandalous behavior now that you are a young lady."

Her father paused and stared at her, his eyes glittering chips of ice. Claudia had a feeling she wasn't going to like what was to come. Was she going to be denied attendance at some of the parties because she'd behaved like a hellion last season?

"I assure you that I regret my behavior last season. It was wrong of me. I hope you'll find a way to forgive me."

Her father smiled, offering her a tidbit of hope, before delivering a devastating blow.

"It is my duty as your father; to make certain you are molded into a young lady and trained for your duty as a proper wife. You won't be attending the season in London this year Claudia; there is no reason for you to be there."

"Father, please; not the whole season. I promise I'll behave. I'll be ever so good if you allow me to come. I'll be respectable and act accordingly when you wish me to meet the gentlemen who are... "

Her father held up his hand as his eyes flared in anger.

"Silence! From here on out, you will speak when given permission. There is no reason to parade you before England's eligible bachelors. You will be wedding the Earl of Brighton." Her father paused to make certain she would hold her tongue as ordered while her mother stared at her, eyes dancing with amusement. Claudia felt as if the world had slipped away from under her feet, but she had sense enough to remain silent.

"You'll be taking the train to Brighton in the morning. Everything you need has been purchased and already packed. Once there, you will be met by a Miss Patton. She is the Headmistress at the finishing school you are going to attend. She is a no-nonsense woman who has quite a bit of experience turning wayward young women into proper ladies.

"Once there, you'll attend each session with the utmost compliance, and abide by their strict schedule and high expectations. This training will last for two weeks. The school and Headmistress Patton have assured me that they will be able to prepare you to be an accomplished and obedient wife.

"They have been my permission to use their more aggressive methods if you so much as speak one word of sass while in their presence, or perform any of the tasks required with anything but enthusiasm. Your future husband, Lord Nathaniel Tarrington, the Earl of Brighton, will supervise the second week of your training.

"When you have completed every aspect of your preparation to the standard that meets his Lordship's approval, you will be taken home and molded to his specifications. After that, I will wash my hands of you, Claudia.

"You will serve the Earl in a way that is befitting a dutiful bride, and do everything he desires, or suffer the consequences. Lord Tarrington will not put up with your abhorrent flirtatiousness or your belligerent manner. It would be in your best interest to learn quickly and never stray from the behavior and obedience he will expect."

Claudia sat for a moment with her mouth open in shock, unable to believe the events that were about to take place.

"Close your mouth or speak. I won't have you gaping like a cod. You have permission to reply."

Claudia's mind was a whirl. She wondered if perhaps she ought to slip off the train at some unknown station and flee the life her father had planned for her. How could she submit to becoming some rich old man's well-trained wife? As if reading her mind, her father squashed any hope she may have had.

"I will be accompanying you on the train and see that you settle in at the school. Papers will be signed giving my permission for you to wed the Earl. You have past the expected age for marrying, thanks to your abhorrent behavior last season. As your father, I will gladly give my approval, and supervise you as you sign a marriage pact with your future husband. Do you have any questions, Claudia?"

Claudia gulped as her eyes filled with unfamiliar tears. What was there to say? Her father would be handing her directly to the Headmistress and the Earl. Her fate was sealed. Somehow, she didn't think her feminine wiles would work with her husband to be.

"No, Sir."

"Very well then; Benjamin, bring the bottle of champagne I selected earlier. It's time to toast my daughter's betrothal."

Tears she couldn't hold back trickled down Claudia's cheeks, and she felt sick to her stomach. How had things gone so wrong? How could her father do such a thing? Her mother was watching Claudia with the same smirk of triumph that she'd had on her face since her father had declared his intentions. How could she? How could they?

Claudia stared at those sitting at the dinner table with her in shock, full of resentment for her parents. She never once thought about how she had brought her fate on herself, and therein lay the problem. Spoiled, beautiful, belligerent, wealthy, and once powerful, Claudia had had the world wrapped around her little finger. Her father knew she would continue to be blind to the consequences of her actions until taught differently. That was exactly where Head Mistress Patton and His Lordship the Earl came into play, for the earl had no intention of having a wayward wife.

Chapter Two

They woke Claudia before the sun had fully risen. Her mother accompanied by her maid opened the drapes to take advantage of the rising sun. Lizzie went about lighting the lamps on the dresser, and the one in Claudia's sitting room, while her mother unceremoniously pulled back the thick quilts, leaving Claudia clad only her nightdress. The action sufficiently put an end to the farce she'd been playing. It wasn't possible to feign sleep when one was freezing.

"Up with you now and I don't want to hear any sass."

Claudia peeped at her mother and again saw the smug look upon her face, yet chose to try and turn the situation around. Her mother ordinarily backed down when faced with opposition.

"Mother, no one besides the servants rise at such an hour. Leave me be and let me sleep. Lizzie, send Beatrice in to light a fire." Her tone was one that had an authoritative note. She sat up just long enough to grab the quilts and yank them from her mother's hand.

"I suppose you think the conversation during last night's supper was only a dream. I have news for you my spoiled girl. Your father will be leaving for the rail station in a little more than an hour. If you wish to be dressed and fed before your trip, you had better get out of bed. He will take you with him either way."

Claudia's eyes shifted as she watched her mother fling open her wardrobe and march back over to where she lay in bed.

"I should like it more if he has the butler toss you over his shoulder wearing nothing but that nightdress and toss you into the carriage, but it isn't up to me. You will either do as you're told or will be made to do as I tell you. You days of commanding people about are over. I had thought we could perhaps discuss what will be happening to you at the school and in the Earl's household, but I will by no means beg you to cooperate."

When Claudia made no move to get out of bed, her mother turned on her heel and motioned to her governess. "Come Lizzie, it appears that Claudia has chosen to be impudent yet again. Leave the lamp. She will have a light, but she won't have any warmth."

Her mother waited as Lizzie did as she asked. Then both women left Claudia alone in her bed, a puzzled frown upon her forehead.

The clock upon the mantle in her sitting room chimed, letting her know it was the ungodly hour of 6:00 in the morning. Claudia groaned, and then stretched, waiting for Beatrice to come and tend the fire, but as the minutes ticked passed Claudia began to realize that the conversation during last night's dinner was, in fact, real. No one was coming to light a fire. No one was coming to help her dress, and no one would be bringing tea and a biscuit. She was being denied all those niceties and realized she had better get out of bed if she didn't want then tossing her into the carriage in her nightdress.

The floor was cold, and she looked around for her slippers, but they couldn't find them. No one had set out her dressing gown either, and Claudia knew no one was going to. Did a life as the wife of Earl mean all the comforts she had become accustom to would be denied her?

The arrival of her maid with water for washing came immediately after a quick knock on the door. Beatrice filled her wash basin in silence and made no move to start a fire or fetch her dressing gown.

"Beatrice, bring me a pot of tea and some breakfast. If I'm to be out of bed at this hour, I need something to eat at the very least."

"I'm sorry Miss but the Master told me to assist you in dressing. I'm to do no more. You are to come to the dining room when you are ready."

"Honestly! This refusing to do things for me is quite ridiculous. I'll wear the blue silk with the long sleeves and the fox lined cape."

"Your wardrobe is empty aside from the gown your father provided. It, your underthings, and the wool cloak are all there is to wear."

"Very well. Set them out as I wash." Claudia quickly washed, muttering about the cold, then returned to her dressing room to find the plainest of gowns, a corset, and a chemise waiting for her. She stood still as Beatrice pulled the chemise over her head and then tightened her corset. The woman was about the help her into the plain wool dress when Claudia pointed out the fact that she was in need of bloomers.

Beatrice quickly put her hand up to her mouth to stifle a giggle at the outrage her very demanding mistress was feeling.

"Why are you snickering? Fetch me my underthings."

"What you see here was what I was instructed to dress you in." Claudia's palm itched to slap her maid. How dare the girl laugh at her plight? She brought her hand up to do as intended but stopped. Claudia sensed the slap would only cause trouble. In the end, she lowered her hand and fixed an icy stare at her maid.

"Never mind! Help me with the dress." Claudia was cold, tired, annoyed, and still stunned by what was happening. She stood still as Beatrice fastened the buttons up the back of her dress, and then tugged at the high neck that felt as if it went all the way up to her ears.

Beatrice helped her with woolen stockings shoes, and then slipped out the door, not wishing for any more confrontations. It had filled the maid with delight to see her mistress taken down a peg, but it was time to go. Her tasks were complete.

Claudia looked at herself in the dressing room mirror and scowled. She then put a hand to her hair and let out a sound of exasperation. The fool girl had left without helping with her hair. Claudia went to the vanity and saw a hairbrush along with a single hair ribbon. Muttering under her breath, she brushed her hair then tied it back with a ribbon, highly upset that she should have to wear her hair like a child.

She took one more look around her set of rooms, noting the emptiness of it all. The fact that all her clothes, powders and scents, jewelry and her hats were gone made her feel an acute sense of loss and foreboding. Claudia hoped they were stored in traveling trunks that were coming with her, but somehow she didn't think so. She fastened the simple cloak around her shoulders and proceeded downstairs, ignoring the tingle of fear running up her spine. She was strong and could take anything her father, the Headmistress, or her new husband had to dish out. She was Claudia Rose Stafford, and if they thought she would cower like a frightened rabbit, they had another thing coming.

Chapter Three

The train ride from Abingdon to Brighton was almost enough to weakened Claudia's resolve. Her father took the time to lecture her about how a proper wife must obey and serve her husband. He told her that he was quite disappointed with her for not cooperating that morning and missing the chance to listen to her mother about matters of submission and her requirements in the bedroom.

Claudia blushed when her father said the words. Despite her wild antics, there was a bit of propriety left inside her, and listening to her father talk about things that were so intimate was unnerving. They had private quarters, and so her father had no reluctance speaking of such things out loud. Therefore, the entire ride held a conversation that had her rattled long before they reached Brighton.

Headmistress Patton along with a footman were there to greet them when they arrived, and much to Claudia's dismay, only one trunk was loaded unto the waiting carriage. It was impossible for all her beautiful gowns, hats, and underthings to fit inside the one trunk. Perhaps her new husband intended to provide her with a new wardrobe. She certainly hoped the outfit she was wearing was only how she would be expected to dress at the finishing school.

After Miss Patton directed the loading of her trunk and joined them inside the carriage, she sat opposite Claudia and her father, eyeing her up and down with frank disapproval. Claudia couldn't figure out why this woman felt she failed in some manner, but she was certain from the looks of her that Headmistress Patton would inform her exactly why she was scowling.

Once the carriage was in motion, Miss Patton clasped her hands in her lap and raised her eyebrows as she stared at Claudia. Claudia stared right back. She was to be at this woman's mercy for the next couple of weeks, and Claudia thought their first conversation would set the tone. The woman looked formidable with her huge bosom, expansive hips, and shoulders that were wide enough to drive a team of oxen. Claudia decided the approach to take was that of someone who couldn't be intimidated.

"The proper response to such a frank look of disapproval would be to lower your eyes. You are an inferior here Miss Stafford. The sooner you understand that, the sooner you will be able to accept the training the Earl has requested."

"I hardly think the wife of an Earl would be subordinate to a school teacher."

"You are not the wife of an Earl just yet, and once you are, you will still be under my authority. Lord Tarrington is meeting us at the school. He wishes to give you the once over and tell you of his expectations. As your legal guardian, your father will sign the papers transferring all authority to his Lordship. The school's chaplain will then marry you."

"So my husband has decided he wants me home with him instead of spending two weeks at your little school. How lovely."

"Claudia, watch your tone." Her father had stayed silent, allowing the headmistress time to see how very insolent and spoiled his daughter truly was. This latest affront was unacceptable, and he couldn't allow it.

"I appreciate your assistance Mr. Stafford and understand your embarrassment over Claudia's behavior. As you well know, she will be instructed in the art of submission, which, of course, includes lessons in humility and showing proper respect. I assure you; her haughty insolence will soon be put to an end."

"Thank you, Miss Patton. I know I am partially to blame for her behavior."

"Nonsense; you were unable to attend to her due to your duties overseas. Mrs. Stafford did what she could. Perhaps it is for the best. Claudia has had a taste of freedom, so she will be more aware of exactly what is being denied her now. It takes time to meld some of them into the perfect wife. Think back to your wife's training. There were some difficult moments, but the school persevered, and she came to understand the way they should be. Is she not the perfect submissive wife?"

Her father relaxed into the cushions with a small smile upon his face. "Yes, Miss Patton, she most certainly is."

"This one will be too. She has no idea what's in store, and therefore she has the nerve to reply with sass. Once she becomes familiar with the consequences, she'll drop her smug attitude. Ah, here we are. I've arranged for tea in the parlor. Come along. Lord Tarrington will be waiting."

Her Father exited the carriage and then gave his hand to Miss Patton, who then stood by his side as he assisted Claudia. She stopped and gazed at the building that held the finishing school. It was an imposing gray stone building with sweeping steps leading to tall double doors which were being held open for them by the butler and footman. Claudia's father offered his arm to Miss Patton, and she took it with a smile but paused long enough to give Claudia a stern look and a warning.

"It will be in your best interest if you submit to all that is going to happen without tantrums or complaint. You are the only one here who thinks you deserving of anything. Mind me now, if you choose to act like a spoiled child, you will be treated like one. You future husband is inside. I'm certain you'll wish to make a good impression. After all, your fate is in his hands."

Claudia was at a loss for words. Miss Patton sounded quite ominous. She couldn't imagine how being married and then spending time at a finishing school learning how to manage a household, plan parties, and make menus her husband approved of could be so hard to learn. Seriously, everyone was looking at her as if she were a calf brought to slaughter.

"I shall be on my best behavior."

Miss Patton sniffed and lifted her chin before turning back to her father and walking up the steps, leaving Claudia to follow or be left standing alone.

The entryway was opulent as was the parlor, leaving Claudia to hope that she would be living in the style she was accustomed to. A handsome gentleman who appeared to be in his mid-thirties was leaning against the fireplace mantle. His eyes were dark and cold; his hair thick and wavy reaching to top of his collar; his lips turned up into the barest of smiles as he stood and looked over every inch of Claudia. He made no move to come closer, nor showed any polite greeting. Claudia's heart beat faster in her chest. She certainly could have done much worse. Some of her friends had been married to ugly old men. She tilted her head in a greeting, but the Earl still did not respond.

When he finished appraising his new bride, Lord Tarrington came forward and kissed Miss Patton's hand, then shook hands with Claudia's father and slapped him on the back. It was obvious the two knew each other. From what Miss Patton said, Claudia thought her mother must have attended school here.

"She's quite lovely, just as you said she was. How old are you girl?"

Girl? Did he call her girl? Claudia drew her eyebrows beginning to frown and pursed her lips. She had an acerbic reply on her tongue but remembered Miss Patton's warning. She also had no desire to embarrass her father.

"I'll be eighteen in three days."

"Your father tells me you attended your debutant ball last season but that your behavior prohibited any marriage match. I suppose that's lucky for me, but it doesn't say much for your character, Claudia."

His use of her first name was overly familiar seeing as they'd just met, and Claudia thought it quite rude for him to bring up her suitors from last season.

"I will admit to making poor choices in my behavior, My Lord. I am older now, and I can assure you I am quite ready to be a proper wife."

Lord Tarrington laughed out loud, making Claudia flush scarlet in outrage.

"My dear, trust me when I say you most certainly are not, but you will be. Miss Patton, is the doctor here? We can't proceed with the marriage without him."

"Yes, of course, my Lord. Right this way, please."

"Doctor?" Claudia looked to her father, but he only nodded and took her elbow in his hand, steering her after Miss Patton and Lord Tarrington.

They all entered a room that had a mix of things from both a study and a physician's office. The man in question rose, and like everyone else, looked Claudia up and down, appraisingly. She was beginning to feel like a horse at auction. Her father escorted Miss Patton to a chair, and then sat as Lord Tarrington took a chair on the other side of the headmistress.

Claudia stood for a moment, unsure what to do. Those around her seemed to have lost their common courtesies. She glanced about but before she could move any further, the man behind the oak desk beckoned for her.

"Come here girl." Claudia had to bite her tongue. Here was another man who felt it was alright to address her as 'girl'. She took slow steps towards the desk, but he stood and walked over to a bench type table with a padded top. "No, no, here. Come here. How do you think I will inspect you if you are standing before my desk?"

"I... inspect?" Claudia looked at Lord Tarrington, her father, and then Miss Patton. All stared at her with a chilling glare that told her none held even a shred of sympathy at her distress. She then looked about for a privacy screen or something to put between her and those who were staring at her.

Her father made a sound of exasperation, aggravated at her lack of cooperation. "Claudia, the doctor is going to examine you before Lord Tarrington marries you. Your mother advised you to get out of bed so the two of you could talk, but you weren't of the mind to listen. If you had been less proud and insolent, you would know about everything that's going to take place."

Miss Patton chimed in right as her father finished. "You are to be married in a short while. The Earl is an important man. He has no desire to wed a woman who has been soiled. Dr. Lancolm will examine you now to make certain your virginity is intact."

"But... Right here?"

Sparing her father any more irritation, Miss Patton answered. The smug look on the woman's face was enough to make Claudia want to give the Headmistress a tongue lashing right back, but she refrained. Claudia felt as if things were already turning from bad to worse all on their own without the help of her usual sass.

"Yes right here, you fool girl. Surely you aren't so daft as to think he can examine you with your clothing on. Remove your dress and underthings."

Claudia tilted her head up a notch, and her nostrils flared with indignation. "I would like a privacy screen." She said the words without a hint of insolence, but they were firmly stated. How on Earth did these people think she would manage to strip in front of them?

Lord Tarrington rose from his seat and grabbed Claudia by one arm, spinning her, so she was facing him. He put a hand under her chin and forced her head back, so she was looking into his eyes. His fingers pinched, not hard enough to bruise, but certainly hard enough to make sure he had her attention.

His eyes bore into her, making a shiver run down Claudia's spine. Her own opened in shock as he held her gaze, his expression saying far more than the words that accompanied it.

"You are going to turn around and I am going to unfasten your gown. We will continue with your disrobing until you are bare. You have no rights, and you are not permitted to refuse. In a half hours' time, you will be my wife, and this is just the first of many lessons you will learn in obedience. Now turn around, Claudia."

Claudia was trembling, not so much out of fear, though there was that, but because Lord Tarrington had a presence that made one very unsure of oneself. She knew instinctively that it wouldn't be wise to anger him. She took a deep breath and then turned around, her head still held high. Just because those around her were trying to bully her, that didn't mean they had robbed her of her pride.

She felt Lord Tarrington's hand as he ran it down her back and over her bottom, and had to bite her lip to keep from snapping at him. He then moved her hair over one shoulder and put his hands at the top of her gown inside the neckline. With a yank he separated the two sides of the dress, the tiny buttons popping off and rolling upon the floor. Claudia squeaked and made a move to turn, but Lord Tarrington put one hand on her shoulder and issued a quiet but sinister 'no'.

The Earl of Brighton then proceeded to tug her dress forward and down, exposing her arms, her chemise, and her corset. As he yanked further, she was left standing in her knee length chemise and her corset. He turned her just a bit, so she was facing Miss Patton and her father, then unlaced the contraption and tossed it to the side.

"There are to be no more of these Miss Patton."

"Yes, Your Lordship."

After divesting her of the corset, he made quick work of her chemise, to leave her standing nude for all to see in just her woolen stockings. Claudia was shocked and appalled. Tears filled her eyes, but she blinked them back. She would not allow them to see her cry.

Lord Tarrington ran a hand over her bottom then pushed his fingers between her tightly pressed knees and slapped each inner thigh to force her to stand with her legs open. He grabbed her hands and then held them behind her back with one hand and moved to appraise his soon to be wife.

He cupped each breast and rolled the nipples between his thumb and forefinger. The buds stiffened, and she let out a little squeak when he continued until a jolt of pleasure traveled between her nipples and the place between her legs. She had allowed the men who chased after her a few quick squeezes before shoving their hands away, but they had never made her feel like this.

"She's thin, and her breasts are small, but I like them. Ones that are large remind me of a cow's teats. She's all legs isn't she? Like a beautiful race horse." the last comment was said with a hint of a smile, and Claudia damned herself for being pleased that he approved of her appearance.

Her moment of pleasure was short lived however when his hand touched the dark brown curls where her legs met. Claudia's eyes grew large as saucers when he touched her there. It was an unheard of thing to do, and in front of her father no less.

"Remove this, but this," he toyed with one of the long brown locks of hair that fell over her shoulder. "This is not to be cut."

"Understood My Lord."

Lord Tarrington slipped a finger between her vaginal lips and gave her a wicked grin as his finger met the slippery evidence that her body had responded to his toying with her nipples. He stroked her clit for just a second, causing her to shiver, and then removed his probing finger and held it up for all to see. "I'm delighted Mr. Stafford. Nice and wet already. She's a whore at heart."

"Wonderful! She's just like her mother. I certainly had my suspicions from her wanton behavior. Let's hope she's still pure. She swore to me that she was."

"We shall know soon enough. Claudia my dear, you are to lie on your back on the table, feet up, legs spread. Tell me girl, have you let a man rut between those beautiful thighs?"

"I... No!"

"That's a very good answer Claudia, because you belong to me. I would be quite upset if the doctor didn't find evidence of your virginity. Your mother spoke of your brazen habit of flirting with men who were considered improper. From now on you will not speak to another man other than your father, and you will never, ever, flirt. Your womanly wiles may have provided entertainment in London, but this is Brighton, and I am Lord here.

Claudia shivered both from the cold and the sinister tone of his words. He smacked her bottom hard, making her gasp and then spun her around. "I said go to the table and lie on your back. Do it now!"

Claudia moved to obey, the tears again threatening to spill over. She lay back with her eyes tightly shut. The table was quite wide, much more so than her hips. The doctor flipped up a pole on each end of the table. Then, to her utter dismay, took her legs one at a time and put her feet in the loops that hung from the top of them. She was spread so wide open in front of her father, her future husband, and Miss Patton, that the feeling she felt went beyond mortification.

Claudia lay there in shock. She was outraged but at a loss for words. Flinging a verbal tirade at these people wasn't going to help matters. She had never felt so vulnerable. The doctor spread some oil between her legs and on his finger, then opened her vaginal lips wide and ever so carefully slid his finger inside her.

Claudia let out a shriek, not because it caused her great pain, but because she was so very humiliated and shocked. She bit her lip, and the doctor move gently inside her. He gazed down at her as he did, smiling at her discomfort and embarrassment.

"It's there; she's intact. You'll be the first."

Lord Tarrington came to the table and drizzled a bit of oil in his palm and slicked up a finger. The doctor stood back and to Claudia's horror Lord Tarrington held her lips wide with one hand and began to strum his finger rapidly over her clitoris with the other.

Claudia whimpered as she felt heat flooding her belly and a blush creeping up her cheeks. She tried to move away, frightened by everything that was happening, but the Earl issued a low growl and moved to wrap his fist in her hair. He bent low, just inches from her eyes and whispered in a voice that let her know how angry she'd made him.

"Don't move. You are never to move from my touch, is that understood?"

Claudia nodded, and Lord Tarrington tightened his grip in her hair. "I didn't hear you, Claudia."

"Yes, I understand."

He went back to his ministrations between her legs, rubbing faster, causing heat to grow in her belly, and a trickle of moisture to dampen the skin in her bottom crack. Then, as soon as he'd begun, he stopped.

"She's wonderfully responsive. I imagine she'll be a shameless whore in my bed. Now we have to make certain she learns proper humility, respect, and servitude. Give her a one of the shifts to wear and then bring her to your office Miss Patton. The lawyer should be here by now. We'll have everything set for the marriage by the time you bring her in.

Claudia lay on the table, still in shock, the place between her legs throbbing while her husband to be rubbed his hands in delight and turned to her father.

"You were right, Patrick. She's lovely and spirited. I look forward to turning her into a perfect little slut. I have a feeling I haven't seen the last of her defiance, but training and discipline are all part of the fun. I've never shied away from those that are hard to tame. Let's have a scotch to celebrate the joining of our families. Well done."

Claudia squeezed her eyes shut and shook her head silently. She felt like her world had not only spun out of control, but had up and sent her to another land where people behaved in a deplorable way and had no consideration for her at all. Yes, it was true that Lord Tarrington was handsome, but he was ever so cold and domineering. How was she going to survive?

She lay there until the doctor moved the poles so she could close her legs and sit up. She stood, and Miss Patton put a loose shift over her head. It tied at the shoulders and sides, leaving a mere tug on the ribbon between slight modesty and complete nakedness. It was quite a curious article of clothing; one Claudia didn't care for one bit.

She followed the headmistress out, feeling humiliated, but despite her shame, the odd tingle in her lower belly accompanied the knot of dread in the pit of her stomach. That and the wetness between her thighs made walking towards her doom quite difficult, but she followed at a crisp pace none the less. Claudia had no desire to be accused of dawdling. Her new husband didn't seem like the sort of man who liked to be kept waiting.

Chapter Four

Claudia's wedding was so unlike the wedding she'd dreamed about since she was a small child that she hardly believed she was married. A few words were said, primarily about how she would honor and obey her new husband. She signed her name, and that was that. She went from a young woman who by law had to obey her father, to a wife who must submit to her husband. It hardly seemed real, and certainly didn't seem fair. She felt more like an object they exchanged than a woman who had just become a wife. She knew that women were just pawns in the games men played to join fortunes and families, but though her new husband was handsome, the marriage was not to her liking at all.

As a girl, she dreamed of an opulent wedding gown, numerous parties, and a ceremony full of tradition and glitz. She thought she'd have a husband who she could control with a pout or some tears, but that had disappeared when she said the words I will.

While it was true, she was marrying into royalty, a step up from where her family was on the social ladder, she had very few illusions about being pampered and catered to. All of the people in the room had put an end to any dreams of luxury that being an Earl's wife might provide.

Lord Tarrington gave her a chaste kiss on her lips when they were pronounced wed, then ask if there was a room to which he could take her. There were things he needed to discuss with his new bride, and he preferred privacy. He bid farewell to Head Mistress Patton and her father before taking her arm and telling her to kiss her father goodbye. Claudia did as told, too stunned to do anything else.

After she had kissed him, her father took her chin in his hand and tilted her head up, so she had to meet his eyes.

"You will do well and grow to love your position as the wife of Lord Tarrington. You must simply do your best to learn and obey. It may be difficult at first, I know I allowed you to be spoiled, wild, and disobedient, but all that has come to an end. You have treated others badly, and gotten the notion in your head that you are the one to choose how life should be.

"I apologize for that, for now you will struggle even more with the bindings they put on you. Be a good girl and don't rebel. There is no point, and with submission comes happiness. We shall see you when the Earl feels you are ready to reenter the world. Goodbye Claudia."

Claudia's forehead creased in a frown. Her father's words were ominous and confusing. "Papa I..."

"Silence! You haven't been granted the permission to speak." Claudia shot a look of resentment at Miss Patton but chose to say nothing further. Miss Patton looked quite angry despite the fact that she did as told.

"All in good time Miss Patton. This one has spirit that borders on insolence. She'll break like all the rest, and when she does, she will be a lovely wife and pet. I shall ring for the servant so she can be returned to you after our chat. She is to have the full procedure done by the doctor at once, and then be given a day's rest. Mind you there aren't to be niceties. She may continue the lesson on humility that began today, but nothing that will impede a quick recovery. I will be checking on her progress frequently. Good day Miss Patton, Mr. Stafford."

Nathaniel Tarrington took Claudia firmly by the elbow as they followed a servant to the private room he had requested. Once the maid had left and shut the door, he set her before him and looked down at her with eyes that held warmth. The fact that he seemed to have anything inside but disdain for her surprised Claudia, and the defiant look she had armed herself with faded.

As he appraised her, Claudia crossed her arms before her and stood straight and tall, doing anything to quash the feelings of nervousness inside. As he stared, the pleasure she felt at the warmth in his eyes changed to uncertainty, and then annoyance. What was he doing, and what did he expect to accomplish staring at her for so long without speaking? It was downright rude. She didn't have the mettle to say anything sarcastic, but she would not cower before this man even if he were her husband.

Nathaniel placed a hand on each arm and lowered them to her side as his expression changed to one more stern. She understood all too well that he wished for her to keep her arms down, but her feelings of disquiet caused by his unblinking eyes was just too much. Without so much as a word and by lowering her arms to her sides, he'd made her feel vulnerable, so she defiantly crossed them again.

"Claudia, you are an intelligent young woman. I am quite certain you knew I wished for you to lower your hands. I am your husband. I own you. Your father, who was your guardian, transferred you to me. I married you. You are mine. I may care for you and treat you as I see fit. I may discipline you or treat you gently. I may spoil you or have you live in squalor. You are mine, do you understand that?"

Claudia took a deep breath, nostrils flaring, mouth fixed into a frown, but she nodded her understanding. Lord Tarrington took hold of her chin and ran a thumb over her lips and squeezing just a bit. He wasn't hurting, but they both knew he could.

"You will speak and do so properly when addressed. If it is I, you will say Yes Sir. If it is Miss Patton or one of her staff, you will say Yes Miss or Yes Ma'am. Do you understand?"

"Yes Sir."

"Good girl." He took his hand away from her chin, and she lowered her arms, causing him to give her a hint of a smile. That slight expression of approval made her feel a bit of happiness as well, but as soon as her mouth softened, she pushed it into a frown once more but did not cover herself again. He was the enemy, and it certainly shouldn't matter if he were pleased with her.

"Claudia you will be attending Miss Patton's school for two weeks more or less, depending on your progress and your attitude. Get this into that pretty head right now, you will submit to anything she, her staff, or I do to you. If you refuse, there will be harsh consequences, and you will not leave here until you learn to be submissive and obedient.

"You will be schooled in housekeeping and cooking. This will include washing floors, doing laundry, chopping meat and vegetables and scrubbing pots."

"I am no maid! Those are not tasks a lady should do."

"You are my wife and if I tell you to get on your hands and knees to scrub floors or empty chamber pots then you will, and you'll do it with a smile and a yes sir. I have a house full of servants who keep my manor clean, cook delicious meals, and do all sorts of tasks. You my dear wife are going to do them as well to help you learn humility.

"Your father knew all too well and therefore I know, that you have been quite spoiled. Doing manual labor, cooking and lowering yourself to do all the things the servants do will make you think twice before you snap about how something must be done. You will not treat the servants badly or toss things here and there for others to clean up. I do not do this to punish you, only to teach you respect for those who toil each day.

"You, my dear, are under the impression that you are better than them, and that is not true. You were simply born into a family of title and wealth. Once you show an understanding of humility and compassion, then your lessons in housekeeping will be altered to teach you how to run the manor in the way I wish. Understood?"

"Yes... Sir"

"Good girl." Again she felt just a twinge of pleasure over the tidbit of praise and again she was angry over her reaction.

"You are not here to learn to sing, sew, play the piano, dance, nor any of the other things you learned as you grew up. I honestly do not care if you can do any of those, as long as you can be a gracious hostess who can instruct the staff in what needs to be done for a dinner party or ball."

Nathaniel raised a hand to the ribbon that held her chemise like garment on her shoulder and Claudia stiffened. Her new husband shook his head slowly, the approval of a few moments before gone from his eyes.

"You are not to move." He unfastened one, then the other, then ran a thumb over the pale skin that was revealed. Claudia took a sharp intake of breath but stood still. He then untied the ribbon at the neck and the garment slid lower, held up only by her small breasts. He cupped them gently and rubbed at her nipples through the fabric until they were stiff, and that feeling of heat once more rose up between her legs. The heat was accompanied by a flush of her cheeks, made brighter by her embarrassment.

"In time you will learn there is no shame in responding to my touch. Some men have the misfortune of having to bed an ice queen for the sake of producing heirs. I will indeed bed you my little spitfire, but there shall be no ice in your veins. Soon your body will be taught to crave me. Just a command will send wetness pooling between your thighs and pleas to fuck you spilling from your lips."

Chapter Five

Claudia's eyes had narrowed at his words, his arrogant attitude filling her with resentment, but the vulgar phrase he said in the end pushed her past the point of reason, making her forget herself.

"How dare you speak to me in such a manner? Have I married an uncivilized lout? I don't..."

"You will be silent!" Claudia tried to take a step back, but Nathaniel's hands grasped her arms before she could move. His eyes were full of fire as his words echoed in the room, making her flinch. He looked as if he'd gladly wring her neck. She gazed at him with wide eyes and then blinked rapidly to fight back the tears that suddenly threatened to spill forth. The days overwhelming horrors were suddenly too much to take, and try as she might, her well of strength had run dry.

One of Nathaniel's hands left her arm and cupped her cheek, his thumb brushing away the traitorous tear that told of her weakness.

"Such pretty tears, but I don't wish for you to shed them out of fear. I would never strike you in anger Claudia. I shall strike you in any manner of ways that I desire, but never while I am in a rage."

She looked at her new husband completely puzzled by his words having no clue to what he might mean.

"Never mind that for now. Come, you have a lesson to learn before I go." Lord Tarrington took her by the hand and led her to a chair. He sat and then tugged at the shift, pulling it down over her breasts and letting it pool on the floor around her feet. He then took both of her hands in one of his and pulled her forward.

Claudia thought he was going to kiss her and then do the things married men do to their wives. She didn't really know what that was, but she assumed he would wish to claim her as his wife before he left, but she was wrong. His other hand and arm slipped around her waist as the hand holding her wrists pulled her forward until she felt herself being hauled unceremoniously over his lap.

"I... NO!"

"Claudia you've already earned a bottom warming, I suggest you refrain from causing yourself a harsher punishment."

"But you said you wouldn't strike me when you were angry!" The tears that had betrayed her came again, and to her horror she began to sob.

"You haven't angered me Claudia. I'm perfectly calm. This is simply one of the many reprimands you will receive from now on. Hold still and do not attempt to cover your bottom."

Before she could protest he released her wrists, wrapped that arm around her waist to hold her tightly. He then gave her bare bottom a few gentle caresses, confusing her all the more, before he raised his hand and brought it down in a sound smack. It wasn't overly hard, but it did sting, and the horror of it all made Claudia cry out and struggle in his grasp.

"Try as you might, my sweet wife, you'll not be free until I am done. Be a good girl now and take your punishment. You were a disobedient, insolent, shrew and I'll have none of it. You are my wife, and I shall do as I please. I may parade you naked down the street, or spank your bottom until it's hot and red. Even if I tell you how I am going to make you beg me to fuck you, and you will say nothing."

As he lectured her, his hand came down over and over, the strength of the slaps getting harder and harder.

'"And you will beg me to fuck you, Claudia. You will beg me to spread you wide and rut like a stag between your legs or bend you over a table and take you like a dog mounts a bitch." She gasped and pounded her fists upon the floor, but the spanks only became harder and his words more crude.

"You will be kept just like a whelping bitch, in the heat, wearing a collar of ownership, and even a lead if I so choose. There isn't anything I can do to you that you will not plead with me to do more of. Your mind is innocent now, Claudia, but soon you will be more skilled than a Parisian courtesan, ready to take my cock wherever I wish to shove it."

The slaps upon her bottom were now coming hard and fast as were Claudia's sobs. She shook her head in denial of his words. That wouldn't be her. She'd never do those things for this man. Husband or no, he was a brute.

His hand never stopped his onslaught but finally the crude words stopped spilling from his lips. Her bottom was on fire and despite being saved from his lecture, Claudia was still crying because of shame and the burning sting on her bottom. Finally, he slowed the slaps and to her relief they turned to caresses intermingled with squeezes that caused a sharp intake of breath each time he did it.

His words took on a honeyed tone, his voice kinder; as soothing as the strokes of his hand on her bottom and back.

"That's my good girl. My sweet Claudia. You shall learn, and all this will be less shocking. That's my good girl." Claudia sniffed and brought a hand up to swipe at her eyes, but before she could, Nathaniel scooped her up, so her hot and painful bottom was in his lap. She could feel the hardness of his cock pressing on her bottom. Though she'd never felt one before, she'd seen the outline of many a man's privates as she flirted with them.

Her new husband wiped her eyes and kissed each lid gently, then placed a chaste kiss upon her lips. "That's my good girl, my sweet Claudia. You'll learn in time."

Claudia looked up at Lord Tarrington; her brown eyes red-rimmed but still a beautiful sable color. She blinked at him, not knowing what to say. The brute had turned gentle, but still, he'd beaten and shamed her. Oddly enough a part of her wanted him to be proud of her, and that longing shocked her.

As she gazed up at him, Nathaniel slipped a finger between her vaginal lips, smiling at the slick wetness he found there. The little minx was responding to pain as well. That was a wonderful thing. He'd had a suspicion she would.

Lord Tarrington watched as his young bride's eyes widened as he slowly stroked her clit. Her lips parted, inviting a kiss, but he didn't give her one. These things took time; she was to be a completely submissive wife and whore. One who could run his household to his demanding standards as well as crave his touch no matter how filthy or improper.

He stroked her clit slowly, not giving her enough to climax, and smiled as her head tilted back, and her eyes closed. When he had her lulled by his gentleness and was so needy that she was arching up and squirming about on his lap, he gave her bottom one last squeeze then set her on her feet.

Claudia's eyes opened in shock, and she groaned at the loss of the beautiful sensation he'd caused between her legs.

"Sorry my dear. There are things that I must tend to, and you have things to do as well. You'll be taken back to the doctor's office, and he will give you a good dose of laudanum. It will make you sleepy and dull any pain the procedures might cause."

"Please don't make me go back there. Please." Claudia's eyes shone with true fear, but it didn't stop her from trying to use her womanly wiles upon him. She batted her eyes but was spun around and given ten hard slaps on her bottom for her actions.

"Now then, you will be taken back to the doctor so your clitoral hood can be removed. Your clit is swollen and ready for him now. All he'll needs to do is give it a good pinch to make it even more prominent, and then slide the scalpel ever so carefully between your clit and the skin that keeps it covered. You'll then have a piercing in each of your pussy lips and the skin on the sides of your cunt so you'll be held wide open at all times.

"You will be kept in a constant state of arousal Claudia, and every brush of your skirt over your clit will make you even needier. It will not matter if we are out at the opera or home playing my twisted and entertaining games."

"I don't understand. Please, I'm not trying to be insolent."

"The spot I was stroking a little while ago is your clitoris. It is where you feel an intense pleasure when touched there. When you aren't aroused, there is a thin layer of skin that slides over it. I wish for that skin to be removed. The procedure won't hurt, and when you are healed, anything that touched you on your sweet little cunt and clit will make you wet and ready for my cock. The piercings will hold your lips open, so you are exposed and so I may view what belongs to me at all times. Understand?"

"Yes, My Lord."

"Such a good girl. Do you wish to be my good girl Claudia?"

It took Claudia a minute to realize that she did for some reason. This man had humiliated her, spoken to her with the foulest of words, spanked her until her bottom was on fire. He'd made her squirm and told her the doctor was going to do something that sounded incredibly lewd, and yet, deep inside she felt a tiny need to please her husband.

"Yes Sir."

"That is as it should be. Behave Claudia. I will return to check on you soon. I expect you to do as they tell you." That said, Lord Nathaniel Tarrington, Earl of Brighton, kissed his new bride on the forehead and walked out, leaving her naked and more than a bit frightened.

Chapter Six

Claudia woke to the feel of dull pain between her thighs. She blinked then closed her eyes as vague images came back to her. She'd been strapped down, spread wide upon a table in the doctor's room, naked and vulnerable. The rest was a blur for she'd been given the laudanum the Earl had promised. The floating feeling caused by the drug remained, and it wanted to lull her back to sleep, but Claudia fought off the cobwebs in her head. She wanted to know just what they'd done to her.

She tried to close her legs so she could sit up easier, but they were bound with straps that fastened to each ankle. She pushed herself up into a sitting position then looked wide-eyed at the thick mitts that covered each hand.

"They don't want you to touch yourself."

Claudia gave a start then turned towards the voice to find a beautiful woman sitting in a chair a few feet from the bed. She had long curly blonde hair that framed her face like a cloud of spun gold, huge green eyes, and flawless skin. She was also nude as the day she was born. Her breasts were full, the nipples large and pink. Each hard nub was pierced by a small ring that held a tiny golden bell that dangled freely from the woman's pert breasts.

Claudia tried to pull her gaze from the other girl's body but was unable to. She looked near perfection with a slightly rounded stomach, curved hips, and shaved vaginal lips that were held open with golden rings that began at the top and continued downward into the crevice between her legs. As Claudia gaped, the girl spread her legs wider, exposing herself fully for Claudia's inspection.

Claudia felt the heat of a blush upon her chest and face, and pulled her eyes away. She looked once again at the lovely face of her visitor and noted a smile and the twinkle of amusement in the other woman's eyes. Claudia shifted her eyes, bringing one mitted hand up to her chest, only to shake her hand as she remembered the things that covered her fingers.

"I didn't mean to embarrass you. We're taught to expose ourselves to anyone's gaze." Claudia turned back, feeling confused and vulnerable, but tried to smile all the same. From the sound of it, this girl was in the same situation as she was.

"You're not one of them?"

"If by 'them' you mean our trainers, no, I'm not. I belong to the Earl of Brighton, same as you."

Claudia wasn't sure why, but she felt a wave of jealousy fill her. This beautiful woman belonged to her husband?

"Please don't be upset. Lord Tarrington sent me here to help you while you're learning what's expected. It can be hard at first to accept all of this, and you'll not find any friends among Miss Patton's staff."

"You live where I'll be living?" The thought bothered Claudia. She couldn't help but compare herself to the other woman, and as she did, she felt like the clumsy, long legged girl with no grace all over again. Her own breasts were small, her hips more sharp than round, and her face plain in comparison.

"I do for now, but I won't be there for long. I was sent here to be trained; same as you, but not for the Earl. I'm to be a gift when I'm ready. I'm afraid I'm quite rebellious despite their best efforts so it may take a while." The girl grinned at her last remark, and then came to sit on the foot of Claudia's bed, the tiny bells making a faint tinkling sound as she moved. She tucked one leg up under herself, and then pushed an errant lock of hair back over her shoulder.

Claudia's eyes were once more drawn to the other girl's nether lips. One couldn't help but look at the rows of small golden rings on each side of her cunny. It held her lips open wide like the wings of a butterfly. It was a beautiful yet disturbing sight. As she stared, Claudia felt a hand upon her ankle. The touch made her jump, and her eyes rose back to the other woman's face.

"I'm Helena." Helena smiled and held Claudia's gaze as she slid her hand up to just below Claudia's knee and then lightly stroked her skin.

Unable to move away from the disturbingly intimate touch because of the bindings, Claudia frowned and placed her mitted hand over Helena's to still the other girl's fingers. "Don't"

"You'd better not say that word in front of Miss Patton. We don't say no here. Well, I still sometimes do. That's one of the reasons I'm not ready to be shipped off to some old goat as a present. You're lucky. Lord Tarrington is young and handsome. He can be cruel when I disobey, but it's easier to take the punishment from him than that battle ax Miss Patton."

Claudia giggled at Helena's description of the headmistress, but then brought her hand up to her forehead as a wave of dizziness hit her. The laudanum was still making its effect known.

"You'd better lie back." Helena moved to slip an arm around Claudia's back and placed the other hand upon Claudia's chest, pushing back gently. Claudia complied. She was feeling weak and disoriented, and it wasn't a feeling she liked one bit. She usually controlled everyone around her, not the other way around.

Helena raised Claudia's head a bit and put a glass of water to her lips. The cool water felt wonderful as it wet her dry mouth and scratchy throat. She drank deeply until the glass was nearly empty.

"Thank you. Tell me what's to happen to me here."

"I will. Let me get the balm first."

As Helena walked across the room, Claudia couldn't help but gaze at the other girl's body once again. Her legs were long too, and her hair fell to the middle of her back. She moved gracefully on silent feet, only the tiny bells on her nipples making noise. Her bottom was rounded and shapely, painted a dusky red with bruises, her hips curvaceous, watching her made a tingle of desire rise inside.

Helena turned after plucking a jar from the dresser and saw Claudia watching her every move. She returned to the bed with slow measured steps, her hips swaying, her gaze turning seductive, her smile provocative. Everything about Helena was sensual, and that fact wasn't lost on Claudia.

"You're lovely. I… "Just looking at Helena made Claudia's tongue tied.

"Hush now and just close your eyes. I have to put this balm on your clit."

Claudia's eyebrows furrowed, and she shook her head slightly.

"It's the little nub at the top of your puss that feels wonderful when someone touches it. The doctor cut the membrane that covers it away, so it's always exposed. It helps to keep you needy and wet. Anytime something touches you there you'll become aroused.

"That's how Lord Tarrington wants you. Wet and ready to be fucked." Claudia gasped at Helena's crude words, but the woman simply smiled and continued.

"Be good now and let me do what I need to. You're never to resist here, and never to say no." Claudia lay still as Helena's hand slid up one thigh. Her other hand brushed the lips of her sex.

"Stop" Claudia tried to move away from Helena's touch, but to her surprise the other woman gave her a sharp slap on her inner thigh. Claudia's eyes opened wide, her expression one of hurt. It wasn't the slap so much as it was the fact that Helena had struck her.

"I'm sorry sweet, but I want you to understand that you've no choice here but to submit. I still sometimes resist, but I don't mind the punishments so much. Your body isn't yours any longer. They will touch you wherever they like and punish you when you disobey or even when you don't."

Claudia's eyes were huge as she stared up at Helena. Never had she imagined a life where she wasn't in control. Since discovering her power over men, she'd been certain her husband would do as she wished and buy her everything she wanted. How on Earth had she ended up in this place without any say as to what was done to her? Reaching deep inside to find the confident girl buried under a blanket of shock, Claudia took a deep breath and let confidence replace the unease that scared her so.

"I'm the Earl's wife. Surely he doesn't mean for other's to touch me. You are... Well, I'm not positive what they are training you to be, but as Lord Tarrington's wife I'm certain I will have the privileges of my station."

Far from being put off by Claudia's words, Helena smiled and stroked the inside of Claudia's thigh before moving higher and gently touching the now baby smooth lips of her cunny. Claudia struggled to sit up, but Helena's hand on her chest and the weakness left by the Laudanum made her give up the effort. Still, her tongue was sharp even if her body was frail.

"I told you not to touch me. I'll ... I'll report your behavior to..." Claudia didn't finish. No matter if she liked what Helena was doing to her or not, Claudia would never report her to Miss Patton. It seemed they were on the same side, and telling the headmistress of Helena's actions would be a betrayal.

"I know you're upset, Claudia. I was too. I certainly don't mean you any harm. It's just easier to adjust to all of this if you come to understand that your wishes and feeling don't matter to them. They are going to do as they like. They will touch you anywhere on your body they wish, punish you in ways you can't even imagine, and make you beg for things you'd think are shocking.

"Now let me tend you. I'm going to stroke you between your legs. I need to put the balm on your clit to help the skin that was cut, heal. I'll do my best only to touch you there, but I find you very beautiful, Claudia. It will be hard not to stroke you everywhere. If you were mine, I'd suck and nip your nipples as I fondled your breasts and slipped a finger deep inside you just to hear you moan in pleasure. After that, I'd put my mouth upon your puss and lick you until you came in my mouth."

Claudia had no reply. Helena's words made the heat of pleasure rise in her belly once again. She never imagined she would want a woman to do the things Helena just described, but now... Helena was nude and so very lovely. Claudia could imagine how her sensuous lips would feel.

"Do what you need to do. I won't resist. I'm sorry I acted so badly. All of this is a shock."

"I know sweet, it was hard for me too." Helena's finger dipped in the jar of balm. She set it down so she could hold Claudia's cunny lips open, and then began to stroke Claudia's clit, her finger sliding easily over the newly cut nub. Claudia shivered and jerked, she couldn't help it.

"Easy now, it's alright. This won't take long. You must get used to anyone who wants, to touching you here, on your breasts, on your bottom, and even in your bottom." Claudia's eyes, which had become almost closed as Helena stroked her clit opened wide once again. "Yes pretty, in your bottom as well. Sometimes as a punishment, sometimes to make certain you're clean, and sometimes when the Earl wishes to fuck you there."

"That's filthy."

"Easy now," Helena's finger was stroking Claudia's clit over and over, and the sensation emanating from the nub was filling Claudia with need. Lord Tarrington had built up the pleasure but left her wanting; Helena's touch had her nearing the edge once again. "It may sound filthy now but you'll change your mind. At first it hurts, but once he's in well... He will stroke you as I'm doing now and fuck you so very deep. I promise you'll think differently once he's through.

"It is wicked. He'll mount you like a dog, mouth nipping at your neck; fingers tugging at your nipples and stroking your clit as he pumps deeper and deeper. Filthy or not, you'll come for him over and over, moaning ever so loudly."

Helena's words and the stroking of her clit had Claudia ready to cum. Her head was tossing from side to side, her fingers curling inside the mitts, her hips coming up off the bed. Though there was some pain from Helena touching the newly cut skin, it paled in comparison to the pleasure she felt.

Helena took her hand away from Claudia's clit, making her cry out in disappointment. She hushed Claudia and moved so she could suckle one nipple, pull and twist the other, and resume the strumming of her finger on Claudia's clit. The sensations drove Claudia wild. She cried out in pleasure, and Helena's hand quickly came up to clamp over her mouth, knowing there would be hell to pay for what she was doing.

Her mouth sucked harder at Claudia's nipple and to her delight, the fingers that weren't stroking Claudia's clit were bathed in the wetness of the other girl's passion. Helena knew it wouldn't be long until she sent Claudia's body spiraling out of control. Knowing she would provide the beautiful girl her first orgasm was a heady feeling. She strummed faster, then faster still as Claudia moaned into her hand, then jerked in shock as the door to the bedroom opened with a bang.

Knowing she had precious little time, Helena stroked Claudia's clit a few more times and was rewarded when she felt the girl begin to quiver and spasm as her body was wracked with its first orgasm. Helena continued to rub Claudia's clit, giving her pleasure, knowing Claudia wouldn't be allowed to cum again for a good long time until she was jerked away from her by Miss Patton.

"You filthy whore! Shame on you Helena. How dare you be so bold as to touch the Earl's property?" Miss Patton had thrown Helena to the floor, but it didn't faze the other woman a bit.

"I was applying the balm as you ordered Ma'am."

Miss Patton raised her hand and delivered a sharp slap to Helena's smug face. "You were told to sit by her bed and keep watch. No one gave you permission to give her pleasure."

Helena shrugged her shoulders and that infuriated Miss Patton even more. The large woman grabbed Helena by the hair and pulled her up to her knees, then dragged her to the straight-backed chair. "Get in position."

Miss Patton then walked back to the bed where Claudia lay dazed, until Miss Patton slapped her as well. "I see you may prove to be as much as a whore as this one. How dare you allow that wicked slut to pleasure you? You were married only a bit ago, and yet I come here to find you writhing in pleasure."

Miss Patton unclipped a leather slapper from her belt. She placed one hand on Claudia's chest and brought the slapped down onto Claudia's freshly cut clit with the other. She gave her five whacks, smiling at Claudia's cries of pain.

"That is all the punishment you'll receive today. You'll get just this one reprieve because you are new and under the influence of the laudanum. You are never to cum without permission let alone allow this one to touch you. Let your painful cunt teach you a lesson and watch what happens to bad girls at my school."

Helena had walked behind the chair and leaned forward, so she was grasping the seat. The action made her stand on her tiptoes and stretched the skin where her thighs met her bottom taut. She gave her bottom a little wiggle when she heard Miss Patton's footsteps returning to where she waited.

"Such a brazen hussy you are Helena, I've no idea why the Earl doesn't toss you out onto the streets. He'll be hearing about your behavior today, and I doubt he'll be pleased that you touched his new toy."

Claudia gasped. "I'm not …."

"Silence! I'll not have you follow in the footsteps of this one. Another word from you Claudia and I'll take a belt to your bottom too."

Both women were quiet as Miss Patton went to the wardrobe across the room. Claudia's eyes widened when Miss Patton opened it. Straps, paddles, canes, and things she couldn't name hung inside the doors, and there were a multitude of drawers as well. Miss Patton pulled one open and removed a large item that looked somewhat like a pointy egg on a base. It was made of carved wood. Claudia had never seen such a thing.

Miss Patton removed a jar from the drawer as well, unscrewed the lid, and dipped the pointed end into the jar. She then pulled it out and held it above the jar for a moment to allow the thick fluid to run off the end and back into the jar. When she was satisfied, she put the jar down, selected a wide leather belt from those hanging, went over to where Helena was waiting. Ever so slowly, shoved the butt plug into the woman's bottom, nodding with satisfaction as Helena let out sounds of distress.

"That just the things for wicked girls. You'll wear this for the rest of the day to remind you not to touch things that don't belong to you." That said, Miss Patton stood back, grabbed the belt by the buckle and rolled the leather around her hand. She then proceeded to strap Helena's bottom, making certain the strap hit the large butt plug buried deep inside the blonde girl.

The strap came down over and over, crisscrossing Helena's shapely bottom with red welts, all to the sound of Miss Patton's scolding. "Such a shameful thing you are. You'd better change your ways if you hope to leave here. It's my pleasure to whip you, you naughty slut, and I'd gladly keep doing it forever, but the Earl wants you tamed. You will learn to follow the rules here and will become a gift worth giving if I have to whip you morning, noon, and night."

Claudia had propped herself up on one elbow and was watching the scene before her with a mixture of shock and fascination. She was dazed by the fact that Miss Patton had shoved the wooden thing deep into Helena's bum. Though sassy and brazen, even Helena had let out cries of pain at the insertion of such a thing, and the ferocity of the blows she was receiving from the belt surely had to hurt horribly.

Helena's lovely bottom was now bright red, the faded marks from past whippings replaced with fresh stripes. Though she bounced just a bit on her toes, to Claudia's amazement she never let out a sound. Claudia knew that in her place, she'd be howling from such a beating. Finally, Miss Patton was done. She took the belt and laid it over Helena's back and then squeezed each crimson cheek. Helena hissed but made no other sound. Satisfied with her handiwork, Miss Patton came over took Claudia's face in her hands, holding her none too gently.

"The mitts will keep your hands off your puss, and the bindings on your ankle will keep you in bed. I hope what you witnessed will be a lesson to you. My school is a place where you will learn both pain and pleasure, but the pleasure won't come from the likes of her."

Miss Patton let go of Claudia's face and moved to open the lips of her sex and then made a face of disgust. "Look how wet you are. Wet as a used whore. Tell me girl, are you wet because that one made you cum or from watching me whip her?"

Claudia flushed; she didn't wish to admit to either. Miss Patton glared down at her, but there was a small curl of satisfaction on her lips. "Perhaps it was when I forced the plug deep into her bum. Whatever it was that you found so arousing, they'll be more of it and then some while you're here with me. I have a feeling you're going to give me as much trouble as that one.

Miss Patton took a dab of the ointment from the jar Helena had left on the bed, and rubbed it on Claudia's exposed clit. Claudia had to stifle the moan of pleasure she felt at the stimulation.

46

"Even with the numbing ointment you're ready as a bitch in heat. Once you heal properly, we'll tend to that cunt of yours good and proper. I'll be back in an hour. Don't move Helena. I'll know if you do, and make certain that the plug stays as deep as it is now." That said, Miss Patton took one last look at her charges and left the room, confident they would obey her. Helena was always a good girl right after a punishment. The problem was, as soon as her bum stopped burning; her rebellion returned.

Chapter Seven

It had been three days since Claudia arrived at Miss Patton's school. Three days of hard work, three days of being ordered about, and three days of being bent over and having that horrid leather slapper Miss Patton wore redden her bum at the slightest provocation.

She'd been a chamber maid; emptying waste, changing sheets, lighting the morning fires. A house maid; scrubbing floors, washing windows, cleaning everything in sight, and a serving girl who stood at attention barely clothed making certain everyone had what they needed while they ate. Everyone meaning those who were in charge or held high positions, not the other women like herself who were there to learn obedience and humility. Now she held the worst position yet. Today she was working in the kitchen.

She'd just gotten done scrubbing the pots and pans from breakfast and was now sitting on a tall stool with a huge mound of potatoes in front of her and a paring knife in hand. Her hands were raw, the chore tedious and difficult because she'd never touched a potato aside from with her fork while eating it. She'd just been reprimanded by Miss Collins, who ran the kitchen for taking too much potato off with the peel, when an older man came through the kitchen door, causing all work to stop.

"Phillip! Come here at once." All eyes went to the nude young man in the corner. While most all the students at Miss Patton's school were women, there were three young men as well. This particular one had been sitting on the stool reserved for those who were in need of punishment and made to wait for it as well. It wasn't the only such stool in the house, but it was the one reserved for those assigned to labor in the kitchen or gardens.

Phillip raised his eyes to look at the man who'd just issued the command. He was a big man who towered over all those in the kitchen, and his hands were the size of hams. Claudia knew she certainly wouldn't want to be facing his wrath.

"I said come here. Do not make me repeat myself again." The man's voice had turned quiet and sinister. There was no mistaking the rage boiling inside him. Phillip slid down from the tall stool and went to stand before the one who'd summoned him, then dropped to his knees and wrapped his arms around the man's legs.

"Please Sir. I'll be good. I swear I will. Please. I'll make you feel ever so good if you'll allow me to." Phillip rose up on his knees and nuzzled the man's crotch. Everyone in the kitchen held their breath waiting to see how the foolish young man would be punished. They were never to make sexual advances.

"Aye you'll suck me. You'll do it until I'm good and hard, and then I'll grease your bum up with lard and give you the punishment that's due." Phillip began to cry and plead with his punisher, but the man wouldn't have it. He pulled Phillip away from his crotch by the hair and unbuttoned himself, pulling out his cock which was huge, even when limp.

"Get to work boy. Lady Ellingsworth received the long list of your misdeeds from Miss Patton today. She sent me right over to take care of you. Perhaps you don't mind a birch being taken to your backside, but I promise you won't like my cock in your arse. Now suck me hard, and I'd better not feel your teeth."

Phillip let out a sob but took the man's cock in his hands and began to lick him, and then pulled back on the foreskin and put the cockhead into his mouth. All of the girls in the kitchen watched in sick fascination until Miss Collins snapped at them. Everyone resumed their chores but snuck glances over at the duo, their eyes widening in disbelief as the man's cock became hard and enormous. All wondered how Phillip was going to manage to take it in his bum.

After a few minutes, the man pulled Phillip back by the hair. "Fetch the lard and make it quick." Phillip scrambled, tears streaming down his face, and went to fetch the crock of lard, and then he once more fell to his knees before the man and offered up the crock.

"On your feet now, I can't fuck your bum with you on the floor. Go over to the stool you were sitting on and bend over it. You'd better hold on tight. Miss Ellingsworth is extremely upset with your behavior. I promised her I would take care of you good and proper."

Phillip rose and bent over the tall chair, his hands reaching to grab the legs on the far side of the stool. The man walked behind him and scooped a large glob of the lard out of the crock with his fingers, held Phillip around the waist, and went to work on his bum hole. He pushed his fingers in, stretching Phillip open, slicking up the inside and spreading the grease round and round. He kept up his work until Phillip was moaning and rocking his hips, his cock becoming erect.

"Quite the whore you are from a bit of teasing, but you'd better hold on now, you'll not like what comes next." The man took his greased fingers and made his cock slick, then took the same hand and closed the fingers around Phillip's erection. He then guided his cock to Phillip's greased bum hole and pressed the tip between Phillip's cheeks.

Phillip began to twist and cry, but the man simply held the boy's cock tighter and with a massive effort popped the head of his cock into Phillip's bum. Once the head was in he wrapped an arm around Phillip and held him tightly as he jerked on the young man's cock intent on filling his bum hole despite Phillip's cries.

"Stop your sniveling. You earned every bit of this punishment. Maybe now, you'll do as you're told."

"I wiiiilllllllllll. Please, oh pleeeassssse." Thomas let out a loud burst of laughter in reply to Phillip's begging.

"You will listen when Miss Patton or any of the other ladies gives you an order. You will scrub this place from top to bottom if they tell you to. You aren't here for your leisure. Your family is giving you to Miss Ellingsworth so she will help your family pay their debts. You are nothing but Miss Ellingsworth's new whore, and that's how you'll be treated for the rest of your life. And last of all, you will never, ever, touch this little prick of yours without permission. Do you understand?"

Phillip managed to squeak out a "Yes Sir" as Thomas began to jerk Phillip's cock and pressed his own into the man.

Once again Miss Collins told them to get back to work, but even she couldn't help but watch. Claudia was watching too, but it was with sick dread. Her stomach rolled, and her hands fisted at her sides, the one still holding the paring knife gripped it so tightly the handle dug into her palm. She felt physically ill as the poor young man before her was brutalized. She'd seen punishments given out, but this was no punishment, this was a vile and vicious deed, and not a soul was trying to stop it.

"Well done Thomas." All of the girls looked at Miss Collins in shock, hardly able to believe their ears. The kitchen mistress who always acted so prim and proper was congratulating Thomas's for his hideous actions.

Thomas spared a glance at Miss Collins, gave her a nod of thanks, and then resumed his work. Phillip bawled and begged.

Phillip's continued cries for mercy rang in her ears, making Claudia's blood boil. Her own eyes filled with tears as she watched Phillip struggle to escape his horrid fate, and her old rebellious spirit returned along with a rush of adrenaline. This was wrong. So very, very wrong. Phillip was being violently assaulted, and Claudia couldn't just stand there and do nothing. With no regard for her welfare, Claudia's fist tightened upon the paring knife in her hand, and she rushed at Thomas, heedless of his size potential to do her great harm.

She flew at his back, shrieking like a banshee, one fist pounding, her other hand sliding down the man's side, the paring knife grazing him as it fell. She'd have stabbed him as intended if he hadn't been warned by her scream.

"Stop it! Stop hurting him. Stop it!" Claudia was screaming at the top of her lungs. The horror and revulsion that had built up inside as she watched Thomas brutalize Phillip was boiling over. Thomas caught the wrist of the hand holding the knife and yanked forward, making Claudia fall away from his back and land on her backside, the knife bouncing out of her hand as she hit the floor.

Claudia rose, and he pushed her back down, swatting her away as if she were a tiny gnat. Thomas spared one more glance to where she lay sprawled on the floor, flashed a malicious grin at her, and then went back to tormenting poor Phillip heedless of the blood running down his side.

She rose to her knees, one hand rubbing the wrist Thomas had grabbed, and then flew at him again. Claudia's shrieked, claws bared, the sound of Miss Collins shouting her name only vaguely registering through the red haze of fury. Claudia leapt upon the giant of a man once more and managed to rake her nails down one cheek. Thomas bellowed and flung his arm back, sending Claudia flying backward right into Miss Patton, who had come running when she heard the commotion.

Arms like iron wrapped around Claudia, holding her arms pinned to her body, and lifted her off her feet, taking away her leverage to get loose.

"Claudia! Claudia! You will stop this instant. Claudia!" Miss Patton shook her like a rag doll, and Miss Collins delivered a sharp slap to her cheek, effectively pulling Claudia out of her sea of rage. Her screams turned to cries of protest, and cries to silence as Miss Patton issued an order and then handed her over to two of the male staff members as all eyes in the kitchen looked on. All were silent except for Phillip, who was still bent over and impaled by Thomas. His little scuffle with Claudia had only made him want to punish the poor young man harder.

"She is to be stripped and bound to the bed in the solitary room. No lamp for light, no fire for warmth."

"Yes Ma'am." Both looked in unison and smiled wickedly.

"Be mindful now, she isn't to be molested. This one is the Earl's wife." Looks of disappointment replaced the smiles at Miss Patton's warning, but they jerked Claudia to her feet none the less. As the men began to haul Claudia away, Miss Patton gave one more directive that made Claudia renew her screams. "Thomas, you may resume. Phillip won't get out of his punishment because some insolent girl thought it was her place to try and save him. The rest of you, get back to work before I line each one of you up and let Thomas have a turn with you.

All of the girls did as they were told, hanging their heads to avoid eye contact with the headmistress. Helena was among them, and hung her head as well, but vowed to find a way to help Claudia. The two had become fast friends, and Helena couldn't bear to think of Claudia cold and alone in the dark. She'd done what all of them wished they'd had the nerve to do.

Chapter Eight

Claudia spent three nights and days in a solitary room. Her only way of knowing if it were night or day was the small seam of light that showed through the heavy velvet drapes covering the window. She had no other way to keep track of time.

The room was kept dark and cold. Her jailers brought no food, and she was made to wet herself upon the mattress. Miss Patton had come sometime during the second day and had released her from her bonds only to bind her to a spanking bench and take a tawse to her bum. The Headmistress had delivered blow after blow telling her that she had no business interfering and that they would deal with her serious disobedience as soon as they were able to contact the Earl. No one, not even the Earl's wife could rush at a man with a knife without severe consequences.

Miss Patton had stood behind her using the tawse on her bottom and thighs over and over until Claudia finally let out a sob. It took more blows than Claudia could count, but once she had evidence of Claudia's suffering, Miss Patton ceased and bound her back upon the wet bed without a cover, lamp or fire. No one else had come except a girl who gave her water and some broth under the close supervision of Miss Patton. Claudia supposed it was only because even Miss Patton didn't dare allow her to die from lack of food and water.

The following day she was released from the horrid room and sent back to the kitchen, dirty and bare and on wobbly legs. Helena had dared to hug her, but the rest averted their eyes, especially after Miss Collins snapped at Helena's display of affection. And so she's done her best to scrub the pots and pans and return to what was considered a normal life at the school.

A week had passed since then, and now she lay in bed swaddled in her sleep sack. Miss Patton assured her daily that she would pay for her crimes, but as of yet she'd received nothing but the usual spanking. She'd also been told that her days of working about the house were over, and her training to be a perfect submissive whore for the Earl would be beginning in the morning.

All sorts of thoughts went through her head upon hearing Miss Patton's proclamation, and her mind wouldn't settle and allow sleep to come. It didn't help that her arms and legs were tightly bound. Her entire body was wrapped tight. She couldn't touch one bit of herself or even try to roll over and rub her needy puss against the sheet. The only parts of her that were free were her head and the area between her legs, leaving her sex open and vulnerable.

She'd found out to her dismay, that this was so Miss Patton could lick, rub, or play with her needy clit. The witch wanted to make certain Claudia was at the height of passion when she was left for the night. It was a torment Claudia knew the old battle ax enjoyed. The sounds of pleasure Miss Patton made as she licked and suckled Claudia's clit were proof of that.

It wasn't just the teasing of her sex that had Claudia wide awake. She was still thinking about the scene she'd witnessed in the kitchen between poor Phillip and that monster Thomas. It had disturbed her so much she was having nightmares of the brutal act. The fact that she hadn't seen Phillip since bothered her as well. She had no idea if they took him away, or if he was just working in a different part of the school.

No matter how she tried, Claudia simply couldn't get the disturbing thoughts about Phillip's welfare out of her head, and to make matters worse she couldn't toss and turn while she fretted. She always found it hard to sleep despite the hard work she was made to do. Each night since she'd been brought back to her room, she was teased to near climax, spanked soundly, and then put to bed early like an errant little girl.

She'd just let out a loud sigh when the door to her room opened, and a tall figure appeared, made dark by the hallway lamp glowing behind him. It was a man, of that she was certain. The figure wore no skirt. She also knew it wasn't the horrid Thomas. Though the figure was tall, he wasn't a hulking brute like Miss Ellingsworth's man. Even so, Claudia twisted in her wrappings, wanting to be free no matter who it was in her doorway.

"Hello Claudia, have you missed me?" It was the Earl, her Nathaniel. Claudia felt her eyes fill with tears. It shocked her how much her heart ached just hearing his voice, but yes, she had missed him; she'd missed him terribly. She tried to twist about in her sleep sack but only managed to rock back and forth.

"My poor wife is all bound up. Quiet yourself Claudia, it will do you no good to wiggle about. You won't get free." He walked to the bed and sat on the side of it, and then brushed silky strands of hair from her face before holding her chin and running a thumb over her bottom lip.

"So lovely. I've been in London on business. I received quite a disturbing post from Miss Patton. She's calling for a public punishment. Do you understand what that means?"

Claudia tried to turn her head away from the piercing gaze of Nathanial's eyes. The room was dim, but still she could discern his emotions. Her husband wasn't angry; he was unhappy. It would be easier to take his ire, but that wasn't to be.

So many people had been angry with her as of late. Too many to count as were the punishments she'd received. She'd learned humility and compassion for those who toiled to keep a home clean and everyone fed, but the constant spankings caused by her rebellious nature seemed to blur together and do little good. She wasn't a spoiled brat any longer, but she wasn't one to let injustice go by without a word.

"Claudia, you are to look at me." She still wouldn't meet his eyes. "We must discuss your offense. What you did was serious."

Now there was an edge of anger to his words because she had failed to obey and look at him. "Did Miss Patton tell you why I intervened? Am I to let others be brutalized?"

"How others are punished isn't your affair. I told you that your life is no longer your own. You'd do best to worry about yourself."

"It isn't my affair when I see things done that aren't right?"

"Don't be foolish Claudia. Do others try to stab the person who is disciplining you? You cannot attack someone with a knife. Are you no better than a ruffian who will slit my throat if I take a birch to you?"

Claudia was shaking her head violently to break his hold on her chin. Her heart ached, and a lump rose up in her throat. She closed her eyes in an effort to stop the tears that threatened to fall, but it was no use. Her heart was breaking. Through it all she'd held on to the hope that she'd been married to a man and not a monster. She'd told herself over and over that he would understand why she'd attacked Thomas.

Nathaniel grasped her head in his hands to still her then wiped at her tears. "Surely you don't think you can justify your actions."

"Yes I do. I was. A brutal rape isn't a proper punishment. If you think it is I'd rather die here and now than be your wife."

Nathaniel's brow furrowed as the look in his eyes changed to one of questioning. His hands went to the ties that laced her into the sleep sack, making quick work of them. When he opened it fully, he saw that she was completely bare inside it. Claudia shivered, gooseflesh rising on her arms, but not from the chill in the room. Nathaniel reached for her, and she flinched, but he ran his hands down her arms never the less.

"Do you intend to repeat the punishment in order to show me how very just it was? Her voice caught in her throat as she said the words; they came out raspy, and though she wished for a brave front, the anger was mixed with fear.

The Earl released her and went to the wardrobe, opening the doors, then turning away when he saw nothing of use. He then went to the dresser and rummaged through the things there. "Bloody hell have you nothing warm, wife?" The question was rhetorical, and he didn't wait for a response. Instead, he went to the bell pull and yanked until a girl came to the doorway.

"Yes M'lord?"

"I wish for a blanket for my wife, and send someone to stoke the fire and light the lamps."

"Tis my job, M'Lord. I'll return in just a moment." Nathaniel looked the girl up and down. Her feet were bare, and she wore only the thin shift that tied at each shoulder and along the sides. He knew they were the required garments, but he hadn't known the sleeping quarters were kept so cold. It was one thing to teach humility and submission, but another to neglect those who were here learning to be a proper wife.

Returning to the bed where Claudia still lay, he pulled her to a sitting position then removed his top coat and wrapped it around her. The stiffness with which Claudia first held her body in response to his touch left her, and while she didn't curl against him, she didn't try to avoid his arm when he put it around her shoulders.

"We've much talking to do Claudia. I suspect what the post told me was not all that happened here. Am I right?"

"Yes, husband." All the women in his life were trained to reply with Yes Sir, but Lord Tarrington chose to let Claudia's response go without reproach. The fear of him seemed to have left her. He wouldn't hear the truth if she were frightened. Women suffering from hysteria could say anything.

The maid arrived carrying a mound of quilts, followed by Phillip, who held a bundle of logs and some tinder. Upon seeing him, Claudia drew in a breath of exclamation. "Phillip! Are you alright?"

Phillip looked from Claudia to the Earl and back, then gave Claudia a small nod. He wasn't about to risk the wrath of the Earl by speaking. Lord Tarrington looked from the young man to his wife, then decided it wasn't worth questioning her about. Instead, he scooped her off the bed, put her on her feet, and wrapped her in one of the quilts. He then sat back down, pulling her onto his lap, and arranging the other quilt over her as well.

When the door closed behind Phillip and the maid, and a fire was roaring in the hearth, Lord Nathaniel Tarrington, Earl of Brighton, crooked his finger under Claudia's chin, forcing her to look up at him.

"Claudia, I am a man who prides himself on being strict and proper. I accept neither nonsense nor excuses from my servants or the women I train. Women have a place, and that place is beneath their husband whether they are hosting a grand dinner party or being fucked like a whore. You are here to learn humility, for you were overindulged and self-centered as a child. You need to learn compassion because you give no care for those who work to make your life easier. You are also here because my wife must be a special kind of woman. She must learn to be submissive to me, in my bed, on my arm, wherever and whenever I choose.

"Just like your father, other men who send their women here to for training, do so because we are the best at what I do."

"My mother? Here?"

"Silence. My grandfather trained your mother. Women are sent here because I teach them to kneel, to obey, to crawl if I so desire. I teach them to accept any and all sexual desires their husbands may have no matter how lewd they may seem, and I do so with a heavy hand. I am not ashamed nor do I feel guilt applying pain when needed. In fact, I teach them to respond to pain as they do to pleasure. That is what makes the perfect sex slave.

We are all part of a secret society, and we will remain secret no matter what. You are receiving training as your mother did before you, and my grandmother before me, and you will be broken Claudia. You will become exactly what I desire. We have a long standing history; you will not come in here and act like a hellion. That said, you were not sent here to receive abuse or neglect. The problem as I see it is our different views on abuse, so you are to tell me here and now exactly what you have been subjected to. Only then will I decide on your fate.

Claudia clenched her teeth, trying to bite back a sarcastic comment. Now wasn't the time. She didn't have to like what her husband was, all she needed to do now was to find out if he was as cruel of a bastard as she suspected he was. It all depended on his views regarding Phillip. She could take the punishment; she could take being fucked like a whore. She already knew her body responded to sexual touches. She would be his wife and be subservient. Women were expected to be, but if he had no care for the violent act committed against Phillip, then she would run away and never look back. She couldn't stay married to a monster.

Claudia took a deep breath and let it out slowly through her mouth in order to make her teeth unclench. She maintained eye contact with the Earl; he was no longer Nathaniel to her, a first name implied caring and Claudia would never care for him if he was heartless and cruel. She would watch his face for any sigh of deceit as she told him of the happenings in the kitchen and her treatment afterward. If his eyes showed real compassion, then there was hope.

"Though I've been unhappy here, scrubbing floors, dumping chamber pots, boiling laundry, and working in the kitchen until my hands were chapped and raw, I accepted each lashing I received because of my insolent tongue and rebellious nature. My mother couldn't tame me, and my father, well I guess he knew you would be up for the task. My life as a girl who was allowed to misbehave didn't prepare me for this place.

"I admit to tears on many nights. I couldn't understand why you would wish for your wife to toil so hard her hands bled and parade around near nude. It hurt my heart to think you didn't care that Miss Patton tanned my bum every chance she got. How could an Earl's wife be so mistreated? These thoughts melted away as I came to understand and have compassion for others. It didn't stop my tears of self-pity at night, but I do understand. I truly have learned humility and compassion. The world does not need to bow down to Claudia Rose Tarrington.

"But the kitchen... That was... I..." Claudia had to take another breath. She damned herself for the emotions welling up and threatening to overtake her. This conversation with the Earl was at a vitally important point in her life. Her husband's first reaction to the brutality committed on Phillip would set the stage for her future.

"Claudia, you were doing well. Tell me what happened in the kitchen."

"I was assigned to the kitchen that day and given a mound of potatoes to peel with no real idea of what I was doing. Miss Collins ordered the kitchen boy to give me a huge bowl full and handed me the knife. Phillip was sitting on a stool in the corner. That's where they put us when we must wait for a severe punishment. You are made to sit there nude, in front of everyone and just wait.

I hadn't paid him any mind. I had work to do, and knew I'd feel Miss Patton's strap if I failed or was too slow. Then all of a sudden this giant of a man comes into the kitchen bellowing for Phillip to come to him. We all looked up, how could we not? Phillip went to him and fell to his knees and began to beg for mercy, but he wasn't to receive any. The man told Phillip to... to suck him hard because when he was ready, he was going to shove it in his bum.

"Of course this made Phillip cry and implore Thomas even more. It made me sick to see it, especially when the man, Thomas, unfastened his pants. His..." Claudia flushed as she stumbled on her words. To tell this to the Earl was embarrassing.

"Go on girl, tell me through to the end. Searching for words leads me to think you're searching for lies."

"No! I... His cock was huge. There, I said it. His cock. You make me confused. Do you wish for a proper lady or a dockside whore?"

"Claudia." There was a hint of menace to Nathanial's voice, and Claudia didn't like it, but she went on with her tale.

"His cock was huge but Phillip complied. Thomas started berating him and telling him how upset Miss Ellingsworth was with his behavior. He went on about all Phillip had done, and when he was ready, he sent Phillip to fetch the crock of lard."

Claudia's voice had become quieter as she told her husband what happened, and her words were mere whispers when she spoke of Thomas forcing himself into Phillip and how the young man had screamed in agony. By the time she was done her body was rigid, and her hands were balled into fists once more. Nathaniel could feel her shaking with rage in his arms. Her story had filled him with a deep remorse. She should never have had to witness such a thing, never mind that the punishment had been completely out of line.

Claudia had watched the Earl's face as she told him about Phillip. She'd stared at his eyes every second, except when she was blinking back her tears, and to her relief she'd seen shock. Her husband, Nathaniel, had reacted with shock and anger when he heard what had happened. She slipped her arms around his neck and began to sob, holding on tight as she told him of being kept in the cold dark room, naked and bound on a mattress wet with her own urine for three days.

Nathaniel held her close as she told him everything, his fury building at the mistreatment she'd suffered. As she cried, the stoic strict man resided, to be replaced by a man who found himself caring for his little hellion of a wife. Brat or no, she should never have seen such things happen to another person, and even though they hadn't been able to contact him, they should never have punished her like that.

"I will make certain those responsible for what happened pay. Both for your sake and that of the boy. I don't condone brutal rape. The lot of you are sent to this school to learn what it is to work hard and be punished if you don't. Any resistance is stripped away. Harsh chastisement is part of that training. You must be obedient and submissive, and your bodies are taught to respond to pleasure and then to pain. All of that is why you're here Claudia, but there is a limit to how far the staff here may go to correct and mold you.

"My dilemma now is the demand for your public punishment. Yes, Thomas had to be stopped, and I would merely defy them all except for the fact that you tried to stab him Claudia. Rich or poor; that is a crime."

"And rape is not?"

"Yes, Thomas was brutal and what he did is against the law as well, but the women here are from upstanding families, some of them even royals. We are an established secret Order, and we must remain so. I stand with you in your commitment that what Thomas did was wrong. He and Miss Ellingsworth, if she issued the order, will be seen to, but I cannot stand by you and say your actions were justifiable."

She tried to pull away from him, but he held her tight, needing her to understand his position. "Listen to me. Thomas needed to be stopped, but you could have killed him. You attacked him with a knife Claudia. You were sent here to learn to be submissive to your Lord and Master, yet you violated the teachings of your Mistresses. You also not only disrupted a punishment, but tried to do serious injury to the one carrying it out.

"Thomas will be dealt with, but I must deal with you in a way that is acceptable to Miss Patton, the staff, and the families who send their daughters and wives here. You raised a hand in anger and tried to hurt a superior. No one will not tolerate that, and I cannot tolerate it either, even if it was justified. We can't set that precedence."

"No, let me go. No!" In the back of her mind Claudia was relieved that her husband did indeed hold compassion inside and knew what was done to Phillip was morally wrong, Even so, all she could focus on was that he was taking their side. He was justifying the punishment because she tried to save Phillip.

Nathaniel set her from him, letting the quilts slip from her shoulders so he could grip her arms. He shook her with frustration. How could he make her understand? Why he cared was something he didn't wish to look at too closely, but he could admit he did care if she hated him.

"Listen to me you little wildcat, just stop it and hear me out. I will bind you nude in front of all and whip you front side and back. You will stay there for all to see for the rest of the day, and be cut down at dusk. They will not be allowed to throw things at you, spit upon you, nor touch you. When I cut you down, I will take you home with me, and you will never return here. I promise you I will take you away from this place. I also vow to see to it that changes made, so no one is neglected or abused again."

Claudia didn't speak, but she stopped fighting him and put her face to his chest, sagging against him.

"You will still be trained to be a proper submissive wife, but your training will take place at our home. I will take you away Claudia, but first you must be punished. Do you understand?"

She nodded; her body and soul exhausted from her days of suffering and heartache. Her husband could still prove to be cruel and unfeeling, but for now it seemed that he would do his best to make certain she wouldn't suffer overly much. When it was done, he would take her home where she belonged.

Chapter Nine

Lord Tarrington set the wheels in motion to have Claudia's punishment take place the very next day. He was in a hurry to take her home, not only because she wasn't doing well at Miss Patton's, but because the girl had managed to worm her way into his heart. The fact that he cared for her didn't unnerve him in the least. He'd felt a special fondness for some of the women he'd been sent to train. The Earl was certain once he had her home, settled in as his perfect wife; the fondness would fade to a more acceptable level.

While it was permitted to care for one's submissive, it was not acceptable to have tender feelings that were so strong they would impede one's ability to remain firmly in control. Meting out punishments as needed, reminding them that they were beneath the men in their lives, never letting them forget that though they were cherished, they were simply another possession. Lord Tarrington had no fear he would be unable to deal with Claudia in the same manner. It was simply the enjoyment he felt from the teaching and taming of a new woman that made his blood race when he held her.

He'd spoken to her at length about what was going to happen to her. He explained how it would feel, who would be watching, and how he expected her to behave. He said that while the things he would do to punish her would be severe, he expected her to maintain the dignity of her station. She was to show remorse and obedience, be respectful to him, refrain from talking back, and always reply with "Yes Sir" when he asked her anything.

Claudia had held her chin up as he sat calmly and told her everything. He didn't have to worry about her composure. Never would she let those watching know how much she was suffering. No matter how degrading or painful, those who demanded she demanded this punishment would not be rewarded with her cries for mercy. The things he divulged her frightened her. The whole idea of being stripped, bound, and punished in front of everyone made her blood run cold. She vowed to him again and again that she would do the same thing if she were to witness another horrid act of brutality upon another person, even when he was done relating the horrors she would experience.

He'd spanked her then, hard and long until she'd cried, but neither her tears nor her blazing bottom would make her take back the words. He'd even humiliated her by making her orgasm, holding her about the waist and sliding that hand under her so he could rub her clit, even as he spanked her to tears. She'd cum hard, damning him for it and had received time in the corner, her red bottom on display and her cum running down her legs for her sass.

In the end he'd called her back to bed, wrapped her in his arms and then kissed her softly after he'd tucked her in. He'd decided she would do as he told her in regards to behavior during her punishment, and had forgone the sleep sack, allowing her to move about, knowing she'd have a sleepless night. His small acts of tenderness weren't lost on Claudia. Though she'd reverted to calling him Sir or Milord, instead of the more intimate Nathaniel, her words were not barbed. She told him good night and thanked him for making certain she knew what was to come. Though she hated what was to happen and why, fear of the known was far better than that of the unknown.

The day dawned sunny and mild; the late spring chill that usually settled upon them at night had taken its leave early. A knock upon the door had awoken her, and to her surprise, Helena came through the door.

"How...?"

"Hush, the rest will be along soon enough. The Earl found me last night and told me he'd made arrangements for me to help you bath and dress."

Claudia's eyes narrowed, and her lips pressed into a thin line. The audacity of it all made her furious. "I'm to be clean and properly dressed before I am stripped and beaten? How preposterous."

"I know you're angry and scared sweet, but it he must do it. If it makes you feel any better, the Earl seems genuinely upset over the whole thing. I think he's taken a liking to you. He told me to give you a hot bath this morning to help you stay calm."

"He hasn't taken a liking to me, he simply doesn't wish for me to embarrass him more than I already have."

Helena wouldn't debate with her on the subject and ignored Claudia's comment.

"You'll do best if you don't tighten up. If your body is tense, it will hurt more and when he takes you in your bum. Try to push back. It will hurt at first, but it doesn't have to hurt the whole time. If you breathe and do your best to stay clam things will be better."

"So I'm to relax while I am beaten and then be calm as he takes me in my bum in front of everyone? That will be a quite a feat. Am I to smile when he makes me orgasm while his cock is in my arse?'

The coarseness of Claudia's words told of her fear. Though she had a willful and rebellious spirit, she also couldn't quite shake her proper upbringing. "There are worse things than cumming while the Earl takes you from behind."

"Is that spoken from experience?" Helena looked pained for just a moment, but it was a moment long enough to tell Claudia that yes, her husband had fucked the lovely woman standing in front of her. Her eyes narrowed this time from anger and jealousy. Like him or not, the Earl was her husband, and it didn't sit well that he coupled with other women.

It pained Helena that the truth about the Earl upset Claudia. They were, only toys to be played with and used when desired. The Earl had taken her in the bum quite forcefully last night when he'd summoned for her. While it was true, he'd fucked her, she also suspected he'd thought of Claudia the whole time. There was a rage in the way he'd slammed into her, fury Helena suspected was caused by what the Earl was required to do today.

"Claudia, let us discuss that another day. I'm not here to upset you. We both know the world we now find ourselves in is crude and vile. Neither of us has any choice about what happens to us. Let me do all I can to help you through this day."

Claudia replied by putting her face in her hands and letting her shoulders slump in defeat. Helena hurried to sit beside her and wrapped the frightened girl up in her arms. "Don't fret pigeon. You're stronger than anything that will happen to you."

She was interrupted by the arrival of the maids with the bathtub and water, neither woman paid much mind as the tub was filled, but both sat up in surprise when they heard Miss Patton's scorn filled voice.

"What a sight, one of the Earl's whores trying to comfort the other. Did she tell you your husband fucked her so hard in the bum so hard he made her cry?"

Claudia refused to react to the Headmistress's words. It was a good thing she'd found out that the Earl found pleasure with Helena a few minutes before. While she hadn't known it was as recent as a few hours ago, the shock factor of Miss Patton's words was greatly diminished.

When neither woman replied to her barbs, Miss Patton walked over to the bed and yanked Claudia up by the hair. When Claudia protested, she was rewarded with a slap on the face.

"You will give me an answer when I address you."

"Forgive me Ma'am. Yes, Ma'am. I know the Earl finds pleasure with Helena. Tis his right as her owner and is not my affair."

Miss Patton scoffed in disbelief but let it go. "You're to be dressed and ready in a half hour's time. Thomas and I will return to lead you to the whipping yard."

Claudia couldn't quite hide the fear she felt when she heard the man she hated would be coming for her. Miss Patton didn't even try to hide her smirk of satisfaction. Fear was what she'd intended to instill.

"Make sure you're ready. Thomas is looking forward to escorting you down to the yard and tearing your clothes off. It's all he'll be allowed to do, so I'm sure he'll make the most of it." After the door closed behind Miss Patton Claudia sank to her knees, face in her hands, body trembling uncontrollably.

Helena sank down beside her and shook Claudia's shoulders none too gently. "Stop it. You are to stop it right now. You heard her. That is all he will be allowed to do. Granted he may get a pinch or a slap in on the way out, but he won't dare do anything but strip you bare once he's brought you to the Earl."

"He didn't tell me." The fact Lord Tarrington hadn't mentioned this brief time she'd have to endure the presence of Thomas upset her. He'd told her so much, all of it she'd thought, but now her mind was spinning. What if he'd omitted other horrid things?

"He told me." Helena simply let the words hang there in the silence that followed. They succeeded in stopping Claudia's trembling, and Helena hoped they helped banish any new fears. It was better to be jealous than terrified.

"What else?"

"Nothing. I know he told you all the rest because it was that one thing he admitted to keeping from you. He crashed about and told me everything, even saying that he'd kept that from you because he knew it would scare you, and there was no reason for you to be afraid."

"And then he fucked you."

It wasn't a question; it was said in a flat tone almost devoid of emotion. Helena suspected Claudia was balancing on the edge between bravado and hysteria. The dead pan sound of her words made Helena think Claudia was leaning toward bravado, and that was for the best. She'd rather hear dead calm then shrieking accusations. Claudia needed every ounce of toughness she had to get through the day before her.

"Yes sweet, and then he fucked me. Let's get you in the tub."

Chapter Ten

Lord Nathaniel Tarrington sat across from Lady Ellingsworth, a table set for tea between them giving the semblance of a civil, social visit. Though each of them had a gracious smile on their face, the gathering was far from an enjoyable social visit. Miss Ellingsworth was the only dominant woman among their secret society. That fact, her behavior made everyone aware of the fact she considered herself special because she was the only female, annoyed Nathaniel since her acceptance into their Order.

For over a hundred years, from the time of Lord Tarrington's great grandfather, their society consisted of the upper class and royal families. All adhered to a strict code of behavior and submission for their wives, and its members exclusively made up of men. The women among them were inferior and held a submissive role. Miss Patton and the female teachers at the school were the few exceptions, but even they were expected to be humble and subservient to the men whose wives they trained.

Because Miss Ellingsworth's family had no male heir to follow in the footsteps and adhere to tradition, she had been accepted as a dominant, but it was under duress. Were it not for her high social standing, outspoken views, and premature knowledge of their Order given to her by her dying father, they would have simply left her family out of the circle until a proper male heir was born. In the Order's eyes, only a male could do justice by the family name.

Her bid for inclusion was rejected over and over until she made such a fuss that the Order was worried she would tell outsiders of their training traditions, and so Miss Ellingsworth was finally accepted. It was her future husband Phillip, a man from one of the Order's families who wished to wash their hands of him because of his taste for other men, whom Claudia had tried to save. They'd had other young men from time to time, but they had been the lovers of the patriarch in their group who needed training, and the discipline they received was never and issue. It wasn't until the annoying Miss Ellingsworth came along that the trouble started.

Miss Ellingsworth always acted as if she had something to prove to the others, and this wasn't the first time her manner of chastisement had come into question. It was however the first time one of the women at the school who were expected to be submissive in all things, had attacked her hired man.

So now, here they sat. Miss Ellingsworth had sent him a post late last night requesting a meeting between them and insisting it happen before Claudia's punishment. Nathaniel bid her good morning but then sat silently as the maid poured the tea. He continued his silence as Miss Ellingsworth stirred in some sugar, wanting her to dispense with small talk and get right to the point.

"Your wife committed quite a crime against my Thomas, and I don't feel he has a large enough part in her discipline to compensate him for being stabbed with a knife. I've never heard of such rebellious and crude behavior by a young lady of her standing. She could have done him serious harm."

"Could have Ethel but did not." Two could play at the game of leaving off titles when addressing someone.

"The fact that she managed only to leave a shallow cut on his side makes no difference."

"The cut was merely a scratch and it didn't stop him from punishing Phillip. Your man was far too brutal. One could speak of his breaking of the law. While it's true, we use anal chastisement as a form of punishment; we make certain we are doing no harm. Thomas is a huge brute and Phillip a small man."

"Phillip hasn't had one incident of needing discipline since then. I would say the purpose was a success."

"Did it not also serve to land him in the infirmary?"

"He needed a small bit of medical care but it was inconsequential. I dare say the act of misbehavior done by your wife was as an act that broke the law as well. My Thomas needed medical care too."

"While I agree a visit to the doctor to have it cleaned and dressed was needed, I would have to argue that it too was inconsequential. I also wish for you to share what the consequence for his behavior was. Truth be told Ethel; we all know he was following your directive, so you should be the one who is reprimanded."

"Why I never. You are a cad sir. I am a woman of the Order, not a submissive girl."

"While it's true you are on equal footing, you need to learn what is acceptable and what is not. I value and will come to cherish my wife. She is to be submissive and will be taught, sometimes harshly, what is expected of her, but it will be done within reason. She is mine to do with as I please, but I don't break my toys Ethel. When Claudia gives her submission, it will be because she has been trained with compassion, and care for her needs and desires, not because she fears me. When she kneels and kisses my feet in gratitude, it will be done with all her heart. She will be there at my feet or riding my cock because there is no place she'd rather be. You will learn that you can teach with brutality and achieve the same results on the surface, but inside Phillip will hate you and fear you."

Lady Ellingsworth gasped at his reply to her and her face flushed crimson in anger. It was all Nathaniel cold do to keep the smile off his face.

"Now I'll ask you if there is a point to this meeting, Ethel? I wish to see my wife before the time to take her downstairs."

"She's being tended. I sent Miss Patton and Thomas to her room already to make certain she would be ready when the time of reckoning came." Her comment made Nathaniel uneasy, but he refused to show he was agitated. He knew Helena was upstairs with Claudia and that she would be alright.

"The point of this meeting Lord Tarrington is that Thomas deserves to whip your wife. Blood for blood."

"You must be daft if you think I would allow that. I will punish her, and I'll do so properly. She will be in a great deal of pain, but I won't mar her skin. I have no desire for my wife's body to be mutilated by someone who doesn't know how to use a whip in the right way. Thomas will strike out and open Claudia's flesh with each lash. I will not allow it."

"Three lashes then. She's pretty enough that you'll still desire your prize with a few lash marks to remind her to stay in her place."

"One, that's all I'll give you, and she walks down under her own power and undresses herself." Lady Ellingsworth narrowed her eyes and pressed her lips into a thin line. She knew her adversary had the upper hand. Many in their secret circle felt she was in the wrong for what she'd had done to Phillip. It wasn't that she cared what they thought; it was that their siding with Lord Tarrington gave him leverage.

"Fine, but he may deliver the lash anywhere on her body."

"Anywhere but her face, and anywhere he can manage with her standing." Nathaniel knew Thomas was unskilled and would never be able to whip Claudia between her legs while she was standing, even though her legs were spread.

"Agreed. That little ruffian is never to lay a hand on Thomas again." The idea was ludicrous, and Nathaniel couldn't hold back a burst of laughter. The idea of the huge Thomas cowering in fear of Claudia was simply too funny to keep inside.

"My wife will be leaving the school with me today. I dare say poor Thomas won't ever have to see her again. While you'll, of course, receive invitations to dinner and balls, Thomas will remain out in the yard or the stables with the other hired hands. He'll be safe as a babe in arms.

"Now if you'll excuse me, I wish to see Claudia before her punishment is to begin. Though I feel you were in the wrong as well when you gave Thomas the order, I do take her misbehavior seriously. You have my word that she will be well chastised for laying a hand on him."

Lord Tarrington exited the room without even a small bow or a look back at Lady Ellingsworth. She sat and stared at him as he left, a knot of fury burning in her gut. The men still treated her as if she were less than them, and it galled her that the cards had fallen in his favor. Granted, Thomas was going to get a chance to whip the girl, but he'd lost being able to drag her to her doom and rip her clothes off. It was a trade she agreed on only because she wished for blood from the little chit, and she knew Thomas did too.

Miss Patton returned just shy of a half hour with Thomas in tow. He grinned at Claudia and licked his lips in anticipation. The two hadn't seen each other since Claudia had tried to stab him, and the malicious intent in his smile was impossible to miss.

Claudia and Helena were sitting on the bed when they entered, and Helena put a reassuring hand on Claudia's knee. Both women held their chins a little higher and sat a bit taller, refusing to be kowtowed by Miss Patton and Thomas.

Helena had dressed Claudia in a simple cotton gown. It was a real dress, not one of the skimpy shifts that were the required uniform of the school. Lord Tarrington had provided the gown to give Claudia just a scrap of dignity as she was led past all those waiting to see her punished. While it was true, the thing was simply going to be stripped off her, it gave her a small sense of protection to be fully clothed while being touched by Thomas.

As Claudia and Helena rose, Lord Tarrington arrived in the doorway and walked straight to Claudia's side, taking her arm and only then acknowledging Miss Patton and Thomas.

"There's been a change of plans. Miss Ellingsworth and I have discussed the fact that neither she nor Thomas feels he is getting what is his due for my wife's crime. We have settled on allowing Thomas to whip Claudia once and only once. Blood for blood is what Miss Ellingsworth feels is fair. She was quite insistent that he be allowed more because a slave who raises a hand towards their Mistress or Master is traditionally executed. I pointed out that my wife is not a slave. Thomas is not her Master. Nor do we reside in the part of the world where a servant is killed because they dared to touch their employer in anger or defense."

"One lash hardly seems just. Claudia stabbed Thomas. She is also here to learn to obey without question. You wouldn't tolerate such insubordination in your home, and we do not tolerate it here."

"And that is exactly why Claudia is being subjected to a severe public discipline. I fully agree that she must learn her place. Such behavior will never be acceptable. That said, she didn't try to stab him because he was carrying out a just punishment.

"I will have no say over what Miss Ellingsworth does in her home with Phillip, and though it is my hope that she is ethical in her treatment of him, it is not mine to decide. My wife, however, is mine, and I am able to decide what's to be done with her. She will walk before all of us unassisted to the center of the yard. There she will strip, apologize to Thomas for taking a knife to his person, and hand him the whip I will be using to give her what is her due.

"Once Claudia has presented Thomas with the whip, I will bind her to the whipping frame, and Thomas will take his turn. One lash, that is all. I've no say as to the force of the lash, Miss Ellingsworth desires blood for blood, but he is not to strike her face."

Helena felt Claudia tremble, but was glad that her face was calm. True she was pale as porcelain, but the look on Claudia's face belied the terror that was making her tremble.

"Claudia, it's time to go out to the yard. You must walk without help and follow the agreement I just laid out to Thomas and Miss Patton."

"I understand Milord and I'm ready." Taking a breath, Claudia held her head high and walked out the doorway, not sparing a glance at Miss Patton or Thomas. She didn't pause or look back to see who followed first, nor did she look at the people assembled in the yard who were there to witness her punishment and shame. Once she was in the center and stood next to the frame she would be bound to, Claudia stared Thomas straight in the eyes as she removed her dress.

Thomas watched her, eyes cold as ice, and licked his lips as Claudia stripped bare, but he got no satisfaction out of seeing her cower with fear. Claudia's hands didn't even shake as she unbuttoned her gown, nor when she stood before him naked and presented the whip.

"I was wrong to assault you with a knife, and for that part of what I did, I am sorry." There were several gasps of disbelief and a chorus of disgruntled whisperings in response to Claudia's apology. She'd been sure to let everyone know that the only thing she was sorry for was using the paring knife. Miss Ellingsworth would not be content with Claudia's act of contrition.

"Have you no control over the girl, Lord Tarrington? Her words were more a slap in the face than they were an apology."

"She is being punished for using a knife. Both she and Thomas committed what would be considered crimes to the outside world, which is why my wife is being publically chastised. Shall we hash over our discussion on how Thomas was reprimanded or get on with what everyone is gathered here for?"

Lady Ellingsworth refused to comment. Instead, she turned to Thomas and said for all to hear, "Blood for blood. Make that insolent chit bleed." Thomas nodded at her and then took the offered whip from Claudia's hands, twisting the looped coils as if it were her flesh between his fingers.

Lord Tarrington took Claudia by the arm and led her to the whipping frame and bound her tight, hands and feet spread wide and tied to each corner. The frame allowed the discipliner to work on both sides of the one being punished. Nathaniel turned Claudia so her back was presented to Thomas, hoping the one lashing would fall on the skin there, but doubting that would be the case.

"Be good and be strong. There is to be no back talk even if he taunts you. Do you understand?" the Earl had leaned in to whisper in her ear, and Claudia nodded her assent. "His lash will cut you, but it is the only one that will. Mine will burn near as badly, but they won't cut your skin. Do not think I will let you off easy though. I cannot do that. What you did was wrong. Now be brave for me."

That said, her husband moved away, leaving her bound, naked, and at the mercy of the man who had brutalized Phillip. She vowed to herself that she would be strong, no matter what happened and how badly it hurt. That resolve faltered though as Thomas came into her field of vision, still twisting the whip in his hands. He backed away until he was satisfied with the distance, then unfurled the whip, letting its coils fall loose as he found the handle and looked her straight in the eyes. Claudia closed hers, but just for a moment, and then met his icy stare with one of her own.

Chapter Eleven

As Claudia stared at Thomas, he stroked the handle of the long whip like a lover. His eyes gleamed as he looked her up and down, and his cock became hard, the shaft becoming clearly outlined in his trousers. The knowledge that hurting her gave him sexual satisfaction disgusted her, and when Thomas grinned and licked his lips, Claudia knew he'd seen the revulsion in her eyes.

"Not so uppity now are you? This whip will teach you to lay a hand on those who are better than you. You're just a little whore now, being trained to do everything you're told like all the rest."

Claudia grit her teeth, wanting to reply but remembering the Earl's warning. It was best to endure the one lash in silence. If he failed in baiting her, he'd be more likely just to do it.

"The uppity bitch has become a terrified mouse. What's the matter Claudia? Are you regretting your attack upon me? If you'd simply let me punish Phillip like you should have, we wouldn't be here. He likes it you know, despite his tears. He likes it up his arse."

One thing Claudia could say about Thomas was that he knew just what would fill her with fury, but she still refused to take the bait. She glanced to the side and saw her husband watching the scene play out. He gave her a small nod, pleased with her silence, and it was that nod that gave her the strength to keep her mouth shut despite what Thomas was saying.

When Claudia looked to the Earl instead of responding, Thomas gave the whip one more stroke and then flung it back over his shoulder. Claudia closed her eyes, and then heard the crack of the whip only an instant before a trail of fire blazed from her right breast, down her body and ending upon her bare mound. She did her best to bite back a scream of pain, but she simply couldn't swallow it all. She pulled at her bindings, wanting to curl up in a ball of agony, but unable to. Tears filled her eyes, but though they clouded her vision, she could still see Thomas, and the look upon his face gave her the strength to stop struggling and raise her chin up in defiance.

Her body was screaming from her nipple to her clit. She could feel something wet trickling down her skin and knew he'd laid her bloody. She clenched her teeth to stop the trembling that threatened to overtake her, blinked to clear the tears from her eyes and then looked back at Thomas full of defiance and fury. Her insolence made him raise the whip again, but a sharp command from Lord Tarrington made Thomas lower it. Nathaniel walked forward, hand outstretched, taking the whip from Thomas, his expression impassive except for the icy coldness in his eyes.

"That's enough. You've had your revenge." Thomas spared one more look a Claudia his eyes full of hate. As he looked at her, Claudia maintained her dignity, but once he'd turned his back, she slumped in her bindings. Her head fell forward as her chin trembled, and she fought to blink back her tears. Her body still felt as if someone had laid a hot poker across it. Claudia didn't know how she would take more strokes from the horrid whip.

In her misery, Claudia hadn't heard the Earl approach. She jumped when he reached out and lifted her chin, but when she met his eyes, strength made her straighten once more. The way her husband looked at her let Claudia know he approved of the way she'd handled herself.

"The worst is over. Close your eyes and breathe. It's possible to be lulled by the pain. I'll build up slowly, and if you allow it, your mind and body will accept the lash and even come to crave it." Claudia's mouth opened to reply, but he let go of her chin and walked away, leaving her to wonder how she could accept the cruel whip. None the less, she did as her husband had said, closing her eyes and taking deep breaths.

The crack of the whip cut through the silence of the morning, and the touch of it left a kiss of fire. It hurt, but it was but a small kiss. Nothing like what Thomas had done to her. She took another breath thinking perhaps she could endure, when Lady Ellingsworth's voice rose above the whispers of the onlookers.

"You're here to punish the girl, Lord Tarrington. I shall expect more than that from you for what she did to my Thomas."

Claudia expected to hear a reply from her husband, but Lady Ellingsworth's words were met with a silence that conveyed Nathaniel's contempt for the woman who had spoken. He kept his back to her, ignoring her completely, and then gave Claudia another lash. It was the same as before, a spark of pain, a kiss of fire, but not the agony she could hardly endure.

Over and over Nathaniel whipped his new wife, the kisses of fire touched her everywhere. Her nipples and breasts, her belly, her back and bottom, even her inner thighs and the opening between her bottom cheeks. She was spread wide enough for him to whip her everywhere, and he did, but he never touched the skin that had been laid open by Thomas. The whipping grew more forceful, making Claudia hiss and moan, the kisses of fire more intense, the pain lasting longer. He focused on her nipples, the lash crossing them side to side, causing a burn on the sides of each breast and a blaze of pain on the tips. Claudia moaned again, wishing he would stop, the pain becoming too much, but then she remembered to breathe.

She opened her eyes and watched as her husband drew his hand from side to side. He saw her watching and scowled at her, shaking his head. His displeasure was felt as the whip crossed her breasts yet again. Claudia shut her eyes one more, taking another breath, and her obedience was rewarded with a stroke that was once more the gentle but fiery kiss of a lover.

Claudia's body was coming alive under the ministrations. Her nerve endings were singing, aroused by the pain. Her heart was pounding, her breath coming as pants unless she focused on her breathing. Nathaniel was moving once again, bottom, back, thighs, stomach, mound, breasts and back again. Each stroke became harder, but the tempo of them remained the same, numbing her mind and indeed lulling her with each lashing.

Claudia had stopped thinking, stopped being aware of the crowd around her, stopped fighting her bonds. She didn't move into the kiss of the whip, but she didn't flinch from it either. Lord Tarrington moved behind her once more and began to lash her bottom and thighs as he had her breasts, left to right and back again, but harder than any others. These bit deep and burned both where they struck and in her belly. They were harsh and punishing, but not once did Claudia feel she couldn't endure. They hurt, oh did they hurt, but her body accepted the pain. It was humming, the endorphins making her light headed. Her world was hazy. The only thing she could and focus on was the sensation of the whip.

Harder now, the lashes erupting in fire, trails crossing her bottom and back, her thighs burning, the pain almost intolerable. She let out a small cry, but Nathaniel only kept on, whipping harder, knowing what must be done to appease those around him, raising welts all over Claudia's skin, but never breaking it. He had to punish her for what she'd done. While both she and Thomas had been in the wrong, this public show of discipline was mandatory. Their secret society ran on strict rules and codes of conduct. Submissive women were never to raise a hand to anyone nor interfere with what those around them were doing. They were to obey, plain and simple, and Claudia had not obeyed.

He gave her ten more, crossing her back, making her shudder with each one though the pain barely cut through the numbness in her head. He then finished with lashes to her bottom, ensuring she would feel this punishment each time she sat for a good long while, raising deep red welts, but still never breaking the skin. Lord Tarrington never broke his toys, and Claudia was a very special toy indeed.

When she cried out with the last of the lashes, Nathaniel slowly curled the whip once more. Those who looked on would have to be satisfied. His wife wasn't bloody, but nearly every inch of her was red and covered with swollen welts. As he walked towards Claudia, Helena stepped forward, taking the whip from Lord Tarrington. She set it aside and then fell to her knees before him, unbuttoning his trousers and pulling out her Lordship's cock. His shaft was only semi hard, for he'd not gotten much pleasure in the disciplining of his wife. It hadn't pained him to whip her, he simply didn't receive the stimulation from the administrations that he normally would have if the punishment hadn't been forced upon him.

Helena paid homage to the Earl's cock by kissing and fondling it, and then picked up a bottle of oil from the table next to the whipping frame. She poured a liberal amount into her palm and began to stroke Nathaniel's cock, making it slick and hard, preparing him to take Claudia deep in her bottom. When her Lordship's shaft was hard and jutted out from his body, Helena moved to Claudia and used more oil to grease her bum hole.

The invasion of Helena's fingers cut through the haze in Claudia's brain and she stiffened, but the slippery fingers running up and down between her cheeks, circling her hole, and pushing in ever so easy because of the oil, soon became pleasurable. All too soon the fingers went away.

Claudia opened her eyes but then closed them again when Helena came into her view. There was nothing to fear from the beautiful blonde woman. Helena stepped forward and slipped her arms around Claudia as Lord Tarrington loosened the bindings on her arm. He brought her hands together, bound them with practiced fingers, and then secured them to a rope that hung from a beam jutting forward from the frame.

The action made Claudia bend forward with her legs still spread wide, her bottom sticking out prominently behind her. Once he was satisfied, Lord Tarrington returned to his place behind her, stroking his oil slicked cock. Claudia sagged into Helena for support, wincing as the bloody lash mark left by Thomas came into contact with Helena's body. A moment later she didn't have time to worry about that pain as her husband's cock was pressing between her bottom cheeks and nudging up against her tightest hole.

"Mind me, you'd better take her hard, Lord Tarrington. Your whipping of the girl left much to be desired. I'll file for harsher disciplinary measures if you don't make the little bitch hurt."

Nathaniel wasn't worried by Lady Ellingsworth's words; she simply disgusted him. Their society would be far better without the woman who dared to take on the role of a man. "Mind you?" His voice dripped with disdain. "I should mind you Lady Ellingsworth? You must be delusional. Do as you wish, and I will answer that grievance with one of my own, demanding to punish your Thomas for his role in all this.

"I plan on taking my wife good and hard. It will hurt her, but my fucking won't cause her harm. I won't injure her regardless of what you'd like me to do. Now kindly close your mouth. Hard as it may be for you to accept, you aren't in any position to give me orders."

The contempt he felt for her was clearly evident, and it let Lady Ellingsworth know she'd never win in a battle between them. Granted she'd been allowed into their society, but even so, the men held all the power. Though they had let her in, she was not their equal.

Returning his attention to the deed at hand, Nathaniel grasped his cock and pushed forward, causing the head to pop into Claudia's virginal bottom. She cried out at the invasion, but he only pressed into her harder. Avoiding injury did not mean the deed would be done compassionately. She had rebelled against authority, and no matter her reason, defiance was not allowed.

The oil made the passage easier despite how tight she was, but easier did not mean the absence of pain. When he'd pushed a few inches of his cock into his unwilling wife, Nathaniel eased back. He nodded to Helena to tell her to hold Claudia tight, and then eased forward again, pushing hard, oh so hard, and then even harder as Claudia tried to squirm away from the agonizing pain.

She fought the bonds that made her unable to move her ankles. Fought Helena who was keeping her steady, and fought the harsh hand that gripped her bottom, making the welts he'd left there burn even as the pain from his cock pushing into her bottom made her wail. No matter how she tried, Claudia couldn't get away, and Nathaniel made short work of it, burying his cock deep inside his wife lovely ass up to his balls, ignoring her cries and focusing only on the exquisite feeling of her virgin bottom squeezing with a scorching grip.

She was so very tight, tight and burning hot, and he had to breathe deeply to avoid spilling his seed prematurely like a school boy. Claudia's entire body shook from this new pain that exploded deep inside her, but Helena's whispered words of encouragement, and her husband's tender stroking of her back over the welts he'd laid there, calmed her to some extent, making her relax and allowing her body to adjust.

Nathaniel felt the tension in her body ease under his hand, and knew it was time to do what needed to be done. He moved his hands to Claudia's hips and slowly pulled almost all the way out, then thrust back in again, pausing just long enough for Claudia to breathe in after she'd gasped. He then began a steady rhythm of thrusting and pulling out, despite the whimpers of pain from his wife.

She had done wrong and needed to pay for it. It didn't matter that she'd done what she felt was justified. The women here did as they were told or were punished, and despite her noises of pain, he knew he was not truly doing Claudia harm. A little pain was good for his insolent bride. He knew that soon she would come to crave it along with the pleasure he ignited in her body.

"You will take my cock up your sweet ass whenever I see fit, and you will never, ever, interfere with those who are your betters. You are my wife Claudia, but that title grants you no privileges. If you defy me, I will do anything it takes to make you obey. This is but the first of many fuckings you will take, so you'd better come to like them. You shall take my cock where ever I chose to put it, and receive it with pleasure, because I am your husband, and I own all of you."

He thrust faster and harder, his thick cock filling Claudia, making her want to get away, but Helena's arm made certain she couldn't. She could hear the other woman urging her to relax her body and to push back, to take her husband's cock, to enjoy his fucking of her. Helena's words were crude and dirty. They went from soothing whispers to a guttural litany, even as one of her hands moved down and found Claudia's clit. Helena began to rub and circle the nub with her slick fingers as her words became even nastier. She was strumming Claudia's clit with a practiced hand, adding a new sensation that melded and helped to ease the painful fucking her husband was giving her.

Claudia jerked as Helena's fingers moved over the skin that bore the mark from Thomas, but then she melted against the woman as the fingers stroked her clit in time to the thrusts of Lord Tarrington's cock. The fire that once was a burning agony was becoming a burn of deep need.

Nathaniel felt her tighten and then release as the pleasure given by Helena mixed with the pain of the whipping and the harsh fucking of her virgin bottom. He moved faster, not relenting, not letting her get lost in a wave of pleasure. This was supposed to hurt. It was a punishment. Yes Claudia would be made to feel shame for cumming while having her ass fucked in front of a crowd, but that pleasure would be mixed with the pain of his cock stretching and filling her over and over.

Claudia's body was a riot of confused feelings. Her body burned all over from the whipping she'd received. Waves of pleasure from the ministrations of Helena's fingers emanated through her, and she felt a deep spark of guttural pleasure building at her very core, put there by the hard painful fucking her husband's cock was giving her.

She began to moan, the sound becoming louder each passing second. Claudia heard her husband telling her to take it like the whore she was, and to let them all know she liked being fucked in her sweet little ass. His fingers dug deep into her hips as he fucked her hard and fast, his shaft moving easily because of the oil, pounding like a freight train as the moan that spilled from his wife's lips became a wail, and the wail a cry of pleasure as all of the sensations came together in her so very deep inside her. They exploded, sending incredible pleasure through her despite the pain.

The crowd's approval reached her ears as they began to shout crude obscenities, urging both her and Nathaniel on. They were telling him to fuck his whore, to pound into her so she'd know who owned her, to fuck her like a bitch in heat, but it didn't matter. She was cumming and cumming hard, despite the pain and the shame of it all. Helena's fingers never stopped their onslaught of her clit and Nathaniel kept up his bruising pace, thrusting into her very center. Claudia felt like he would split her in two, and then she finally heard him grunt out his pleasure as his cock pulsed and his hot cum spurt inside her.

The onlookers gave more applause as the Earl gave one last thrust, then ground his hips against his wife's well punished ass. Claudia was shaking, the ropes and Helena's body being the only thing that held her up. Otherwise, she would have fallen long before her husband was done with her. She felt him shudder as an aftershock of his orgasm went through him, and she followed as Helena gave her clit one last rub. Then there was nothing behind her but cool air as Lord Tarrington pulled his cock from her bottom, the head popping out of her still tight hole. As he left her body, his cum dripped out and down her legs, leaving her bare, used, and punished for all to see.

Claudia choked back a sob as full blown shame filled her in the wake of her orgasm. She buried her face in Helena's shoulder as the woman moved her hand away from Claudia's swollen puss and wrapped her arms around her friend.

"Hush now. It's done. Just hush now. You survived."

"H...he.. just left me. He used me like a whore and left me here in front of them." Claudia having never been taken felt wave after wave of vulnerability and shame wash over her. She needed him, needed to be held.

"This was a punishment, sweet. There are no niceties with a punishment. You'll be all right."

Claudia clung to Helena until Lord Tarrington came and took the other woman away. Then Claudia was alone with all eyes upon her and nothing to shield her from them. Thomas came and stood near, tossing insults at her as her husband's cum dried on her bottom and thighs. Finally, her husband came and took her down. Claudia had no idea how long she'd been there. She'd done her best to recede to a place deep inside where the shame and the pain couldn't find her.

"We'll be going home now Claudia. You've had enough. I'm proud of you, my sweet little wife. You did well." Claudia didn't reply. She couldn't understand how he could be proud when she felt so wretched. "You'll be bathed and cared for when we get home, and then put to bed. It's over now."

Claudia nearly fell as the restraints were taken from her ankles and wrists, but Nathaniel caught her and scooped her up into his arms. She moaned as the still red welts protested his touch, and he placed a kiss on her forehead. "That's my good girl. We're going home."

His good girl? Was she? His words were confusing but oddly comforting. She let her mind drift as he carried her through the school and to the waiting carriage. She felt his arm around her and then a soft quilt being pulled over her as she slipped into sleep. It had been a horribly trying day. One filled with pain and shame, but also pleasure. She was still light headed from what her husband had done to her body, and gladly welcomed the sweet darkness of sleep.

Nathaniel looked down at his sleeping wife as a very unladylike snore escaped her lips. He smiled at the sound, knowing she needed the sleep that had claimed her. The one he'd chosen for his own was not like the other pretentious women he often came across. She had a tough façade but a soft heart. He like that, and thought breaking in his little wildcat would be a delight. Her training would begin first thing in the morning. His cock stirred at the thought, and he smiled again, and tightened his arm around Claudia, who was blissfully oblivious to his wicked intentions, lost deep in sleep, unaware of what the morning would bring.

Chapter Twelve

Claudia woke to bright sunlight streaming across the bed as the maid pulled back the heavy velvet drapes. She blinked, the last vestiges of a dream flitting away, and then groaned as the events of the day before came back to her. She lift her arms, placing her hands over her face at the remembered shame of it all and whimpered as tears threatened. Her body hurt, inside and out, and the very vivid horrors of yesterday squeezed her heart.

"You'd best let me help you sit up Miss. I'll brush your hair too. You had a bath last night though I doubt you remember, but your hair is a mess. I imagine the Earl will come to see you this morning, and Miss Reagan will be here any minute."

Claudia uncovered her face as she rubbed her eyes, and then moved to sit up only to stop as her body protested in pain once again, and she realized she was quite naked.

"May I have a dressing gown?"

"Oh no Miss. Miss Reagan would be livid."

"Who is Miss Reagan?"

"She's the head of his lordship's household. You won't want to be making her angry."

The maid came over to the bed and helped Claudia sit up, fluffing a pillow for her to lean against before heading to the dressing table to pick up the ornate hairbrush. Claudia winced yet again, her bottom hurting both inside and out, and then pulled the sheet up to cover herself. She watched the other woman for a moment, then looked around the room. It was opulent with its velvet drapes, Persian rug, and carved mantle. A bedroom fit for the wife of an Earl much to Claudia's surprise.

"Are you one of... I mean does Lord Tarrington... are you here to learn... things?" Asking the question made Claudia flush red. While she was in no way a prude, she still was unnerved by the ease with which her husband and those around her spoke of and did such intimate acts.

"Oh no Miss. I'm just a servant, though I'm to be your lady's maid when you're allowed one. My name's Rebecca."

"Oh," Claudia couldn't think of anything else to say though she knew she had to sound and look like a fool with her mouth agape.

"Most of us are just employed by the Earl. We know the way of things, but the amount of our pay_ensures our silence. You've no worry about the spreading of tales, Miss. We mind our own business and don't gossip. There's to be none of that. Miss Patton or the Earl himself would take a birch to my backside if I dared to tell of the goings on here."

Claudia knew that many men disciplined their staff, and was relieved that her husband didn't share intimacies with the maid before her. Though he'd been cruel and demanding, he'd also done things to make her punishment a bit easier. She couldn't say she liked her husband, but she was also glad he wasn't intimate with Rebecca.

Rebecca brought her a wet cloth with which Claudia gladly wiped her face. Though someone had given her a bath, her eyes still felt gritty from crying.

"Sit up a bit Miss, your hair is all tangled. I wasn't to brush it last night. You slept through your bath, but I'd have probably woken you if I'd have pulled at your hair." Claudia sat forward so Rebecca could get at her hair more easily, and then tensed as she heard the clack of heels in the hallway. Rebecca's hand moved lightening quick to tug the sheet Claudia was covering herself with out of her hands only a moment before a tall, regal woman entered the room.

Her hair was jet black and pulled back so tightly that Claudia mused it must hold her eyes wide open. Her nose was long and thin, her eyes a steely gray and her lips were two pale lines that pursed together when she saw Rebecca sitting on the bed behind Claudia. She wore neither the clothing of a maid nor the finery of a lady. Her skirt was black, her blouse white and heavily starched, accented only by a large cameo pinned in the center of the high collar. The only other adornment she had was a wide belt that held a wooden paddle and a leather strap. The sight of them made Claudia groan inside. She was all too familiar with the implements.

She walked towards the two women, scowling at them as if she'd caught them committing a grave sin, stopping a few feet from the bed, looking down her nose at the both of them with obvious disdain.

"Leave her."

"Yes Miss." Rebecca rose quickly with the bob of her head.

"Prepare her cleansing."

"Yes Miss."

"And mind you fill it. We will treat her like any other." Rebecca nodded her assent and hurried through the door of the bathing chamber. When she had gone, Miss Reagan turned her eyes upon Claudia with a look that made her want to wither. Her normal sass had seemingly fled in the wake of her punishment and Miss Reagan's icy stare.

"Lower your eyes." The command was snapped in a tone that left no room for defiance. Claudia did so as her hands grasped the sheet she wanted to pull up to her chin again. Miss Reagan snatched it from her and threw back the quilts as well, leaving Claudia bare.

"Lie back" Claudia chanced a quick look up but then looked away and did as ordered. There were times to fight back, but this wasn't one of them. Claudia pulled the pillow out from behind her and then slid down so she was lying flat, naked as the day she was born. Her experience from the day before, lending her courage.

"You're all legs with hardly a curve to your hips." Miss Reagan touched Claudia between her hip and her navel, and Claudia had to fight not to move away. "I suppose your tits are pretty. They're small but round, and your nipples are big and a nice dusky rose color. He'll be wanting to clamp them or pierce them and put little bells on you. It's a shame that idiot was allowed to whip you. That lash will leave a scar if we don't tend it properly. The Master won't like it if that pretty skin marred."

Claudia's first reaction was to snap that the Master had indeed marred her quite well himself. The way Miss Reagan's finger's pressed into her hip when she made a noise of outrage convinced Claudia she'd do best to keep her opinions to herself. Still, she looked up and met the other woman's eyes. Meekness might procure a bit of mercy, but a bit of insolence let an opponent know you weren't a timid weakling.

Claudia's direct gaze brought raised eyebrows from Miss Reagan along with a wicked glimmer that promised reprisal as she called to the maid. "Rebecca, bring me the ointment."

The woman scurried out of the bathing chamber bearing a tray of bottles and jars. She set it down and quickly headed back where she'd come from, her task there apparently not finished.

Without a word, Miss Reagan dipped her fingers in a blue glass jar and scooped up a fair sized dollop of its contents, and then began to spread it on the long open cut made by Thomas. Claudia hissed at first contact, but then closed her eyes as Miss Reagan continued to apply the ointment between her breasts. She made her way down Claudia's stomach, coating the wound all the way to its end so very near her clit. The salve left a numbness in its wake giving Claudia relief from the pain, but Miss Reagan had more in mind for the new Lady Tarrington.

"That is the only nicety you'll get from me today. You'll find your brazen look a bit costly, Claudia. I'm certain you will come to understand that those tiny shows of defiance aren't worth the cost. Now spread your legs."

Claudia's eyes narrowed, and her mouth opened but then snapped shut. She had no power here. Doing as told, she spread her legs and then looked away, her jaw clenching to bite back words that would only make things worse.

"You'll not be getting the regular ointment upon that exposed clit of yours today little miss high and mighty. Oh no, I've something special just for those who think rebellion is a proper form of behavior."

Miss Reagan dipped a finger into a different jar and then put the dab of cream on Claudia's clit, rubbing it in as was done every day to make certain the exposed nub never got overly dry. Lacking the covering of a natural membrane meant great care had to be taken. Claudia didn't react though even the nasty Miss Reagan rubbed, her body was just too tired from the trauma of the day before, but then she felt the heat and her eyes opened wide.

"That will teach you girl. A touch of hot pepper oil will leave you on the edge between misery and need. Now roll over." Claudia closed her legs and turned onto her stomach, her clit ever so hot. She squirmed upon the sheets but regretted her actions a moment later as she heard Miss Reagan unclip the wooden paddle that hung from her belt. The woman then proceeded to give Claudia more smacks than she could count upon her already sore bottom.

"You'll not wriggle about like a whore trying to ease the ache between your legs in this house. We forbid that activity. Only the Master can provide such relief. Think of that brazen look you chose to give me every time your need for release drives you mad."

Rough fingers spread Claudia's bottom cheeks making her hiss, but an insult was added to injury when Miss Reagan poked her tender puckered hole. Claudia squeaked, and Miss Reagan chuckled.

"You have a shapely bottom despite how skinny you are, and pretty little crinkled hole. It's nice and red, just as it should be. He fucked you good and proper didn't he? It wasn't more than you deserved. As his wife and his whore, you'll get a lot of use as long as you keep him happy. Anger him and you'll wind up bound wet and needy. Remember than when you're tempted to act like a shrew. Good little sluts still get their share of pain, but they don't have to suffer from a needy cunt. Bad whores get the pain, but no release for their aching clits."

After she'd finished her inspection Miss Reagan once more dipped her fingers into a jar and this time, her fingers came up coated in a greasy ointment. Claudia closed her eyes, saying a silent prayer that the stuff wouldn't cause her misery. Miss Reagan spread Claudia's cheeks once again and went to work on her bottom hole. She shoved her fingers in none too gently, greasing Claudia up, making her yelp when the woman delved deeply, and when she was through, she gave Claudia a stinging slap on her bottom.

"Up with you now. It's time to get you cleaned out."

Claudia moved but couldn't bite back her reply. "Rebecca said I had a bath last night." Her response brought a gale of laughter from Miss Reagan, and Claudia itched to slap her.

"That was for the outside. Now march to the bathing chamber girl." Claudia did as told, the sound of Miss Reagan's heels clicking behind her as she went.

Claudia stopped in the doorway of the bathing chamber, a puzzled look on her face. Besides the commode and bathtub, there was a dubious looking low table and a rubber bag with a long nozzle hanging from a hook in the ceiling.

Miss Reagan once more gave Claudia a stinging slap on her bottom. "Get on your hands and knees, head down, bottom in the air. You may have had a bath last night, but you've got to be clean inside and out now that you're in the Master's house." Claudia didn't move. "You were told to get on the table. Do it now, or I'll take a strap to your already sore bum and then you'll get on the table when I'm done. It makes no difference to me either way. You've no choice but to submit."

Claudia squeezed her thighs together to quiet the heat radiating from her clit that was now intermingled with dread in the pit of her stomach. She didn't know what Miss Reagan was going to do. But she knew she wasn't going to like it one bit. Swallowing her pride, and her fear, Claudia climbed upon the table on her hands and knees and then lowered her head, making her bottom stick up in the air.

"I see you're smart enough to do as you're told. You're going to get an enema. I will put a nozzle in your bum and then I'll release the clip on the bag. Your bowels will fill with soapy water and then I'll plug you up, so it stays in there until I think you've had enough."

Claudia heard Miss Reagan moving about and then the woman's fingers were spreading her cheeks once more. She felt something long and thin invade the place that had so recently been assaulted, and then warm water began to fill her stomach making it cramp.

"Please." That was all it took to make Claudia ask for mercy. "Please stop, I can't take anymore."

"You can and you will. We've only just started, and I'll not stop until every drop is swelling your stomach and making you beg. I'll remind you again of your insolence. It's best you learn that I have many ways to make you suffer if you choose to sass me."

Claudia felt as if her stomach was so bloated it would burst, and the cramping brought tears to her eyes. "I'm sorry I was disrespectful. It won't happen again."

"Oh, it will. I know your type. It takes more than a lesson or two to break that rebellious streak. You were spoilt your entire life. Waited on hand and foot, never appreciating any of it. The Master told me all about you. You ran wild, behaving scandalously, refusing to obey your poor mother, well that life is over Claudia. You may be the Lady of the house in public, but you've no power here."

Claudia moaned as sweat dampened her brow. She felt nauseated, and the cramping was too much to bear. She let out a whimper, knowing words wouldn't save her.

"There we go. It's all in. I imagine you're feeling nice and full. I'm going to pull out the nozzle and push in a good thick plug. Perhaps we can wash away some of your wicked behavior." Claudia felt the nozzle slide out and was gripped by panic, feeling as if she'd never be able to hold the water. She clenched her bottom cheeks together in desperation until Miss Reagan pushed them apart and popped the plug in place. A few moments later Claudia felt the plug expanding and heard the sound of a ball being squeezed.

"Twenty minutes. That's how long you'll wait before I allow you to get on the commode." Claudia moaned and shook her head from side to side. "Oh yes, you will. Poor, poor Claudia. Does your stomach hurt?" Claudia refused to answer. Miss Reagan put her hand on Claudia's swollen belly, rubbing it as she began her litany about what happens to spoiled wicked girls again, and then she put a finger on Claudia's clit.

"Noooo... Please, not that. It hurts."

"Your belly hurts but I imagine your needy clit is burning from the pepper oil." She strummed Claudia's clit and let out an evil snigger as the girl at her mercy moaned and rocked her hips.

"Please. Please stop." Miss Reagan rubbed Claudia's clit a little longer before pinching the little bud and pulling her hand away. She wouldn't give the girl relief, not even if it were mixed with the pain in her belly. Only the Lord Tarrington would provide that for his wife. All she could do was give the girl enough pain and misery to make her understand that her pampered life had come to an end, and she was now owned by a husband who had very particular tastes.

"You've fifteen minutes yet. I think you should use that time to think about how helpless you are here in your new home. I know just how to tend to bad girls. Rebecca will help you when the time is up. I imagine you'll feel a bit miserable for a good bit. We'll spend the day talking about the household, how it's run, and what's expected of you. Later on, you'll be prepared and presented to Lord Tarrington. He'll further your education this evening."

Claudia said nothing. Her stomach felt like it was about to burst and despite her misery, her clit throbbed with need. She'd spent only a day in her new home, but already she knew that though handsome, her new husband was the devil in disguise.

Chapter Thirteen

True to her word, Miss Reagan had let Claudia suffer for what seemed like an eternity before giving Rebecca the order to unplug her and help her to the commode. The entire experience had been horrid. Not only had her belly cramped and her bottom hole become extremely sore, the embarrassment she'd felt sitting upon the commode with Rebecca hovering and Miss Reagan watching from the doorway had been humiliating.

After the enema, Miss Reagan had led her to a straight-backed, wooden chair that was too hard for her punished bottom to bear where she'd sat naked for the longest time. She'd wiggled about, trying to become comfortable all under the watchful eyes of the evil matron. Claudia saw the gleam of satisfaction in her eyes as she saw the evidence of Claudia's discomfort.

She had spoken of the household, told her of the staff, and informed Claudia of the different ranks of those in power. She was educated about the fact that there were two different types of dinner parties, social evenings, and visitors. There were those who, like the Earl, had sadistic tastes, and those who consisted of the rest of society who came for business or expected social engagements. Miss Reagan assured her that soon she would know what was expected at each. She was also reminded time and again that no matter what, her immediate obedience was expected in all things, or there would be dire consequences.

When the lecture was over, Miss Reagan had her lie back in bed, tying her hands and her ankles so she was spread wide, but not before shoving a hard plug into her torture bottom. She then put more of the hot pepper oil on Claudia's already aching clit before covering her with a rough sheet that scraped at the hypersensitive bud with a mixture of discomfort and pleasure. When Miss Reagan was satisfied that Claudia was helpless and under duress, the witch had smiled with glee. When Miss Reagan got over her glee, she informed Claudia she was to take a long nap. Later in the day she would be woken so preparations could commence before Claudia was presented to her husband.

True to her word, Miss Reagan returned as the sky outside Claudia's window was turning pink with the brush strokes of dusk. The woman unfastened her hands and ankles, rubbing each appendage to increase circulation, but snapped at Claudia when she'd moved to close her legs.

"No one told you to close your legs, girl. You're always to show your cunt. Whether standing, sitting or lying down, you're to be exposed to any who wish to look." Punishment always accompanied that admonition and Miss Reagan didn't fail to administer it. Five sharp slaps were delivered with the leather strap upon the part of her that must always be exposed. It amazed her how fast Miss Reagan could unclip and fold over the hateful thing.

Claudia thought back to the first morning she'd met Helena. The woman had told her the same thing, and it had been true. Whenever she'd pressed her thighs together, she'd received a slap upon her thigh or a twist of her nipple. The lesson had taken some time to sink in. Ladies were supposed to sit modestly. Claudia had been raised hearing that among the litany of items a proper lady did and didn't do.

"Up with you now. There's much to be done. Rebecca will do your hair while I prepare the rest of you."

Claudia stood, only then noticing Rebecca who was sitting silently in a shadow darkened corner. The maid rose and turned up the gas lamps in the room and then went to the dressing table. Taking that as a cue, Claudia went to the table as well and sat down on the cushioned bench, saying a silent prayer of thanks for the padding under her tender bottom.

"Two long plaits, one on each side of her head. Then pull them around and up." Claudia bristled at Miss Reagan's orders to Rebecca.

"I'm not a child who needs little girl braids."

Miss Reagan ignored her. Claudia curled her hands into fists and gritted her teeth in an effort to stay silent. Ignoring her was just another means by which Miss Reagan was reminding Claudia that her opinion and wishes didn't matter. Rebecca went to work brushing her long hair as Miss Reagan pulled various jars and bottles away from the rest on the vanity top. She glanced at Claudia's lap, and Claudia immediately spread her legs wider, narrowly evading more spanks upon her clit. Miss Reagan raised an eyebrow and looked down at Claudia making certain she knew she'd come close to another lesson taught by pain.

The matron picked up a jar and a tiny paintbrush, moving in front of Claudia as she dabbed the brush in the jar. Without a word she set the pot down and began rubbing, pulling and pinching one of Claudia's nipples. It didn't truly cause enough pain to make Claudia cry out, and Claudia knew to keep her mouth shut. Miss Reagan stopped when Claudia's nipple was a hard pebble, and then used the brush to paint it a dark red. She repeated the process with Claudia's other nipple and then painted her lips as well. The taste of strawberries danced on her tongue, and she gave her lips a quick lick.

"Stop that. They are flavored for the Earl, not for you." Claudia chanced a grimace at Miss Reagan and was rewarded with a sly smile that spoke volumes. She'd only been in the house a short time, but she knew that look all too well. It said, "I will be punishing you for that before too long."

Miss Reagan toyed with Claudia's exposed clit until she felt a pool of her juices wetting the cushion underneath her bottom. When Claudia let out a moan of pleasure she couldn't hold back, Miss Reagan looked at her in disgust and proclaimed her a wanton whore. Claudia shot the woman another look that she knew she'd pay for, but she couldn't help it. To tease her where her body received the most pleasure and then call her a whore for responding was idiotic. There was no other word for it.

"You'll regret your sass, Claudia. I'd put more pepper oil on your whore's cunt, but the Master won't want that in his mouth." Claudia's eyes opened wide at the statement. So she was finally going to become intimate with her husband. The fact that he'd put his mouth on her puss didn't have the power to shock her anymore. Helena had told her all sorts or sordid things a man and woman did for pleasure.

"I can still put a touch of clove oil on before I paint your clit though. I hope he leaves you begging tonight. You don't deserve to cum." Miss Reagan did as promised and oiled not just her clit, but the folds of her puss and the edge of her opening with the clove oil before painting the area with the strawberry tint.

Claudia couldn't help but wiggle about as the brush teased her clit. She moaned once more, not able to help it. Miss Reagan then dusted her body with a silky powder that tasted of honey, making Claudia feel much like a sweet treat.

When Rebecca was finished with her hair, Miss Reagan had Claudia stand before the wardrobe. The doors held mirrors on the inside, and Claudia couldn't help but gaze at herself. Despite the childish hairdo, her red lips, tinted eyes and painted nipples and puss made her look lovely. The makeup Miss Reagan had applied enhanced her big brown eyes. Her skin shimmered from the powder, and the red hue made her nipples look like over ripe berries waiting to be eaten.

Claudia was pulled from her self-appraisal by a slap on her bottom. "You're not here to gawk at yourself. I shall have to tell the Master of your vanity. You'd better learn humility girl. You may be the Earl's wife, but you are not special in the least."

Miss Reagan took a sheer white gown from the wardrobe and slipped it over Claudia's head. It fell around her body like a shimmering waterfall, stopped only by tiny ties made of lace on each shoulder. The garment, if you could call it that, left her almost completely exposed, her red nipples and puss still very prominent.

"Arms up." Claudia obeyed, too fascinated and horrified by the piece of clothing to give a care about what Miss Reagan was doing. The woman went about tying little lace bows down each side of her. Afterward, she drew back the fabric from a slit in the front to draw it up and away, exposing her sex, and doing the same for the back. The last task successfully putting Claudia's whip striped bottom on display as well. The effect did more to frame them than anything else since the fabric was so sheer, but it added to Claudia's overall feeling of being near naked.

Footsteps could be heard approaching in the hall, and Miss Reagan pulled Claudia to a place in the center of the room as the door opened to admit Lord Tarrington, Earl of Brighton, Claudia's husband. He paused, taking her in, and then stepped into the room with a smile of satisfaction on his lips. Claudia appraised him even as he looked her up and down.

Her husband was an attractive and virile man, not a bit old and ugly like so many of her friend's husbands. No one in her social circle married for love. Marriages were arranged for the benefit of the families involved, which often meant being wedded to a man twice your age or repulsive in some way. Despite the pain, embarrassment and degradation she'd received at Miss Patton's school, Claudia could find no fault in the Earl's good looks. The smile upon his lips suggested that he felt the same about her.

"Well done Maude. She's perfect."

"She certainly thinks she is."

"Did she give you trouble?" He asked the question of Miss Reagan, but his eyes stayed on his new wife, quite enchanted by her.

"Nothing that she won't be accountable for. I'm just telling you, so you know she needs a bit more humbling."

"Ah, well she'll have a good dose of that tonight at dinner. Thank you for getting her ready. That's all for tonight. Rebecca, your mistress, won't be in need of you for quite some time. I'll ring when I'm finished with her."

Claudia lifted her chin and glared at the Earl. He would ring when he finished with her? He made her sound like she was a thing, or worse still, a trollop who was bought for the hour.

"I see what you're referring to Maude. Claudia, you'd do best never to look at me in that way again. I own you. You are my wife, but you are also my pet, my sexual slave, and now exist solely for my pleasure."

As she was being scolded, Miss Reagan and Rebecca left the room, leaving her with an angry husband. His spoke the words softly, but they were laced with disapproval. Claudia lowered her chin, but not her eyes, still, she didn't dare glare at him.

"I understand Milord. I'm sorry."

"No, Claudia, you do not understand, but you will." His gaze turned from one of anger to one of pleasure as he began his appraisal of her once more. His fingers ran down her neck, teased her nipples, and then stroked her sides. He strutted around her like a cock with a new hen, more than pleased with himself and his new acquisition.

Stopping behind her, Lord Tarrington's hands cupped her bottom cheeks. His thumbs tracing the still vivid marks left by his whip, and then Claudia felt a hand on her back pushing her forward. She began to take a step, but his hand moved to her hip to stop her.

"No, bend for me. Legs wide, hands upon the floor." Claudia took in a deep breath and did as she was told. His hands returned to her bottom, the heat of them and his nearness reminding her of his harsh taking of her bottom in front of the crowd.

He spread her cheeks and to her horror; Claudia felt her juices trickling down her inner thighs. She told herself it was only because Miss Reagan had tormented her clit all day. Still, when Nathaniel pressed against her bottom, his hard and prominent cock pushing between her spread cheeks, more moisture flowed from her and whatever the reason, Claudia was horrified.

Claudia's fingers tried to grasp the smooth floor as her husband ground his cock against her bottom. She feared she would topple over, but then to her relief; he backed up. That relief was short lived when she felt him running a finger up one thigh and then the other, gathering the evidence of her desire.

"That's my good little harlot, wet and ready for her Master. Would you like my cock in your bum again pet?"

"I'd prefer not, Sir. I'm hurting from the taking and what that wit... And from the enema."

"At least you are honest, and you caught yourself before calling Maude a bad name. As for the fucking, we shall see. I will use you tonight wife. My cock with thrust in your mouth, your cunt, and your bum, probably many times. You are going to cry and beg for me sweet whore. You will do anything I tell you and do it with pleasure. I'll fill you in ways you didn't know were possible, but first we must go to dinner."

His hand had slipped around the front of her and began to tease her clit with slippery fingers. His nasty words and ministrations filled her with a need she could hardly stand. It didn't matter if he was speaking to her like a two bit whore. She'd been brought to the brink so many times, her body would have responded to anything.

"So slick and wet. Stand up straight for me. That's a girl." She straightened and felt one finger slip inside her vagina ever so carefully and make small circles at her entrance. Claudia moaned, her hips moving with the rhythm of his touch on their own accord.

"That's right. You're my whore Claudia. And you'll always be wet and ready for me. You're going to cum and cry for me tonight my sweet virginal wife. You're ever so tight, but I will thrust deep as you cry, and then you'll wrap your legs around me like the whore you've become. My sweet slut will hold on tight as I ride her into the floor or the bed, or where ever I choose to fuck you."

So very nasty were his words and so wonderful his finger in her puss. "Please, I need to cum. Please Milord."

"Oh no, my pet. You won't be allowed release that easy. You'll work for it later." He removed his finger and move it up to push into her mouth. "Taste how wet I make my little whore." His finger slipped over her tongue, and the flavor of her desire filled her mouth. She suckled his finger like a babe with a sugar teat, and he laughed at her eagerness, but pulled his hand away all the same.

"There will be much more of that, but not until after dinner. Get on the bed on your hands and knees, bottom in the air. I want those cheek to be as red as your lips when we go downstairs."

His words cut through the haze of pleasure, and she jerked against him, trying to turn and face him, but he placed his hand on the back of her neck and held her still. "Do not disobey me, Claudia. You are never to question an order. Do I make myself clear?"

His words had turned sinister, his voice a harsh whisper against her ear. When she didn't respond immediately, his fingers entwining in her long plaits. He pulled back, his hot breath caressing her neck, and then nipped her earlobe as he hisses his command once more.

"Get on your hands and knees on the bed and push that ass up high. You've earned some extra attention now. You will also crawl there to help you remember your place is at my feet. Now do it."

He released Claudia, and she dropped to her knees at once, the sheer material of her chemise falling open even wider across her back and bottom. She paused a moment to gather the material on each side up and tossed it across her back in an effort to avoid ripping it. Nathaniel growled in impatience and tore the flimsy cloth from her body.

"There are others, and I've no patience for delay. Crawl to the bed, Claudia and get into position. Do it NOW!"

Claudia squeaked and obeyed, crawling over to the big bed and scrambling up into position. She lowered her head and thrust her bum up, making sure her legs were spread wide. She had no desire to anger him further, and the burn in her sex throbbed incessantly, making her want to feel his hands upon her again, even if it was in a way that would hurt.

Chapter Fourteen

Nathaniel stood and admired his new wife. Her breathing had quickened; her body flushed giving testament to the fact that blood and adrenaline were both coursing quickly through her body. She let out a little whimper as he made her wait, and then smiled as a tiny trickle of moisture ran down her inner thigh giving testament of her arousal in spite of her fear. Despite the trouble at the school, Miss Patton and her staff had managed to begin the training of his willful wife.

Once done with his inspection, Nathaniel walked to the dresser and picked up the heavy silver hairbrush that had an ornate pattern which included the family's crest, and then turned back towards Claudia. He went forward slowly, knowing a knot of dread battled with the desire inside her, making her wait, building both the pleasure and the panic in the woman who waited for his wrath. When he stood directly behind her, he reached forward and grabbed both of her long plaits in his fist. He yanked her up so her back was arched, and her head tilted back, and then whispered in her ear.

"Open your eyes." Claudia obeyed and found her face just inches from his. Nathaniel gave her the gentlest of kisses on her jaw line before bringing his face back to hover mere inches above hers.

"You have a willfulness about you that I will not tolerate. There are many lessons to be learned here in your new home, but not all of them need to be taught through pain. It shall be your choice my little wife, but I can assure you, they will be taught.

Tonight's lesson is one of humility. You've been spoiled all your life, but that stops here and now. You will be taken down to dinner without a stitch of clothing now that I found it necessary to tear the garment you were wearing. You will be introduced to the servants as my wife and the new lady of the house, but your nudity and well-punished bottom will make it clear that you are also mine in every way.

"The women in my home are submissive whores. The only exception is the servants. They aren't trained to love the lash and to crave a good hard rutting, and while they are reprimanded for disobedience or laziness, it is as all men punish those he employs. Up until a few weeks ago you were an uppity little bitch. You never paid any mind to those who served you, and worse than that, you treated them with scorn and disrespect. There will be none of that here, and to make sure you learn to be humble, you will be presented to them in a very degrading manner."

Claudia was shaking, both from his nearness and his words. The feel of his breath upon her cheek, his unmistakable masculinity, and his whispered words telling her of the evening to come, all had her trembling. The hand holding her hair pushed her head forward, so it was bowed, and then he thrust the silver hairbrush before her eyes.

"This my dear is going to warm your backside before we descend for dinner. My family's crest is engraved in the silver. Your bottom will bear my mark once I spank you with it for days to come. Think of it as my branding of you Claudia. My mark of ownership so to speak. Kiss it now and thank me for the punishment that is to come."

Claudia's mouth was dry, and her mind muddled by all the warring sensations in her body. She didn't mean to make him wait; she wasn't a fool, but found herself unable to speak.

Nathaniel gave her a little shake. "Kiss the thing that will give you pain and thank me for what is to come. Do it now!"

"Thank you Sir for… for punishing me and teaching me humility." The sentence came out in a rush of words, and Claudia then closed her eyes and gave the brush a quick kiss.

"Good girl. Your belated obedience won't save the skin of your arse, but at least we can now begin. Get back into position."

He released her, and Claudia once more dropped to her hands and thrust her bottom out to be spanked well and proper by the Earl. He stroked the soft skin, admiring the sheer beauty of her bottom, and then wrapped an arm about her waist.

"You are not to struggle nor are you to move."

Her first thought was to wonder why he held her so tight if he didn't expect her to struggle. That question was answered as his hand brushed the skin of her belly then moved to her clit. Claudia jumped, not able to help herself. Her nub was so sensitive. She had no clit hood any longer, and he'd stimulated her to near orgasm only a bit ago.

"Pain and pleasure my sweet whore. That's what you'll get at my hands. Though I love how wet you are for me, there won't be any release for you. You've been a very bad girl."

Nathaniel stroked her bottom with the back of the hairbrush then lifted it high and brought it back down with a loud crack upon Claudia's bottom. She jerked, but then made herself still. Jerking only served to increase the pressure of his fingers on her clit, and she knew if she moved about and made herself orgasm there would be even more hell to pay.

It wasn't long before all coherent thoughts left her mind. Nathaniel brought the brush down upon her bottom and upper thighs without mercy. The brush was heavy and carried a hard impact that left the one being spanked almost breathless. He spanked her hard, going from the middle of one bottom cheek down to the tender spot where her ass met her thighs and then lower still. It was these that finally made her cry out and beg him to stop. She'd held her resolve to refrain from begging until his attack upon her thighs. It was too much. The pain too intense.

"You will learn to obey wife. You will do as I wish before I even have to ask. You are mine for life, and I intend to make certain that a day doesn't go by where you will feel my ownership of your body. You will be a whore, a dutiful wife, and a lady, whichever I require. You will learn to crawl for me, learn to pleasure me and yearn for my touch and my approval of you. No desire of mine will be too filthy for you to perform. Do you understand?"

"Yes, please Sir. Please."

"You will ache for me every day Claudia, in your cunt and on your bottom, breasts, and thighs. I will adorn you as I see fit. Punished as I like, and pleasured until you are moaning and as wet as a bitch in heat, and each day you will thank me for choosing you to be mine."

Her bottom was a blaze that was so intense Claudia thought he was surely taking the skin off, and still he spanked her without mercy as he lectured her. He spanked though she begged him to stop, he spanked until she thought she would go mad, all the while tapping a finger upon her clit to make all the sensations war inside her. If her mind had been able to produce a coherent thought, she would have wondered how her traitorous body could feel the pleasure despite his cruel treatment, but her head was filled with a red haze of pain.

Finally, he stopped, and Claudia gasped, drawing in a breath she hadn't known she was holding and releasing it a second later in a huge sob. She buried her face in the quilt to muffle her cries, hating him and hating the life she was now destined to live.

Her entire body shook as she fought to compose herself, and she jerked as if burned when he began to stroke her back in a soothing manner Claudia found absurd. How could hands that had hurt her so badly now seek to give comfort? Did he take her for a woman who had no fire or spirit?

Nathaniel continued to stroke Claudia's back until her trembling ceased. He then pulled her up, so she was once more on her knees, and wrapped his arms around her, his hard body pressing against her back and well punished bottom. One hand cupped her breast, thumb rubbing ever so softly over her nipple. The stern man who'd inflicted so much pain, replaced by one that was gentle. He slowly stroked her belly, gave her a soft kiss upon her neck, and then tilted her head back and kissed the tears on her cheeks, mystifying Claudia further.

"You did so very well pigeon. You stayed in position as told, took all I felt was your due, and kept your composure. I'm proud of you my sweet wife."

His words confused her, and just a hint of Claudia's anger melted away. She leaned her head back against his shoulder and took deep breaths that allowed her body to relax. The brushing of his thumb over her nipple was more of a soothing gesture than one meant to stimulate, and when he wrapped an arm around her waist holding her tightly, she couldn't help but feel comforted.

"Such a good girl. My sweet, sweet wife. We shall be happy together. I've chosen well." His words made her bristle, but when he whispered the word mine over and over as he kissed her, her irritation and anger once more began to fade. When Nathaniel moved to scoop her into his arms, and carried her to the wingback chair in the sitting room, Claudia nuzzled into his chest. His arms were so strong, his presence so virile, his continued words of pride for her making her feel cherished despite the pain her bottom felt as it came into contact with his lap.

He held her close and then pushed her knees open, moving her just a bit, so she was fully supported by his arm and the chair. He stroked the insides of her thighs, and then moved up to slide his finger between her swollen pussy lips. Claudia let out a gasp. Despite the pain, she was so very needy. All day long she'd been built up to the brink of orgasm only to be denied, and the pain from her punishment hadn't dampened her arousal.

Claudia buried her face in Nathaniel's chest, ashamed at her desire. His finger slid so easily between her lips, up and down, swirling just inside her virginal opening and then up to rub her clit with a slick finger. She shook her head even as her hips thrust forward, needing release.

"Part of you is saying no and part of you is screaming yes. No is forbidden Claudia."

"I'm not saying no to you Sir, but to myself." The words were muffled because her face was still buried in his chest. She could feel the heat of her shame in her cheeks and wanted to hide.

"There is no shame in desire. That is what I wish from you."

"To be your whore." The words held venom once more. Despite her desire and his sweet words, Claudia hadn't forgotten all the nasty things he'd said.

"Being mine takes away the shame of desire. You have no control over your body or what's done to you. You are free to simply feel without the burden of shame. Many women remain cold and unfeeling in their marital bed, the words about always being a lady keeping them from tasting pleasure. You've no such burden wife."

"I don't feel free, husband. I feel trapped."

Nathaniel let out a small chuckle which made Claudia stiffen in his arms. "I am not laughing at you wife; I am finding joy in the fact that one day soon you will understand how free you truly are. As long as you obey, there will be no misery. I will do many things to you, but I tell the truth when I say you will desire them all. Now hush. We're already late for supper. You must still be introduced to the servants."

His reminder of what was to come made her anger rise up, but the rapid movement of his fingers over her clit and up soon made her need to cum override all else. She spread her legs wider, not caring if she was acting the whore. All that mattered was the heat building in her core, coiling tighter and tighter as an exquisite pleasure spread from her clit through her entire body.

Claudia moaned loudly and tossed her head back, hips moving as her husband moved his fingers in circles around her hard bud. He went back to rubbing ever so fast, making her cry out even as her well punished bottom rubbed the scratchy fabric of his trousers. A blur of images went through her mind as he played her body with practiced fingers. Helena on the bed touching her. Miss Patton rubbing oil into her exposed clit. The humiliation of being bound and punished before all. Her husband forcing his greased cock into her bottom as Helena pleasured her. All the sensations came back to her, the pain, the pleasure, the denial, and the disgrace.

It was the last memory that made her arch up her back; her body stiffened and then shook, hips pumping as an exquisite pleasure exploded inside. Fire raced from her core through every nerve, liquid heat spreading through her entire body, and still Nathaniel rubbed. He rubbed as she jerked in his arms as she bucked and cried out, shaking her head, lost in the wild sensations until finally his fingers slowed and turned gentle, bringing her back down.

He pulled her close as she whimpered and trembled, enjoying each shiver of aftershock that ran through her as his finger ever so lightly and slowly brushed her clit. His lips claimed hers. His mouth demanding. His tongue plunging in, sweeping side to side and then curling around hers. He kissed her breathless and then pulled away and looked down at her, loving how her lips stayed parted. Her once plaited hair was a tumbled mess and a flush of passion stained her cheeks. Her eyes were hooded and heavy as she tried to gaze up at him.

Nathaniel hadn't planned on allowing the little minx to cum until he was thrusting inside her in their marriage bed that night, but he found her untamed spirit bewitching. He had wanted to see her go from anger to wild abandon, and so he'd given her release. Now she was looking up at him sated and sleepy, but it was time to go downstairs. She wouldn't like it one bit, but her wishes didn't matter. He was her lord and master.

Before she knew what was happening, Claudia had been set on her feet and received a slap on her already well punished bottom. She cried out in shock and turned accusing eyes upon him. Nathaniel gave her a no nonsense look that made it clear the tenderness and pleasure had come to an end.

"You've had your need met my little Jezebel, and now it's time for dinner." He took her hand, but she pulled back, her innate defiance rising up despite her spanking.

"I'll have none of that now. Come along." He led her to the vanity and quickly undid the plaits in her hair, and then brushed it with the same brush he'd used to spank her without mercy. When he was done his eyes met hers in the mirror, and he gave a curt nod.

"That will have to do. Come now."

"Nathaniel, please. I have to have something to wear."

"No Claudia, you do not, and you are to call me Sir or My Lord. You must make amends for all the years of uppity spiteful behavior towards the servants at your father's house. Though the people are different, their stations are the same, but you will be respectful of them. Your position as lady in this house doesn't guarantee you respect. That is something you will have to earn from them."

"Naked!?" Claudia stomped her foot in a show of temper before thinking about what she was doing. Her spoiled ways were not so far gone as to make tantrums a mere memory. She regretted the action the second she did it though, and shame at her childish behavior flushed her cheeks.

"I believe you just confirmed your need for a bit of humility." He smirked at her, and Claudia wanted to slap the smug look from his face but instead curled her hands into fists. Nathaniel noticed of course and was pleased with her show of restraint. He spun her around and took a quick look at her bottom then turned her back to face him.

"You're already showing my mark of ownership on your sweet backside. All will know that you are mine and that the taming has begun. Off we go now, pet, don't dawdle."

Chapter Fifteen

As they left her chambers, Claudia felt the cooler air upon her skin. It was a gentle caress, but one that made her painfully aware of her nudity. Only her bottom enjoyed the change in temperature; the rest of her broke out in gooseflesh either from the chill or because of her anxiety over being present to the staff without a stitch to cover herself.

She slowed her step for a moment, breathing deeply, and then shut her eyes and lifted her chin in a small but needed show of pride. Nathaniel had allowed the falter in her steps, but when he saw her prideful display his fingers squeezed the elbow he'd taken.

"It's your misplaced feelings of superiority that make it quite necessary for me to force a bit of humility into that arrogant head of yours, but it appears you haven't been listening my dear. I would have thought the day's activities would have taught you that your haughtiness isn't what I wish from you."

Claudia's eyes had flown open as her new husband spoke. His words wounding her and making her flush. She had to grit her teeth to bite back a scathing comment despite the harsh spanking she'd just endured. Though it had enflamed her bottom in a very painful way, it hadn't erased years of feeling superior to those around her. She would be damned if she'd allow his servants to see her cowed because of her lack of clothing and her well paddled bottom. Since being brought to Brighton, so many had seen her naked that she'd lost count. Still, she decided to sweeten her words with honey instead of snapping at Nathaniel like a shrew.

"The pride in myself that my upbringing taught me wasn't what made me lift my chin. It's the determination to make you proud of me no matter what you make me endure." Claudia peeked up at him through lowered lashes, the picture of sweetness.

"I'm not a mere boy you can manipulate Claudia. I've had more than a bit of practice taming women who are uppity and full of self-importance. I've no use for batted lashes and coy looks. You will learn humility pet. There are all sorts of lessons that you won't like one bit to teach you appreciation for those who see to your needs. Tonight is merely the start. I've no tolerance for conceit. You are an owned plaything, Claudia. Despite being my wife, you're nothing more than what I make of you, be it whore, pretty bauble to show off at dinner parties or scullery maid."

He began to propel her along towards the grand staircase as he said the words, and suddenly they were at the top. Claudia found herself gazing down at the expansive foyers well lit by a glittering chandelier. The floor shone like polished glass, and waiting there looking up at her, were at least a dozen men and women in clothing that identified their status in her new home.

Her step faltered, all of her bravado leaving her in a rush to be replaced by panic. She became acutely aware of her nudity once more and pulled back when Nathaniel tried to move her forward.

"No." She shook her head, this time raising her chin in an effort to stop the tears that threatened from falling.

"Oh yes pet. They've all been wondering about the new lady of the house. It's only proper I_introduce you."

"Please, Sir."

"Though you remembered how to address me properly, your begging makes no difference. Move down the stairs now, or get on your hands and knees with your legs spread and be spanked with your already punished bottom and quim on display."

Claudia took a deep breath, her breasts rising and falling and then took the first step down towards the waiting servants. She saw Nathaniel smile with satisfaction at her submission, and hated him for it, vowing that she would find a way to make him pay for this humiliation.

He chuckled as if reading her mind, and then whispered in her ear that she was expected to meet their eyes, before giving her a nip on her earlobe. She looked up, her face a mask of indifference. Two could play this game. Yes, she was horrified, but she was stronger than he suspected. It would take more than a parade past the servants without a stitch of clothing to make her cower.

They walked down the rest of the steps, and Claudia did as she'd been told, looking straight at those who stood there judging her every curve and feature. Nathaniel's hand held her elbow securely as he steered her towards the first of the servants. Their dress told her they were the butler and head housekeeper. Nathaniel made formal introductions as if she were the new bride coming home for the first time, the staff properly line up to greet their new mistress. Though their words were polite through the introductions, many an eye strayed from her face without reprimand from her husband.

The girl who'd been her ladies maid, Rebecca, was there. Claudia was grateful when she saw the sincere smile upon the maid's face, thinking that at least she had one friend in the depraved household. Last but certainly not least was the already despised Miss Reagan who looked down at Claudia with disdain. Claudia stared back with a look that let the formidable Miss Reagan know she hadn't beaten her. Nathaniel saw her expression and of course disapproved.

"Claudia, Miss Reagan is your Nursemaid and you will show respect."

Nursemaid?! Was he joking? That thought was immediately followed by one that rang much truer. Of course, her husband wasn't joking. The Earl of Brighton was hell bent on putting her in the position of submission, and having a nursemaid as if she were a child was simply another bit of degradation she would be made to withstand.

Claudia bowed her head hoping to appear much like a well-chastised child, but was, in fact, doing her best to hide her simmering rage. Time and again everyone around her did their best to make her feel like a thing of no importance, and she'd had about enough, but now wasn't the time for rebellion. The squeeze upon her elbow let her know that Nathaniel was not fooled, and that obeying was the better course of action for the moment.

"Forgive me Miss Reagan, I forgot my manners. It's a pleasure to see you again." Claudia glanced up as she said the words and gave Miss Reagan a tiny curtsy if one could call it that without a skirt to hold out, fuming all the while. The woman before her had shoved a nozzle up her bottom and filled her with soapy water, and then toyed with her puss as her poor stomach cramped painfully. The woman was a nasty bitch, but Claudia could play the game her husband demanded she play.

"You're forgiven my dear. I so look forward to taking care of your special needs. Tell me Lady Tarrington, has your bum hole recovered from yesterday's fucking and today's enema?"

Claudia flushed. Even she hadn't the will power to keep the crimson stain of her embarrassment from flushing her cheeks, but shame or no, she wasn't going to grovel or let the old battle ax get the best of her.

"Why yes Miss Reagan, thank you for asking. I'm feeling quite well."

"Claudia," Nathaniel said her name in a sinister tone that let her know she'd suffer for her words. She felt a flutter of panic in her stomach at her husband's single uttered word. It said in no uncertain terms that there would be more pain in her future.

Without further ado, Nathaniel steered her towards the dining room, and then to her seat at the opulent table. China, crystal, and silver graced the table settings, and a grand candelabra cast a glow that reflected in each piece upon the table. Her chair was pulled out for her, and Claudia sat at once, grateful to be half hidden beneath the table despite the pain her bottom felt when she sat.

The meal was somewhat uneventful, servants bringing one course after another, and more of them clearing the dirty dishes. Claudia spoke only when spoken to, and behaved in a very restrained manner, doing her best to be a picture of submission. She knew Nathaniel was already going to punish her for her poor manners when speaking to Miss Reagan. She wasn't going to add insult to the injury of her bottom by confronting her husband where the staff could hear her being insolent.

"Claudia." She'd been daydreaming. Being a meek and submissive woman was boring, and she'd become lost in her thoughts.

"Yes, Sir?"

I asked you if you'd like to know how and why I chose you to be my wife. I'd have thought that would be of interest to you."

He had her full attention. Meek and submissive or not, she truly had wondered why she was the one who'd been selected as a suitable wife for the Earl. "I am Milord. Very much so. Please continue. Forgive my inattentiveness."

Nathaniel looked at her critically; eyebrows raised. He wasn't sure he liked this passive little thing that his fiery wife had become.

"Stop it, Claudia. We both know I haven't subdued your bad behavior that easily. It's one of the reasons you're here. I enjoy women with spirit."

"So you can beat her!" The angry words rushed out before Claudia could stop herself. Nathaniel was quite right that she hadn't been bullied into submission.

"So I can tame her, and mold her into the perfect wife and whore." Claudia looked at her husband, her brown eyes full of rage.

"I've known you since you were a gangly young thing running about like a heathen. Your father and I belong to the same secret order as you are now well aware, and though only a child, your temperament, and wild ways intrigued me.

"When your father was sent away for work, he asked me to keep an eye on you. Not to try and control you, but to watch you and see if you did indeed prove to be a woman I would want as a wife. Countless girls come to us here in Brighton. Our society is large with many of the noble families as members. Not all of the girls are sent here for training, but a good many follow in their mother's footsteps."

Nothing he'd told her was really any news, and her bored expression conveyed the fact. "So I've been told."

"As I said, you sparked my interest, especially when you grew into those long legs of yours and developed such delightful curves. I followed you the season you went to court, watching or having other's watch to make certain you didn't allow all those fawning lads to do anything more than paw at you. I had to confirm my suspicion that you had a wild streak that would make taming you a welcome challenge.

"All those times you slipped into the gardens, one of my men was there. I witnessed behavior that made me want to haul you over my knee and give you the spanking you so well deserved, but I contented myself with watching you act the harlot and tease. I knew that as soon as your father came home you'd be mine, and so here you are, naked and well spanked at my table and in my home."

Claudia's expression had undergone a remarkable change. Gone was the boredom, gone the look of complacency. She now had fury in her eyes as she stared at Nathaniel in disbelief.

"You had me watched? You... you..." Claudia thought over all the times she'd tease some poor hopeful suitor, flirting and even allowing his hand to cup her breast as her body pressed against his growing erection. Nathaniel had been watching? How dare he?

Furious that she'd been spied on in an effort to see if she'd be exciting to tame, Claudia's fingers tightened on her water goblet seconds before she threw it at his oh so smug face.

The crystal flew just inches past his head and then shattered upon the floor behind him. The servants who had been standing, waiting to clear a dish as soon as it was empty, made little sounds of disbelief, their eyes nearly popping out of their heads. The women whom the master of the house trained didn't usually have so much spunk, let alone the gall to throw something at the Earl.

"My, my Claudia. I thought you'd have the sense to know that I wouldn't tolerate childish temper tantrums. Daniels, are my chambers prepared?"

"Yes, Sir. As specified." The butler spared a glance at Claudia and smiled, knowing what was in store for his lordship's wayward new wife.

"Very good. Tell the staff they won't be needed anymore tonight. I'm not to be interrupted."

"Yes, Sir."

"And leave the mess. My wife will clean it up tomorrow."

"Very good Sir."

That said Nathaniel rose from his chair and then jerked Claudia's chair away from the table. She tried to evade him and dart away, but he caught her about the waist and swung her up over his shoulder with ease, her head hanging down over his back, fists pounding to no avail. She was also doing her best to kick, but her feet met thin air, and wiggling free wasn't an option either.

Nathaniel's arm held her just behind her knees, her stomach resting on his shoulder, her bottom thrust up into the air. He began raining stinging slaps down upon her well positioned backside as he carried Claudia from the dining room. His actions left no doubt in anyone's mind that the Earl had his hands full with the woman he'd chosen to be his wife. Not that anyone had reservations about him being up for the challenge. Soon the mistress would learn to behave. Lord Tarrington had many ways to subdue those who didn't comply.

Chapter Sixteen

Nathaniel carried Claudia up the stairs, down the hall and to his chambers slapping her bottom all the while. He entered, kicked the door shut, and then walked through the dressing room to the bedroom where he deposited his still shrieking wife upon the bed in a heap.

"You will stop that screaming this instant."

Claudia's mouth snapped shut, but her eyes shot daggers at her husband. She rolled over and scrambled off the far side of the bed, then headed for the door. He watched her flee, his face impassive, showing no emotion, let alone anger. He'd played many such scenes with the women he'd chosen to be his submissives over the years. Therefore, Claudia's behavior hardly fazed him.

"Do you plan on running away without a stitch of clothing, or had you forgotten that you're quite bare?"

His words halted her in her tracks. She turned, looking for something else to throw at him, her eyes landing on a vase on the fireplace mantle. He saw her intent and cocked an eyebrow, his mouth twisting in a sardonic grin.

"It appears your pretty bottom isn't warm enough yet pet. You may throw the vase, but I promise you will clean up the mess just as you will the mess you created in the dining room. While it's true, I enjoy spirit in a woman; childish behavior is quite unappealing. Haven't you had enough pain Claudia?"

"Haven't I had enough? Are you serious? I most certainly have. Has it not occurred to you that it is your behavior and that of the wretched Miss Reagan that brought me to this state?" Her new husband remained silent, the mocking grin still upon his face. "That... That woman gave me an enema and then put her fingers where they most certainly didn't belong. She..."

"Miss Reagan prepared you as instructed. You had better get used to such things as they will often occur."

Claudia barely registered his words. She was so intent on screaming out all the indignities that had been done to her that day.

"I was painted and dressed like a whore, and then you... you."

"I spanked you for your bad behavior just as you'll be punished for your temper tantrum when you're finished having it." He voice was so calm and his manner so indifferent that it only stood to infuriate her more.

"It was much more than the spanking that has me in a rage. You paddled me so as to brand me as yours; you paraded me naked before your staff. Naked! In front of the servants! How dare you? You've done everything you possibly can to humiliate me and make me feel like a... a thing instead of a woman. I am your wife! This was to be my wedding night. That is the one thing that has kept me from going insane despite the vile treatment I have received. Though you have proven yourself despicable at times, you have also shown a shred of decency as well. Now you've only become a brute who tries to break me by hurting me inside and out. I had hoped this night would bring us together but instead all you've done is made me hate you."

Claudia's eyes shimmered with tears, and she damned herself for them. She had no desire to appear weak before the monster that was her husband. He would only use her tears against her to wound her further.

Before he could do anything in response to her tirade, Claudia marched to the small table. She yanked the tablecloth from its top, causing the crystal decanter of scotch and the accompanying glasses to shatter upon the floor. She quickly wrapped herself up, stepped carefully over the mess, and then walked out of the room, leaving the Earl stunned but torn between amusement and remorse.

Miss Reagan appeared in the doorway and looked from the mess to her employer; her eyebrows arched and her look one of shock.

"Shall I fetch her and put her in the punishment room for you Lord Tarrington?"

There was a gleam in the eyes of the woman he employed that told Nathaniel she'd like nothing better than to do as she asked.

"Leave her be. I'll find her. She can't go far dressed in a tablecloth, and get someone to clean up this glass. I'll not have her feet cut even though she's the cause of the mess."

"Yes, Sir."

Nathaniel turned away from the door, dismissing Miss Reagan, and entered his bedroom. The sheets were turned back, the rose petals that Claudia hadn't noticed or hadn't commented on were still strewn upon the bed though they were crumpled. She had told him it was to be her wedding night, and he had ruined it by tormenting her, and a furrow caused by uncertainty creased his brow. He'd been hard on her, but to be fair, he was hard on them all. Making her accept her new life left no room for tenderness, at least not until they learned to obey.

He picked up some of the rose petals and brought them to his nose to inhale their sweet fragrance then let them fall back upon the bed. Nathaniel then walked to each corner and moved the restraints that were always in place, onto the bed. He was going to give his little hellion the wedding night she wanted, but it wouldn't all be done her way. Claudia was his wife, but she was also his submissive. While it was true, he hadn't had a wife before; he saw how the wives of the other men in their society acted, and it certainly wasn't in the manner Claudia was behaving.

He walked out of the bedroom and then into the hall, his steps ringing on the marble floor, his stride purposeful. He was going to find his errant wife, and when he did, she would end this tirade of disobedience. There was more than one way to tame a wildcat, and it was time he used a different method to make Claudia pull in her claws.

He walked the second floor, opening doors and looking about with no luck. The little hellion was running about clothed only in a tablecloth. She wouldn't have dared to go outside would she? While it was true, he'd paraded her before the staff bare as the day she was born, Nathaniel was sure his wife was still in the house. Giving up on the second floor and doubting she'd be on the third floor where the servant's rooms were, Nathaniel went down the stairs, his face somewhat puzzled. While it was true, he could and would tame Claudia; he was unaccustomed to such rebellion.

"Sir"

Roberts, the butler, met him at the bottom of the staircase. Nathaniel had been lost in thought and had nearly plowed into the man. "Have you seen Lady Tarrington?"

"Yes Sir, this way."

Nathaniel followed the butler down the hall and back to the dining room. There he spotted Claudia. She was on her knees picking up the shards of glass that littered the floor. The tablecloth was pooled around her knees, the hand she was depositing the glass in was bleeding and trembling, a telltale sign that she was highly agitated.

Nathaniel went towards her, but Claudia didn't react to his footsteps, she just continued her task as if she were alone. He stood silently behind her for a moment, waiting for her to acknowledge his presence, but she wouldn't turn around. Intent on picking her up, Nathaniel grasped Claudia under her arms, but she pulled away, losing her balance her hand coming down on the glass shards.

"Leave me be!"

"Let me pick you up, you little fool."

"The servants have no need to clean up my mess. You said so yourself when you carried me out of here like a brute."

"My intention was to bring you back in the morning and give you a broom and a dustbin, not to have you kneel in the glass and pick it up with your bare hands."

"Why do you care how I clean it up? You've certainly inflicted your share of pain upon me. What is a bit more?" Claudia reached for another shard, but the butler intervened, kneeling down with a whisk broom and dustbin.

"Allow me Lady Tarrington."

"Give me that." Claudia dropped the glass she'd been holding and reached for the tiny broom. "Don't act as if you think I'm the lady of this house. I've seen the looks all of you have given me. My husband has made certain I've earned no respect from any of you."

Roberts looked more than a bit flustered. While it was true the new lady of the house received treatment that humiliated her, she was still the new Lady Tarrington.

"Give her the brush and the bin Roberts. It's clear my wife wishes to atone for her fit of temper." A scarlet flush of rage spread over his wife's body and up her neck, at his words.

"If your only wish is to torment me further, then I beg of you to leave me be. I shall clean this up and return to your chambers. I imagine I've earned yet another punishment."

Nathaniel stared at Claudia, marveling at her determination. Most women would have admitted defeated by now and done whatever he told them to, but not his new wife. Her skin still held the flush of her anger, but her back was rigid with resolve and the trembling of her hands had stopped.

"As you wish Claudia. Roberts, see to it that Lady Tarrington doesn't get lost on her way back and have Rebecca bring supplies to bandage my wife's hands." Nathaniel knew that Miss Reagan's presence would only add to Claudia's distress, and though she deserved a bit of humiliation for her tantrum, she'd suffered enough for one day.

"I'll be waiting for you pet, don't be long. You and I have things to discuss."

Claudia didn't reply. Instead, she began to clean up the glass from the goblet she'd broken, ignoring her husband, her back stiff with pride. She didn't know what awaited her when she arrived in his chambers, but whatever it was, she wouldn't accept it meekly. Oh, she would bend for her spanking, she wouldn't fight him or break any more glass, but she wouldn't be silent and meek. If Lord Tarrington wanted meek, he should have chosen a different wife!

Chapter Seventeen

Nathaniel rose from the chair before the fire when Claudia came through the door on soundless bare feet. She stopped, within arm's reach, her chin lifted in silent defiance, her eyes challenging. Nathaniel met her gaze, refusing to be intimidated by his cheeky wife, and then looked her over from head to toe, noting the spots of blood that marked her trail into his chambers.

He looked her over again, this time putting his hands on her shoulders and spinning her from the front to back and around again, searching for wounds. Happy she seemed to have escaped injury any place other than her hands, he slid his own down her arms and lift her hands palms up, to assess the lacerations.

Both had small cuts. One, on her fingertips, the other on her palm. He bent and kissed her hands gently, the tenderness of his lips surprising Claudia. She wasn't expecting gentle treatment at her husband's hands.

Nathaniel led her to the bath chamber, still without a word. No scolding, no sinister whispers of anger. He seemed far too calm considering the events of the evening, and his composure unnerved her in a way his anger never could. Bandages and salve had been placed by the wash basin, and after washing the blood from her hands, Nathaniel carefully assessed each cut, searching for small bits of glass. He picked one shard out with the gentleness of a mother tending her babe, then applied the liniment and bandages.

"That should be sufficient to keep the cuts from festering." It was the same salve that had been applied to the cut on her chest left by the whip. It seemed to have a numbing effect as well as healing properties, and though she'd never say so, Claudia was glad to have her hands tended to. It wasn't that the wounds had been painful; it was the tenderness they had brought out in her husband that left her feeling a good deal better.

"Thank you, Lord Tarrington."

"Claudia when we are alone, and especially when in my chambers, you may be less formal. There will be times when Sir will be expected, but this is not one of them."

"I wouldn't care to risk your wrath by becoming confused, Milord. I imagine there will be a price to pay for my disobedience as it stands."

"While it's true, we will attend to your behavior, we are celebrating our wedding tonight. I wish to hear my name when you address me. You are to call me Nathaniel."

"Will I be accorded the same courtesy? I wish for you to stop calling me your pet and your whore."

Lord Tarrington's eyes narrowed, showing just a hint his displeasure with her sass, but he let it pass. She was still learning. "There will come a time when you understand those terms are not meant to be demeaning."

"Forgive me... Nathaniel, but all you've done tonight has been demeaning. You speak the word whore as if it leaves a revolting taste in your mouth, and pet as if I am an animal you own. I hardly see how they cannot be construed as ways to belittle me."

"This is getting us nowhere. Sheath your claws kitten and come here." He didn't give her a choice, pulling her to him and slipping his arm around her. He fisted his hands in her hair and pulled back, tilting her head to the side and baring her neck. Nathaniel placed a trail of kisses up the long column, interspersing the kisses with tiny nips until he'd reached her ear. He kissed her behind the lobe as his arm tightened around her even more, then nipped her earlobe before licking the shell of her ear ever so slowly.

"You are mine Claudia, and before the night is over you will want nothing more than to belong to me. I shall have you wife, in every way possible. Your body will thrill to my touch as I make your every nerve cry out with passion."

His whispered words and the heat of his breath upon her skin left Claudia in no doubt that what he was telling her would be true. She was already aching for him to touch her again despite her anger, and she silently damned him for what he could do to her. Her only solace was that though her body responded, her heart remained a lump of ice.

Upon feeling her shiver in his arms, Nathaniel captured her lips with his. His mouth was demanding, and she opened her own, letting his tongue slip inside her mouth and circle around hers. She responded, waging a battle for dominance by tangling hers with his, but it was a fight she'd never win.

His fingers stretched out over the back of her head, holding her still as he kissed her hard. His mouth was practiced in this art of seduction, and his tongue continued to swirl about, never letting her come up for air, never ceasing until she was trembling and breathless. Finally, he pulled back, but it was only so he could take her bottom lip between his teeth. He nibbled, loving the sweet taste of her before finally relenting. He trailed a line of kisses from her mouth back to her ear as one hand moved to cup her bare and still sore bottom, pushing up against her and rubbing his hard cock upon her belly.

"Do you feel my need for you Claudia? It is time I claim what is mine." He scooped her up and carried her from the bath chamber to the bedroom, his dark eyes smoldering as they stared down into hers.

He laid her on the bed, and she looked about as the silkiness and heady scent of the rose petals filled her senses. She hadn't noticed them before; her anger had blinded her to their presence. The sweet thoughtfulness of the gesture melted away some of the resentment she carried inside.

She lay there unmoving, her body aching from the torment of the last few days and the need that was rising up in her core. Nathaniel had told her on the day they were wed that she would be taught to crave his touch and become his whore as well as his wife, and his words now rang true. Though Claudia hated the word, the need that grew inside her from any kind of touch be it pain or pleasure upon her sensitive skin had her wet with desire and flushed with need.

He spread her legs then slowly crawled up between them like a sleek panther. Taking one arm, Nathaniel lifted it over her head and slipped a silken rope around Claudia's wrist. Before she could do more that draw in a breath of surprise, he grasped her other wrist firmly and bound that arm as well. Claudia's eyes had been hooded and smoldered with desire, but now flew open wide as she tugged on her bindings.

"No. Why?"

"Yes, and because I wish it. Hush now sweet wife. This is the way of things. I do as I wish with you, and in exchange you are given incredible pleasure." His knee was between her thighs, pressing against her swollen lips and exposed clit, and he could feel the heat of her through the fabric of his trousers. "Even now in all your fury, your body is primed and ready for me."

Once more his lips descended, trailing little kisses down from her ear to the hollow of her neck. He repeated the sweet kisses on the other side and then traced each trail he'd made with his tongue, ever so slowly before rising to his knees. Nathaniel's fingers reached to toy with her nipples, his thumbs and fingers set to roll them, pulling and pinching. He paused in his ministrations, staring at where the red welt of the whip mark marred her porcelain skin.

The shadow of guilt filled his eyes making Claudia want to scream accusations at him if only to wound him inside because of all that had befallen her since becoming his wife, but she held her tongue. The truth was there would be many more of the marks covering her body if he hadn't intervened.

Nathaniel kissed the welt between her breasts, suckled just long enough on each nipple to make her moan and close her leg around his knee in an effort to apply more pressure.

"Ah, ah, ah. None of that now. I decide when that cunt of yours is to receive more pleasure. You must crave what I have to offer sweet Claudia."

His dark eyes bored into hers, drinking in her frustration and need. Claudia wanted to fling hateful words at him for making her be the whore he'd foreseen. Even so, the fire of her rage melted like butter as she lay upon the bed beneath him, bound, wet, and trembling.

Nathaniel watched with satisfaction as the passion in her core waged war against her anger and won. She was well and truly his now, no matter her ire. Like it or not, she needed him. He had won this first war of wills, turning the angry wildcat into a purring feline who was ready to be stroked and petted. Granted he'd done it with arousal, and hadn't touched her heart or mind, but it was the beginning. First they submitted because they were made to, and then they came to love being owned. There would be battles in the future; her spirit would see to that, but for tonight while they celebrated their wedding, his new wife would sheath her claws and silence her barbed tongue.

"If this is not yearning then I don't know what is Milord."

"You are to call me Nathaniel, and you've only begun to hunger." Without another word, he lay atop her, his weight pressing her down upon the silky rose petals. One hand cupped a breast, one stroking her side as his mouth took her nipple between his lips, suckling and swirling his tongue round and round. Claudia tried to arch up, but he had her pinned down, causing her frustration and need to spiral up inside her. He began to pinch one nipple as he licked the other, a brief touch of pain alternating with the lovely feel of his hot mouth and tongue upon the other nipple.

Just when she thought the dual sensations would drive her mad enough to scream, he moved his lips and his tormenting hand, running one down over her leg, and the other leaving kisses upon her belly. When Claudia moaned beneath his lips, pulling upon her restraints and damning him once again, he rose. It was time to play a new game.

"No." Claudia hated that she needed him so, but the loss of his lips, his heat, his touch, left her feeling abandoned though he was still on the bed with her.

"The answer is yes, sweet wife. You are always to say yes. Yes, you may fuck me, yes I need to be punished. Yes, I am your whore. Yes, yes, yes. Say it now Claudia. Tell me you want me to do incredibly nasty things to your body. Tell me you want me to fuck you, to consummate our union, to make you feel things you never dreamed were possible. Tell me yes, Claudia. Say it now."

She tossed her head from side to side. Though her body betrayed her, he couldn't have her mind and heart. Not with all she'd suffered through. Not with all she'd lost. He'd stolen her dignity and her freedom and replaced them with shackles, humiliation, and pain.

"No."

"Yes. Say it Claudia. Tell me yes." It wasn't that he needed her consent for anything he might wish to do, but a part of him wanted her heart as well. While it was true, she would come to worship him as all submissives did their masters; he wanted more from her than adoration. He wanted her love. She was his wife, the one he'd chosen for life, and her submission wouldn't be enough.

"Tell me yes, Claudia. Whisper the words. Call me by my name and say yes."

Nathaniel climbed off the end of the bed, standing to unfasten his trousers. He was fully erect, his body more than ready to take what was his. He stood for a moment admiring the beauty who was his upon the bed, long dark hair spread out like the halo of a fallen angel around her head. Her skin was a pale canvas touched here and there by the marks left from his whip. Her dark nipples a dusky pink, their color and that of her lips lush and ripe, her cheeks flushed red like the rose petals beneath her.

Nathaniel knelt upon the bed once more; his hard cock brushing her inner thigh, and then moved so it pressed directly upon her unsheathed clit as he positioned himself between her legs again. She trembled as the head of his cock slid across her sensitive bud in a way she was powerless to ignore.

"Say the words, wife. I can feel your desire. You're trembling with need and your cunt is slick and ready to be satisfied."

"You can make my body do as you wish, but I will always detest you Nathaniel. You find joy in my pain, and only wish to crush me."

"The pain is not to crush you. If you stop resisting everything I do, you will find pleasure in the torment. There is an ecstasy to be found in each touch, but not if you continue this defiance."

Though his cock was throbbing with need, he resisted the urge to thrust into her. It would turn the shrew into a wild but willing tigress, but he wanted more from her than her passion. This compulsion to wrench something other than submission and adoration from Claudia was a desire he hadn't experienced before. He was smart enough to know that a night full of exquisite sensations that were a blend of pain and pleasure wouldn't thaw the ice around his new wife's heart. It would begin to melt it though.

His hesitation when he was poised so close to entering her confused Claudia. She wouldn't lie to herself and profess to not want what he was about to do. It was all she could do to not raise her hips and rub her clit upon his cock.

"My body will yield and I will do my wifely duty. Do as you must."

"Don't be a hypocrite Claudia. You'll not lay there like a cold fish as I take my pleasure, so save your speech about wifely duties."

Moving up, the length of his cock sliding across her clit until the base of it was nestled upon it, he resumed his assault upon her nipples. He nipped then began sucking each in turn, upping the amount of pain he gave her, and then bathing the tortured peaks. He brought his head up and looked into her eyes, loving the wild passion he saw there, but seeing the loathing as well.

He lapped each nipple in turn as he stared into her eyes, licking, sucking, then biting hard, making Claudia cry out, the base of his cock bumping against her clit the whole time. She was getting close to orgasm, and Nathaniel knew it. Changing his tactic, wanting to make her mad with desire, he delved his fingers inside her sopping pussy. Nathaniel then brought them up to wet her nipples, and bent down and slowly licked Claudia's juices from the peaks before smiling up at her like a Cheshire cat.

"God you taste heavenly, Claudia. Delicious and delicate, honey and spice." He dipped his fingers inside her once more, and this time brought them to her lips. He coated them with his wet fingers, and then kissed her, his tongue swirling and filling Claudia's mouth with the sweet taste of her need. She felt the heat of her passion rolling in her belly and bucked up against Nathaniel, wanting to end her torment.

"That is not allowed Claudia."

The mumbled curses said under her breath made him smile yet again. She'd been born and raised a lady, but her spirit was that of a tavern wench.

Nathaniel moved down her body nipping and squeezing, then roughly yanked her thighs apart as far as they could go. He shoved her feet up and bound them quickly with the silken ropes that hung from the bed canopy, then sat back on his heels to admire his prize.

"No." Claudia had no idea what he would do to her next, but the feeling of being utterly powerless made her anger flare up once again.

"Will I never be allowed to participate in my own fucking?"

Nathaniel arched his eyebrows at her comment. "I can assure you that you'll be very much a part of your 'fucking' my dear. All that time working as a servant has had an appalling effect on your language. I was led to believe I'd married a lady."

Nathaniel knew it was the wrong thing to say even before the fire of rage blazed in her eyes.

"If you wanted a lady in your bed you shouldn't have gone to so much trouble to make me behave like a common whore."

"Enough Claudia. Hold your tongue. I'll not have us bickering when my intent is to woo you as we celebrate our marriage."

"Woo me? I..."

Nathaniel's hand came down upon Claudia's sex and exposed clit, giving it a stinging slap that sent shivers of pleasure shooting through her along with the pain. She gasped, and he did it again, lighter but still hard enough to make her cry out.

"I... said ... hold... that... tongue!" Each word was punctuated by a slap that held both agony and ecstasy. Her clit throbbed, and the lips of her sex swelled. Even as she cried out in pain from each slap, she raised her hips to receive the next blow, whimpering when he stopped, confused and so very needful of his touch.

Claudia twisted upon the bed, damning him and the ropes that bound her, still unable and unwilling to keep quiet. "If it's begging you want, I'll give you your wish. Please, Nathaniel, please untie me."

Instead of replying, Nathaniel turned a deaf ear on her pleas and lowered his head between her spread thighs instead. Her pussy was so very swollen and now had turned a lovely shade of red. Her clit was a shiny pearl which sat atop the slit of her sex. Every inch between her legs was wet from her passion and glistened in the lamp's light.

It was a sight Nathaniel couldn't resist. He lowered his mouth with a growl of hunger and fell upon Claudia's hypersensitive pussy like a man long starved. His action caused her to let out a shriek as his lips wrapped around her clit, and he began to suck. He drew the nub in and lashed his tongue back and forth across it, sending jolts of pleasure racing through her body.

Claudia pulled harder on her restraints, the combination of intense pleasure and inability to move driving her mad. She wanted nothing more than to curl her fingers in Nathaniel's dark hair and hold his head to her sex until he finished what he'd begun. All she could do was raise her hips mere inches off the bed. Her legs were spread wide, ankles high above her head in an obscene pose, her wrists bound tight, forbidding any movement. She tossed her head in frustration even as a cry escaped her lips to attest to the incredible pleasure he was giving her.

Nathaniel heard her cry and knew she was on the edge, waiting to tumble into the sweet abyss. Part of him wanted to send her there, to keep licking her hard nub until she was wailing. His wife was caught between the mad desire for him to continue until she was driven mad, and the need for him to stop so she could come back from the brink of insanity. It was right where Nathaniel wanted her to be.

He lifted his head, and Claudia let out a sound that could only be described as a growl. "Noooo. You can't, please, please. Don't stop."

"Tell me you want me to fuck you. Tell me yes. I must hear it Claudia. Say yes Nathaniel. Yes I want you to fuck me hard."

Claudia let out a tortured cry then grit her teeth and shook her head, determined to defy him. She would beg, and she would be the wanton whore he'd made her, but she wouldn't call him by his name. That was an intimacy she refused to give him. Yes, he was her husband, and yes he'd wooed her with roses and a few sweet words, but there was nothing intimate about being trussed up like an animal.

Nathaniel licked his lips, savoring the taste of her, wanting to delve his tongue between her folds and torture her engorged clit, but theirs was a war of wills. He'd not dealt with such tenacity and stubborn pride, and though it made him admire her, the dominant in him still need to make her bend to his will.

He rose up on his knees again and then hooked an arm around one of her legs, resting his head on the inside of her knee and looked down into her eyes. "Say yes Claudia." She shook her head, and he gave her a stinging slap right between her legs. Her clit pulsed from the shock of pain delivered right where she needed his talented tongue. The sensation marring the line between pain and pleasure. If he did it again, she feared she'd climax, and while her body screamed for release, her mind didn't want to succumb to such degrading treatment. He'd told her it was a night to celebrate their wedding, but he was treating her like anything but a cherished bride.

He rained a flurry of little slaps upon the wet folds of her sex and her clit. His action caused her to arch her back to the extent that she was able and scream at him. Her fury did not come from the pain, but from her rage and the sensations of a climax so intense it made her crazed.

This wasn't what she wanted, not to cum in this depraved way, but she was powerless to deny the orgasm that had been building for so long. As her body fell over the brink and into ecstasy, Nathaniel slapped her puss one last time. The sound of his hand squelching in her wetness gave testament to how much her body loved what he was doing even if her mind was rebelling, and then to her shock and dismay, he stopped.

"Did you hear that sweet? The sound the juices from your cunt make when I slap you there? Your face shows your dilemma sweet. Your body is mine to play like the finest violin. To coax the sweet music of your passion from you however I wish. Such a needy thing you are Claudia, you tremble as the first sensations of your bliss send sparks racing through you.

"Shall I slap your wet cunt again and again and wrench your orgasm from you, or shall I mount you and make your body spiral out of control. The pain of my ripping away your maidenhead will mix with the pleasure of my cock burying deep inside you as my body raking across your little unsheathed nubbin will make you half crazed. However, I take you, you'll scream for me, Claudia. You shall cry and cum for me because I wish it."

Claudia was near mad with longing, and it took all of her strength to focus on his arrogant face and form words in a mind that was spinning and unable to produce rational thought.

"I hate... you."

Chapter Eighteen

Her caustic words and the look of pain on her face made Nathaniel pause. He'd heard the words before, many times, in fact, when he was breaking someone new, but shattered hope accompanied the accusation in her eyes. Nathaniel reached to stroke her face, but she jerked away as if his touch was vile. Here she was, trembling with the beginning of ecstasy, and yet still she was able to hold on to her despair.

He looked and her; at the bindings that held her, at her bandaged hands, at the rose petals meant to woo, and then back at her face, and felt a stab of guilt. It was a feeling he didn't have to face often, and it didn't sit well at all. Claudia was his wife. Granted she would also be his submissive whore, but she wasn't here to merely be made to submit. She was his wife. His partner for life. Did he genuinely wish for her to hate him?

He bent to kiss her but Claudia turned away, causing his lips to graze her temple. The heat of his body as he lay over her. His hard cock was nudging between the folds of her nether lips. The intense feel of his gaze was upon her even though she refused to look at him. It made her let out a cry of dismay. No matter how she felt about him in her mind and heart, her body needed what he could provide.

Nathaniel slid his hands up her arms to the wrists that were bound, then lay a trail of kisses upon the tender flesh before unbinding her. Once free, he lifted each palm and lay kisses upon them as well before sitting up so he could release her ankles. Once done, Claudia lay there unmoving, unsure as to what he intended, refusing to allow even a flicker of hope to spark in her soul. The Earl, for that, was what he was, not her husband Nathaniel. Never that, while he treated her with such degradation, most certainly had a plan to torment her even though he'd unbound her.

"I don't wish for you to hate me Claudia." He didn't wait for a reply. This woman before him was strong on the inside despite her body's delight in all things erotic. Instead, he began to make love to her with the intent of making her feel cherished instead of owned. His mouth trailed kisses, his hands stroked and teased, his body covered hers pressing her down into the bed, but never in a way that felt overbearing. He maintained his role of dominant, but he changed the way in which he ignited her passion. Little touches, soft words, the tiniest of nips here and there until Claudia's eye were glazed with passion and held no hint of disdain.

He knelt between her thighs, his hot skin hovering over hers, one hand holding the wrists she'd willingly offered up, the other keeping him propped up so he could look into her eyes. Sliding the hand that held her down and trailed a finger around the shell of her ear, across her jaw line and to her chin, and held it firmly but gently. She would do as he wished for he controlled all she felt and could never give up that control, but his commands had to be made delicately so as not to awaken the wildcat.

He lift her up and slid her out from under him, and then moved so he was sitting with her legs straddling his waist, his well-muscled thighs beneath her bottom. He held her and placed sweet kisses on her neck as her head lolled back then suckled each nipple offered up to him by her arching back.

"Put your hands on my shoulders, Claudia." She obeyed without resistance, and Nathaniel pulled her forward, so his shaft was in direct contact with her slick folds and needy clit. He put his hands on her hips and slowly moved her up and down and jiggled her from side to side as his cock rubbed her in all the right places. They were both slick with her juices, and it made the movements fluid as she sat on his lap, legs spread and spread wide behind him.

"So sweet, my Claudia. Feel my need for you wife." He lifted her up and down again; his cock nestled in her folds, the head bumping and rubbing her clit with each up and down movement.

Claudia moaned and gazed at him with hooded eyes. They were warm and rich now, the brown lush as sable, and glossy with need. Her mouth was open slightly, her breaths coming in small pants, her nipples dark and dusky and hard as tiny stones.

"Do you like that sweet? Does it make you want me to take you with my cock?"

"Oh God yes." There was no denying anything any longer. He had changed his seduction from one that took away her dignity to sweet words and touches that she couldn't resist. She hadn't any reason to deny her passion, not any longer.

"Do you want me to take you now Claudia? I can thrust in hard and fast or slow and sweet. I can give you an ecstasy you've never known and the release your body craves. Tell me love, for I need to hear it from your lips. Do you want me to make you mine?"

"Yes."

"Who am I Claudia?"

"My husband."

"Yes, I am that but it's not what I need from you. Here and now, in this bed, celebrating our union there is no room for the hurts from the past. I want to take you as you cling to me with wild abandon. I want to thrust so deep that I touch your core and make your body fill with white hot passion as it explodes around me. I want to bury my cock so deep inside that you know you are well and truly mine and are inseparable."

He lifted her again, his cock hot and hard, sliding between her folds, so close but so far from where her body needed him to be. The friction against her clit would send her over the edge, but he wanted to be buried deep inside her.

Up and down, sliding, sliding, rubbing, making the fire of need so hot neither could take much more. "What do you want sweet wife? My Claudia. Do you want me inside you?"

"Oh... God, Yes, please yes. Yes, Nathaniel. Please."

It hadn't been the begging he'd been holding out for, but the sound of his name said without a hint of scorn or hatred was enough. Now that she'd come to a place where it was only them here and now, only the sweet passion in their marriage bed, he could take her and make her his wife without need for humiliation.

"Do you want me to fuck you now my beautiful wife?"

Claudia threw back her head and moaned as she ground her throbbing sex against Nathaniel's silky but rock hard shaft. She needed him, and soon, or she was going to scream. There was a void inside her that she felt with an acute need. One never filled before, but still it ached for what only Nathaniel could provide. Just when she thought she couldn't hold on anymore, Nathaniel lifted her up and poised her slick sex over his shaft. He held her still a moment, savoring what was to come.

"Here we go my passionate girl. Take me in all the way. I'm going to delve so very deep. Going to open you up for my pleasure and yours." He lowered her so just the tip of his cock was inside her, making her gasp as her walls fluttered, clamping and releasing then clenching again.

"Oh Claudia, so tight. Let me in love." Nathaniel couldn't believe how incredible she felt, scorching heat and silky satin squeezing his shaft within her folds, making him ready to pop like a school boy. He'd had virgins before, but she was his virgin. There would never be another man entering her like this. She belonged only to him, and he would keep her for life.

"Hold me tight sweet wife." Claudia wrapped her arms around his neck and pressed her forehead to his shoulder. "That's a good girl, breathe, Claudia, relax and let me in." When he felt her take a deep breath and then slowly let it out, he lifted her up and brought her down hard, sheathing himself half way in. Claudia struggled, her movements making the muscles clenching his cock flutter. Nathaniel had to grit his teeth to keep himself in check.

"No man's had you but me, and no man ever shall. You're all mine. With this pain will come exquisite pleasure if you simply let it. It's time to learn to take my cock wife, for you will be doing it often. Stop fighting me. It's time for my passionate little whore to come and play."

Claudia cried out at his words, and he felt her nails biting into his flesh, but he was too much in need to mollify her now. There would be time for that later. Right now, he needed to be buried deep inside her. The little minx would love being fucked if she let her body lead the way.

Nathaniel lifted her and brought her down hard once more. Her breath caught as he forced his way past her maidenhead, plunging deep until he buried himself to the hilt. She pushed at his chest and thrashed on his lap, but he held her tight and thrust his hips forward, so her clit was trapped between the cock inside her and his hard stomach. It was time to mix pleasure with the pain. It was a lesson she would learn every day of her new life with him, so she might as well begin to understand.

"I will not halt my taking of you Claudia. My cock belongs deep inside you. Embrace the pain, for you will come to love it." He wasn't sure if it was her pride, or the pain she felt that made her fight him anew after being so passive, but he didn't care any longer. She was his wife, wedded and bedded, absolutely owned by him. She could fight like a wildcat, but he had no intention of backing down. If his sweet wife wanted a hard, rough and tumble, that's what she would get. Sharp claws and angry fists wouldn't get her slow, sweet lovemaking.

Nathaniel began to move her upon his shaft despite the fact that he was hurting her. Yes, he could slow his movements and allow her body to adjust, but that wasn't what he needed, so he continued to lift her up and down so his cock pushed deeper. He knew the rubbing of her clit would mix the two sensations, and her passion would overtake any desire to be free.

Though she felt as if he was tearing her apart, Claudia was keenly aware of the pressure on her exposed nub, nudging her forward, past the burning inside, into the realm of pleasure. Her hands that had curled into claws to rake upon his back turned to ones that clung as Claudia sought something to hold on to. When that wasn't enough to steady her world, her arms wrapped around his neck and her legs curled about his waist. Her desire to be away from him changed to an undeniable need to have him go even deeper.

Nathaniel smiled as she went from a fighting tigress to a woman lost in a turbulent sea of sensations. Though he had known he would make her cum regardless of any pain, it was wonderful to feel the transformation. The walls of her sex now fluttered around his shaft as her pleasure swelled. He hadn't worried about her finding pleasure as she was initiated into the art of fucking, it was out of her control, but it still pleased him to know he had taken away her choice in the matter.

Now that Claudia was responding to the primal pleasure, it was time to ease things back to the level that would both tease her and prolong their joining. Nathaniel wrapped one arm around her waist and began to jiggle her up and down, rubbing her clit with each bounce. This new activity wasn't to her liking because she wanted so desperately to go over the edge. There was still lingering pain from where he'd torn away her maidenhead and sunk deeply into her depths, and Claudia knew the pleasure of an orgasm would take the pain away. She struggled to take him a bit deeper and to move her hips, so her clit received what it needed, but Nathaniel refused to let her take control.

"Hold still wife. You deserve to be fucked good and proper, and that is what I'm going to do. I shall take you for as long and as hard as I want Claudia, however I want, and you've no say in the matter. You're mine, and I shall have all of you. You'll get used to my cock. The first time always hurts love. Take it like a good girl."

Nathaniel stroked her hair then brought his mouth down on hers. Claudia whimpered and tightened her legs around his waist. Her body was in a tailspin and she didn't know if she wanted him to move into her hard and deep, or keep up the jiggling against her clit that had her on the edge of the precipice of unimaginable pleasure.

Nathaniel began to lift her up and down on his throbbing shaft, making sure his body still rubbed her sensitive clit. Up and down they rocked, Claudia wiggling her hips back and forth, squeezing her muscles, driving him wild. She was full of fire and passion, responding to his taking of her as if it were all she lived for.

"So full of fire my beautiful wife. Your passion belies all your anger. If you stop all your arguing and shrewish behavior and let me lead you as I am meant to, you will always find pleasure with the pain."

The small amount of wiggling wasn't enough to keep his appetite satiated, so Nathaniel pulled at the arms that were twisted around his neck, pulling them loose. "There now, I just told you not to fight me. Do as I wish and put your hands on my shoulders, move with me Claudia, it's time to get down to the serious business of fucking you."

Despite his crude words, Claudia did as he asked and placed her hands on his shoulders. At first, she just held on. As Nathaniel began to move her, thrusting hard as he brought her body back downward to sheath his cock in her silky hot depths, Claudia began to follow the rhythm. She pushed against his shoulders to aid in his lifting of her, and then dug her nails into his flesh as he pushed ever deeper. Not because he was hurting her, but because she was turning into a wild thing that was crying out and taking great joy from their coupling.

Though the position they were in allowed him to go deep, Nathaniel had a need to feel her writhing beneath him. When he lifted Claudia up, he leaned forward, toppling her backwards, so she lay under him. Their bodies stayed joined for her legs had been wrapped around his waist, and now they tangled with his. He slid an arm under her hips to tilt them just right, practiced skill making him know the perfect angle as the other hand grasped one wrist and pushed it up over her head. Knowing she'd fight him and bring the other hand up to pry his hand off hers, he caught it deftly and easily held both her wrists in his big hand.

"You are not in control sweet wife. Never try to be, for it will only lead to disappointment however brief. If I wish to have you pinned beneath me, struggling to match my passion with fire of your own, then I will. I don't mind the fight Claudia, it adds fuel to my pleasure, and the way you are squirming under me lets me believe it adds to yours as well."

His words spoke the truth, and so she continued to do her best to twist beneath him, moving her hips, so his body moved against her clit. Her efforts drove her pleasure and his to an even greater plateau. Both of them were panting, hearts pounding, as he thrust forward into her like a runaway train, taking, hurting, pushing them on, she was a wild thing that thrashed about and made him all the more rough in return.

If she had had any reticence before he had claimed her, it was long gone, and the harsh cry each thrust drove from the depths of her soul chased any remaining inhibitions the way of the wind. There was no room for a shy maid in their bed as both fought to get the pleasure that would take them over the edge from the other.

Finally, unable to wait any longer, Nathaniel moved his arm out from under her. He lifted it up, intending to take one of her wrists in it, but Claudia had other plans, her passion making her bold and fierce.

"NO!" When Nathaniel loosened his hold on her wrists, she snatched them away and raked her nails upon his back instead. Nathaniel cursed under his breath but also to drive into Claudia's scorching depths even harder, finally making them both begin the spiral of orgasms that would bring the satisfaction both craved.

Claudia moved about beneath him so wildly that he wasn't sure if she were fighting him or rejoicing in the intense pleasure. Then the squeezing of her walls around his cock made him know it was the latter. His wife was a she-devil, spitting fire and clutched him to her as the heat that had built up in her core exploded, sending white-hot pleasure to every part of her body. She was frenzied, awash in incredible pleasure, and she was lost in the crazy spiral of sensation that became ever more powerful as Nathaniel cried out his own pleasure and began to come deep in her depths.

They clung tightly to each other as their orgasm ebbed and then finally waned, taking them on a ride of searing pleasure that lift them up before crashing down in the depths of each other's bodies, taking and giving what the other needed.

When the sensations subsided enough for their minds to stop spinning, Nathaniel once again wrapped his arms around Claudia, rocking her as he moved gently from side to side. Shocked at the intensity merely taking his wife had created inside him. They hadn't had a long session of pain and pleasure to whet his appetite and yet it had been far more pleasurable than the taking of any other woman had been, no matter what game he had played with them.

Claudia kept her eyes closed tightly, and allowed Nathaniel to rock her as aftershocks of pleasure rippled through her. Their lovemaking had been amazing despite how violently she had reacted at times. The things he had made her feel were incredible, and even if he proved cruel enough to taunt her with her wild abandon, she would not regret her actions. They'd behaved like uninhibited mating animals, but the pleasure had been breathtaking. There was no shame in it.

A flutter of kisses upon her face chased away her fears. Despite her behavior, Nathaniel was going to be loving. The gentle rocking continued as his lips sought hers for dozens of sweet kisses, stealing the breath she'd only just gotten back. Finally, he contented himself with kissing her forehead and turned onto his side. He held her close, letting her nuzzle up into his chest as he pulled the blanket over them, rose petals fluttering around them as he did.

"Sleep now sweet wife. We both need a rest. Sleep tight my passionate creature, I'll wake you when it's time to love again." For once, Claudia did not resist. She did as she was told to do, letting herself drift away amid his warm arms into a sea of rose scented dreams.

Chapter Nineteen

True to his word, Nathaniel roused her time and again, his need for her not ebbing, until there wasn't an ounce of strength left in either of them. They slept soundly, undisturbed by a house full of servants who knew not to intrude until his Lordship tugged the bell pull. Even then, nearly a full day went by before he summoned a maid, telling her to bring food when she arrived. They both needed something to eat, or their bodies would never sustain their passion. Even then, the household didn't see the Master, for he had no desire to leave his chambers.

When they'd finished their meal, Nathaniel took Claudia by the hand and pulled her up, into his arms. She melted against him, her body seeking his warmth and the exquisite feelings he could create with his masterful hands. She closed her eyes and tilted her head back; lips parted in anticipation of a kiss that would make her weak in the knees, but Nathaniel had other plans. He nipped her bottom lip, causing her eyes to open wide and pull the injured skin into her mouth.

"I have other plans than to stand here and kiss you. Last night was delightful, but there are other things you must learn."

Claudia's expression darkened, thinking of the spankings she'd received as well as the whipping and his taking her deep in her bottom. She worried at her lip, her eyebrows drawing together, not pleased with the direction things might be taking.

"We could go back to bed." Her hand came up to rub his cheek and then began a journey downward before he grasped it, stopping its descent.

"You are not to decide what it is we do, and you are not to touch me without permission." Claudia pulled back, her expression one of anger and confusion as she thought of how she had touched him all night.

"When did you change the rules Nathaniel? Only an hour ago you were calling me your luscious whore as my hand was stroking your cock."

"That's enough."

"Enough of what?" Claudia was genuinely perplexed.

"As my wife you are mine to play with when and where I choose. You stroked my cock because I wanted you to. I encouraged you, because I was preparing to fuck you."

Claudia felt as if she could see the man who was her tender lover disappearing. He had turned his back and left the room, replaced by a man who angered easily and expected her to obey without question. The way he used the word fuck to describe what they had done all night cut her to the quick. It had been romantic and passionate, tender and wild. He had made her feel things she hadn't known were possible while taking her over and over in the big bed, asserting his claim as her husband.

Claudia was being given a choice to make, obey and enjoy what he had planned, or argue and earn another spanking. She had no idea what he intended to do, but imagined it would be preferable to being tossed over his lap or a chair and paddled like a child.

"I am yours Nathaniel. What is it you wish me to do?"

The smile she earned was almost worth swallowing the hurt he caused her by being so callous about their wedding night. Almost, but not quite. Still, she smiled at him and stood waiting. Nathaniel, evidently pleased, stroked her cheek as the other hand absently played with one of her nipples. It was sore as was all of her, and he played with it a little harder when she hissed, enjoying how his rough handling hurt her. Claudia didn't make a fuss, though her nipple ached, there was a pool of hot desire forming in her belly, one that was growing rapidly because of his touch.

"Close your eyes and don't move."

Claudia did so and listened intently for a clue to what he was doing. Soon she felt the whisper of silk over her closed lids, and then the tightening of the scarf behind her head. Her hands came out instinctively, searching in the newfound darkness. His hands touched her shoulders and then slowly pushed her arms down as they stroked from shoulder to wrist.

"I'm right here. Do as I say, follow every command, and you will find all you need."

He took her right hand and held it tightly, tucking it through his arm as he came up beside her. When he started to walk, moving her as he went, Claudia faltered, unsure in her blindness.

"Trust me Claudia. You must trust me and obey."

She moved along side him as he walked across the sitting room and then paused before a door. Nathaniel opened it and led her inside, the sun streaming in through the open drapes lighting his way, and only her arm looped through his showing her the course.

"Almost there now. That's a good girl. I won't let you fall."
They walked a few more steps and then stopped. His arm and
body then moved away, her anchor and stability taken from her.
Claudia wanted to reach out, but sensed he would be pleased if
she remained still, so though she felt fright mix with the desire
he had created, Claudia didn't move.

His lips suddenly brushed hers, and it was too much of a
temptation. She reached out, not because the sexual desire was
overwhelming, but because she was blind in a sea of darkness,
and his lips didn't give her all the steadiness she needed. "Ah,
ah, ah. Hands down now. I'm here. Trust me Claudia."

His breath bathed her ear in a soft warmth. "That's a good
girl, step and step, trust me Claudia. It's all about trust." Her
world was tilting; her sense of feeling heightened because of his
heated skin on hers, the pressure of his arms and the movement
of his lips upon her ear as he spoke. The words were all she knew
in the darkness. They lured her back as surely as his arms did,
the whispers giving soft commands as her feet took steps back
into the unknown.

"Good girl, that's a good girl." Nathaniel stopped and then
the arms, body, and lips vanished. She sighed and swayed just a
bit, but resisted the nearly overwhelming urge to reach out and
feel the space around her.

"Your obedience pleases me." The words came from in
front of her and were not accompanied by a touch. Claudia's
mouth formed a large O, and a sigh escaped her, but no words
and no movement. She did as he wanted, knowing he expected it
of her. The man who demanded obedience had returned when
they were in the sitting room.

"Take a step back." That was it, no guiding hands. Claudia
hesitated but only for a moment before moving. "Again." Claudia
complied. "That's my girl. Good girls get good things." Claudia
heard his feet as he moved around her and then felt his hand on
her hips. "Back now, just a little." Claudia took tiny steps until
her back made contact with what felt like smooth wood. "There,
perfect. Now turn around." She did, her hands reaching out for
him, unable to stop herself because she knew the wood was
there. He caught her hands, lacing his fingers in hers for a
moment, giving her a quick kiss, and then pulling the scarf off
her eyes.

Claudia blinked at Nathaniel and then looked at the thing
in front of her. It was a two long smooth boards crossed at the
center, so they made a large X. "What?"

"No, no. Questions aren't allowed. Turn around again and then come closer." Claudia complied even though she was full of questions. "Good, now lift your hands. Try to stretch up each part." Claudia did, and Nathaniel quickly secured her wrists with straps of leather that were fixed to the cross. "Ankles too. Spread your legs. That's a good girl." Nathaniel stood after he fastened the leather straps on her ankles. He came around to stand behind her, then ran a finger up the inside of one thigh to the place between her nether lips, gathering the moisture there before beginning to circling her clit.

Claudia gasped and did her best to move her hips forward, loving his touch, wanting more. "That's my little wanton whore. So nice and wet for me. Good girls get good things Claudia, and you were a good girl."

"Ahhhhhhhhhh." Her hips wanted to pump but were up against the cross, so all she could do was a small wiggle.

"Such a dirty girl. My Jezebel. You want my cock don't you?"

"Yes. Please."

"My name is Sir and you will ask properly."

"Please Sir, Please take me."

"Oh no Claudia. That won't do. Where would you like me to take you? To the opera? To church?"

"No, no. Please Sir..."

"Tell me Claudia, there is no room for the shy maiden to make an appearance. I want my little whore. Please fuck me with your cock sir."

"Yes, yes. Please Sir," Claudia gasped as the intensity of his fingers rubbing her clit became faster, and he pressed up against her body, trapping her between the cross and the length of his body. "Please fuck me with your cock Sir." The words came out and were only accompanied by a tiny blush. He was correct that there was no shy maiden in the room. He had sent her packing as he fucked her over and over throughout the night.

"Tell me again."

"Please fuck me with your cock, Sir."

"Where?"

"In... In my cunt." She had learned the answer to that question last night. Though there wasn't pain when he took her in her bottom, she preferred to have him deep in her womb.

"That's a very good girl, but no, not now."

Claudia gasped and almost let out a string of words that surely would have caused him to paddle her scarlet, but clamped her mouth shut just in time to stop herself. He moved around the cross again so she could see his face.

"That was hard wasn't it?"

"Yes, Sir." It still was. Claudia wanted to scream at him in frustration. He'd made her need him so badly and then stopped cold. Right about then she would have used the word bastard instead of sir, but she held back. Good girls got good things. Claudia had a feeling she would come to hate that phrase.

"I think we need the scarf again. Today I will teach you about all the things your body can feel. I'm going to touch you in many different ways Claudia, and you will learn to love all of them. If I take away your ability to see, you will feel things more acutely. Do you understand?"

Though Nathaniel was speaking in a quiet tone that suggested what he had planned was perfectly reasonable, Claudia wasn't as sure as her husband was that she would enjoy it. He brushed his thumb over her cheek, and Claudia realized she was just staring at him even though he'd asked her a question. Being unresponsive fell in the bad girl realm of things, so she quickly replied.

"Yes, Sir. When I was walking and couldn't see, all that was there for me was your voice and your touch."

"Yes, exactly. You learn very quickly Claudia."

That was all he said before he put the scarf back over her eyes. Walking away, leaving her bound and blind, her nude body pressing on the wooden cross, waiting for the things he wanted her to feel. Her body was heated with the desire his touch created, but there was distress inside her as well. Fear that ran deeper than what she felt while moving around guided only by his voice and touch. What did he have planned? She thought it would hurt because he seemed to like hurting her. If she were good and took it without complaint, then she imagined he would reward her with pleasure. Claudia just wasn't so sure it was an even trade.

She stood stock still, listening for a clue what Nathaniel was doing, but when her ears picked up the sound, it was one she couldn't identify. The noise was one that made a swishing sound over and over. It neither sped up or slowed, and she didn't feel anything. At first. Claudia was straining her ears, trying to figure out how Nathaniel was going to touch her, when she began to feel a slight breeze caress her back. It was nothing but air moving close to her skin, nothing more, lulling her as she stood there, the breeze just kissing her skin, and then something a little more.

Claudia jumped when the falls of the flogger passed over her skin, not from pain, but from surprise. The sensation took up the pattern the breeze had taken, lightly caressing her skin again, but only for a short bit. Nathaniel's strokes became harder as he moved forward, slowly introducing Claudia to the feel of the flogger, not wanting it to hurt, at least not at first. His aim was to build up the sensation all over her back and bottom. He wished to stroke her skin not with his hands, but with the swish of the leather, over and over, step by step coming closer until what Claudia felt was a thudding strike upon her back, moving from side to side, covering her sensitive skin, touching the muscles that ached from their long night of passion.

She made a small sound, almost a coo as Nathaniel changed things up and began a criss cross motion that covered her back. With a stroke that was harder still and grew in intensity until it nearly took her breath away. Just when she thought it was too much, Nathaniel altered the strokes so the flogger was striking her bottom, over and over. The falls touching the surface of the pool of desire deep inside her, spreading the need through her body even as the thud became hard to take.

She stood their bound and absorbed the feelings Nathaniel was creating and cried out as the thuds became harder still. They crashed into her body, shaking it from the force, reminding every part of her that ached from Nathaniel's bedding of all the things he'd made her feel. She was oh so sore, but though the thing striking her bottom reminded her muscles of how she'd been used, it also stirred up the embers and fanned them into flames. Her hands fisted, and she threw back her head, calling his name as she had during the night, calling for him until he let the flogger dangle from his hand and walked to where she stood quivering.

"Please Nathaniel, please."

He pressed his body against her tender flesh and every nerve from her shoulders to the tops of her thighs came alive. Where moments before they had been struck hard, demanding her to feel, the length of him hot and hard, his lips kissing the shell of her ear and then teeth nibbling upon her neck was like a soft song sung to the very heart of her.

She was dizzy but so very aware of each little sensation, aroused but too overwhelmed to even press back into Nathaniel's body. He must have stripped off his dressing gown before he'd begun to wield the flogger for his skin was hot and bare where he molded himself into her back and bottom.

"Please..."

"Tell me Claudia."

She shook her head no. No, she didn't want to play the begging game. She didn't want him to fuck her; she needed him to hold her. Her world was in a tailspin, and she needed him to help her set it right. She was cold, but also hot. Feeling dead inside without the rhythm of the flogger's falls striking out the beat her husband had chosen, and yet more alive than ever because what he had done. Now he was pressed to her back, awakening every inch of her inside and out.

"Hold me. Please Nathaniel. Hold me."

He had planned so much more, but it was clear Claudia couldn't take it, not right then. She was new to the ways in which he liked to play, and she would come to take so much more, but for now she needed to be curled up in his arms and resting. She was his wife, and they had a lifetime. Despite their rough start, despite her sass and stubborn will, she had bent hers to him, and for now she'd had enough.

He quickly unbound her ankles and then pressed her up against the cross once more as he unfastened her wrists, scooping her up with practiced skill before she could collapse, and carrying her through the sitting room and into the bedroom to lay her on the rumpled bed.

When he pulled away so he could climb in as well, she held up her arms like a desperate child wanting to be held, and he gladly complied. Despite the fact that his cock was rock hard and would have to stay that way, it had been a delightful afternoon spent with his new wife. He would hold her now and whisper the sweet words good girls got to hear as she settled down from the flogging. Later they would eat, and he would have her once more, but for now it was enough to embrace her as she floated in the haze only their distinctive type of play could create.

Chapter Twenty

True to his word, her husband appeared within an hour, and true to her spoilt upbringing, Claudia was still in the tub. If he was going to treat her as if her opinion and wishes didn't matter, she was going to do the same. Claudia was well aware that her backside would suffer for her defiance, but she couldn't find it in herself to care. His sweet words and passionate lovemaking of the night before were hollow, and therefore Claudia would be damned if she'd behave like a dutiful wife.

His footstep made a sharp staccato on the wood floor as he walked across the sitting room to where she was bathing. Claudia had closed the door and even had the audacity to lock it in her fit of temper, and couldn't keep the hint of a smile from her lips as she heard the doorknob rattle. The action was followed by his furious words, made more amusing by his obvious shock. She'd sent the maid away so there would be no witnesses to their argument. Claudia was wise enough not to throw kerosene on an already smoldering battle. Therefore, the laughter that bubbled up inside her and over her lips was heard by no one but the man on the other side of the door calling her name and releasing a string of obscenities.

"Claudia Rose, you have no idea what will befall you if you continue this charade of defiance."

"Charade? My defiance is no charade husband. You can trust it is very real. Perhaps your other women allow you to terrorize them with brute force and threats, but I am not them."

"That much has been made clear, wife. Regardless of that fact, you are to open this door this instant. There are many more ways to discipline you than taking the skin off your lovely backside, ones you couldn't even dream of."

"Will I not be subjected to your depraved desires and brutality no matter my behavior? You said I was to be your pet whore. I hardly think you plan on accomplishing that with tenderness."

"You have already become my pet whore. Have you forgotten how you moaned and begged for my touch and my cock? It mattered little where I put it, cunt, arse or mouth; your reaction was the same."

"Finding pleasure in sexual acts does not make me a whore." Her voice had risen an octave, a fact that made her furious, but she couldn't help it. She had begged for more with every lewd thing he'd done to her, her body exploding in orgasm time and again.

"Ah, but it does wife. It makes you my passionate little toy because your body is being taught to crave it. Open the door Claudia, there is no winning this argument."

"I wish to finish my bath."

"Shall I ring for a key and invite the staff up here to watch as I lift you from the tub and fuck you on your hands and knees like a bitch in heat and then take you to the training room with a collar and lead?" To his satisfaction, Nathaniel heard her sharp intake of breath followed by splashing. He'd gotten under her skin with his threat. He didn't imagine she'd be keen on the idea after her nude introduction the night before. Claudia knew none of his threats were idle.

Nathaniel heard more splashing and then the sound of wet feet slapping against the tile floor, followed by the key turning in the lock. Claudia swung the door wide and stood before him, silhouetted in the afternoon sun streaming through the window. She was wet, naked as the day she was born; chin tipped up in defiance, water flowing down her body to pool on the floor around her feet. The sight was quite bewitching, and Nathaniel suspected she knew it. His wife wasn't one who lacked knowledge when it came to womanly charms or the power of her sexuality.

Nathaniel gave her a cool appraising look that went from head to toe, traveling the length of her slim neck. He paused to admire her breasts, the creamy flesh dotted with bruises from his fingers and teeth, with hard little pebbles for nipples. He further his inspection by watching as the water trickling down over her stomach ran in a path over the baby smooth lips of her sex, still puffy from his rough taking of her. When his eyes traveled back up, they met hers and challenged the defiant stare she dared to direct his way.

He grasped her shoulders and shook her hard enough to make her pinned up locks come loose and tumble over his hands where he held her. Claudia's arms came up to break his hold on her, but he was too strong. He shook her once more knowing it would do nothing to erase her defiance nor make her more sensible, but it appeased his anger at her audacity all the same. When he stopped the look of defiance still shone from her eyes, but Nathaniel felt no fury. Instead, her rebelliousness upped his determination to tame her strengthened. He put moved one hand up behind her head and tangled the fingers in her hair, then pulled back even as his other arm snaked around her, moving her forward to press against him.

The water on her skin soaked his shirt, making the fabric between them feel as if it were nonexistent. The fabric of his trousers was rough against her sex, scratching the shiny pearl that was never able to hide. He growled as he looked down at his struggling, still disobedient wife, then held her in an iron grip despite a kick to his shin. He merely stood and held her tight, giving himself a chance to get his anger in check.

"Despite the ounce of common sense that made you come out of the bath, the willfulness that caused you to behave in such a way won't be tolerated. You tell me to treat you with respect, but then act like an obstinate child, showing your annoyance by locking the door in an effort to make me cross. Well, you've done what you set out to do, but I doubt you'll enjoy what wet skin does for the intensity of a spanking."

Claudia's eyes narrowed, shooting daggers at Nathaniel despite the fact that he'd just gotten done shaking her and was threatening a spanking. "Violence seems to be your answer for everything, husband. I was raised to believe genteel people spoke with one another to resolve their conflicts."

"Well, as a matter of fact, some of us genteel people spank our wives quite often. If you'd listened to your mother, you would have known that. As it stands, you've hardly shown the manners of your upbringing. Quite the opposite actually. It seems you attempt to thwart any of my attempts to be gallant. "

"Gallant!" Claudia tried to twist away, but Nathaniel wasn't about to let her go, nor was he about to listen to any more of the tirade he knew was coming. He took his hand from her hair, spun her in order to gather her wrists behind her back. Before she knew what was happening, Claudia was propelled towards the straight backed chair where she'd sat for her breakfast. Her wet feet slid on the floor, giving her no chance to halt their procession. Once there, he sat down, grabbed her around the waist and pulled her over his lap, a move that was becoming all too familiar.

Claudia struggled fiercely, but Nathaniel was expecting as much, and just tipped her forward, so she was off balance. He then placed a firm hand in the small of her back, exerting his dominance and thwarting any escape.

"You can choose to struggle and perhaps fall off my lap, or you can stop your defiance. If you fall, I'll only haul you back up here and start over. You must accept the fact that I'm going to spank you. I will do so until I think you will behave more like my lady wife and less like a child who should have had a strap taken to her backside at the first sign of insolence."

"You husband, are an insufferable brute." Claudia kicked her feet and pushed her hands down onto his leg in an effort to gain her freedom, and true to his words, Nathaniel let her tumble to the floor. She sat there, wet and naked, body still dripping, looking indignant and shocked. It was all Nathaniel could do to stifle his laughter, but though amusing, his goal wasn't to humiliate her.

"We haven't time for this Claudia. I've other plans for you today. Come here so I may warm your bottom. Perhaps the sting will help to remind you how you are to behave at least for a few hours."

He was looking down upon her like she was a naughty child instead of his naked wife, and it was that look that made her comply. How could she expect him to respect her if she played silly games to taunt him and had fits of anger? Granted he was an arrogant tyrant, but even a tyrant could be tamed with sweetness and compliance. Claudia gazed back at him, but then willed the insolence that made her wish to scratch out her new husband's eyes, leave her body. She bowed her head, doing her best to appear docile, and then rose to stand beside him, the picture of a perfectly compliant wife obeying her husband's command.

Nathaniel didn't believe for a moment that Claudia had accepted her fate, but he wasn't one to let the opportunity slip through his fingers. Still, their battle of wills was fast becoming a full-blown war, and Nathaniel couldn't help but test her resolve to appear docile.

"I've changed my mind. Bend over the chair and place your hands on the seat, legs spread, head down, mouth shut." Claudia allowed herself to glare at him for just a moment but then complied. She'd provoked him, and this was her fate, besides, she was beginning to shiver.

Nathaniel stood and went to the huge armoire. He selected a leather strap, and then came back to his wife; He laid the strap over her back, just above her hips, and then went to the bathing chamber to fetch the bath sponge. His wife had chosen to be wet when he arrived, and he would damn well make her regret her decision. After soaking the sponge, he carried it dripping to where she waited, belt over her back, and squeezed water over her bottom and down her thighs.

"Nathaniel!"

"You are to stay still. Don't stand, and don't move your hands." He wanted her to thank him for each lash but knew the willful girl would replace the compliant woman in an instant if he gave her that command. Seeing the wide stripes the strap left on her bum would be enough.

Nathaniel doubled the leather over and snapped it tightly between his hands, smiling when he saw the prickle of gooseflesh rise on Claudia's skin. He took a step back and to the side, and delivered a stinging blow to the center of her bottom, leaving a two inch wide welt. Claudia yelped but didn't rise. He swung the strap again, catching her bum lower, the strap kissing both cheeks and leaving another trail of fire. The third was a bit higher but well placed, striking the top of her cheeks and causing her to bounce up and down on her toes.

Nathaniel put a hand on Claudia's back, to steady her, and felt the quivering of her body. Though she would never admit it to him, the pain of the strap on her wet skin was driving his displeasure home. The next blow caught her where her thighs met her cheeks, and Claudia let out a hoarse cry as it struck. From where he stood, Nathaniel could see his wife face. Her eyes were screwed up tight, her mouth a thin line. The pain was etched upon her pale face that hung upside down, framed by her long dark hair. He noted how the knuckles of her hands were white in her effort not to let go of the chair to rub her blazing bottom and felt a surge of supremacy.

The last blow landed squarely on her upper thighs and made Claudia lose her composure. Her eyes flew open; her expression one of agony as her dark, accusing eyes met his. Nathaniel knew from her gaze that the emotion that was forefront in her heart was hatred, and the thought made a twinge of guilt rise inside him. Most of the women became docile and almost clingy after a strapping, striving to appease him and make him pleased with them once more, but not Claudia. Though tears she couldn't hold back told of her pain, there was nothing in her expression that said she was sorry and wished to be forgiven as he held and soothed her.

Nathaniel dropped the strap to the floor and took Claudia's elbow in one hand, but she pulled it away. "May I stand, Sir?"

"Yes Claudia, you may stand. Your punishment is over." She rose and took a step back from him, her expression changing from despondent to resentful and back again. She didn't rub her bottom, and the few tears she'd allowed herself had fled in the wake of having to face him.

"I apologize for my childish behavior. It was wrong of me to lock the door. I find myself hopelessly incensed time and again with no course to follow to damper it. Everything that has befallen me has left me despondent. I have no say in what happens around me and even less for what happens to my person. You feed me tidbits of tenderness only to call me a whore when I find pleasure in those crumbs. Some would say my best recourse would be to obey silently, but I am simply not made that way, husband. If my spirit is such that it pains you so, then I fear we shall never find happiness with each other."

A single tear escaped despite her best efforts, and she swiped at it before raising her chin once more. Her gaze held no contempt or fury as she searched his face for the answers to her predicament, only the misery of a young woman picturing her long life before her as a path that held only sorrows.

When Nathaniel reached for her, Claudia flinched, and her reaction made a knot of self-reprisal form in his stomach next to the seed of doubt put there by her words. He kept his hand raised until she stilled, and then brushed a lock of hair behind her ear and ran his thumb across her cheek.

"This is all new Claudia, and I know it's confusing to you. Given time, our marriage will thrive and become a loving union. Tuck away your pride, and allow me to lead you."

Her forehead creased, and her eyes filled with anguish before she was able to stop the emotion that belied her stoic façade. "If I allow my pride to be stored away on some abandoned shelf, what will I have left? I now know the wrongs of thinking I am better than those who serve me. I understand that my birth into a genteel family does not make me better than others nor bestows upon me the right to have everything done the way I wish. That right is for the men in this world. The spoilt girl has fled, husband, and though my spirit causes me to rebel when I see or feel injustice, do you truthfully desire to break it?"

Chapter Twenty-One

"I wish to banish your rebellion, not turn you into a meek little mouse. There is a difference. If you would simply accept your life as my wife and embrace the role I have chosen for you, all of the punishment for defiance will cease. I cannot understand why you won't allow yourself to submit and be the wife you ought to be."

"Allow myself? I..." He silenced her by holding up his hand and giving her a steely look.

"While I realize you have more spirit than most, you will be better off if you give yourself over to the pleasure that can mix with the pain. Embrace the fire that blazes inside you when I fuck or play with you, and your life will be simpler. I've never met a woman more obstinate that you. The others accept their role as dutiful wives, loving the intimate service and the joy that comes from being the one who is allowed the grand undertaking of seeing to their master's every need. Perhaps you must see how blissful their lives are, how they adore their husbands and live only for his pleasure."

"They grovel and pretend."

"Silence wife. They do no such thing. I see there is no way to open your eyes to the truth. That is something that will only come with time. Come along now, you've training to do and we are already behind schedule. You've created quite an uproar in my household young lady. The sooner you find your place, the better. Your body already knows what it needs, I wish your mind would follow suit. These walls will be your home until the day you die. It would be to your benefit to accept it."

Though tears shimmered in her eyes, Claudia wouldn't let them fall. It pained her to have her opinions dismissed as folly and to be told to swallow her pride and embrace her new life as a puppet that only moved or thought when Nathaniel decided she should. Though it seemed so easy in his mind, to Claudia it was impossible to tolerate. She was loathe to shut off her mind and become a mere shell of herself just to please him.

Taking her silence as a show of submission, even if it was forced, Nathaniel deemed the conversation over. He picked up the discarded dressing gown, and then wrapped it around his still wet wife, thinking it wouldn't do to have her catch a chill. Claudia stood unyielding as he laid the garment over her shoulders, pleased she wouldn't be forced to walk through the house unclothed, but still raging against her husband.

They saw no one as Nathaniel led the way down the long hall and to the narrow steps at the end. It was the staircase used by the staff to come and go from their rooms on the third floor. Claudia felt a knot forming in the pit of her stomach. Was she to be humiliated before the servants again? If so, for what purpose. Her fearful contemplations made her open her mouth to ask what they were about to do, but then she closed her lips in silence. Her husband would almost certainly refuse to tell her at any rate, and Claudia had no wish to give him the satisfaction her anxiety would cause.

To Claudia's relief, they passed the doorway that led to the servant's quarters and continued to climb the very top floor of the house. The stairwell opened upon a vast expanse under the eaves that spanned the entire length of the manor. Unlike many attics, the home of the Earl had a room that was clean and free of clutter. That did not mean it was empty though. There were pieces of furniture throughout the room, but there were open spaces as well. Nathaniel went about turning up the lamps upon the four walls, and the effect combined with the sunlight streaming in through the windows on one side made the room awash in brightness.

Nathaniel turned to stare at her and remained silent as she studied the odd pieces of furniture in the room. Some looked like things you might find in the dungeon of a castle, and the sight of them renewed the anxiety inside Claudia. Other things resembled the spanking bench she was already familiar with, and one was simply a cage. Distress filled her despite her nerve and earlier impertinence. She could not imagine sitting in a cage like a dog. Would her new husband truly humiliate her in such a fashion?

"Discard the dressing gown." His words in the silence broke her from her musings. They were hard and clipped. Commands issued by a man who was confident his demands would be carried out without haste. Claudia narrowed her eyes, though she had indeed been submissive to Nathaniel on more than one occasion, the tone of his voice and his smug arrogance still annoyed her. Nathaniel met Claudia's small show of irritation with more silence. He wasn't a man used to issuing orders twice.

Not wishing to incite Nathaniel's anger, Claudia dropped the dressing gown and stood before her husband. The act caused no shame. Nudity was low on the list of things she was now enduring on a daily basis.

"Get on your hands and knees and crawl for me."

Claudia's eyes went from being narrowed in mild annoyance to opening wide and filling with fire. She pressed her lips into a thin line to bite back the words that immediately came to mind, and then took a deep breath to calm herself. Straightening her shoulders and lifting her chin, she looked at Nathaniel in defiance.

"I will not."

"Yes you most certainly will Claudia. It wasn't a request it was a command."

Claudia weighed her words. On one hand her bottom was still blazing from her recent whipping, on the other was her pride. She knew he would force her to do as he said. What she needed to decide was if her pride held more value than the skin on her backside or the humiliation she had no doubt would befall her if she continued to defy her husband.

"You have me mistaken for an animal, Milord. I am your human wife, and I move about on two legs." There, it was a polite refusal that conveyed her point of view while giving him something to ponder.

"You are my human wife who is in need of taming, for she forgets her vow to obey each time I tell her what I wish. Get on your hands and knees and come to me Claudia. Do it now."

His words were soft and free of menace. Nathaniel was well aware that Claudia would bristle if threatened. There was no need for it. In the end, Nathaniel was certain his wife would obey. The consequences that would befall her if she refused would be carried out matter of fact way as they had been on all the other women he had owned in the past.

"I will do as you ask only because I am weary of this battle. Today I shall grovel and pretend for you Nathaniel, but you should not think that you have won this battle. I will act the part of your puppet and suffer in silence, but my heart and my mind will be rebelling. I can only hope the time comes when you understand that you will never have a wife who cares for you if you continue to degrade me."

Claudia gave him no time to react as she got on her hands and knees and crawled across the floor to where Nathaniel stood. When she was within touching distance, Claudia sat back on her haunches, hands still planted on the floor at Nathaniel's feet, and hung her head. She would not look at him nor speak. If he wished for a puppet, then he would have one. She would keep all her fire and spirit inside, giving him nothing of herself besides her physical body.

"Good girl." Nathaniel patted Claudia on the head as he spoke the tidbit of praise, but his words did nothing to cheer her. How could they when she was on her hands and knees being treated like a well trained dog?

"Lift that arse up now girl. You are to crawl at my side until told you can stop." Nathaniel pat his leg to indicate where he expected her, and then turned and began walking, leaving Claudia no choice but to follow on her hands. Refusal would only spark another volley of hurtful words and anger.

Her body ached from the activities of the night before, but she did her best to keep pace, feeling both foolish and furious. How could he do this to her and what was his purpose? They made one circle around the room that spanned the manor from end to end, Claudia crawling quickly, her fury mounting. Her rage balled into a lump that was nearly impossible to swallow, and lay on her tongue, needing to be spewed forth to put an end to the humiliating act.

Just when Claudia thought she couldn't be silent any longer, Nathaniel stopped. "Sit up now so you can see." Claudia rose and sat back on her feet, looking at the chest before her, pointedly ignoring the man at her side.

"The key to winning your obedience is through your body's desires." He opened the trunk and picked up two small silver things that looked like hairpins. "These will help you enter the proper state of mind for today's lesson." Nathaniel brushed his knuckles over one of her nipples and frowned when her body failed to respond. "You will be trained even if you don't wish to be Claudia. It is the way of things here. You are mine for life so it would behoove you to open yourself up to learning how you will be expected to behave."

The hand went back to her breast and cupped it gently, and then rubbed her nipple with his thumb. The creamy flesh held small bruises where he'd nipped her during their lovemaking the night before. Nathaniel worked the bud gently but with persistence and finally gained his intent when Claudia's nipple hardened. He quickly placed one of the silver pins over the bud and slid it down, so it pinched with enough pressure to make Claudia hiss.

"There we go. Now the other one." Nathaniel repeated the process as Claudia remained stone still, refusing to look at him or even acknowledge his presence and what he was doing to her body. Tingles of pleasure were running from her lower belly to each nipple, but Claudia didn't resent her body's response, it was a natural thing she couldn't control.

When both clips were on her nipples, Nathaniel stood back and gave each one a flick, smiling when Claudia shivered. "Do they feel nice Claudia?"

"Yes, Sir." She would use the term of respect and answer, but her heart and mind would remain cold and closed off from him as long as he continued to degrade her with humiliating acts.

"Stand up, spread your legs, and clasp your hands behind your neck. I want your pretty titties pushed out." She did so, keeping her mind blank, not acknowledging him or his lewd requests beyond simple compliance.

To Claudia's surprise, Nathaniel knelt so his mouth was at the same height as her sex. "Perhaps paying your cunt some attention will chase the ice maiden away." Nathaniel reached out and gripped both bottom cheeks and then stuck out his tongue. He wiggled it lewdly when she glanced at him and then began to run the tip over her exposed clit, all the while squeezing her tortured buttocks.

Claudia did her best to remain still, knowing full well her body would respond to him but determined to remain aloof. His tongue lapped at her clit, then made circles around it lashing it gently over and over, making molten desire build in her core. When he began to suckle her gently, pulling the bud between his lips Claudia gasped and rocked onto her heels, her legs becoming weak. Nathaniel chuckled, knowing the pleasure he was giving her was cracking the ice, if only a little.

He licked and sucked upon her clit and then darted his tongue deep inside her, piercing her sex and swirling his tongue about. The action caused pain along with the pleasure because her body so sore from his claiming of her virginity. As she reached the pinnacle and was teetering on the edge, the molten heat ready to explore and send ecstasy coursing through every nerve, Claudia lowered her hands and grabbed Nathaniel's shoulders. Then, knowing she was about to receive the ultimate pleasure, he stopped.

"Noooooooooo."

"Yes. Though your puss is tasty, I have no desire to make you cum for me. Making you teeter on the brink of satisfaction is much better."

Nathaniel slipped a pin just like the ones on her nipples over her clit, squeezing the hypersensitive nub and almost sending her over the edge. "There will be no cumming for you Claudia until I wish it. Hands back up now. Let's see how long you can remain aloof. Perhaps you should ask yourself why it is so important to be defiant and cold. I think it would be easier to be a good girl so you can have the carnal delights your body craves. Tell me wife, is your cunt in need? Is it still easy to pretend I'm not here?"

Claudia was weighing the satisfaction she would receive from kicking her husband right in the middle of his smug face when he stood up, most likely saving her bottom as serious lashing. A kick to the shin didn't hold as much appeal, and so she returned to position, legs spread hands behind her neck even as her clit throbbed. There were worse things in life than lusting for her husband's touch. While it was true, his puppet was needy, she was still very much enraged by being made to crawl. Perhaps other women came to enjoy this disturbing way of life, but Claudia swore she would not become one of them.

Chapter Twenty-Two

Claudia's afternoon with her husband consisted of crawling about at his side while maintaining a proper pose. She was to be on her hands and knees like an animal, but hold her head up and arch her back in a way that made her bottom stick up. All the while she kept the ridiculous pose; she had to keep a up pace that kept her next to, but slightly behind Nathaniel as they circled the room. It was an introduction into what her life would consist of whenever they climbed the stairs and entered what he referred to as the playroom.

She found out quickly that it was wise to learn the exacting standards of her position as she moved. Nathaniel held a long crop that would either tap upon her or lash out to deliver a sting accompanied by words such as higher, faster, arch that back, push out your bottom, etc. To say Claudia grew weary of the exercises long before Nathaniel lost interest in his games was an understatement, for he kept her in his special room for most of the afternoon.

Claudia received an introduction to each piece of equipment as she crawled about. Nathaniel initiating her by explaining how to arrange herself and letting her in on just what would occur when she was upon it. His manner was cool and reserved towards her, but Claudia was certain Nathaniel was enjoying their time spent together. His eyes would shine with a hint of merriment if she failed to hide her reaction to what her life would be like in the days to come. Claudia did her best to be the ice queen he spoke of earlier, but could not always contain her shock. The clips upon her already sore nipples and the one on her very needy clit also made her determination to remain aloof a difficult task.

And so they went about, Claudia crawling to the best of her ability, biting back the words of anger when he lashed her with the crop or gave orders as if he were training a dog. On she would go, mounting furniture that put her in degrading positions that exposed her sex, her bottom thrust up, her hands bound, or her entire body trussed up for his liking. As the sun began its descent, the afternoon rays lowering in the windows, they came to the last piece of equipment in the room. It was a chair but with modifications that made it very different from that which you would see in an average home. The chair was on a platform, putting the seat at the level of her husband's crotch. There was a large cutout V in the center of the seat to make room for a hand, an implement, or even a person to fit between her spread legs as she sat. A stubby but fat peg was in the middle where one would sit, and the arms had straps at the ends to bind her wrists. The thing looked like it belonged in some medieval dungeon, not in a respectable home.

Nathaniel paused in front of the chair and tapped her bottom with the crop. "Sit."

The command had lost its potential to infuriate her because he had issued it too many times before. Claudia sat back on her heels, spread her legs wide, and put her hands behind her neck. The fight for her dignity wasn't worth the effort. Nathaniel would do as he pleased, and no protest that could pass her lips would change that. The best she could do was offer up a silent protest in the form of remaining detached. If he wished to treat her like an animal, she would remain mute and dispassionate.

"Good girl." He tossed out the bone of praise, but if he expected her to respond with joy, he would be disappointed. "I've saved the best for last. How well you cooperate and show your appreciation for the attention I am bestowing on you, will determine if I allow Helena to dine with us this evening."

They were the only words that could have a positive effect on her attitude. She would do nearly anything for a chance to see her friend. The days when they had been together were really the only days that had not been horrid since she had come to live in Brighton. While they had suffered indignities, they had survived them together. The other woman was the only one who really understood how hard it was for Claudia to be submissive or harder still, contented, with what the word obey meant when it came to Nathaniel. The thought of spending time with Helena brought the day's only genuine smile to Claudia's face, and Nathaniel noticed the change in her immediately. He recognized the fact that he finally found something to break through his wife's stoic demeanor.

"I see I have found a chink in your armor. While I will continue to school you day in, and day out until you have become submissive and live only to please me, I am happy to have found a way past your frosty attitude."

He looked as if he expected her to speak, but Claudia had nothing to say. Was she to congratulate him? He had to know the slight smile on her face was not for him. Her emotions for her husband ebbed and waned depending on the hour. Last night she had dared to hope her life would take on some semblance of normalcy. He had treated her with a bit of dignity though she her body had reacted in a way that some would consider shameful. He had also allowed her to sleep late, making her feel almost like the lady of the manor if only for a while. All that, of course, had changed as she crawled along as if she were a dog, clips on her nipples and her nub, stirring up pleasure.

As if reading her mind, Nathaniel rubbed a thumb over one nipple. "Breathe deeply now." Claudia had learned that when he said those words, pain would follow. She breathed in and slowly let her breath out as he slipped the clips from her nipples. The blood rushing back into the tormented buds made her cry out with the intensity of the pain. Claudia took another breath and let it out, absorbing the agony, helping her body to accept it. Nathaniel did the same with the clip on her clit. It didn't hurt for it hadn't been that tight, but the nub throbbed upon its release, heightening her sexual desire, which she steadfastly ignored.

A frown creased Nathaniel's brow as he waited for her to squirm or possibly beg him to touch her sex, but when she remained silent and still he found only disappointment. A finger slipping between her folds, sliding about with ease told of her body's arousal, and it was enough to make her husband happy.

"Do not forget your behavior will be crucial to my decision regarding Helena."

"If I am a good whore you will allow me to see my only friend?"

"If you wish to put it so crassly, yes. If you allow yourself to accept the passion and respond in kind, you will see Helena. If you remain aloof, she will dine in her room."

"Then your puppet will without doubt be animated Milord."

Irritation flashed in his eyes, but Nathaniel chose to ignore her insolent attitude. She would learn. They always did. Granted his wife was proving to be troublesome, but he had time. She was his for life. "Stand, turn around and bend over. Feet spread."

Claudia obeyed, her heart beating faster from anticipation and a tiny bit of fear. He unscrewed the lid from a jar on the table beside the chair and scooped up a dollop of cream with two fingers. Without a word he proceeded to use the cream to lubricate her bottom hole, and as soon as he did, Claudia knew that the peg on the chair seat would be going in her bottom. The thing wasn't huge, but it was fat enough to make certain she knew it was inside her.

After he had worked the cream inside her still tender hole, he took another dollop and spread it on the peg. "There we go, sit down wife."

"Sir please, my bottom is sore."

"Your bum will become accustomed to being well used. Get to the chair, hover your arse over it and then slowly sit down. That peg is going inside you. I can force you onto it, or you can lower yourself slowly. The choice is yours."

Thinking of Helena, Claudia closed her eyes and pictured the beautiful blonde-haired woman, remembering her scent, the softness of her skin, and the touch of her hands. Claudia was a bit shocked as she realized her thoughts of seeing Helena had become erotic, but accepted the images nonetheless as she positioned her bottom hole over the peg and slowly sat down on it.

A yelp escaped her as the tip of the chunky dowel pushed inside of her, but she did not give in to the pain. "Ahhhhhhhhhhhh..." Claudia raised and lowered herself, eyes squeezed shut as the peg pierce her tight crinkled hole and invaded her anus.

"That's a good girl. Push yourself down now. Think about my cock thrusting in. Think of the pleasure it gave you." Claudia was thinking of Helena and the wonderful feelings the other woman gave her as Nathaniel had fucked her in the bottom before the crowd. She let out a sound that was far different from the one of distress, and Nathaniel took it for desire sparked by thoughts of him.

"All the way down sweet whore. You will push until it is all the way in, and then I will fasten your bindings. That's a girl, all the way in."

Claudia grunted then wiggled until the peg was somewhat comfortable, then parted her legs and moved her hands to where the straps were. Nathaniel buckled her up and then took a step back to admire his handiwork, thinking how very lucky he was to have chosen a wife who was so full of fire, even if she was obstinate. Despite her silent objection, she was bound and ready to service his needs. She was a passionate thing even though she refused to accept her life.

It was a widely held belief among refined society that one should refrain from lewd sex acts with one's wife. A genteel woman was to accept her husband's advances in the bedroom, but forcing her to suck on her husband's cock or take his member in her anus was not acceptable. Gentlemen were expected to use a prostitute for such things. Nathaniel and the rest of the men in the Order of Blackguards disagreed with this belief. They knew the value of training their wives to receive any sex act no matter how vulgar or sadistic. Why fuck a sullied and diseased whore when you could have a wife that would fulfill all your needs no matter how base they were?

"Husband, if you have a mind to use me while I'm all trussed up, I beg you to do it now. This chair is far from comfortable."

"Sometimes discomfort can lead to sexual delights. I know you find the peg up your bum distasteful, but you will survive. I have no doubt you will enjoy yourself when you stop being so unyielding. I am going to reward you for the obedience you exhibited this afternoon. Once you learn that good behavior leads to exquisite pleasure, your life will be richer."

"There are pleasures in life that do not require degradation."

"Yes, there are, but satisfying the flesh is one of the finer things, and despite your belief to the contrary, living to serve your husband can be gratifying and enjoyable. I have no desire to trap you in a life that you will hate, Claudia. If you would only trust me and allow yourself to feel, all this would be easier."

"All I feel is humiliated."

"The path towards pleasure can be found when one rises from the depths of emotions. Your humiliation will make the final reward sweeter, and learning to do everything I command without hesitation, will make your role as my wife more fulfilling as well."

"Nathaniel, I've no doubt you can make my body feel, but what of my heart and mind? How am I to disregard the sorrow there?"

Nathaniel bent to one knee between Claudia's spread legs and cupped her chin, using his thumb to stroke her jawline with uncommon tenderness. "Simply stop resisting. When you understand that what we do is normal and not immoral, you will find the joy your heart yearns for."

Claudia lowered her eyes. His stare was too intense. He honestly believed what he was telling her, which made it all more disturbing. Did all the women actually find love and satisfaction when treated in such a way, or did they simply abandon their pride and carry out their wifely obligation suffering in silence as their husbands ignored their pain?

Nathaniel had no more patience for his new wife. She would come to accept the life she had been given. He rose, so he was looking down at her once more. "Now then, it's time to continue your instruction. This is a very special chair. As you can feel, it penetrates your bottom to keep you focused as well as spreading your legs so I may do what I wish with your cunt. However, there is one more unique feature."

Nathaniel reached down and began to turn the crank on the side of the chair. When he did, the whole thing lowered, causing her legs to straighten and stick out in front of her, putting her mouth on the same level as his crotch.

"As you can see, there are many things one can do to a person while she sits in this chair. Today's final lesson will be on oral servitude. You will now learn the proper way to use your mouth. I have grown weary of your sharp tongue. Remember, if you act like a harpy, Helena will dine in her room. On the other hand, if you do as I say and pleasure me as a good wife should, there will be rewards."

He stepped between her spread legs once more and unfastened the buttons on his trousers, reaching in and pulling out his half-hard cock. He was close enough for it to touch her mouth, and that is exactly what he did. Nathaniel held the shaft and pulled back the foreskin, so the smooth bulbous head came into view, he then began to rub the head back and forth over Claudia's closed lips.

Claudia closed her eyes, somewhat revolted, the sight of her husband's cock reminding her of the things he'd done to her during the night. Now here she was, restrained once again. Would he ever allow her to do things of her free will? She despised the straps that held her down so much that had he only asked; she would promise good behavior. She turned her cheek to tell him as much, but Nathaniel grasped a handful of her hair and moved her back to center.

"The only reason you are to open your mouth is to pleasure me. My cock is going inside no matter what you wish. Be a good girl now and open wide." Claudia obeyed; there was no avoiding what was about to happen and she desperately wanted to see Helena. "Open your eyes. You are to look at me as I tame you."

Claudia complied, and Nathaniel moved his hips forward, so the head of his cock was in her mouth. Claudia wanted to gag and could barely contain the response. She breathed in through her nose only to smell the scent of their sex than had permeated the bedchamber last night.

"Close your lips over the head and suck now. Nice and gentle girl, cover your teeth with your lips." His cock head lay on her tongue as she tightened her lips around it and began to suckle. "That's right, look at me wife, your eyes will tell me how this makes you feel. Right now, all I see is disgust. That will change. Open."

Claudia did so, and Nathaniel pulled her head back just a bit with the hand entangled in her hair. "Lick me now. Stick out your tongue and lick me up and down. Each time you chose to speak your mind, you shall find my cock filling that sassy mouth." He held his shaft and moved it about as Claudia's little pink tongue darted about, flicking his cock and then laying the flat of it upon the smooth skin and lapping harder. Claudia drew her tongue from the base of her husband's penis all the way up the shaft to the head. He gave a groan of pleasure, and she noted that the more she licked, the harder he became. With each movement of her tongue, his cock stiffened, and his pleasure written upon his face. When she took the head back into her mouth and sucked, Nathaniel groaned again.

"That's my good girl. Service your master. You can't be brazen and disagreeable when I'm fucking you here." Though the words incited her ire, she was still fascinated by the way he was responding. He still held the upper hand, his fist held her hair tightly, directing her movements, but Claudia sensed that she too held power when Nathaniel was in such a vulnerable state. His desire was overriding a bit of his dominance to indulge his sexual need. Claudia was a quick learner and far from foolish. Giving him intense pleasure would mean good things for her, and so she began to suck a bit harder, and use her tongue to swirl around his cock as she did. The outcome of her actions wasn't exactly to her liking however.

Nathaniel loosened his fingers from her hair only to grasp the back of her head. His fingers tightened and then began to move her head forward further than she could stand. The head of his cock hit the back of her throat making her gag before he pulled out to allow her to regain her composure.

"Easy girl. In time, you will swallow it all, but today we'll go easy." Claudia sucked harder as Nathaniel began to piston his hips forward and back, fucking her mouth. Her hands were bound, and he held her head in a tight grip, taking away a control she had, but again Claudia noted the intense pleasure his expression conveyed, and felt his cock pulsing upon her tongue.

Feeling him throb in her mouth, using to the sound of his moans to guide her, Claudia did her best to please her husband. When he pulled his shaft almost all the way out, she sucked him like a hungry babe would a bottle as she ran her tongue around and around. When he moaned louder and relaxed his grip on her head just a little, she slowly slid forward and back of her own accord, taking as much of him inside her mouth as she could. There was power in this pleasuring of him, and Claudia was working to find what he liked best, because when he was completely wrapped up in the passion, he in turn became weak. As she sucked and bobbed her head, his control of her lessened despite being strapped into the chair. He needed what she could do for him, and needed it badly.

"Oh God, Claudia. Yes. That's a good girl. Suck me now."

Nathaniel growled deep in his throat as the blood pulsed in his manhood. Gratification overcame Claudia's reluctance as she heard his moans of pleasure, knowing she satisfied him, pleased she could make him need what she could provide, but her control was short lived. He thrust forward, burying himself deep and then began a steady rhythm as she did her best to suck him. His hips thrust forward with a punishing rhythm, fucking her mouth with no mercy, completely taking away any power she had.

Watching as her sweet little mouth took him so deep, loving the rush of power and adrenaline he felt along with the intense sexual desire made him half crazed. He held her head in both of his hands, grunting as he fucked her mouth. He paused on the brink of orgasm, needing to watch her face as he spurt into her mouth for the first time.

"Suck now girl. Suck me harder. Take it all and suck."

Claudia's lips stretched open, surrounding his cock in a hot wetness while her tongue ran circles around the head of his shaft. He was burying himself in his wife's mouth, ready to explode when running footsteps and a cry of anger sounded on the stairs. Nathaniel turned to see who dared to intrude upon his pleasure and saw Helena come flying through the doorway at the top of the stairs with Miss Reagan on her heels.

Chapter Twenty-Three

Claudia tried to turn her head, wanting to see what the commotion was about, but Nathaniel gripped her head too tightly. Though he paused the thrusting of his hips, his cock lay heavy and pulsing on Claudia's tongue. The way it throbbed told Claudia her husband was very near his fulfillment, and knew as well that whomever it was that had burst in on them was not likely to receive anything but Nathaniel's ire.

"To your knees." The words were clipped and cold. Nathaniel was barely suppressing rage. Claudia heard a plop caused by bare skin hitting the wood floor a few moments before Helena came into view. The blonde woman was crawling towards the Earl, her face seemingly innocent except for the twinkle of merriment in her eyes. Still, she hung her head as she came nearer, knowing that Lord Brighton would most definitely be angry with her.

Helena stopped just feet from where Claudia sat, and Nathaniel stood, and then bowed low, her fingertip sliding across the floor to a spot almost touching his foot, her forehead resting on the floor. Claudia wanted to turn her head for a better view of Helena, and did indeed try to, but Nathaniel gripped her chin.

"Forgive me Lord Tarrington. She..." Nathaniel held up his hand, putting an end to Miss Reagan's excuse before the flustered woman could begin.

"Silence, no one is to speak. Claudia dear, finish what you started. Suck me good and hard until I tell you to stop." Claudia's eyes shifted back and forth. On one side of her husband was the nude and prone Helena, her back arched, flaxen hair shimmering like a golden pool about her head, the ivory skin of her bottom marred with stripes new and old. On the other, stood the red-faced Miss Reagan, lips pressed together tightly, eyes fuming as she stared at Helena.

Strong hands squeezing her jaw brought her eyes back to center where they met with Nathaniel's. Despite the interruption, he didn't appear particularly fazed, and his cock was still hard and smooth upon her tongue. Before he had to issue his command a second time, Claudia sucked inward, her cheeks hollowing as her tongue working to move over Nathaniel's shaft.

"That's a good girl. Do not stop sucking me. We now have an audience, so I expect you to strive for perfection. Bob your head now and move that tongue around the tip." Claudia began to move her head forward and back, taking in as much of Nathaniel's cock as she could without gagging. Her effort was rewarded by her husband's sharp intake of breath as his manhood seemed to swell even larger.

"That's my sweet pet. That's it. Now for the benefit of those watching, you are to squeeze the wooden peg in your bottom as I count to five. Squeeze now. One, two, three, four, five. Good, now relax. Again Claudia. Your face is flushed my dear; I dare say you enjoy that feeling. Again now, squeeze harder. One, two, three, four, five, and release. Why Claudia, is that desire I see in your eyes. Don't worry pet, I shall fuck your bum later."

Nathaniel had her continue to squeeze and release as she bobbed her head back and forth, a sheen of sweat dampening her upper lip at the effort she was using to clench the wood knob in her bottom.

"Faster Claudia. Faster now." Once more Nathaniel gripped her head in back, fingers anchored in her hair. He made deep grunting noises and began to thrust his hips once again. Claudia gagged once more, but Nathaniel seemed not to notice for he never slowed his rhythm. His ball sack slapped against her chin as she sucked and slurped, doing her best to open her throat.

He let out a roar and thrust forward, holding Claudia's head tightly so she could not back away as his cock slid deeper into her throat. He spilled his seed into her wet hot mouth, staring into Claudia's eyes as he pumped and ejaculated. Claudia pulled at her bindings and tried to turn from him, but it was no use, even in the throes of orgasm, Nathaniel was in complete control, keeping her face exactly where he wanted it. She began to swallow though it turned her stomach, it was that or have his semen spurt from her lips, and Claudia knew defiance would come at a cost.

When he'd spent the last of his seed in her mouth, his cock lay upon her tongue like a wet heavy thing, twitching as the aftershocks of pleasure coursed through him, he patted Claudia on the head. "You did well, wife. We will work on your ability to take the entire length of me in your mouth, but for the first time, you performed admirably."

He pulled his cock from her mouth and wiped a trail of semen from her chin as he spoke. Claudia's eyes narrowed none too pleased with his comment or his patting her on the head, but set her anger aside at his next words.

"Now then, as for you Helena, it's clear you've managed to find yourself in need of punishment though you've only just arrived."

"It was not my intent to interrupt your pleasure, Sir. Miss Reagan..."

"Silence. Come and clean my cock Helena. Claudia, watch how she makes certain everything has been licked off."

Helena glanced at Claudia, her eyes apologetic, and moved into position. She cradled Nathaniel's shaft in her hands ever so gently and then began to clean it with little licks. Her pink tongue darted out, covering his manhood from shaft to tip and then move to lick his balls as well. When she finished, Helena looked up at Nathaniel, waiting for instructions. Her ministrations had left him semi hard.

Claudia watched as Helena licked her husband's cock. She felt a surge of desire fill her as the other woman's tongue moved about, but then also felt a tiny twinge of jealousy. To her surprise, Claudia realized both emotions came bubbling to the surface because of her feelings towards Helena, and not Nathaniel. It was an insight that made her uneasy. The lust was somewhat understandable, but the jealousy? It was not a feeling she expected or particularly desired.

Through the pleasuring Nathaniel found with Claudia, to the bathing given his cock by Helena, Miss Reagan watched the proceedings with a face flushed by anger, her mouth made into a thin line from pressing her lips together to bite back her words. Miss Reagan had her arms crossed in front of her, and her fingers were white at the knuckles where they held each elbow, all her anger manifesting in the grip she had on her arms.

"Excuse me Lord Tarrington. Would you like me to remove that one? Miss Reagan dipped her head in Helena's direction. "I was just about to give her an enema and a good scrubbing."

"Please Sir; she is a spiteful old witch. The enema bag was full of cold water and the scrub brush one with wire bristles."

"I've no desire to hear any excuses for your behavior. It is clear you fled from Miss Reagan, and you dared to come to my private sanctuary uninvited. Both are punishable offenses. You are going to satisfy Claudia for she has earned her release, and then I will put you in the cage until tomorrow morning with your chastity belt on, unable to get your own pleasure or disturb this household. Tis a shame Helena. Claudia was looking forward to having you there at dinner. I dare say it's what kept her on her best behavior all afternoon. Pity you ruined both her reward and yours because you insist on being defiant."

If Nathaniel thought allowing Claudia to have sexual gratification at the hands of Helena would endear him to his new wife, he was mistaken. As Helena crawled on all fours and began to lap at the sensitive bud between Claudia's legs, Claudia completely forgot about her husband. She ached to be able to wrap her fingers in Helena's golden hair and hold Helena tightly as the woman's warm wet tongue slid up and down Claudia's slit, collecting all of her juices, slurping noisily as she did so.

Miss Reagan made a sound of disgust, not at all pleased with her employer's decision. Both women were clearly enjoying themselves as Helena's head moved between Claudia's legs. Lord Tarrington's wife was making little mewling sounds of pleasure as her hands fisted in their bindings; her faced flushed, her eyes closed. Miss Reagan knew the woman was on the brink of orgasm, and good behavior or not, Claudia had committed too many crimes to deserve sexual release.

Helena's tongue swirled round and round Claudia's clit and then slipped into her sex, wiggling there, rubbing the tip along the side that pressed against the wooden peg in Claudia's bottom. The mix of intense sensations combined with the desire she felt for Helena, soon had Claudia crying out as her body peaked. Every nerve ending sizzled with intense pleasure spiraling out from her core. Claudia's body clamped down on the peg in her bottom, squeezing without conscious thought as she tumbled over the edge with an orgasm so intense it made her head spin. Through it all, Helena licked, lapped, and suckled her, driving Claudia's orgasm on and on until she was crying out in near desperation because of the intensity of the sensations.

Helena sat up on her knees and nuzzled Claudia's belly, planting tiny kisses on her exposed clit as Claudia shook from the power of her orgasm. She slipped her arms around the young dark haired woman and pressed her cheek to Claudia's quivering thighs, hugging Claudia before Nathaniel pulled her away.

"Enough." Nathaniel ignored Claudia's small cry of distress as she lost the comfort of Helena's arms. If he had not been so intent on punishing Helena, he might have guessed at the bond that was building between the two women, but he either did not see it or else he did not care. Miss Reagan however saw the brief look of yearning that passed between her employer's wife and the whore he had trained.

"Miss Reagan please put on Helena's chastity belt and put her in the cage. She may have water in a dish, but no food. It certainly will not hurt her to hunger for something other than sex. Perhaps it will help her realize her days of disobedience are over."

"Yes, Sir. It will be my pleasure."

Nathaniel nodded, but it was one of distraction, his days of lusting after the voluptuous blonde woman were over. The slim woman with sable hair, who was slumped in the chair, already captured his attention. It was time to remove her bindings. He moved forward, dismissing both Miss Reagan and Helena, to loosen the straps on Claudia's wrists and ankles. She looked up at him; eyes half mast, leaden from passion and exhaustion.

"Time to put you in bed. I dare say you need a long nap before dinner. Perhaps my good girl will be too exhausted for the formal table."

Claudia registered the fact that her husband was pleased with her, but she didn't find much pleasure in his sweet words. This man seduced her with honeyed words and rose petals one moment, and made her crawl about like a dog, stuffing his cock down her throat the next. While she didn't loathe him, love and tenderness certainly hadn't blossomed in her heart. It would take more than a nap before dinner in a soft bed to soothe her ire. Claudia thought that there was perhaps a decent man inside Nathaniel, but she also suspected the years of following his family's traditions just might have made it impossible for him to ever see her as more than a play thing.

Nathaniel pulled her up off the wooden peg that had pierced her sore anus, and despite his gentleness, she made an involuntary hiss of pain. Claudia did not care for her husband's fondness for shoving things in her bottom. She turned in an attempt to catch Helena's eye as Nathaniel gathered her in his arms, but the other woman was already crawling across the room at Miss Reagan's heels. Claudia felt a sadness fall upon her heart at the sight of her friend submitting to the awful Miss Reagan, but she supposed a punishment of wearing a chastity device and put in a cage with no food would make anyone do as they were told. She sighed; neither her fate nor Helena's was just, but it was clear rebellion wouldn't help anything.

Nathaniel heard her sign and held Claudia close, mistaking the reason for her discontent. "Don't fret Claudia, you shall soon be in a warm bed. Good girls get good things." His words brought the absurd image of herself rolling on the floor on her back offering her stomach up for a good rub like a favorite pet hound to mind, causing a wry smile. The thought was both amusing and disconcerting. How on Earth had her life taken such a turn? She should have been in London, but instead she was being carried to bed, her bottom hole sore from the crude wooden peg that had been stuffed in it, the juices of desire put there by another woman drying on her thighs.

Chapter Twenty-Four

Nathaniel carried Claudia down the stairs, stopping at the second floor to take his wife to her rooms. There wouldn't be a formal dinner for her that night; just something simple brought on a tray after Claudia had time to nap for a bit. As he carried her, her eyes remained closed, but Nathaniel had no doubt she was feigning sleep. While he didn't doubt she was worn out, he did not believe she would fall asleep so readily in his arms.

He was torn about the day's training session. While she had submitted to his will, crawling, mounting the furniture, and sucking his cock, her spirit had not followed. His wife had yet to grant him her submission by her own free will. The fight in her remained, as did the wall around her heart. This ability of hers to remain aloof instead of embracing the compliance that meant delightful things for her body, and an affection for the man who provided her pain and pleasure, was troubling. Never before had a woman refrained from falling into his arms, adoring him as a submissive should her master.

When they reached Claudia's bedchamber, Nathaniel laid Claudia on the bed. His wife's bed had been turned down and readied for her in case the Master decided to put her there instead of taking Claudia back to his rooms. He pulled the bell cord to summon Millie, his wife's maid, and then looked down at her, not surprised in the least to see her staring at him.

"I see you've awakened from your slumber."

"Will I be allowed to remain here for the night?" Her question aggravated him. By this time, she should be ready and willing to serve him in any manner despite being fatigued.

"You have earned your rest."

A look of fury flashed in Claudia's eyes before she lowered them to hide the emotion. She had no desire for her husband to see that he could, in fact, make her feel anything. She had submitted to him all through the long afternoon, but that didn't mean he had captured her heart.

"Is your anger because you wish to be in my bed or simply left over defiance you were unable to give voice to during your training today?"

"Does it matter?"

"Answering a question with a question is not acceptable."

"And now I must be punished? You said only a moment ago that I had earned my rest."

"That was before I was met once again with your sass, but no, I won't punish you for speaking your mind."

"Pray tell husband, is that just this once or always?"

"Why must you fight me? I am your husband and you vowed to obey me."

"I was married against my will."

"Most girls of good breeding are. You don't differ from them."

"I find it hard to believe that most girls crawl like a dog at their husband's side, have things rammed into their bottoms and suck their husband's cocks. The matrons with their eyes keen as a bird's when searching for a tidbit of gossip could neither hold their tongue about such acts of debauchery nor engage in them at their husband's command."

"Your mother did just that."

"My mother was never like them. She lacked their fortitude and narrow-minded attitude."

"Things aren't always as they seem."

"Spared me your lies. I refuse to be spoon fed deceit."

Nathaniel sighed; he was weary of the shrew he'd wed. Granted time, and continued training would produce the wife he wished for, but he'd had enough for the day. "Roll onto your stomach."

"Nathaniel, please. My bottom is painful both inside and out. I shall cease my arguing and be a model wife if only you will spare me your wrath."

"Did I not just tell you I had no intention on punishing you? Use your ears girl and stop trying my patience. Now roll over." Nathaniel damned the slip of a girl and her ability to goad him. He disliked the loss of control she could cause in him, and he didn't care for it one bit.

Claudia complied with a huff of irritation that Nathaniel chose to ignore. Millie arrived with a pitcher of hot water and poured it in the basin on the bed stand without a word. She set a folded cloth next to it before giving the master of the house a small bob of her head and quickly exiting the room.

When Claudia felt her husband's hands pull her bottom cheeks open, she hissed in pain, hoping he would be a man of his word. She felt the touch of cool air on her bottom hole, the sensation making her feel vulnerable which she didn't care for in the least. When he poked at the red puckered aperture, Claudia couldn't keep quiet any longer.

"I would be grateful if you stood by your word. I cannot take anything more where you are probing."

"It isn't my intention to punish or fuck you Claudia, I intend to cleanse the oily residue off before allowing you to rest. I cannot help but touch you. I imagine you would find the sight of such a tender place stimulating as well. While I found my pleasure in your mouth not long ago, the evidence of your time upon the chair makes my cock stir."

"A man who enjoys the torture of his wife is a despicable monster."

"Not in this house. Now stop that shrill chatter. I've had more than enough. I cannot promise continued freedom from punishment if you do not shut up."

Claudia was no fool, and so she pressed her lips together despite wishing to fling more accusations at her husband. Granted her continued defiance wasn't in her best interest, but she simply couldn't be the submissive ninny Nathaniel wanted her to be. It wasn't in her to be docile.

Nathaniel welcomed the silence as he dipped the soft cloth in the hot water and then began to wipe the oil from between Claudia's bum cheeks. He wasn't particularly gentle as he rubbed at her crinkled rosebud, in fact; he couldn't help smiling when she hissed in pain. She deserved much more, and she would get it as well, but that would have to wait until tomorrow. Despite her insolence, she had done all he required in the playroom. Her words of anger and continued disobedience were things he wasn't used to from women. All of them were compliant, from the maids to Headmistress Patton. It was a woman's place to do as men bid.

When he was finished washing her, Nathaniel set the rag aside and ran his hand over the plains of her back and bottom, slowly stroking the valley and hill. Touching ever so gently, from her shoulder all the way down to the spot behind her knee, loving how soft she was, and for a moment how submissive. She didn't sigh nor toss barbed words of anger; she yielded to his touch as she always should.

As he stroked Claudia, Nathaniel thought about his feelings towards the girl he'd married. While he didn't love her, he did feel possessive. She'd wormed her way into his heart like it or not. The softness he felt for her there was uncommon. Granted he'd had favorites among the women who'd come before Claudia, but Claudia's spirit seemed to enamor him to her. He wasn't sure why he should feel such a thing. The girl pushed back each time he tried to teach her the joy of submission, but the tender spot was there nonetheless. He just wished she'd do as she should. A bit of spirit was fine, it made for a more enjoyable bedmate, but the sass simply had to stop.

"Pardon me, Lord Tarrington, but Sir Hastings has arrived."

"Sir Hastings? Did Miss Reagan fail to tell me of dinner plans?" He had whirled on the maid when she interrupted him, and now she took a step back, seeing the annoyance on the Earl's face. Lord Tarrington was fond of disciplining his house servants.

"I don't know Milord. I was just told to give you the missive."

"Never mind. Run and tell him I'm on my way, and make certain the kitchen staff is aware that I have a dinner guest."

"Yes Milord."

"And send word that Miss Reagan is to join us in my study." He was more than a bit angry that Helena had managed to free herself, and now it appeared his head housekeeper had forgotten to remind him of a dinner engagement. He had planned to allow Claudia at the supper table and to have Helena brought down as well. How had Miss Reagan forgotten his dinner guest? Perhaps Miss Reagan was focusing too much of her energy battling with Claudia and Helena.

"Yes Milord."

Nathaniel watched her go and then turned back to Claudia. His wife's eyes were once again closed, and her breathing was slow and deep. He thought perhaps she was asleep this time. "Rest Claudia. You've earned your peace and quiet." He would make sure Millie stayed in attendance so a supper tray could be fetched upon her waking since it appeared he had forgotten about his dinner plans. It was probably best that Claudia was sleeping. Nathaniel didn't think she was ready to be presented to his friends. She was far too rough around the edges.

When Claudia heard his footfalls going towards the door, she opened her eyes to watch him. His gentle stroking had indeed made her sleepy, but though she was weary, she couldn't help thinking of poor Helena, confined like a dog with only a bowl of water to drink. Claudia rolled over as her eyes traveled upward to where her friend remained imprisoned in a cage, her heart heavy at the injustice of it all.

Slipping from her bed, groaning at the ache that enveloped her whole body, Claudia went to the wardrobe and pulled out a dressing gown. When she turned around, Millie was in the doorway, eyes wide as saucers as she watched her Mistress.

"Don't tell. If he finds out I'm gone, tell him you found the room empty when you came back but didn't want to interrupt his dinner."

Millie worried her bottom lip beneath her teeth and wrung her hands.

"Please." Millie still hesitated. She did not enjoy the feel of the Master's strap. "I just want to go upstairs. I swear I won't leave the house."

The maid finally nodded, then turned and took flight, allowing the new Mistress of the house time to flee. Claudia wasted no time. She hurried to the narrow stairs that led to the attic, knowing that if Millie had returned, then Miss Reagan must have received her summons to Nathaniel's study, leaving Helena alone.

Her feet were bare so her journey upward was soundless aside from a small creak or two, which wouldn't be discernable from the rest of the noise the old manor made. When she reached the top of the stairs, Claudia paused on the landing just out of sight, listening, and was met with silence. There were no sobs coming from the room that held so many things designed for torture and debauchery, but Claudia didn't expect to hear crying. Helena was resilient no matter how they punished her. It was her tough, rebellious spirit that was causing her to behave in a way that those in charge found intolerable.

She did a slow count to ten and then stepped into the room. The afternoon sun had slipped below the line of small windows, leaving the attic shrouded in blacks and grays. The shadows cast by the hideous furniture looking akin to the beasts a child might expect to find under the bed. Claudia dismissed the slight flutter in her chest, knowing the true villains of the manor were currently below in the study.

Moving forward, the gloom becoming thicker moment by moment as the sun sped its way toward complete descent, Claudia made her way to where the cage that held Helena sat. The flaxen-haired woman sat with her back against the bars facing away from any who might venture upstairs to torment her further. A small creak gave away Claudia's presence, but Still Helena didn't turn. Claudia surmised that her friend had her fill of any who might be approaching.

"Save your breath and your horrid games. I won't cooperate no matter what you do."

"Even with me?" Helena moved to her knees in a flash, spinning, so she faced Claudia.

"How? Claudia!"

"Never mind how. Did that old hag take the keys?"

"No. The ring is there on the beam."

Claudia squinted and debated lighting a lamp, but then made out the metal ring holding the keys to the various pieces of furniture that locked the unwilling into place. She quickly pulled it off the nail it hung on, making a face as she wondered which would fit.

"You're going to get in trouble."

"How can things get any worse?"

"They can. You've no idea."

"I think I have some. My life here has already been a nightmare."

"Still, I saw how he gently picked you up. Lord Tarrington has feelings for you."

"Don't be ridiculous. The man only wished to take care of his new toy." Claudia knelt beside the cage door and began to try the different keys in the lock, making a small sound of triumph when she found the right one. She swung the door open then stepped back.

"Hurry."

"Thank you for the dramatic rescue, but I can't go anywhere."

"Of course you can. Here, take my dressing gown."

Helena slowly shook her head. "And where am I to go? They will just put me back in here with new aches and pains for causing trouble."

Claudia shrugged her shoulders. Helena was right. Neither of them had any place they could go for refuge. Their families wouldn't help them and the townspeople certainly wouldn't either. They had one dressing gown between them and no friends but each other.

"Well then I shall keep you company." Helena's eyes widened, and a smile big enough to be seen in the gloom lit her face. Claudia crawled inside the cage and sat down against the bars, holding the dressing gown up so Helena could curl up beside her.

"This will only lead to trouble, but thank you just the same."

"I couldn't leave you in here. Besides, you are right. No one will help us."

"That's not true for you. He cares about you."

"No. He's a beast and just wants to play his twisted games."

"You're wrong. Miss Reagan knows it too. I saw how she watched when he carried you away, and I can assure you that he has never carried me anywhere. If I had him, I wouldn't rebel. Well, at least not so much."

"How can you say that? He made me crawl beside him all afternoon and then put me on that horrid chair with the peg in my bottom."

"I know, I hate the crawling and the worst of the whippings, at least those I get from Miss Patton or Miss Reagan, but I like the other stuff." Helena's hand found Claudia's under the robe squeezing tightly. "You liked it when I licked you."

If the attic hadn't been near darkness, Helena would have seen the blush staining Claudia's cheeks. Her response to her friend's mouth on her sex was about the only thing that could make her feel shy. The rest of it was too forced. There was nothing that could do about it.

"Yes I liked it. Your mouth felt wonderful. He can make my body feel all those things too, but my heart holds no feelings for him at all."

"He's not that bad, Claudia. There are worse things, much worse."

Claudia thought about Helena being married to the old man Nathaniel had mentioned, or worse, her being given to Lady Ellingsworth. She pulled the hand Helena held to her chest and tried to see Helena's face in the growing darkness. "Listen to me, you have to leave here."

"No silly, I..."

"You don't understand. That horrid Lady Ellingsworth wants you."

"Claudia, they will send me where they want. If I go to her then, I shall battle her each second of the day until she dumps me upon the Earl's doorstep crying good riddance."

Claudia's shoulders slumped in defeat. She would have done anything to help Helena. Maybe she could charm him into getting her way. She doubted it would work, but it might be worth a try. Her husband wasn't like the boys she'd teased during her season in London, but it wouldn't hurt to try.

"I could do my best to enchant Nathaniel. According to you, he has feelings for me." Claudia found the idea ludicrous, and her doubt came across loud and clear.

"He does. I suspect he would be against the idea no matter what he feels. The two of us under the same roof would be a risky venture. Just think of the chaos we'd cause." Claudia laughed at the idea of wreaking havoc in Nathaniel's household and making Miss Reagan rue the day she was born, then sobered and settled down next to Helena, pulling the dressing gown around them.

"Don't fret pigeon. I'll be alright no matter where I land."

"I shall miss you Helena."

The sun had set leaving the attic in complete darkness; the sliver of the new moon not affording the cavernous room any light. Just as Claudia was laying her head on Helena's shoulder, the clatter of footsteps sounded from across the room. Someone, make that more than one, was coming up the wooden stairs in a hurry. The circle of light that proceeded the intruders came into sight first, followed by the pinched and furious face of Miss Reagan. She held the light high as she stormed towards the cage; her eyes taking on a murderous shine when she spied Helena and Claudia inside.

"There! Take them to the Master's study while I tell Lord Tarrington of this new affront to his authority."

Both men came forward but then hesitated before grabbing Claudia, effectively stopping them from obeying Miss Reagan's command. The new mistress was in the center of the cage now between them and Helena.

"What's the matter with you? I can assure you that he doesn't wish for that one to be up here."

"Perhaps they know what you refuse to see." Helena's words dripped with venom as she flung them at Miss Reagan.

"Silence girl. I'll take the skin off your backside for this."

"Stop it. Helena did nothing. She is still in this horrid cage where you left her. I shall speak to my husband."

"Why you uppity little trollop. Just because he fucked you sweetly doesn't mean he won't enjoy punishing you."

"He'll enjoy it, and come to care for her all the more because of it. I know you aren't blind to the Earl's affections for his new wife. Go ahead Claudia. I will be right behind you. I would advise everyone to keep their hands to themselves."

Claudia crawled out, and Helena came at her heels. Miss Reagan raised a hand to slap Helena, but Claudia stepped between the two women, eyes blazing.

"Don't touch her."

"I don't have to take orders from a whore."

"But you will." Claudia wasn't quite as sure of herself as her words implied, but they had the desired effect just the same. Miss Reagan lowered her hand and turned towards the stairs. Claudia hooked her arm in Helena's. If they had to face the wrath of her husband, they'd do it together. Standing tall, gloriously nude, the two women went towards the stairs as well. The footmen fell in behind, holding their lanterns higher to admire the view, both exceedingly happy they hadn't had to lay hands on the new Lady Tarrington.

Chapter Twenty-Five

Lord Tarrington was blissfully unaware of the drama that was unfolding under his roof. Had he been privy, skirts would have been raised; bloomers parted, and birch bundles applied to all involved. He was sitting in the study with Sir Hastings, sipping whiskey and filling each other in on what had transpired in their lives since last they saw each other. Nathaniel rarely left Brighton, but Sir Hastings was fond of London and society even though it was simply a ruse that he was seeking a girl of good breeding to wed. Like Nathaniel, Bryce's family belonged to the Order of Exultant Blackguards, and therefore would marry a girl raised in a family who believed in strict punishment, sexual service, and absolute female submission.

The men had settled down in front of the fire after Nathaniel finished reprimanding Miss Reagan, giving the woman ten lashes with the tawse before sending her on her way. All under his roof were subject to physical punishment no matter their gender or station. Lord Tarrington ruled with an iron fist, and the fact that he had been interrupted while teaching Claudia how to suck his cock was inexcusable.

Bryce had watched the scene from beginning to end as Nathaniel lectured Miss Reagan on her duties and had her lean over the birching wedge so he could apply the tawse to her ample bottom. The fact that Nathaniel had made the woman who held a high station in the manor bare her own bottom had received an enthusiastic nod of approval from Bryce as had the whipping itself. When he had finished, Bryce had applauded, watching poor Miss Reagan swipe at her eyes as she tugged her skirt down and left the study, feeling shamed and well reprimanded.

Now the two were discussing Bryce's visit, and conversing about the fact that the London season was coming to an end. The end of the season meant Bryce couldn't put off marrying any longer. It wasn't that he couldn't continue to go to London whenever he chose; it was the fact that his bachelor days had come to a close. Nathaniel knew Bryce wasn't dismayed by the idea of being wed, for in their homes marriage had benefits other men of their station didn't have.

"That was an outstanding demonstration Nathaniel. Does she give you cause to whip that ample rump often?"

"No, Miss Reagan does her job well. She seems somewhat distracted of late."

"How do she and your wife get on?"

"You are quite adept at getting to the root of the problem. I must admit that Miss Reagan and Claudia despise each other. To say my wife is high spirited would be to put it mildly. She struggles to comply with the confines of her new life. Miss Reagan is quick to pass judgment and to punish. The two cause a good deal of tension in the house."

"Miss Reagan has run your home for a good many years. Wasn't she here while your father was Duke?"

"Yes, and she has been in charge of the others."

Bryce nodded, seemingly in quiet contemplation.

"Is something troubling you? I have to say I've found it odd that you've enjoyed London and the young ladies you can't touch more than your home full of girls who must bend to our ways."

"Life in Derby is duller than you can imagine."

"Surely London and the endless suppers with twittering girls and their hopeful mothers must get tiresome."

"True, you have to remember that the school is here, Nathaniel. You've more nubile submissive women at your disposal."

"Once you've chosen a wife you shall have whatever your desire, and there is no reason you can't travel to London once the training period is over. No one would think anything of you paddling the girl even there, and we engage in the more lewd sexual acts behind closed doors."

"Women talk."

"Not our women! She is yours for life, and when taught how things should be, she won't even wish to be free."

"And your Claudia. Is she a perfect example of this submission?"

"Hardly. The girl rebels at every turn. She is learning though, and she's incredibly passionate in bed. Her lessons are a delight."

"Are you being harsh with her?"

"By harsh do you mean whipping the girl for her failure to obey?"

"That and the rest. The humiliation and forced groveling, the taking them in the bum and the rough sexual service."

"You make everything sound so sordid Bryce. Our mothers were content with their lives, and our wives will be too. You have put too much thinking into this. You must remember how delightful it is to have a woman kneeling at your feet as she sucks your cock or quivers beneath you as you thrust into her bum. I know you have had such delights and saw your mother gladly submit to these things. The women come to love their station in life. You know that."

"I do. I imagine my misgivings are because those who attract me in London are the ones who are high-spirited and full of sass. Those who stick close to their mamas and haven't an ounce of mischievous fire bore me."

"Claudia is certainly mischievous. She is as spirited as they come."

"But will she still be once you break her."

Nathaniel looked at Bryce, his eyebrows drawn together, wondering just where the conversation was going and not understanding the man's aversion for their lifestyle. Bryce was brought up to know the distinctive place women held in their world. How could he disagree when the pleasures were so numerous and enjoyable?

"What are you getting at Bryce? Are you saying you wish to wed a girl who isn't a daughter of our Order?"

"Heavens no. I'd never break from our tradition. What I'm getting at is, are all of the girls indeed submissive? What if some are not. Your Claudia could be an example. She is fighting you every step of the way. I've no doubt you shall win in the end, but will your victory extinguish the flame inside that makes her so full of passion? I've no desire to crush my future wife's spirit nor do I wish for her to hate me."

"The women don't grow to hate us; the come to idolize..."

The sound of Miss Reagan's voice accompanied by multiple footsteps interrupted Nathaniel. He rose so as to see what the commotion in the hall was, and was shocked to see Miss Reagan leading the way down the staircase followed by Claudia and Helena, who were both nude. Two of his footmen brought up the rear of the odd parade. Claudia was snug in her bed the last time he saw her, so her presence was baffling. He had enlisted Millie to watch over her to make certain she was safe. How on Earth did she wind up with Helena and Miss Reagan?

"What is the meaning of this? Claudia, you were to stay in bed."

"Forgive me Lord Husband, but you never forbid my rising." What his wife said was true, but it did nothing to calm Nathaniel nor did it answer his question.

"Be quiet Claudia. Miss Reagan, I hope you have an excellent explanation for why my wife and Helena are being paraded naked through the manor."

"The two were found together in the upstairs chamber."

"Don't mince words woman. Bryce is a member of the Order. You know that. Otherwise, these women would be clothed."

"This one," Miss Reagan pulled Claudia forward roughly, "was in the cage with this one." Miss Reagan grabbed Helena and thrust her forward as well. They were both inside it, embracing under a dressing gown."

Nathaniel wasn't pleased with how roughly Miss Reagan handled Claudia, but he was more incensed about the disobedience and mischief going on, especially since Bryce was here to observe it all. His friend had risen and was standing in the doorway of the study watching the upheaval of his authority unfold.

"It appears things at home can be as interesting as the theatre," Bryce said the remark with dry humor, but Nathaniel knew the fact that both of the women in the hall acting anything, but submissive, shed an ill light on his control. Bryce already had doubts, and the defiance taking place right in front of him would add fuel to the fire.

Chapter Twenty-Six

Bryce had a smirk on his face as Nathaniel stared at the calamity that was his head housekeeper, his wife, Helena, and two of his footmen. He was at a loss for words for a moment, his anger almost choking him. To make matters worse, Bryce was devouring both Claudia and Helena with his eyes. Nathaniel had little care if his friend did indeed devour Helena. The woman had been a thorn in his side for nearly two months, and he would be glad to be rid of her. When it came to Claudia though, Nathaniel had the urge to cover her with his frock coat.

All eyes were upon him, waiting for the next cue from Nathaniel as if they were trapped on a stage in the theater, lost without the director's prompts. He met each set of eyes, always needing to be the one in command, and shot them a piercing gaze until they looked away. His footmen averted their eyes at once, showing deference, but the three women, and most particularly Claudia and Helena, in fact, had their chins in the air. They were striking haughty poses in defiance of whatever was to come next. Nathaniel was torn between strangling his wife and the queer desire to cover her again. Her nudity shouldn't matter; the entire crowd had set eyes on her charms when he'd whipped her in the square, but he couldn't shake the urge. He could however use his iron will to overpower it.

Helena finally withered under Nathaniel's icy stare, but Claudia still refused to look away, and to make matters worse, she had the gall to speak even though his eyes were as hard as flint.

"Husband, Helena didn't have a hand in any of this. It was I who opened the cage and crawled inside. I..."

"Silence, I will hear your pleas for mercy after you both have had a taste of the birch. A bit of fire upon your backside will make sure the words ring true. Niles and Simmons, you may go. Miss Reagan, remove that chastity belt and then leave us. I will speak to you later. Helena and Claudia, march into my study at once.

"This is a perfect example of being in over my head, Nathaniel. I don't know if I'm ready to deal with a household let alone the misbehavior of a wife as she learns the fine art of complete submission."

"In that case, you shall watch and learn. All you need is a firm hand. This type of defiance may rear its ugly head at the beginning of your marriage, but before long peace will resume. I've no doubt all involved will be eager to show me they have seen the error of their ways by the time I finish with them."

"By all means, show me, for I am at a loss with misbehavior of this extent." Bryce turned to follow the women into the study, most appreciative of the back view he was afforded as he did so. Both women were lovely but in very different ways. Helena was voluptuous and fair, her curves ample, her hips filled out in a way that would afford the man fucking her luscious handles to hold. Claudia, on the other hand, was thin and dark. Her legs were sleek and long, her hair cascading like a silken wave of sable silk down her back. One could never describe her curves as ample, but there was no doubt she was a woman. Both sported the evidence of recent chastisement, which only made Bryce more aware of his desire for them. Perhaps his doubts about how they lived really were unfounded.

Nathaniel turned and closed the study door. The entire household needn't be privy to all that took place under his roof. Having Bryce watch was enough of an audience. He didn't mind teaching the man. They all had to learn by example; it was that stubborn wish to cover Claudia and keep her from Bryce's gaze that gnawed at Nathaniel.

"Helena show Claudia where one stands while one is waiting for punishment." Helena gave a toss of her head. The action told all she hadn't a worry nor regret despite the upcoming punishment. Claudia did the same, though she did indeed have a knot of fear caused by the unknown twisting in her belly. Helena went to stand along the wall that held numerous rows of books on tall shelves, and then raised her hands and laced the fingers behind her neck while taking a stance that spread her legs. Claudia again followed suit though to stand in such a way before a stranger caused her unease even though she'd been nude before so many people she'd lost count.

Bryce smiled as he appraised the women, noting the exposure of their clits and their how their nether lips were pulled open and held that way by golden rings. Again he noted the stark contrast between the two, and again he thought either would be a pleasure to bed. Though he struggled with the deliberation of taking command in the way Nathaniel did, he certainly had a love for the female form. He also had a voracious sex drive that kept his mistress in London on her back with her legs spread wide.

"I'll start with you Helena. Though my wife comes to your defense, the entire lunacy of the afternoon's events began with your defiance. You were brought here to prepare you for your new husband, not to disrupt my household. Position yourself on the birching board."

Helena walked to the board that had a forward slant and rose up to waist height before it met another slanted board which joined it at the top and went down to the floor. She leaned into the contraption and bent over where the two boards met, and then reached down to grasp two pegs near the bottom. The action made her already red bottom thrust up in the air, displaying her sex and readying her for a sound punishment.

Her exposed clit rubbed upon the board as she stood against it, already stimulating her. Though there was pain in the punishments meted out by Nathaniel and the others, Helena couldn't deny the pleasure she found as well, especially when positioned on the birching board. Though her bottom would soon feel as if a swarm of bees was furiously stinging her flesh, the nub that gave her pleasure would stroke the board each time she moved. It was a twisted merging of intense pain and dark pleasure, dreamt up by someone with a sick sense of humor.

"Now then." Claudia and Bryce turned from the delectable sight of Helena bent over the birching board and looked once again at Nathaniel. "Helena will receive five lashes with the birch bundle for the trouble she has caused. I'll not have you women being willful towards me or any of the staff."

"We women?" Claudia had broken the pose, her eyes glittering with rage. "I am your wife and yet you wish me to bow before the staff? While I have learned I am not better than they are, I most certainly should not be expected to..."

"Claudia!" Nathaniel was livid. How dare this slip of a girl come into his well run home and toss all he had achieved into upheaval like a ship at sea in a raging storm? When the two women had bonded, he had assumed Claudia was following Helena in her show of rebellion, but now he was made to wonder if his young wife was not as guilty.

"You will be silent." That was it, nothing else. A simple command no one could mistake for permission to speak. Claudia pressed her lips together and resumed the stance Helena had shown her. She knew that if she indeed continued to make her husband furious, it would be Helena's bottom that would suffer, at least for the moment.

Nathaniel walked to a crock near the birching board and selected a bundle of twigs bound by a cloth that had been wrapped around one end and tied securely. He gave is a few test swishes through the air that to his delight made his wife's eyes grow wide, and then took up his place behind and beside Helena.

"You will not move."

"No Sir."

"You will hold fast to the pegs."

"Yes, Sir."

"You will not find your pleasure during your punishment."

"No Sir."

Both Bryce and Claudia looked stunned by his last command, but Nathaniel scarcely paid them any mind. He was well aware of Helena's love/hate relationship with pain and how she responded to having her greedy nub rubbed even as agony spread across her bottom. Without further ado, Nathaniel raised the birch bundle and swished it across Helena's bottom, causing the woman to cry out.

Red welts appeared almost instantly, and her bottom moved as she did her best to shake off the pain. Her clit rubbed the board beneath her as she moved.

"You shall receive five more if you orgasm." That was all he said. His arm rose again, and again the birch bundle left dark red stripes all over Helena's bottom, two of which oozed tiny drops of red. Again and then again, in quick succession, Nathaniel's arm rose and fell, birch in hand. Helena's bottom that had been purple from bruising when she arrived at Lord Tarrington's home became crisscrossed with so many red lines that they all seemed to connect in an intricate web of pain.

Helena moved her hips, deliberately mixing pleasure with the agony rolling like waves through her body, and grit her teeth as she waited for the final blow. It came hard and fast, catching her low, so some of the branches swept across her upper thighs and jangled the rings on her pussy lips. She yelped as the fire blazed across the before untouched areas, feeling tiny droplets begin to trickle down from her tortured skin as the welts oozed pinpoint of blood.

Helena rubbed her sex upon the board, knowing she had to mix the pleasure with the pain before she was ordered to stand. Nathaniel saw her and hissed in fury. While it was true, they wished for the women to find pleasure in the darkness of the pain they were subjected to; a harsh punishment had no room for desire to mask the horrid agony.

"Stand up at once. You'll not pleasure yourself in my presence. Return to your spot on the wall, and there is to be no wiggling. Claudia, assume the position on the board. Bent over, hands on the pegs, just like Helena. You dear wife will receive five as well. Though I am tempted to give you one extra for your antics."

Claudia opened her mouth to speak out against the unjust punishment, but Nathaniel held up his hand to silence her. Claudia sensed imminent defeat, so went to the board and assumed the stance Helena had just displayed. She too felt the hard board press against her clitoris but had no desire to intensify the feeling. Her stomach was too knotted to think of sexual pleasure.

Nathaniel began with a lighter stroke. His wife had never received a birching, and so he wished to spare her just a bit of the pain. She cried out with the first stroke none the less. The second had her yelping and bouncing on the balls of her feet; the third caused a cry that cut off as all the air left her, leaving Claudia with nary a squeak to protest. Her legs shook, and her hands clutched at the pegs, feeling like they were the only anchors in a sea of agony.

The fourth elicited a sob that went straight to Nathaniel's heart despite his anger, and the fifth left Claudia trembling and sobbing in a heap. The fight beat out of her. Bryce was silent as her sobs filled the room, and he looked from Nathaniel to Claudia and back again. When Claudia's misery caused a look of pain to come over Nathaniel's face, Bryce looked away and focused his eyes on Helena, doing his best to give his friend and Claudia privacy.

Nathaniel helped Claudia stand and led her to Helena, allowing the other woman to comfort his wife at a time when he knew he couldn't. As much as her pain caused sorrow and dismay, if he backed down now and coddled her, his authority would be put in jeopardy. Nathaniel felt as if he had to stand firm.

Claudia would have sagged to the floor if not for Helena's support. She held Claudia tight and whispered words of tenderness and encouragement into her ear, trying to give the girl some of her strength. Helena didn't mind the pain, but it was clear Claudia had been destroyed by it. Her rebellious spirit snuffed out like a candle flame.

"Hush now, you're alright. It will pass. Hush now." Helena rubbed Claudia's back and shot an accusing look at Nathaniel, who turned away, not needing Helena's disapproval to make him feel remorse. That was something that filled him already. Still, his stubborn pride and his ridged upbringing had him believing swift punishment with no sympathy was the best course to take to re-establish his authority and bring harmony into his home.

Nathaniel looked at Bryce, doing his best to look nonchalant. "See there. I doubt these two will cause me any more trouble."

Bryce looked uncertain. While he'd witnessed the birching of many a woman while he grew up, the extinguishing of Claudia's fire made him uneasy. He would hold his tongue for now in front of the women. Even so, Bryce planned on bringing up the idea that some women simply weren't submissive, and to make them so would be to harm them deep in their souls.

"Helena, walk with Claudia and help her up the stairs. We're returning to the attic." The moan of despair that escaped Claudia at the news cut deeply into Nathaniel's heart. He pressed his lips together so hard they became a thin line as he fought off the unfamiliar feelings of tenderness he felt for his wife.

"Come sweet. I'll be with you." Helena kissed Claudia's eyes and wiped her tears from her cheeks before taking the girl's chin in her hand. "Look at me." When Claudia complied, Helena rested her forehead on Claudia's. "You can do this. Don't let him see your pain." Only Claudia heard the whispered words, and they had the wanted effect. While she couldn't stand tall with the pride that she's come in with, she ceased her tears and clasped Helena's hand. They turned towards the door, not looking at Nathaniel, who had become worse than Satan himself in his wife's eyes as she wondered how he could hurt her so and with such a nonchalant attitude. Maybe Miss Reagan was right. Perhaps he did regard her only as a whore and a plaything. Men who treasured their wives didn't hurt them so badly.

Taking strength from her only friend in the world, Claudia walked beside Helena, wondering what was next on her husband's list of terrors? Still stunned by the acts he planned on inflicting, all because she'd wanted to comfort a friend.

The women led the way once they reached the staircase, Nathaniel walking behind them in silence. Neither woman was hurt badly enough to hinder their pace; it was Claudia's mind that slowed her steps at times, not her physical condition. Her head and heart had shattered into jagged pieces that cut ever so deep. Even so, she fully believed Nathaniel would lay the lash upon them like a slave driver if their steps faltered. The idea made her climb briskly even though she was full of dread as she wondered just what would happen to them in the attic room.

"You needn't fear our fate. His lordship has put me through my paces on everything in the attic, and I have survived."

"You are stronger than me. I can't find pleasure in anything he does when it is meant to hurt me so gravely or crush my heart. None of it feels the least bit good."

"That is mostly because you haven't yet learned to combine the things that hurt your flesh with those that give it pleasure. Unlike you, I don't have a heart that grieves when Lord Tarrington does as he pleases.

"My heart does no such thing. It's my pride that will never accept all of this."

"Pride can be a dangerous thing, especially for a woman who has no choice in who she marries, and you said only a moment ago that it crushes your heart when he does these things. Perhaps if you would relent and embrace..."

Claudia stopped and whirled to face Helena, which also put Nathaniel in her line of vision. "I will never embrace my life here with him." Claudia gave a nod in Nathaniel's direction. "As long as he keeps treating me like a whore and a toy. I find pleasure in the passionate things he does to my body, but the other things... Never! I am no weak pathetic girl who opens her arms and kisses her husband feet simply because he is a man and my father chose him to lord over me."

Claudia spun back around before Nathaniel could reply. If he they had been alone, he would have told her that he didn't wish to crush her heart nor did he want a woman who was a timid field mouse._Unfortunately, the stairs were no place for that discussion.

"She is as spirited as an unbroken filly. I will not deny you've much more experience with this sort of thing, but, if she were mine..."

"She isn't." Nathaniel's words were clipped with anger though it was aimed at Claudia and not at Bryce, but one shouldn't put oneself before a firing squad as they were primed to shoot.

Bryce shut his mouth quickly at Nathaniel's decree. Still, he couldn't help but feel his old friend was handling his new bride with a hand that was far too heavy. The girl was a delightful mix of beauty and fire. He would be loath to snuff out her wildness in fear of losing the best part of her for the sake of making her obey.

Everyone had become quiet for the rest of their ascent to the attic, and Nathaniel felt as if all were judging him in their silence. He knew both women had to learn a lesson. Both had been far too disobedient since coming to Brighton. He had to make an impression on Claudia so the girl would understand that to please him was to find a reward, and to anger him was to find correction. Claudia was a passionate woman, but he wanted her passion given to him without her harpy's tongue.

Helena, on the other hand, had to be made to yield so she was what any man in the Blackguard's Order would desire. Granted her new husband would mold her for his particular tastes, but she was far too disobedient. The school was to have done that, but that of course, hadn't happened, and private time with him hadn't taken her sass and penchant for misbehavior away either. Both women were frustrating, and it would be the perfect opportunity to show Bryce how things were best handled while showing both women what noncompliance brings.

As they arrived above, one of the maids was just finishing with the lighting of the lamps along the long walls of the attic. While Nathaniel enjoyed the fact that his staff saw to his every need, her disliked knowing they were privy to all that went on. It soured his mood even further.

The women paused at the entrance of the room, but Nathaniel put a hand in the small of their backs, and pushed them forward. "There is no use in hesitation now. It is far too late for that. To the poles with you both."

Helena groaned but led the way to where long poles, close to the size of Claudia's hand and carved into a blunted triangle were placed upon supports that resembled ladders with closely spaced rungs. Claudia looked at the things when they stopped, remembering that Nathaniel hadn't had her mount it as she crawled around the attic that afternoon.

"The two of you are too different in height to straddle the same pole. That doesn't mean I can't arrange them, so you can see the misery on the face of your friend and co-conspirator. Helena, you first, come."

Helena went to stand over one of the poles and raised her hands over her head. Nathaniel expertly fastened a loop around her wrists and then pulled the rope tight using a pulley above the woman's head. He then moved each end of the triangular pole up the rungs of the ladder supports until one edge of the pole nudged tightly in the folds of her pussy.

"Ohhh... Milord, please not so deep."

"Nonsense, you wished to rub that clit upon the birching board to get your whore's fill of pleasure, surely you want to rub it again. You can also find relief by standing on your toes. Bad girls get bad things. I have no pity for your pain."

Helena stood on her toes so the edge of the pole wasn't quite so tortuous on her clit and sex, but knew she wouldn't be able to hold the pose for long before her calves cramped. It was one torture device she was hard pressed to mix pleasure with the pain.

Nathaniel moved another of the poles into place on the support rungs. "Come here Claudia. Face Helena and straddle this pole. She is the reason you are being punished. Leaving your bed, coming up here, and unlocking her cage were all things done without permission. You will learn that my word is law wife, like it or not."

The words that passed between the women on their way to the attic and those Claudia had thrown at him with vehemence still rang in his ears. He would never let her have the upper hand. Nathaniel roped Claudia's wrists as efficiently as he had Helena's, and then raised the pole, so a sharp edge nudged his wife's clit and pussy, nodding in satisfaction when she hissed. The pole had a rounded edge, but it was still very uncomfortable when one's entire body weight was resting upon the edge supported by only one's clit and sex.

"Standing on your toes will provide relief. Be glad I have allowed you the option. I will return in an hour. Bryce, we can discuss my methods over dinner."

"Gladly. I have a few questions, and I have an interest in owning the fair-haired one."

Though he was surprised, Nathaniel led the way back to the staircase. He wished to give the women time to talk alone, for though Helena was rebellious, he had not missed the fact that she believed Claudia cared for him. He imagined Helena knew that he cared for Claudia as well. Helena rarely missed anything, and he wanted for Claudia to hear of his tenderness because it was in fact something that existed. Granted his actions were harsh, but the age-old tradition dictated his deeds. The wives of the Order were obedient, period, and the way to accomplish that was with an iron will and a heavy hand.

Chapter Twenty-Seven

Nathaniel was lost in thought as he and Bryce went down the stairs, and Bryce chose to keep his questions in check until they reached the dining room. What had just occurred was troubling, but he imagined Nathaniel would do his best to dismiss any concerns, holding fast to the heritage of their families.

The servants scrambled into action when the men arrived. It wasn't uncommon for dinner to be set off schedule by other more pressing needs in the Earl's household. The cooks were accustom to finding ways to keep the meal hot while not allowing it to become unpalatable. The butler emerged with a bottle of wine as the men took their seats, deftly pouring as Nathaniel and Bryce got settled.

"Now then, you have questions for me, Bryce?" The fact that the butler was in the room as well as a serving girl who came from the kitchen mattered not. Nathaniel knew his servants had the utmost respect for his privacy in regards to what occurred in his house. They might gossip among themselves, but his family's business never went beyond the walls of the manor.

"You know the blond woman well?"

"If you are asking me if I've taken her, yes, I have. Several times."

"Is that common with women from the school?"

"If you're wondering if I use the school as my personal pleasure den of inequity, no. Helena is in the habit of breaking all the rules. She is difficult for them to handle, despite the harsh punishments she received there. When Miss Patton has had enough, Helena comes here for a few days."

"What offense did she commit at the school this time?"

"This time she is here because she will be leaving the school for good. She is as ready as she will ever be, and is here to either be wed to Mr. Bruaer or else to be given to Lady Ellingsworth."

"A woman?"

Nathaniel made a face of disgust. Lady Ellingsworth may be part of their Order by right of her birth, but Nathaniel knew he would never feel the woman had a place among the men.

"She is the daughter of Viscount Ellingsworth. The only child as it happens. He felt it was permissible for his daughter to take the place of domination in our Order because he lacked a son. We disagreed of course, but the viscount's ancestors were founders of the Blackguards. He was adamant that his family shouldn't be by-passed over because of his lack of a male heir."

"Surely this problem has come up before."

"Yes, of course. In the past when this situation has arisen, the family keeps the truth from their daughter and the father approves of a husband from within as is the norm. It's that, or he speaks to his daughter's husband after they marry. The Viscount opposed our tradition, saying that his daughter was quite capable of running a household. As you know, once in a while a male child is born who lacks the skills to be an effective dominant, or worse, they have an unhealthy attraction to other men."

"Forgive me, but what does this have to do with Helena? I dare say she would not make a good husband."

"No, of course not. Lady Ellingsworth dislikes Helena both because the girl is bold, and because I have taken up her training on occasion. Lady Ellingsworth and I do not see eye to eye. I believe she is of the mind that if she acquires Helena, her rough treatment of the girl will cause my distress."

Bryce thought about the punishment he'd witnessed that evening. It had been harsh. "If questioned, I'd say what took place tonight was harsh. Am I correct that Helena was placed in the cage for running away from Miss Reagan and disrupting your time with Lady Claudia?"

"Yes. What are you getting at? I fear you've been away from home and the teachings of your father for too long."

"Nathaniel. I'm not passing judgment. You've much more experience than I. My question is a true one. I want to understand your methods and your reasoning. You put Helena in the cage as a punishment, she remained in the cage as commanded, and yet she received the same birching and placement on the pole as your wife. The girl didn't run or even move from where you demanded she stay?"

"I see your point. My wife and Helena have bonded. Helena was here when Claudia first arrived, and I gave her the task of helping Claudia adjust."

"But you knew she was disruptive and insolent. Nathaniel, it seems that their bond was of your making and now you are angry with them for the very thing you created."

"There is more to it. Claudia struck Lady Ellingsworth's hired man who is technically a superior to my wife. A penalty was demanded, and I allowed Helena to help ease my wife's fears and to make the actual punishment more bearable."

"And now they are friends."

"And now they are accomplices who find ways to rebel at every chance they get."

"You reprimanded Helena to aid in your chastisement of your wife."

Bryce wasn't asking; he was making a statement, one which Nathaniel didn't deny. "It doesn't matter. Helena will leave here in a day or two, and Claudia will conform. She has no choice."

"I must be honest and tell you I fear for her spirit. It's clear she is feisty and full of pride that makes her rebel, but that pride adds fire. Do you truthfully wish to put it out? You may turn her from a feisty wife into a silent mouse."

"Claudia behaves like a wild thing and speaks to me like a shrew. I won't allow that."

"I'm sure you know what's best, Nathaniel. Just remember she is your wife, a Lady, not some random girl of lower birth."

"Even the wife of the Earl of Brighton must know her place is beneath me. I am her husband, and as such she must obey and do as I command."

Bryce knew he would never turn Nathaniel from his course. Perhaps one day when Claudia was but a shell of the woman who had so much fire, he would realize what he'd done. It might very well be too late then.

"I'd like to declare my desire to marry Helena formally."

"Bryce, I don't think you could handle her. You've become soft from too much time spent in London."

"While I agree that I've grown used to girls who speak and act like any high-bred lady, it's the girls who show a bit of rebellion that catch my eye."

"Helena is more than a little rebellious."

"She is full of fire and passion."

"Fire that will burn the one who doesn't know how to tame her."

"Forgive me Nathaniel, but have your methods worked so far? How long has she been here in Brighton?"

Nathaniel sighed. Bryce did have a point. He couldn't deny it, but he feared his friend would be too permissive. Their Order had a strict code of conduct and expectations. "While you are right that we haven't tamed her, the fact that you questioned my actions worries me."

"I'm not saying the girl doesn't need a firm hand. I'm saying she is both passionate and wild, and perhaps if given an outlet for that fire, she would stop fighting her submission."

"If one beds her more often she'll behave?"

"Not exactly but yes, bedding her very frequently would be part of it."

"Tell me more of this plan."

"I don't have a precise strategy, but Helena needs an outlet for all that wicked naughtiness. Perhaps I would take her to run wild and swim nude in the forest. Maybe allow her a chance to visit London and go to the opera or dance to her heart's content. I'll spank her soundly in the carriage before the party and bed her with a fervor that matches her fire when I get her home. It would be a shame to turn that wild beauty into a timid mouse, or worse a cold lump upon the sheets instead of a squirming vixen in bed."

"I will put your bid for her hand before the Order. Her father is deceased, and her brother is out of the country. He placed her with Miss Patton before he left, and directed us to do as was best, knowing full well his sister was an unmanageable heathen,"

"Well, I'd like to marry that heathen."

"The matter will be discussed. The Order is well aware of her behavior. We seek someone with a firm hand. That is the only reason we have considered Lady Ellingsworth. Helena might be too much for Mr. Brauer."

"A discussion is all I'm asking for."

The serving girl put a plate of roasted boar before him, and Bryce picked up his fork and his knife. They had talked through the soup course, and he was starving as well as highly aroused. Talk of Helena and the thought of her being his wife had sparked an ember of hot desire in him. He couldn't wait to see the woman again, and while he thought Nathaniel might be persuaded to allow him to bed her after her time on the pole, Bryce kept mum. He had put in his bid, and that was enough. The lovely Helena would have to wait.

While the men enjoyed their supper, Claudia and Helena spent their time alternating between standing on their toes as long as they could and resting their tender sexes on the triangle pole. Claudia was abnormally quiet and before long, silent tears trickled down her cheeks, the sight of them going straight to Helena's heart.

"Claudia, move off your toes before they cramp and off the poll before it becomes unbearable, and don't hold your breath."

Claudia looked at her friend with eyes that were made bright by her tears. There were so many thoughts running through her head, and they were the real reason she wept, not the pain, though it was substantial. What hurt worse than what was happening to her, was the fact that the man she was wed to could so easily treat her with disdain and punish her so harshly.

"My tears are from my broken heart. How can I spend the rest of my life with that monster? I hate him."

"I don't..."

"And don't tell me he cares for me. I won't believe it. My father would thrash me, and the punishments were well deserved. I admit to being an incorrigible girl. I didn't care a lick for anyone but myself, and I treated the servants horribly. That shallow and foolish girl is gone. Am I to pay for the reckless and cruel actions of my youth for the rest of my life?"

"Lord Tarrington was raised to believe that all women are to be submissive to men. We all know men feel that way. They think we are ninnies without brains. We shouldn't be allowed to make decisions or speak our minds. The men of the Order are even more narrow minded. They have added perverse sexual service to their husbandly rights."

"I didn't mind being bedded. To be honest, I found pleasure in it, but I'm not a whore to be tossed aside nor am I a dog. He acts as if it's right to have one's wife scurry around on her hands and knees, and he put you in a cage! We would be better off being one of his hounds. They aren't starved or beaten."

"If you try and please him, things will be better. And before you protest, understand that I agree. This treatment isn't right. I can't believe all of the wives come to love being treated like this. I think many are like you, and finally just accept things in order to be treated with a shred of dignity. Good girls, get good things."

Claudia winced at her last words. It seems they were all told that, or at least it was a phrase her husband embraced. "So I should swallow my pride, hide my intelligence, and instead remain mute to my objections and follow his lead without question?" Claudia's tears resumed at the thought of suffering through the humiliation for the rest of her days.

"Yes, for now. Not forever. Claudia, he does care for you; I can tell. He doesn't become angry when he has to punish me. He finds pleasure in it. With you, it's different. He is frustrated and out of sorts. You are his wife, the one who will be with him all of his life, and yet you fight what he feels you should embrace."

"But I can't embrace how he treats me. It's wrong. Look at us hanging here torn between the agony of staying on our toes or the pain of resting our most sensitive places upon a hard edge. One day he takes me in a bed covered with rose petals, making me feel cherished. The next he makes me heel at his side and mount each piece of furniture in this room as I listen to his tales of debauchery."

"I believe he is trying to show you how your life will be, so you resign yourself to it."

"That will never happen. I am a lady, and even if I were a scullery maid, I wouldn't feel as if it were just."

"As you grew up, were you ever given reason to believe you would choose your husband?"

"I thought; I mean. I was spoilt and incorrigible. When I came out during my first season in London, I spurned those my mother wished me to meet, and flirted with those whom I found exciting and dashing. I thought if there was a man I fancied; I would charm him into asking my father for my hand."

"And yet you are here. How did you become wed to the Earl? Was he in London last season? From what I understand, the men of the Order don't choose their wives that way."

Claudia slowly shook her head. It had all gone so wrong so very quickly. Hers was no whirlwind romance; it was more a tale of tragedy.

"My husband didn't find me in London. He wasn't there, though I dare say I might have toyed with him. My father came home from overseas. That crushed my dreams of a second season in London. One night at supper I was told I was to being wed, and the next morning we were on a train for Brighton."

"Claudia, I know how unhappy you are, but when it all seems too horrid to take, think of those of us who will go to men who are old and ugly. We will have to accept that, as well as their ruling their homes under the ways of the Order. At least being touched by the Earl isn't revolting."

"I suppose I must agree that is my only saving grace, though the longer I know him, the more I hate him."

"Come closer, sweet. At least we have each other."

"But you are to go to..."

"Hush, I don't want to worry over that now."

Helena leaned forward as far as the binding would allow, taking all of her body weight onto her tender sex just to be closer to Claudia, who had begun to weep in earnest. Claudia did the same when she saw what Helena was doing, and wiggled about until she could touch foreheads with her friend. The two stayed that way, enduring the pain of their bodies in an effort to banish the pain from their hearts. Fate had been cruel to them, landing each in a world where their obedience and submission determined their worth. It might all be easy to swallow for a woman who never thought on her own nor wished to run free. For Helena and Claudia, submission to someone who didn't tell them they were cherished, was too hard to take.

Chapter Twenty-Eight

The women continued touching foreheads, silent in their misery as the men finished their supper. When footsteps sounded once again on the stairs leading to the attic room, they remained motionless. There was no one in the manor who could appear that they'd wish to see. It was true that they were in extreme discomfort, but the bond between them and the touching of each other, was a scrap of solace.

Nathaniel stopped at the top of the stairs and looked at his wife and Helena in surprise. Each had shimmied forward as far as possible, straining their arms behind them and taking most of their body weight onto their most tender area. Their behavior befuddled him and at the fact that neither moved in an effort to look up caused even more confusion. In the past the women whom he'd punished in this way were more than grateful to be released from the torturous pole, kissing his feet in reverence when taken down.

"Bring them down, and do it gently." Though he was angry at their display of affection for each other, he was also concerned that they had harmed their sexes. Their tender clits could incur damage by the constant weight of their bodies. He had no desire for Claudia to ruin the bundle of nerves that made her so passionate in bed.

As the footmen began to untie their bindings, Claudia stretched forward as far as her strained arms would allow and bestowed a sweet kiss on Helena's lips. It only lasted a second, for she was lifted up off the pole in the next moment. Claudia cried out in pain as her arms were lowered, then once again, louder as the blood was able to rush back into her clit.

"Give her to me." Nathaniel cradled Claudia gently and placed a kiss upon her forehead, but his wife refused to open her eyes and look at him. She felt broken inside. There was no fire with which to fight him, nor any to make her care what was to come of her now. Her body hurt everywhere, the most horrific of the pain being where Nathaniel had birched her, as well as the tender place between her legs that had suffered such torment.

"That one is to be placed back in the cage." Her husband's words struck a spark Claudia thought had gone out. Her eyes flew open, and the look she gave Nathaniel was one of pure hatred.

"She has suffered enough. I was the one who opened the cage. It was me! If you've any feeling in the lump of ice that must be your heart, have pity on Helena."

Nathaniel had an inkling that if he went through with his order and did indeed have Helena placed back in the cage, his wife would never forgive him. This day would stand as a fortress between them. Claudia would come to care for him, and what's worse, would fight him day in and day out through all the years of their marriage. It was time to call a truce somehow, and find a way through the wall of resistance around her heart.

"Take Helena to her room, and send for one of the maids. See she gets a hot bath and is put to bed. See that you stay by her door. If she gets the chance to run free in this house, she will not be the only one punished."

"Thank you." The words that came from Claudia were curt and cold, but he was able to hold her gaze for a moment before she closed her eyes and shut him out once more.

"Send for Millie. My wife is to have a bath and a supper tray."

"Yes, Milord. The footmen not holding Helena left at once, and Nathaniel followed, calling over his shoulder to Bryce.

"Make use of my home as if it were yours. You are welcome to stay until it's time to make a decision about Helena. Just tell one of the maids that a room should be made ready and that I wish you to have whatever you need." Bryce called out a quick thank you, but his words found Nathaniel's back, not his ears. The man in question was quickly descending the stairs.

Nathaniel took Claudia to his rooms. Once inside he lay her on the bed, then traced a gentle finger along her jawline. Her mouth was set in a line of fury; her teeth clenched, and Nathaniel wasn't certain how to calm her. Several thoughts swirled through his head before he settled on a phrase he hoped would better the situation.

"Helena will be treated well."

"Only because I insisted on it. You were going to have her put back in the cage!" Claudia flung the accusations at him, not appeased by the knowledge that Helena was being tended.

"I will not argue the point. I don't want to upset you further."

"There is only so deep one's soul can sink. You have already managed to cut me to the quick. I doubt my heart can become even more brittle."

"Claudia, I have no wish to make you hate me or see me as a monster."

Claudia made a sound of disbelief and stared at him with icy eyes, saying nothing.

"I am a compassionate and just man. You are my wife. My chosen mate, and yet you defy me at every turn. In this house, under my authority, you must obey. Wives are to do as their husbands bid and yet you protest time and again. My family are members of the Order, Claudia. We have pledged to each other to maintain our way of life. We swear an oath each time we meet, and I must stand by my words."

"You swore to love and comfort me as well."

"And you to obey and serve. I don't think you will find a winning argument in our wedding vows."

Claudia turned away from Nathaniel, not having the strength to do battle. What did it matter? Surely if her husband had any intention of treating her with respect he would have done so. The only tenderness or comfort she had received at his hand had been on their wedding night, yet even that had come at the price of her dignity.

Millie came and proceeded to the bathing chamber to run a bath for her mistress. She was keen to notice the tension between them, the silence in the room as quiet as a tomb. His Lordship appeared flustered, his cheeks red, his mouth a grim line as the girl peeked at him from the bathroom.

Miss Reagan arrived with a swish of skirts, her face also twisted with anger. It seemed no one was to be happy in the Earl's household any longer. Millie shrank back into the shadows of the small room at the appearance of Miss Reagan. None of the servants cared for the head of the staff who was quick to punish and tell the master when someone made a mistake.

"Excuse me Milord, but there seems to be some confusion in regards to Helena."

Claudia's eyes shift to her husband, and she held her breath, waiting for his reply. Would he stay true to his word and allow Helena gentle treatment?

"Miss Reagan, Helena isn't your concern."

"I have always seen to her care."

"You have always tormented her!" The vehemence behind Claudia's words was as powerful as a slap upon the face of Miss Reagan. She visibly flinched in shock but then took a step towards the bed where the new lady of the house lay naked, her eyes red from the tears she'd shed while seeking solace from Helena.

"Leave us. See to my home and my servants, but from here on, stay away from Helena and my wife."

"Yes Sir." Miss Reagan shot Claudia a look that promised retribution before she spun on her heel and left. Claudia wasn't intimidated at all by the housekeeper's expression. She planned on her own vengeance against the woman who had a hand in causing Helena so much suffering.

"If you've no imminent plans of punishment for me, I'd like to be alone." The words were polite, but Nathaniel heard the barely controlled anger all the same.

"I'll leave you to your bath, but will return." Nathaniel bent to kiss her, but Claudia turned her cheek, her husband's small tokens of affection not welcome. "Millie, you're to put the healing ointment on my wife's wounds."

"Yes Milord."

"Is her bath ready?"

"Almost Milord."

Before Claudia could move away, Nathaniel picked her up once again and carried her to the bath. He set her in the tub gently, paying no mind to the water soaking his shirt. Claudia winced as the water touched the small cuts on her bottom and her tormented sex, the water feeling as if it was burning hot for a moment. Nathaniel paused but then put her all the way in when her expression turned from one of pain to one of relief. He then twisted her long hair up and out of the water, still paying no mind to his clothes.

"Fetch me the hairbrush." Millie went to retrieve it at once hurrying back and handing the Earl the brush. Nathaniel took it and then began to brush the tangles from Claudia's hair, but saw that she was holding herself stiff in her anger. He sighed, giving up, not sure how to appease her, and handed the brush back to Millie."

"Tend your Mistress." Nathaniel rose without another word. He was not used to women who were so contrary, and he certainly wasn't accustom to allowing such impudent ways. Claudia was his wife, and he had agreed to comfort and protect her. The problem was; she thwarted him at every turn by being so willful. How was he to treat her gently when she defied him? He gave his tender caresses as rewards that came from obedience. She was to earn the things she desired, not just have them handed to her.

As he walked from the room to check on Helena, Nathaniel wondered for the first time if other men dealt with such outrageous behavior while trying to tame their wives. Surely not all of them did, or methods to overcome such resistance would have been developed. Still, if things went on like this any longer, he'd have to ask, even at the risk of appearing incompetent.

"Excuse me Lord Tarrington." Nathaniel ignored the woman. Of all the things plaguing him at that moment, Miss Reagan's troubles were not one of the things he cared about, but she was not to be put off.

Miss Reagan sped up to catch Nathaniel when her employer didn't slow down. "Lord Tarrington."

"Miss Reagan I've no interest in speaking with you. There's tension in my home, and your actions seem to be part of the woe. If Helena hadn't burst into the training room earlier, I wouldn't be in such a foul mood. As it is, you are one of the few people I would take great pleasure in horse whipping. Now leave me be. There are other matters to see to that don't involve being in my company, namely making certain Lord Hastings is being tended to in a fashion I would approve of."

"Yes Milord, forgive me."

"That may take some time." He had paused during his tirade, but he picked up the pace once more intent on paying a visit to Helena. Nathaniel wasn't in the habit of consulting women, but though the blonde had suffered the same fate as Claudia and worse, she didn't seem to hate him at all. Perhaps Helena could tell him why Claudia was so very angry or better yet, how he could appease her that did not compromise all of the things he believed.

He found Helena soaking chin deep in a tub of hot water, the smell of lavender filling the air. Her eyes were closed, and a small smile turned her lush lips up at the corners, making her look like she was having the sweetest of dreams. Helena's eyes remained close though Nathaniel knew she'd heard his footsteps. He tilted his head towards the door to indicate the servant woman should leave them alone, and then pulled a chair from the writing desk into the bathroom, settling down in it while enjoying the view. His pleasure in gazing at Helena's curves didn't last long though, he was too distraught at his inability to tame his wife.

"You seem no worse for wear."

"Ummmmmmmm the bath is delightful. Much better than I expected."

"You've Claudia to thank for it."

"Oh, you can be assured I am well aware of what her presence has done to improve my lot."

"Only for today."

The small smile turned to a frown as Helena recalled what Claudia had told her about Lady Ellingsworth. "Would you indeed give me to that shrew?"

"Perhaps." In truth, Lady Ellingsworth was the last person he wished to see Helena go to. It wasn't because he held an abundance of fondness for the blonde; it was because he despised the Lady in question.

"What of your friend Bryce?"

"You are overly familiar."

"Perhaps." The smile appeared once more, replacing the look of distaste. Helena never kept a bad mood for long.

"I would horsewhip you, but you'd find a way to enjoy it."

"I didn't enjoy my time on the pole."

"You weren't meant to."

"Your wife didn't either, and I think you aren't so blasé about how Claudia feels."

"Perhaps."

"She cried a good deal, and it wasn't from the pain."

"Go on."

"She won't conform; I don't know if she can."

"Wives are to obey their husbands."

"Not all of them find that easy. She has too much pride."

"The arrogance of her youth isn't something she needs here."

"I think you mistake my meaning. Claudia isn't prideful because her family is wealthy or because she is highborn. She fights because she feels you do her a grave injustice. She thinks it would be better to be one of your hounds."

"So she has said. Crawling for me is a way to show her submission, the cage a punishment. It was she who chose to go in there."

"Are you truly so foolish? That makes no never mind. She cares for me, and you sentenced me to spend the night in there. It hurt her to think of me treated like an animal."

"But you don't care Helena!"

"Claudia doesn't understand that. She never will. Are you so blind to your crimes against her? You made her spend the afternoon on her hands and knees. Birched her for coming to my aid. Flung words that spoke of your coldness towards her feelings at her, and then finished the day by stringing her up in a way that forced the most sensitive part of her onto the edge of that pole."

"I'm guilty to it all. She will not bend her will."

"You are a fool, and I will not beg your forgiveness for those words." Their eyes locked, his brooding and full of anger, hers pleading with him to understand.

"Am I to give her all she wants and allow her run of the manor so she can live her life the same as she did while growing up?"

"Claudia would make an elegant and regal lady if given the chance."

"Perhaps, but I am her Lord and husband. For over a century, my family and those of the Order have kept our females submissive and in sexual servitude. There is no reason for them to be anything but. I have watched as the wives of the other men have fawned over them and obeyed the slightest command. There is no speaking out of line, no sharing of views, and certainly no disobedience."

"Then they are like me and obey only because they find pleasure in the pain, or they have become empty headed ninnies made so because their spirits are broken. Isn't there even a small part of you that admires her mind and loves her fire?"

"Her fire and passion please me. I've no use for her sharp mind if all I receive is sharp words."

"Claudia told me she enjoys your touch. I believe she could come to be content here, even in service to you. All wives are expected to obey, but if you continue to dishonor her, you will lose her."

"She is bound to me for life."

"True, but it is possible to be in this manor without being here at all. Would you wish for her to be a shell of the woman she is now?" Helena's question was much like Bryce's, a fact that wasn't missed by Nathaniel. Still, Claudia's resistance hurt his pride and sensibilities.

"Right now she is a tireless shrew who cannot silence her mouth."

"Perhaps, but a woman who cries because her husband treats her in a way that breaks her heart, cares for him."

Nathaniel gave Helena a looked that made her want to box his ears to put some sense into his head. When he saw her look of exasperation, he answered with one of irritation. "Marriage isn't meant to be this difficult. That is why those of us in the Order hold fast to the old ways."

"Claudia is a woman, not a doll. You act as if she should be at your feet when you wish to play, but sit mute and unmoving when the need passes. Behave as if you have some sense, and your problem will solve itself."

"That's enough. Mind that mouth." Helena knew any chance of getting through to Nathaniel would vanish if she angered him.

"I'm sorry, Sir. I did not intend to be insolent. I truly wish for the two of you to find a way to make peace. Claudia feels an emotion akin to hatred, and yet her heart can't stop hoping you'll treat her tenderly. She believes that if she can just make you understand how you make her feel, things will be right between you. She doesn't argue to anger you; she does it because she can't accept that she will spend the rest of her life with someone who enjoys causing her pain and humiliation."

"But I have treated her well., and she makes me regret it with her atrocious behavior."

At Helena's look of skepticism Nathaniel's need to defend himself grew more acute. "I wooed her with romance the night I first bedded her. I know she was pleased. She lay curled up by my side, purring like a kitten when we finally settled down to sleep."

"And when did her anger return?"

"When she was made to do something that didn't appeal to her."

"You are a dolt!" Helena splashed water at Nathaniel in frustration. He jerked away but ended up with pants as wet as his already soaked shirt, his expression one of perplexed confusion.

"I've no idea why I thought speaking to a woman would help. You are all empty headed ninnies with no ability to comprehend such complex things as the need for strict obedience."

"You're here because your wife is a woman, and you wish to understand her. One might wonder why you are unable to comprehend that!"

Nathaniel grabbed Helena's wrist with a crushing grip. His patience gone. One woman who defied him was more than enough. He didn't need Helena's sarcastic tongue as well. "Behave, or I'll make arrangements for you to go to that Ellingsworth bitch."

"I was speaking the truth. Do as you wish to me, I will survive. Claudia will not. If you break her, you won't be able to put her back together again."

"Enough. You are not to speak of this conversation to anyone." He gave her wrist a squeeze then released her hand and abruptly rose from the chair, knocking it over in his haste. "Not to anyone."

Helena shook her head mutely as Lord Tarrington gave her one final glare before storming from the room. He left Helena with little hope that anything she'd said would help the Earl and his wayward wife see eye to eye.

Chapter Twenty-Nine

Nathaniel paused outside in the hallway, unsure where he might find some peace. It seemed everyone in the manor had something to say about how he was conducting himself in his treatment of Claudia and Helena. Never before had he felt such uncertainty, and that uncertainty was not sitting well. He was raised in a home where the women were submissive. His mother had knelt at his father's feet, kissing them with reverence even after a punishment. How could Claudia be so different? Was forcing her to submit wrong? Both Bryce and Helena said he would break her, but Nathaniel refused to turn his back on his family's tradition.

As he'd grown older and turned from a boy into first an adolescent and then a young man, he'd been privy to the punishments of his mother and the servants. He had also been taken to the school numerous times to witness firsthand how some of the women fought the life that was given them. He saw how their resistance was overcome with pain and consistent discipline until they became loving, passionate things that would do anything they were told, and performed sexual acts some would consider perverse, with evident pleasure. Finally, when he was considered old enough, he'd sampled the sex acts and come to love some of the more unusual ones, as well as the different forms of punishment.

Nathaniel was an only child and so he hadn't any real experience as to how young girls were raised before they came of age. Granted he'd been told of the Order's decision as he was told about and shown their ways, beliefs, rituals, and rules with which one was to run one's home. As expected, Nathaniel's mother had been married to a man in the Order when his father had died. He'd taken care to choose wisely for he loved his mother dearly, but he hadn't asked her if she preferred one of the men who had bid for her hand over the other. His mother knew it wasn't her place to voice her opinion and that Nathaniel wouldn't care what she desired. Expressing one's opinion would lead to punishment. His mother knew that and embraced the knowledge that her son would make the best decision, so why couldn't Claudia start her journey down the same path? Why did she resist time and again?

A peal of thunder that shook the house jarred Nathaniel from his thoughts. He looked up as the sound of the wind whistled through the rafters, feeling as if the storm that was beginning to rage outside matched his mood perfectly. His wife occupied his set of rooms. Miss Reagan could conceivably come around the corner and begin her unwanted groveling at any moment, and Bryce was most likely in the study sipping an excellent brandy and enjoying the warmth of the fire.

Thinking Bryce was the least of his nemesis; Nathaniel headed for the stairs. He'd had enough of women at least until it was time for bed. If he were lucky, a nice bath and a good meal would have put Claudia's attitude to rights by the time he wished to go to bed. If not, he would put a gag on the woman and bind her in a sleeping sack so he could get some rest. Being permissive and allowing her errant behavior to continue wasn't the answer. It simply couldn't be. The Order had been training their women for over a century. His way of life simply couldn't be wrong. He refused to question all they taught him since birth. He wasn't bull-headed or stupid, he was following in the footsteps of his father and grandfather. He was expected to, and damn it; it was how it would be.

Another rumble of thunder shook the house, and a shutter began to bang somewhere as Nathaniel made his way to the study, the thunder matching his thunderous mood. He and Bryce would reminisce about their boyhood escapades and leave talk of Claudia alone for the night, enjoying cigars and brandy would be the first step in setting his mood upon a better path. Putting thoughts of Claudia out of his mind would be the second.

The aroma of cigar smoke wafted through the air, telling Nathaniel that his guess had been correct. Bryce was enjoying one of his fine cigars. He entered his study and took the chair next to Bryce before the fire, and put up his feet as he reached into the humidor for a cigar.

"I wasn't sure you'd be returning."

"Matters were settled." That was all Nathaniel intended to say, and Bryce was quick to note his friend's foul temperament lying just below the surface. Though he took the pose of one who was relaxed, and puffed upon his cigar as he lit it with flourish, Nathaniel's hands gripped the thing so tightly his knuckles were white, and his eyes were anything but cheery. A flash of lightening lit up the windows and was soon followed by a tremendous crack of thunder, making both men jump just a bit.

"Good thing I chose to stay. I pity anyone forced to be outside." Bryce lifted his glass of brandy and gave a nod in Nathaniel's direction after Nathaniel had filled his glass. "Here's to good company and hospitality. My thanks."

"You're always welcome here Bryce. You're like the brother I never had. I was thinking on my way down that it would be gratifying to reminisce about our exploits. I believe we kept our nannies..."

The rest of his thought was cut short by a peal of thunder so loud it made speaking impossible. Rain lashed at the tall windows even as another flash of lightning appeared to announce the arrival of more thunder. It sounded as if the manor was being battered by a host of warships.

"I daresay it's a good thing my home has sound bones. She's old but solid." Another flash of lightning and ear splitting thunder caused both men to wince and look towards the window as if expecting the branches scraping on the glass, to come crashing through.

"Milord! Milord! Come quick. Oh, may the lord have mercy on us. Come quick Sir, Miss Claudia has been hurt. Oh Milord, please hurry."

The knot of fear that punched him in the gut at Millie's words shocked Nathaniel, but he didn't have time to give thought to his terror. Both men stood up; Nathaniel grabbing Millie by the arm and shaking her.

"Stop your ranting and tell me what happened. Where is she?" A ruckus in the hall made Nathaniel release the maid and hurry towards the sounds so he could see for himself, dread twisting his insides. The sight that met his eyes didn't put an end to his fear, on the contrary, it made it ten times worse. Coming from the back of the manor was one of the footmen, carrying an unconscious Claudia in his arms.

Claudia was wet and disheveled as well as being unresponsive to the servants clustering around her. One foot was bare, and on the other was one of Nathalie's boots. She was dressed in his clothing, the wet trousers clinging to her legs and the oversized dress shirt and topcoat swallowing up her slender frame. Her hair was a matted with mud and blood, her hands, and feet were muddy as well. Her forehead had a long cut from which blood was dripping to pool on the marble floor along with the rainwater that streamed from both his wife and the footmen.

"Bring her in here. I expect someone to tell me exactly what happened." His eyes first landed on the face of the footmen, but then he looked at the other servants who were clustered about, When he saw Millie, his eyes flashed with rage. The maid shrank back, turning pale under his gaze, but opened her mouth to speak regardless of her fear.

"The Mistress wished to be alone in her bath. She sent me to check on Miss Helena and fetch some hot tea. The tea on her tray had grown cold."

"You could have rung for more." His voice was flat, almost void of inflection, but his face was thunderous, belying the calmness with which he spoke. Nathaniel was struggling to remain composed. He wanted to shake the maid and scream at her.

"Milord, she told me to go. I did not wish to disobey her."

"I am your Master. What of my orders?"

"Oh, please Milord. I beg your forgiveness. I did not know I wasn't to leave. I would have remained with her had you told me to."

"That's enough." Nathaniel dismissed anything else Millie had to say, but the woman was quite certain it wasn't going to be enough. The Master would have more to say on the matter all too soon. "Where did you find her?" Nathaniel was asking the groom now, Millie forgotten for the time being.

"The stable boy heard a ruckus, and he thought it was just the horses reacting to the storm, but then he heard hoof beats. He ran out of his quarters and saw someone riding out of the stable."

The groom had put Claudia down on a chaise in the study, and Millie was pulling a blanket over her. Nathaniel looked at Claudia's pale cheeks and the blood still running from the cut on her head. "We need clean towels. I need to tend her head."

"They are being fetched Milord, and the stable boy has gone for the doctor."

The news didn't change Nathaniel's grave expression. All in the room knew the doctor was a good distance away. The manor house was in the country and outside of Brighton. The doctor would struggle to get there quickly in the fierce storm. A maid arrived with some towels and Bryce immediately took one and splashed brandy on it before taking it to where Claudia lay to wipe the gash on her head. She whimpered when the alcohol burned into the cut.

"Sorry, sweet. I have to clean this."

Nathaniel didn't care for Bryce's familiarity with Claudia but let it go. He needed to hear the rest of the story. While it was clear his wife had dressed in his clothes and made her way on top of a horse racing out of the stables, he wished to hear the rest.

"Tell me the rest."

"When the horse got to the courtyard, the boy seen it was the Mistress on it cause the lightening flashed, but then when the thunder cracked, the horse spooked. It reared up, and the Mistress fell. The boy started hollerin', and I heard him from the kitchen. I went out and saw her in a heap on the ground."

"How long ago?"

"Just a minute before I brought her in."

Millie knelt by Claudia's side and held one of her hands as Bryce cleaned Claudia's face. Another of the maids wrapped a towel around her wet and muddy hair to keep it out of the now semi-clean cut. As they tended her, Claudia began to shiver despite the blanket that covered her.

"Millie, she needs to be warmed up. Run the bath again and then warm the bed. I want her clean and dry. Fever will take hold if we don't warm her."

"Yes Milord." Millie raced from the room, nearly knocking Miss Reagan over as she went out the doorway. The maid didn't give the head housekeeper a second thought, but Nathaniel did when he spied her there.

"Miss Reagan I would expect you to lead the effort to tend my wife."

"I've no skill at doctoring."

Nathaniel found her answer infuriating. "I don't expect you to doctor her. I would think you would be making certain we had all we need." As he spoke to Miss Reagan, Nathaniel had picked Claudia up. He strode to the doorway where Miss Reagan stood, and gave her a chilling look as he went past. "You are to make certain there is a basin and clean hot water upstairs when the doctor arrives. Despite your dislike of my wife, you are still an employee of mine. See that you act like it."

The expression of fury on Miss Reagan's face was lost on Nathaniel. He was already past the woman, and heading up the staircase, clutching a cold and wounded Claudia to his heart like she was the most precious thing on Earth.

Chapter Thirty

Claudia remained limp and for the most part unresponsive as Nathaniel put her back in the tub. He washed her hair, taking great care not to move her head about in a way that would hurt her. He spoke to her in a tender voice throughout as he tended the cuts and scrapes, and pressed a clean towel to the cut on her forehead. By the time the doctor arrived, Claudia was in bed with a cloth tied about her head to keep the wound from bleeding. Though she opened her eyes from time to time, she neither spoke nor kept them open when Nathaniel was in her line of vision.

Millie had managed to get her to drink a bit of tea when Nathaniel moved away from the bed, for though she had been in the hot bath, Claudia continued to shiver. Ointment was put on her hands and the other scrapes as well as on the cuts made by the birch bundle earlier in the day. The liniment helped take the pain from those wounds, but the cut on her head required attention from the doctor.

When the doctor arrived, Miss Reagan, whom also had fresh linens and a water basin, preceded him into the room, but when Claudia's trembling increased in the woman's presence, Nathaniel shooed her from the room.

"Give me more light." The doctor bent over Claudia, looking into her eyes with a scope. Millie turned up the lamp on the wall and brought another over as the doctor gazed into Claudia's eyes again. "Her eyes appear normal. They react to the light. Her head needs sewing. Does your head hurt Lady Tarrington? I mean more than just where the cut is."

"I can endure it." They were the first words Claudia had spoken since the footman brought her inside after her aborted run for freedom. When she spoke them, she was looking at Nathaniel, and he knew she was damning him for all the pain he taught her to withstand.

"I'll give you some laudanum. Then I'll sew up that cut."

"You'll not use chloroform?"

"Yes, of course. I just want to dose her with the laudanum before I put her out." That way when she wakes up, she'll not have an ache in her head. I will leave some as well. It will help with headaches and to make sure she can sleep."

"Mix this in a glass of water. Five drops per glass." He handed a small bottle to Millie and turned to Claudia. "You'll drink it down and then we'll see about that cut. Tell me what you did to get a gash like that on your head."

The doctor was not the same man who had examined her at Miss Patton's school. He was one who cared for the whole town, and was not aware of what went on behind the doors of some of the homes in Brighton.

"I fell from a horse."

"The storm came up while you were riding?"

"Yes."

"It was pretty late to be riding, Lady Tarrington." The doctor looked at Nathaniel but let the subject drop. Millie brought the glass of water with the laudanum mixed in and helped Claudia sit up so she could drink it. She made a face at the taste but drank it down.

"I'll only use a bit of chloroform. Bumps on the head can cause the stomach to become upset. We don't want her vomiting when she'd unconscious. You won't feel the stitching though. I'll make sure of that. Close your eyes now and breathe deep."

Claudia did as he instructed and was out in a few minutes. The doctor stitched up her wound and then rose as he gave final instructions.

"Keep her on her side as she sleeps and watch over her. Wake her every three hours. Speak to her and listen to how she speaks. Does she talk nonsense? Is her speech slurred? She may be concussed, and confusion or trouble talking will indicate that. When she wakes, the laudanum will help with the pain, but when it wears off, Lady Tarrington is going to have a nasty headache. I know she said it didn't hurt badly, but I think that was her dignity talking. She can have laudanum every six hours. I'll be back to check on her tomorrow."

"Thank you doctor. She will make a full recovery?" Nathaniel's voice was thick with worry. The sight of Claudia in the footman's arms, wet and bleeding, continued to flash in his mind. It shook him up and made him face the fact that even though she was insolent and stubborn, he cared for his wife. Her desperate wish to flee in a raging storm spoke volumes about how unhappy she was.

"There can be complications with any head injury, but it's good she was awake. Take care she doesn't ride any more horses in a storm."

"I'll do that. My wife is headstrong." Both men knew Claudia's version of the events sounded false, and that Claudia's temperament had little to do with her injury, but the doctor was not going to speak against the Earl.

"Very good then. I'll see myself out, but will be back tomorrow morning."

Millie busied herself stroking Claudia's head and tucking the blankets around her, not wanting to meet Lord Tarrington's eye. She was afraid he would resume his verbal discipline of her, now that they were alone, but she didn't have cause for worry.

"Take care of Lady Tarrington and under no circumstances leave this room. Ring for anything you need, or if she takes a turn for the worst."

"Yes, Milord."

"Do exactly as the doctor said. Tell me now."

"I'm to dose Lady Tarrington every six hours and to wake her every three. I am to ask her questions and listen to see if she is confused or speaking strangely."

"Very good. I would stay, but I don't think my wife wishes for me to be at her side." Millie had no idea what to say to her employer. She ducked her head and fussed with the blankets again. "I'll come back to check on her."

"Yes, Milord."

Nathaniel leaned down and kissed Claudia's forehead before leaving his chambers without another word. He knew Claudia would not want him there. It would be best if he waited in the study or tried to get some rest in one of the guest rooms. He debated going to speak to Helena, but then dismissed the idea. The last thing he wanted was to have Helena look at him with accusation in her eyes. He certainly did not need her to tell him this was his fault. Any fool could see it was.

He made his way back to the study, in need of another brandy. If Bryce were there, perhaps it would be advantageous to discuss Claudia once again. This time he would abandon his belief that he knew everything about women and how to tame them. Perhaps it was time to listen to Bryce when he said that the methods and beliefs of the Order might not work for all women. The idea gnawed at his gut, but Claudia provided proof that the way he was training her was not the right way to go about making his marriage anything other than a war.

He arrived in the study to find it empty. Bryce was gone, as were any trace of his servants. It was just as well, the mood he was in was thunderous. He needed to have a long talk with Miss Reagan, but now wasn't the time. The woman had run his household for ten years, but if he were to change his views about what was best for Claudia, then Miss Reagan would have to accept them, like it or not.

The servants had removed all evidence of his wife's ordeal aside from the water stain on the chaise, and for that, Nathaniel was grateful. The fire was dying, but Nathaniel used the poker to stir it and then added a log. He preferred privacy over the need to do it himself. Once the hearth was giving off sufficient warmth, he settled down in one of the chairs before it and poured another brandy. Instead of sipping the drink, he tossed it back and refilled his glass. Nathaniel wasn't a man who drank in excess, but he certainly felt the need tonight. All the same, he would drink the second glass more slowly. He did not need to become intoxicated. Claudia might need him during the night. He had to suppress a burst of cynical laughter at the thought. His wife certainly was not going to ask for him. He was the last person she would want tending her.

As he was sipping at the liquor, his eyes went from the flames to the portrait of his father above the mantle. The hard eyes staring out from the canvas made Nathaniel feel like a child once more. The painting never had that effect before. Nathaniel was certain it was his own guilt eating away at him.

"Did they all comply?" His father, of course, had no answers. "You raised me to believe our course was the only way. Didn't any of them rebel as much as Claudia? I have no desire to have my wife braving the elements and throwing common sense to the wind in order to escape her marriage. What am I to do? She cannot be the only one. Must I choose between loyalty to the Order and Claudia's happiness?"

His question was again met with a stare that seemed to accuse him of misconduct. "You made me believe all the wives were happy. Claudia hates me. SHE HATES ME!"

He accompanied the last of his angry tirade with the shattering of crystal as he threw his glass at the mantle. The impact scattered the glass everywhere and caused a brief flare up in the hearth. Still, the portrait of his father offered no words of wisdom, even when Nathaniel was done bellowing at him.

Shaking his head, fed up with the turn his life had taken, he ran his hand over his face in frustration and yanked on the bell pull. Footsteps soon sounded, and the butler appeared in the doorway.

"Yes Milord?"

"Have one of the maids prepare a guest room for me. I'll be up after I check on my wife."

"Yes, Milord." The man left with his instructions, and Nathaniel watched after him. Being turned out of his rooms was an embarrassment mollified by the fact that Claudia was injured. It was the only reason a man could hold up his head after sleeping in one of the guest rooms. As for why he was not at her side, let those who gossiped be damned. The turmoil under his roof was hardly a secret. His firebrand of a wife had caused chaos since arriving. Hell, she caused chaos even before stepping foot in his home.

Shaking his head and feeling like a fool, Nathaniel went back up the stairs. He went as far as the bedroom doorway in his chambers but left when Millie nodded and gave him a small smile. Her chair was close to the bed, and she was busy with her needlepoint. Nathaniel was certain the woman would become aware of any change in Claudia. There was no need for his presence. It would only serve to agitate his wife. It was time to get some rest. He went down the hall to where light spilled from one of the guestrooms. The maid was busy turning down the bed. She gave curtsied, and turned to leave, but Nathaniel called her back.

"Yes Milord?"

"My boots. Remove them for me."

"Yes Milord." Nathaniel sat, and the servant girl knelt in front of him, pulling off one boot and then the other.

"Will there be anything else Milord?"

Nathaniel had half a mind to bed the girl but knew an image of his wife's pale face would haunt any pleasure he meant to have.

"No. Get out and close the door."

"Yes Milord."

When she left, and Nathaniel was once more alone with his thoughts, he rose from the chair and laid down on the bed fully dressed. He hadn't the energy to disrobe, and there was a chance, however slight, that Claudia would need him. If anything changed, he would be ready to go to her.

Chapter Thirty-One

The soft knocking upon the door did not wake Nathaniel, so the maid stepped inside with trepidation. She knew things in the manor had not been running smoothly, and having to bother the Master of the house was not something she wanted to do. She was only here because she didn't have a choice in the matter. Miss Helena had herself in a fury and was demanding to see the Mistress. Ordinarily the women's wishes did not matter, but things seem to have changed in that regard, besides, Lord Hastings had sent her, not Miss Helena.

"Pardon me Milord." She knocked again, harder but to her dismay Nathaniel still didn't wake up. The maid decided to give it one more try and then she would leave and find Richard. He was the butler and usually tended to all matters that concerned Lord Tarrington. She was just about to leave, deciding that was the best course of action without knocking again, when Nathaniel woke himself with a snort.

He looked about in confusion, and then spied Clarice in the doorway. The memory of Claudia being hurt came rushing back as the cobwebs of sleep fell away. "Claudia?"

"No, Milord. The other miss. Miss Helena. She wishes to see Lady Tarrington. She's quite adamant about it."

"My wife is well?"

"Yes, Milord. She is sleeping."

"And you disturbed my rest at the request of Helena?"

"Well, no Sir I... Lord Hastings decided I should wake you."

"Lord Hastings is with Helena?"

"She asked after Lady Tarrington at breakfast and Lord Hastings told her of the Lady's accident. Miss Helena wanted to rush upstairs, but Miss Reagan wouldn't allow it. Lord Hastings declared Miss Reagan's objection to be rubbish, and sent me to wake you."

Nathaniel had looked at the window covered by the thick velvet drapes when the girl mentioned breakfast. He was shocked that he had slept for so long. Apparently, the events of yesterday combined with the good helping of brandy had granted his rest despite his worry over Claudia.

"My wife is still sleeping?"

"Yes Milord. Each time Millie woke her, the Mistress said her head was aching. Millie gave her more laudanum, or so I was told. I believe Miss Reagan said the doctor would be returning to see her soon. I may have heard his carriage only a moment ago.

"Everyone is to stay downstairs while I go and see her. If it was the doctor, he may be brought up, but no one else."

"Yes, Milord." Clarisse quickly retreated. She could tell the Master was in a foul mood. Perhaps visiting the Mistress would cheer him.

Nathaniel did his best to straighten his clothing, washed his face in the basin, and combed his hair back with his fingers. He knew he still looked haggard, hell; he was still wearing yesterday's clothes. The trouble between he and Claudia wasn't going to disappear if he was neatly dressed and well groomed, so what did it matter? His good looks had not charmed her so far.

Nathaniel stood in front of the mirror for another minute, sizing himself up with a critical eye. The events of the night before played through his head as he looked at his reflection. He had eyes like his father, but his mother's softer smile. How had she felt being kept under his father's thumb and doing things that would make the London whores balk? He couldn't remember her ever having an opinion of her own. Thinking on it now, Nathaniel didn't even know if his mother was an intelligent woman. To be honest, he even had to work to remember her voice. Was that what he wanted for Claudia and his children?

She was beautiful and full of fire, headstrong and impudent, impulsive and quick to disagree. Her behavior never failed to light the fuse of his anger. The only time she had been pliable, doing as he asked and accepting all his commands without an argument had been the time they spent alone. He could not stand here looking at himself and deny the reason for her smile and ease of obedience; it was because he had romanced her and treated her tenderly. The rose petals, the little kisses, feeding her breakfast, allowing her to talk to him as a person and not someone of lesser importance. He spent those two days acting as if she was important to him. Could he say the same for the rest of the time Claudia had been in the manor?

The answer to that question was painfully clear. Staring at himself, and seeing his father stare back at with those eyes of dark blue, still gave him qualms about abandoning all they had taught him and all he'd believed in since he was young. Women were to serve and obey. It was their lot in life. They were the weaker sex, and could not be trusted to make rational decisions, society agreed with the Order on that point, but what of the other? What of the deeper form of servitude expected from the wives of the men in the Order of the Blackguards? His father and his grandfather before him stuck with the ideals that demanded more of their women. They were of the belief that a woman be trained to do everything a man needed her to do. It didn't matter if it was degrading, painful, or caused their unhappiness because a man was a woman's lord and Master. But what were his obligations to her?

Nathaniel knew what the Order believed, but what about Claudia? Bryce had suggested that perhaps not all women were submissive, or at least not as submissive as the Blackguards required. Was it possible to have Claudia be a dutiful wife, serving his needs but being happy to do so? Was it really so wrong that she couldn't accept crawling on the floor at his side like a dog? Would he wish to crawl like a dog? What if he were in her place, punished for having an opinion about how he was treated and given painful and degrading lessons until he finally stopped fighting? What if the shoe were on the other foot?

Nathaniel ran a hand through his hair once more and then turned from the eyes of his father. He needed to see his wife. Claudia's accident had frightened him terribly, and the fact that she was running from him made him feel as if someone had punched him in the gut. Her behavior spoke one thing loud and clear. She would rather die than stay married to him. No matter that she responded sexually, no matter that she had orgasmed when he'd done degrading things.

He was a member of the Blackguards and was trained in the arts of giving women pleasure, but just because her body felt the thrill, didn't mean it was all okay. Though she had clung to him in passion, and, flown high on the rush that the flogging gave her, Claudia had also cried as she picked broken glass up off the floor as her hands bled. She stayed mute and did as he asked, crawling like a beast even though it had killed her inside so that she could see Helena. So many times she'd shown him honest emotion and begged with her tears, words, and actions for him to treat her as someone who mattered, but he'd remained blind, deaf, and dumb. Well, now he was going to set things right, for Claudia, and for Helena. The women were two peas in a pod and the best of friends. He couldn't go forward determined to find a way to live some of the Orders teachings, and at the same time treat his wife as though she were precious to him. He also could not leave Helena to a terrible fate. Claudia would never forgive him, and that is what he needed most if he was going to win her heart.

Secure in his course and ready to face Claudia and declare his intentions, Nathaniel went to the doorway only to run into Bryce.

"Come quick man. There is something wrong with Claudia."

Nathaniel wasted no time asking Bryce what was wrong. He led the charge to his set of rooms and rushed through the door to find the doctor in the chair Millie had occupied. Helena was on the other side of the bed holding one of Claudia's limp hands. Millie stood back looking terrified and wrung her hands, and Miss Reagan stood at the foot of the bed with a look that bordered between boredom and glee. Despite his command to have everyone wait downstairs, the room was full.

Claudia lay back upon the pillow; her eyes closed, her skin pale as ivory, her dark hair fanning out like a tarnished halo around her head against the white cotton bandage wrapped around her head.. Under her eyes were dark circles, and her lips were nearly bloodless. The sight of her so void of life made Nathaniel's heart skip a beat. He couldn't lose her now, not when he was finally coming to understand.

"What's wrong with my wife?"

"Her maid tried to wake her a short while ago and she wouldn't stir. I've tried the smelling salts, but no luck with them either."

"Millie, did you wake her during the night as I ordered?"

"Aye, milord. I woke her twice as the doctor said we should. Lady Tarrington woke on her own several hours after the doctor left, and then I woke her a bit after midnight and again before dawn."

"And she was talking? Did she know her surroundings?"

Though his face was puzzled, the doctor decided Millie was the one to ask. It appeared that Lord Tarrington hadn't been in attendance while his wife lay sleeping.

"Yes, Sir. She asked for water and another powder, saying her head hurt. She was befuddled just before dawn, but I thought she was just sleepy.

"Was there any retching?"

"She coughed up the water early this morning but said it had gone down wrong. She didn't vomit, Sir."

"Was there weakness or slurred speech?"

Millie began to weep. "I held the glass for her. She sounded like a person woken from a deep sleep."

"Well, she isn't responsive now. When was she last awake?"

"I believe it was perhaps 4:00 or nearing 5:00. The sun hadn't risen."

The doctor patted Claudia's face, calling her name as he waved the smelling salts under her nose once again. When Claudia remained unconscious, he set the bottle down and lifted her head off the pillow, running his fingers over her scalp.

"She has a lump back here. It's no doubt she is concussed." The doctor took his scope from his bag and waved his hand towards Millie, who brought the lamp closer. He lift one eyelid and then the other, gazing into Claudia's eyes. "Move the light close." He repeated the examination of Claudia's eyes as all watched in silence.

"Her eyes are responsive, which is good, but she is deeply unconscious. The must be pressure on her brain. Swelling could cause her to enter a state of utter unresponsiveness like this."

"When will she wake?"

"That isn't something I can answer."

"But she will wake up."

"I'm afraid that isn't always the case." A sniff from Miss Reagan drew Nathaniel's eye towards the woman who was his head housekeeper and co-trainer of the women he'd brought home to be his mistresses on occasion. Before she brought a hand up to her mouth, Nathaniel saw the hint of a smile. He realized Miss Reagan's sniff was an effort to keep her glee from the others and not the beginning of tears caused by worry. Her eyes were wide, and her chest heaved as if containing laughter, and at that moment in time Nathaniel could have gleefully strangled her.

Now wasn't the time for loud confrontation. His wife lay still as stone, possibly dying. He turned eyes that were hard as steel upon Miss Reagan and quietly told her to leave. She looked surprised for a moment, but then simply spun on her heel and exited the room. Before she'd even left, Nathaniel's attention was back on Claudia.

"What can you do for my wife? There must be some way to wake her."

"I've read of some who have cut the scalp to let the blood flow out, but sometimes they find the bleeding inside the skull. Then no blood drains when they cut the skin."

"Is that why she won't wake up?"

"It's possible. Some have tried boring a hole through the skull."

Millie gasped, and Helena made a sound of protest while Bryce put a hand on Nathaniel's shoulder to steady him.

"I can't... No, I won't have you drilling into her brain."

"Then we wait."

"How long?" Nathaniel wanted answers, but the doctor didn't have any, at least any he wished to hear.

"I can't say."

"That's not good enough!"

"You just have to wait. Have her watched around the clock. Talk to her, try the smelling salts once an hour. It's too late for a cold compress on the bump. Had she told me of the pain in the back of her head perhaps we could have kept the swelling down. Now it won't make a difference."

"There's nothing else?"

The doctor shook his head and eyed up Nathaniel, still wondering what exactly Lady Tarrington was doing on a horse in a storm. "Sit with her, talk to her, keep watch over her. She may wake in an hour or could be unconscious for days."

"But she WILL wake up?"

"I told you there were no promises. There are some things you can't control, no matter if you try to command them. Right now, Lady Tarrington and that lump on her skull are beyond your orders. I'll come back tomorrow. Send word if she wakes up sooner."

With that the doctor packed up his things and took his leave. Bryce began to say something in an effort to boost Nathaniel's hopes, but Nathaniel cut him off.

"Go, all of you. Leave us alone. Millie bring a basin of water and a cloth. Her lips are dry. I have to wet her lips. I..." Once again, Bryce put a steadying hand on Nathaniel's arm. "I'm fine; we'll be fine. I'll ring for anything else we need."

Once Millie returned with the requested basin and filled it with cold water, all who were attending Claudia's side began to drift out. As Helena walked past Nathaniel, he stopped her, placing a hand on her arm.

"I've been wrong. She isn't like the others. I've been so wrong."

"You'll have a chance to tell her." Helena placed her hand on his and squeezed. "You'll have a chance."

Nathaniel closed the door after all were gone and took up his place beside Claudia. He wet the clean cloth, and then dabbed at her dry lips before opening them just a bit and squeezing a trickle of water into her mouth. When he was done, he pressed a kiss as gentle as a summer breeze on her bandaged head and then took one of Claudia's limp hands in his. Bowing his head, he said a prayer to a God he hadn't spoken to in years, asking for one more chance to tell Claudia the things he needed to say. He was sorry, and he had to tell her. He was ever so sorry, and she had to hear him say so.

Chapter Thirty-Two

Nathaniel took the seat so recently vacated by the doctor and sat looking at his young wife. She was still lovely of course, dark shadows under her eyes and paler than normal skin couldn't hide true beauty. She looked like she was merely sleeping, lost in sweet dreams. In truth, aside from the flush of her skin, she looked much as she had during their long days and nights of passion. He'd often woken then and quietly watched her dreaming, thinking how perfect she was both in beauty and spirit. Now the flush of desire was absent as was the fiery spirit. She was a mere shell of herself, and that was what Bryce had warned him about.

Of course, she hadn't become this way over time as he ground down the rough edges and forced her to conform with the ways of the Order, but he had killed her spirit all the same. The only difference was that he'd snuffed it out in one fatal blow, not only murdering her fire, but nearly doing away with Claudia as well.

Nathaniel took her hand in his, marveling at how slim her fingers were, how delicate they looked. Women were the fairer sex, but society put a huge burden on their shoulders, at least it did if they were of the lower class or perhaps a wife of the Order of the Blackguard. Did Claudia really deserve to have her beautiful hands become callused because she was expected to crawl at his side much of the time instead of standing beside him as his cherished wife?

"What am I to do Claudia? You've made me doubt all the things I've held tight to my heart. My path in life was clear, and then you arrived and disrupted all I've envisioned for our future. What will I do with you? If you come back to me, I simply must change my ways, but what of the Order? The decision you've thrown my way isn't an easy one. Bryce thinks it is possible to follow the teachings of the Order without breaking you and Helena, and I hope he's right. I cannot take the chance that you would try to flee again, risking life and limb in the process, just to get away from me."

Nathaniel placed Claudia's hand gently onto the bed, and then stood, looking at his wife, feeling both desperate and angry. He had no experience with being helpless. The doctor said it was possible she could hear him, and if so, perhaps she could feel his nearness as well. Though he was loathed to admit it, it might be best if he wasn't hovering over her. The fact raised his ire. He was in change damn it, and yet here he was, begging God to save Claudia and doubting everything he held dear.

Nathaniel began to pace the room, moving back and forth like a caged tiger, trapped by what he believed, and the truth he was confronted with. Looking at Claudia lying still, and silent upon the bed told him what was right. He couldn't mend her now, but he felt as if he would do anything to get a second chance.

Nathaniel walked to the window and parted the heavy drapes, allowing a thin shaft of bright sunlight to penetrate the dark room. It came to rest on Claudia's face, highlighting the dark shadows under her eyes. They were the marks that told of the strain she'd felt, the marks that spoke of her pain. Of course, her injury contributed to them, but if he thought back over the past weeks, Nathaniel had to admit that there had been clear signs of the torment Claudia had received since arriving in Brighton.

"Can you feel the sunshine Claudia? Feel it warming your face? It's daytime now sweet. It's time to wake up." Of course, Claudia didn't stir or respond to his words. Why would she? Claudia equated him with pain and humiliation.

"Helena came to your side just as she always does. She's so worried about you Claudia. And Millie is as well. Everyone cares for you. I... I care for you Claudia. Things will be different when you wake up. I swear they will be."

Nathaniel let the curtain fall back into place, dousing the spotlight that had illuminated Claudia and made the plight of her condition even more apparent. It was just as well; he couldn't stand to look at her when the results of his actions stared him in the face. He walked back to the bed and sat down, almost certain his wife wouldn't want him there, but not willing to leave. His actions towards Claudia were going to change, and being here for her was the first step. He wanted to be the first person she saw when she woke up, wanted her to know he was taking up vigil by her side. She had to believe him when he told her he cared for her, and if she wouldn't listen, then he would show her. Life was going to change for Claudia Rose Tarrington, and it would be a change for the good.

A soft knock upon the door startled Nathaniel. He realized he must have dozed off. He straightened from his bent over position of arms folded on the bed and forehead resting on them with a grimace.

"I don't wish to be bothered." As he responded to the intruder, Nathaniel wrung the cloth out in the basin of water and then trickled some between Claudia's lips before wetting them with the wet rag. Her eyes didn't flutter in response to his words or his actions, something that made the knot of worry in his belly grow.

"Excuse me Sir. Lord Brauer has arrived. He is expecting to meet with you about Miss Helena. Miss Reagan wants you to know that she will take care of things because you are indisposed, but Lord Hastings advised me to tell you."

Nathaniel realized he had forgotten about his appointment with the man to discuss Helena. If he had arrived, then Lady Ellingsworth would arrive soon as well. He seemed to be forgetting all the other things happening in his life since Claudia came to be his wife. The little chit has his world turned upside down. Now it was time to deal with Lord Brauer and Lady Ellingsworth. The woman was quite serious about becoming Helena's new owner.

"Tell Miss Reagan I will deal with things directly. I wish for Helena to take up watch over my wife. I'll be down once she is in place."

"Very good, Milord. Will you need Richard?"

The question made Nathaniel look down at his rumpled clothing and realize how unkempt he was. His tongue felt like a bloated dry thing in his mouth. Though he didn't much care about anything right now aside from Claudia, Nathaniel realized it was best to put up a stoic front for his company. The Order would hear of his change in behavior towards Claudia soon enough.

"I believe I can groom myself. Have Richard make certain Lord Brauer and his company are comfortable and seated in the study. Tell them I will be down shortly."

"Yes, Milord."

"And Millie."

"Yes Milord."

"Tales of my wife's accident will be most unwelcome."

"Yes Milord. As long as Miss Reagan hasn't told them, I'm certain the rest of us will remain mum."

Angry words sprang to his lips at the thought of Miss Reagan telling outsiders about Claudia's disastrous escape attempt. If the woman truly had overstepped her bounds, he would send her packing. That was a serious possibility anyhow. Miss Reagan and Claudia despised each other. How could he make good on his promise to better Claudia's life if she had to come face to face with Miss Reagan day in and day out?

Nathaniel went to the wardrobe in his dressing room and pulled out a fresh shirt. Everything else could wait. He wasn't going to a formal dinner. Stripping off the shirt he wore, Nathaniel went to the basin in the washroom and splashed his face, scrubbing the crumbles of sleep that were in the corners of his eyes. He dried quickly and then brushed his teeth, not taking even one extra moment to look into his own eyes. Nathaniel knew they were haunted. He couldn't shake the guilt that lay heavy on his shoulders.

As he was donning his shirt, a knock sounded at the door announcing the arrival of Helena.

"Come." Nathaniel would face the blame in her eyes if need be. He was guilty after all. Still, he was glad to see Helena's expression was one of concern and not accusation.

"Sit with her. Hold her hand."

"I will. Has she moved at all?"

"No, there's been no change. Talk to her. The doctor said she might be able to hear."

"I will. I promise. She'll be in good hands."

"I care for her. I never wanted this."

"Of course you didn't. No one would think you wished for this, no matter how she behaved."

"She most likely does."

"Her heart is wounded."

"I treated her badly. I've never had anyone react like Claudia has."

"You've never had a wife before. She looks at things differently Sir. She sees her whole life, all those years to come. I think some women can't accept this kind of marriage."

"You are bold Helena."

"Yes, Sir. I always have been."

"And yet you bend to my will."

"I enjoy many of the Orders activities."

"Claudia does not."

"There are things that gave her pleasure. I believe she cares for you."

"Don't be a fool. Claudia risked life and limb to get away from me."

"If she felt only hate, your actions would not have broken her heart."

"What I broke was her spirit in a fool attempt to tame her."

"Claudia will wake up. When she does, you can start again."

Nathaniel made a noise that told Helena he did not have much faith in her view. "Has Lord Hastings told you of his interest?"

"He mentioned it at breakfast."

"I imagine you would prefer him over Lady Ellingsworth or Mr. Brauer."

"Lord Hastings is young and handsome."

"He is."

"Only a fool would wish to belong to Lady Ellingsworth."

"Lady Ellingsworth is not fit to own anyone; not even you who likes the way we take pleasure."

"I have no respect for her and would find it hard to bend to her will."

"And Lord Brauer?"

"I do not know Lord Brauer, but Lord Hastings is very pleasing."

"Has he done much of this pleasing?"

"Oh no, Sir." Helena raised her skirt to her waist so Nathaniel could see the chastity device she wore.

"Miss Reagan put it back on you?"

"No Sir. Lord Hastings did. I think he finds me pleasing as well, and didn't wish to show you disrespect by touching what didn't belong to him. If you must know, I was brazen and expressed my desire to pleasure him. He not only refused, he bent me over a chair and took a strap to my bottom. I believe I can still feel the heat of his wrath. "

"That gives me hope that he could control you. I know what Claudia would wish. Stay with her. They expect me below. I'll send Millie up if we need you. It is common for the interested parties to examine the woman in question, but Bryce has had his fill as has Lady Ellingsworth. Lord Brauer saw you when he arrived?"

"Yes Sir."

"All right then. Sit with her. Talk to her. Tell her you believe me when I say I'll treat her better, if you trust me of course."

"I won't lie to her. She would know. I have faith you will try to do right by her."

Nathaniel leaned over, kissing Claudia and stroking her cheek. "You can wake up now. I'm leaving. There will be no one here to torment you." Nathaniel closed his eyes for a minute, and Helena wondered if he were praying or silently beseeching Claudia to listen. "Where is that fire? Have I doused it completely? Please Claudia, you must fight this. It's in your nature to do battle, so now I wish for that spirit that made me so angry to return."

Chapter Thirty-Three

Nathaniel heard the sound of an approaching carriage as he came down the main staircase. Lady Ellingsworth had arrived. He grimaced but then thought how very livid she was going to be when told she was not going to acquire Helena. Nathaniel didn't care that her family had been in the Order since its inception. The woman was a sadistic bitch who had no idea of how to properly train and care for anyone. One merely needed to watch how she had her hired man mishandled those she was to train. While the Order believed in full sexual submission and service without question, they also believed the women must be cared for and have all of their needs seen to. While many in the Order had a vicious streak, they knew they were to train their wife in such a matter that she came to enjoy the pleasure and the pain. Lady Ellingsworth was utterly cold and cruel.

Richard was opening the door and bowing as Lady Ellingsworth made her way into the foyer, nose in the air, skirts billowing. Thomas was on her heels and gave Richard a look of disdain even though the two men were of equal station. Nathaniel observed it all with pressed lips and hard eyes. He had no patience for Lady Ellingsworth today. He never did, but at the moment she was bound to be more trying than any other because his place was at Claudia's side, not entertaining a woman who didn't know her place.

"Richard, are Lord Hastings and Lord Brauer in the study?"

"Yes Milord."

"Please show Lady Ellingsworth the way." His face held an expression that anyone in their right mind would recognize as one of barely controlled impatience. Lady Ellingsworth either didn't care or didn't have the brains to see that Nathaniel was teetering on the edge. His manners were being presented, but it wouldn't take much for his civil façade to disappear.

"Why Nathaniel, women are usually entertained in the parlor. Have you forgotten?"

"You are playing in a man's world Ethel." Nathaniel paused a moment for the slight to sink in. If the bitch wished to address him without his title, then he would refrain from using hers. Lady Ellingsworth was a lady by birth alone. Her temperament was a cross between a spoiled child and a brute who enjoyed pulling legs off insects.

"Yes I am and play I shall. I am prepared to offer a substantial fee for the chit."

"The 'chit' as you refer to Helena, isn't bought by the highest bidder. This isn't a slave auction. You must show your knowledge of training, ability to support her, and in your case provide a reason why Helena would be better off with you. Most would think than a husband with whom she can bear children and continue to provide descendants for future generations of families in the Order would be a better match.

"Please follow Richard to the study. We will discuss this matter in the presence of everyone. Richard, after you finish escorting Lady Ellingsworth, take Thomas back to the kitchen and see refreshments are provided."

"Why I... Thomas needs to stay with me."

"I promise my staff is quite capable. Would you like tea? It's a bit early for brandy."

"Sir, Anna is serving refreshments."

"See there Lady Ellingsworth. You needn't worry. Come along." He offered her his arm only to speed up proceedings, and walked her to the study. When they entered, the smell of cigar smoke was thick in the air, causing Lady Ellingsworth to wrinkle her nose.

"I hope you don't mind that I took the liberty of enjoying a cigar. Lord Brauer thought it was a grand idea as well."

"By all means, they are meant to be enjoyed."

"Why I never." Lady Ellingsworth was working up to a grand snit when Nathaniel turned to face her, his expression clearly showing his disdain.

"If you wish to play the games of men and dabble in the rituals of the Order, then you need to be quiet. Having a tantrum or swooning over the smell of smoke will only make all of us more convinced that you do not belong here. Now sit down. You are new to these proceedings. Anna, pour Lady Ellingsworth a cup of tea, unless she wishes to leave."

Though she looked as ruffled as an angry hen, Ethel sat down on the edge of a chair and accepted the cup of tea from Anna without a word.

"Now then, we are here to discuss the matter of Helena. Her father passed away, leaving only one surviving son who is old enough to serve as her guardian. Niles is the guardian of Helena's three younger sisters and two young brothers as well, but he is washing his hands of Helena because of her wild antics."

"What of the girl's mother?"

"The woman is very obedient and highly skilled. She has a new husband and is allowed frequent visits with her children. Helena is nothing like her mother. She is as wild as an unbroken filly and has proven hard to tame. Both the staff at the school, and I have struggled to make her a wife who is suitable for one of the Order. Part of the reason for our failure and her continuing resistance is that she enjoys our games. The rougher, the better seems to be what she needs and wants.

"She is full of sass, enjoys being punished no matter the implement or method. She has graced every piece of furniture in the attic and had a smile on her face when taken down. She enjoys pleasuring both men and women and has much experience using her mouth. She has also been conditioned to not only accept, but enjoy being taken anally. Her maidenhead is still intact. Her family is a large one as has been the case with past generations, which means she is apt to produce many children.

"This is a woman who needs a strong hand and a level head. You must be crafty in your punishments, or she will misbehave to earn more of the same. I'll hear your cases now."

"Lady Ellingsworth, please go ahead. You are an equal here." Bryce flashed his most winning smile at the woman through the haze of cigar smoke. She pressed her lips together, knowing Bryce was feigning gallantry, but then proceeded.

"Helena is incorrigible. She is defiant, disrespectful, headstrong, and undisciplined. The woman does not deserve marriage nor does she deserve any title that comes with it. In my home, she would be treated in accordance with her behavior. The chit might as well be a scullery maid during the day and a whore for my men at night. Let her have a taste of games she doesn't enjoy and see how long her sass and cheery disposition last.

"As for being a good brood mare, is that what we want? Do we wish to have her produce more girl children who will be so defiant and cause this much trouble? I think not. Any children she bears will be bastards who take their rightful place as servants. Let her sisters and brother carry on the family name. Helena would not produce heirs the family could be proud of, not even if she were wed to a noble husband. The chance for another heathen is too high. Save the aristocratic title and proper marriage for a girl who will obey. Let this one find only hard work and humiliation as the whore of my household."

The three men and even Anna, who was to serve but never react to those she worked for, were motionless as they regarded Lady Ellingsworth. While it was true, the woman had made her point crystal clear, what she proposed was unthinkable for Helena. Though she was destined to be the wife of a man who lived by the standards of the Blackguard Order, she would never be cast aside for a life of sexual depravity that included serving as a prostitute for any number of men. Her husband would use her sexually and provide tasks that he felt would better her as a wife, but never would she become a common trollop. It was unthinkable.

Nathaniel broke the awkward silence by clearing his throat. "Thank you, Lady Ellingsworth. Lord Brauer, please share your thoughts."

It was customary for those presenting their bids to refrain from commenting on the other's opinions. A debate could be held later if two views, both of which had merit were proposed, but not until after everyone had their say. In either case, Lady Ellingsworth comments would not be up for discussion because of the inappropriate suggestions contained in her bid.

"Though I only saw the girl in question for a few minutes, there's no doubt she's lovely. At my age, her comeliness isn't enough. I feel as if I wasn't informed about her faults and unwanted behavior before I traveled all this way. I've no use for a wife who is combative and downright belligerent. Although she would provide satisfying sexual gratification, her behavior wouldn't be worth the pleasure. I've no doubt I could break the girl. I've been at this for forty odd years, but I simply don't wish to. I will gladly trade fire and passion for obedient and quiet.

"Brisban's daughter Mary has come of age. He sent an invitation to see the girl, but I declined because I received Lord Tarrington's invitation first. In hindsight, I would have saved myself the trip here. Mary is said to be obedient and shy, the type of girl I seek, therefore, I am withdrawing my bid for Helena. She's all yours, Hastings."

Lady Ellingsworth made a sound of indignation, clearly outraged at the ease in which the men had dismissed her bid, but then settled a steely gaze on Lord Brauer, under the delusion her sentiments mattered. "I do not appreciate the way you snub me, Lord Brauer. The decision of where Helena is to go isn't yours. You shouldn't count me out."

"Though I don't want the girl, there are standards that must be adhered to. Your family may have a long history in the Order, but you clearly cannot comprehend the complex and careful way in which we train our wives."

"Well, I never."

"I agree, you have never learned the proper and expected relationship between a man and his wife. You are a woman and an annoying one at that. You are incapable of the finesse it takes to establish and maintain control in relationships such as these."

Lady Ellingsworth stared at Lord Brauer, her mouth gaping like a fish, and Bryce seized the moment. He could see Nathaniel was reaching his breaking point. There was no doubt his friend wished to be back at Claudia's bedside.

"I believe I am to have a chance to own the woman in question as well. Here is my proposal." Bryce knew his theory about how to train women and how to handle one who was wild would make waves. He would never convince those who were steeped in the history of the Order that some women just were not naturally submissive, so he had been careful when planning his speech.

"It's simple really. I have spent time with Helena, have seen her punished and have seen how she reacts to the different forms. She is precocious, strong-willed, mischievous and disobedient, but even so, I like her. Her defiance is harmless, her insolence meant in jest, and her headstrong impertinent behavior just a means to right what she sees as a wrong.

Instead of wishing to douse her fire, I wish to rise to the occasion and match her quick intelligence and sass with a wit of my own. She is a challenge plain and simple, and I am up to that challenge. Some love to tame a wild horse, I thrill in taming, but not breaking this spirited woman.

"Any children we bear will be will have her love for life, but they will also learn at my hand. Our sons will be better able to demand obedience from their women without ripping away their self-respect. Unlike the wild heathens Lady Ellingsworth fears will come from Helena's womb, I see children with bold intelligence and an understanding of how to treat those in need of dominance, as well as how to submit to the men chosen as their husbands.

"Helena is lady from an upstanding genteel family. Her marriage must be to one of equal birth. With Lady Ellingsworth, Helena will never marry and bear children as she should. Misbehavior and a fire that makes it difficult for her to obey are not reasons to take a woman of noble birth and toss her to the servants to be nothing more than a prostitute."

Nathaniel was quick to jump in, leaving little room for Lady Ellingsworth. Bryce had summarized his views of Lady Ellingsworth's proposal. That was not the norm, but having a woman in the game at all wasn't normal.

"I agree Bryce. Helena is in need of taming, not condemnation. Lord Brauer do you have any thoughts?"

"We should not be punished our whole lives for mistakes we make in our youth. The girl is from an aristocratic family. Lord Hastings will make a good match. One that society expects and accepts."

"The girl is wild. If she were gentle and deserving, then I would not have made my proposal. The Order does not need the likes of Helena holding the title of lady."

Nathaniel didn't wish to argue the issue further, but Claudia would never forgive him if Helena were given to Lady Ellingsworth. It was time for them to finish the whole fiasco. All present knew Lady Ellingsworth came to make her bid without truly having a chance to walk away with the prize.

"Ethel, word would get out that Lady Helena has disappeared while in Brighton. Whispers will reach the ears of those in power, and we will attract unwanted attention because we turned a woman of noble birth into a whore and a scullery wench. Lord Hastings is a good match; Helena will go to him."

"You are bias. Lord Hastings has been your friend since you were a boy."

"And now I'm a man and am in a position to decide where Helena goes. Her brother entrusted her to me. Helena will marry Lord Hastings. That is my decision. The matter is now closed."

"You will rue this day Nathaniel. The Order will know of your favoritism. I'm not through yet."

"Perhaps, but we are." Nathaniel tugged on the bell pull, and Richard arrived at once. "Fetch Thomas from the kitchen and have Lady Ellingsworth's carriage made ready. She is leaving."

"Yes Milord."

Lady Ellingsworth stood up, her face red with rage, her mouth hanging open in astonishment but Nathaniel ignored her.

"Lord Brauer, may I offer my hospitality? You came a long way and are leaving without a bride. Please be my guest and enjoy that which my home has to offer in compensation."

"Thank you no, Nathaniel. I have a mind to drop in on Baron Brisban. I plan on telling others in the Order what took place here and that you made the right decision."

"I appreciate your support."

"As do I. I plan on wedding Helena as soon as possible. There is no reason to delay. She's trained to the best of the school's ability."

"Excuse me, Milord. The Lady's carriage awaits as does her man."

"Thank you, Richard. Lady Ellingsworth, I will see you out." Nathaniel took Ethel by the elbow and propelled her through the door and towards her carriage. Truth be told; he would have enjoyed giving her a mighty push, but knew restraint had to be in order.

As soon as Lady Ellingsworth was on her way along with the scowling Thomas, Nathaniel went up the stairs two at a time. Richard would see Lord Brauer out, and he would send Helena downstairs so she and Bryce could get better acquainted. The chastity belt would remain in place, however, until after they wed. There were procedures that had to take place and traditions of the Order they to be abided. Miss Reagan was quite capable of helping Bryce prepare, and the woman needed something to do. He was still of the mind to find her a position somewhere else. Claudia hated her, and therefore Miss Reagan had no place in the manor.

Chapter Thirty-Four

Nathaniel opened the door to his chambers but then paused because he heard... conversation. It wasn't just one voice; it was two. He walked on silent feet to the doorway of the bedroom trying to tell himself not to be disappointed if the voices were those of Millie and Helena. As he peered into the dim room, and his eyes focused, it became apparent that only Helena sat by the bed. The voices he was hearing belonged to Helena and his wife. Claudia was awake.

A board squeaked, giving away his presence. Helena spun around to see who the intruder was, and then gave Nathaniel a weak smile as her eyes widened with a look that urged caution.

"Claudia is awake?" He tried to keep his voice level and managed to refrain from rushing to the bed,

"She woke a few minutes ago."

Nathaniel came forward slowly, well aware that his presence was not cause for celebration in Claudia's mind. He put what he hoped was a soothing smile on his face, and came closer to the bed. His wife was indeed awake. She lay in the center, eyes wide and wary, bed sheet pulled up to her chin like a child who just had a terrifying dream.

"You've nothing to fear from me, Claudia."

"Liar." She whispered the words, but they held a vehemence that was loud and clear. She turned her head away, unwilling to accept Nathaniel's presence in the bedroom.

"I've told her the same thing, but it may take more than words Milord."

"It took more than words to make her hate me." Not a soul in the room could refute the statement, and Claudia chose not to acknowledge it. Her head remained turned so she would not have to set eyes on the man who'd broken her spirit as well as her heart. "And it will take more than words to convince my wife that I mean to change."

At this statement, Claudia did turn to look at Nathaniel, but it was so she could stare at him with incredulous disbelief. "You'll never change. You haven't the decency or the will. Your beloved Order has been tormenting women for too long."

"Leave us."

"I wish for her to stay and you to go. If you mean to change, start by allowing me to choose who I keep company with."

Though her tone rankled the man who was brought up believing women never spoke to men in such a way, and her words were not what he wanted to hear, Nathaniel swallowed his reprimand and objection. His actions now would be the first test of his resolve to treat Claudia better. While he had no intent of allowing her to rule their marriage, doing as she wished in a time like this would show her he did indeed have decency within him.

"I've no wish to upset you, not after I almost lost you. I will return in the morning so we may have breakfast together."

"And if your presence upsets me then?"

"Then we will discuss it. You are my wife. I do not intend to spend the rest of our lives apart. Sleep well Claudia, I shall see you in the morning." He turned and left without trying to kiss her though he very much wanted to. In the face of her near death, he wanted nothing more than to hold her close and never let her go. It wasn't time for that however. If he intended to prove that her feelings mattered, he had to start by showing her he cared about her wishes.

True to his word, Nathaniel stayed away except for when the doctor arrived. As soon as he'd gone, Nathaniel left Claudia in peace, but on the morrow, he entered along with Claudia's breakfast. Though she'd tried to convince Millie to bring the tray earlier, the maid had refused, citing an order from the Master of the house stating breakfast was not to be brought until he was ready to arrive along with it. Though Claudia expressed annoyance, Millie had only brought tea.

"How are you feeling this morning Claudia?" His wife was sitting up in bed; cheeks flushed by her anger over his presence, but Nathaniel welcomed the color no matter what the cause. It replaced the unhealthy pallor of yesterday.

"I was feeling quite well before your arrival."

"Claudia, I told you of my intent. We are husband and wife, and I plan on spending time in your presence."

"The manor is large and I don't need much space. Surely you could grant me the privacy of a few rooms."

"I could, but won't. Besides, you are in my bed, in my chambers. I can hardly avoid these rooms."

"Then I shall ask Millie and Helena to help me take anything of mine back to my room."

"Claudia, this sparring of words will get us nowhere. Would you like to eat breakfast at the table or shall I sit by your bed?"

"I have no appetite."

"I heard Millie telling cook you were famished."

"Your presence turns my stomach."

"That's enough Claudia. While I will pay more consideration to your wishes and discuss the things I wish you to do in the attic room, I will not allow you to become a shrew. If you want me to treat you with decency, then you need to find your manners."

"I knew you wouldn't change."

"Oh, but I have. The behavior you've just displayed would have earned you a very painful trip over my lap. You are lucky I am choosing to be lenient. I won't tolerate your sharp tongue. You will speak in a civilized manner, or I'll remind you that a lady refrains from berating her husband."

"So you will continue to beat me?"

"You will be disciplined when you choose to act in a way that is not befitting my wife. I will listen to your wishes, but that does not mean I will grant them all, nor does it mean I am allowing you to act rude. Now I will ask again, do you wish to have your breakfast in bed or would you prefer the sitting room? If you cannot decide, I will make the choice for you."

"I will come to the table." Claudia sat still, waiting for Nathaniel to move away.

"Shall I carry you?"

"I am able to walk." Still she did not move and neither did Nathaniel whose patience was running thin.

"Claudia I will not allow you to walk to the table without my assistance. The doctor said you might experience dizziness. I've no intention of allowing you to fall."

Knowing she would not win this battle, and it would be childish of her to continue to protest, Claudia flung back the covers and sat on the edge of the bed. Before she could stand, Nathaniel put her slippers on her feet and then held her dressing gown so she could slip into it, doing the things a lady's maid would do without complaint. He was quite serious about not allowing her to fall. His day and night spent in solitude made Nathaniel all too aware of what it would feel like to lose Claudia.

Nathaniel took Claudia's arm and steered her to the table, only letting go after she sat down. Truth be told, if Claudia were asked, she would say she was glad to have Nathaniel's steady hand to help her. Though the laudanum took away the headache that still plagued her, it left her feeling wobbly.

Claudia plucked two sausages from the serving dish and a square of toast, and then busied herself with a cup of tea, doing her best to avoid her husband's eyes.

"Claudia look at me." She graced him with a cold stare.

"I meant every word I said yesterday. I've no wish for you to be so desperate to flee from me. That isn't how I want you to feel about our marriage."

"And yet you just told me I will still receive beatings."

"Spankings. You shall receiving spankings just like you did from your father. A man must rule his home."

"My father never birched me and he never made me stand with my hands tied and my sex upon a painful beam."

"Perhaps if he had birched you I would not be dealing with such an obstinate wife."

"You feel that hurting me will make me behave as you wish but all it makes me do is want to leave here as soon as I can."

"You are not going to leave my home, Claudia."

"Some husbands and wives live apart."

"Don't be foolish."

"All I received from you are words that call me a fool and actions that leave me bruised and in pain. Why can't you see they only make me feel resentful? I am aware a husband rules his home as he sees fit, but shouldn't the husband then care for his wife and see he treats her gently?"

"My anger is what makes me cross. You incite me at every turn. Where is the obedient wife who vowed to obey? I shall care for you Claudia, but so help me I will not allow you to run wild. You will follow the rules I set for you, or I will spank you. I shall leave the birch bundle for the servants but will employ a paddle, hairbrush, or strap if need be."

"I will not allow you to put me in a cage, and I refuse to crawl at your side. That is demeaning and demoralizing. If you force me to act in such a way, I will fight you in any way I can."

"We will use the furniture in the attic room, but it will be for pleasure, not punishment."

"You are a barbaric heathen."

"Stop it Claudia. Look me in the eyes and tell me you found no pleasure on the cross in the room next door or on the chair as Helena licked your puss with the peg in your bum. Things that bring pleasure are not barbaric. A woman must allow her husband sexual relations. Be happy I care about your pleasure as well."

"The things you do are depraved and repulsive."

"Don't be a hypocrite."

"Why can't you understand that the things you do to me would be welcome if only you would treat me with tenderness?"

"You are a passionate wildcat in bed Claudia. I have the scratches on my back as proof."

"I don't need to be reminded of my behavior. Doing so humiliates me. Can't you understand that I was free to be a woman without shame because it was then I felt you cared for me?"

"There is no shame in pleasure whatever the means."

Claudia hung her head, choosing to remain mute. He wasn't listening to her. He was simply too bull headed to understand.

The silence stretched between them like a vast chasm, neither feeling that the other understood. On one side was Claudia wanting Nathaniel to show her respect and tenderness, on the other was Nathaniel wanting Claudia to accept that the pleasure they found in each other's bodies wasn't shameful in the least.

"Claudia, when I do things that arouse you I do so because I wish for you to have pleasure."

"Good girls get good things." She spat the words at him, hating the phrase he used so often. "I am not a horse to train; I am your wife."

"And as my wife I may bed you anytime I so desire."

"It is not the bedding; it is the demeaning way you do so. If you treat me like a harlot and not a treasured wife, then I shall always feel sullied no matter the act. When we consummated our marriage, you wooed me with roses and sweet words. I felt safe in letting go and taking pleasure from all you did because you made me feel cherished."

"Am I to bring you flowers each night before I take you to bed?"

"No."

"What do you want wife?"

To her dismay, Claudia felt tears welling in her eyes. They were the last thing she wanted Nathaniel to witness. "I want Helena. I want you to leave me in peace and send Helena."

"Why can't you care for me as you do her?"

"Helena is the only one who gives love without wanting something in return. She cares for me, truly cares for me, without strings, without expecting me to be a good girl."

"Why is telling you you're a good girl so heinous?"

"I am not a hound. I don't wish to have you scratch my ears and pat me on the head for a job well done."

"Do you honestly feel as if I don't know you are a woman and not a dog?"

Claudia shook her head, full of frustration. Nathaniel just could not comprehend her outrage, and speaking to him of her feeling was not getting them anywhere. Deciding words were not enough; Claudia looked Nathaniel in the eyes; her stare not wavering.

"Do it." She said the words quietly, but the expression of uncertainty on Nathaniel's face had nothing to do with misunderstanding her.

"What?"

"You do it. Strip off every stitch of your clothing, get on your hands and knees, and then crawl to the bed and back. I will let you know I am pleased by calling you a good boy."

"Claudia that is out of the question. Men are not naturally subservient. Crawling is… well it would be improper."

"It is unseemly when you make me crawl, and while I must defer to you in all things, I do not do it because of my disposition. If you truly wish to mend my heart, crawl upon the floor Nathaniel. Crawl on your hands and knee without any clothing to hide your shame, and then tell me I shouldn't feel mortified by doing the same."

Nathaniel saw the tears welling in the eyes of the girl who was once full of fire. Her spirit was waning, being killed by the battle for dignity. Holding her gaze, Nathaniel slipped from the chair onto the floor, taking up a stance on his hands and knees. He did not remove all his clothing; he couldn't go that far, but he did indeed begin to crawl across the floor as Claudia looked on in shock but said nothing to stop him. When Nathaniel returned to the table, he didn't wait for permission to rise, but stood and silently slipped into his chair, still remaining mum.

"How do you feel?"

"Mortified. Ashamed." He said the words quietly. All of the wind had left Nathaniel's pompous sails, and at that moment, he did indeed feel shame. He felt horrified because of his actions. No matter how innocent he thought them, no matter what the Order believed, Nathaniel finally understood. No one could force him to crawl upon the floor again, and no amount of pain or sexual pleasure could ever make him like it. To think otherwise would be idiotic. He knew then that he had grievously wounded Claudia, and if he wished her to remain by his side, he had to change. Never again would he force her to do something so humiliating.

"I'm sorry Claudia. I truly am. I was wrong." The feeling of guilt welling up inside Nathaniel was unfamiliar and most unpleasant.

Claudia watched Nathaniel as a change overtook him. The once confident man was gone. In his place was a man who was facing the consequences of his deeds. It didn't matter that he was taught by his father and the Order. Her husband's shoulders were weighed down by remorse because he knew he should have realized that Claudia was different long before she tried to flee upon an unsaddled horse during a raging storm.

Though he'd done her terrible wrongs, Claudia reached for his hand. It was time to begin rebuilding the trust and caring that had blossomed during their blissful time alone.

"Nathaniel, I just want to be treated as if I am important to you, not as if I am a mere possession. I don't wish to be discarded like an old toy when you've had your fill of me."

"You are important to me. Please don't doubt that. I've been sick with worry. I care for you Claudia and you've made me understand. It may not be easy for me to change, but I swear I will."

"Perhaps we can start by locking the door."

"Your head is wounded."

"So is my heart. Both need tenderness to mend."

Nathaniel thought about Bryce and Helena. He thought about Lady Ellingsworth possibly stirring up some form of trouble. He knew he needed to dismiss Miss Reagan and to set about a change that would show the household that Claudia was indeed Lady Tarrington, and mistress of the manor. All of them were things that had to be done, but none was as important as healing Claudia's heart. He walked to the chamber door and twisted the key in the lock, and then walked back to his bride, holding out his hands. The world would simply have to wait.

Chapter Thirty-Five

Claudia rose to greet Nathaniel as he held out his hands to her. A flush painted her cheeks a dusky rose and a smile lit her face. He wrapped one arm around her and placed the other under her chin to tilt her head back, but it wasn't a kiss he was seeking. He was transfixed by the expression of sheer happiness on Claudia's face and wondered if he had seen her smile before. The fact that he had doubts was sobering. He'd done his best to crush her and force her to comply, but never again. His control would span their marriage to keep Claudia safe, protecting her from the ills of the world, and at the same time making the decisions about what was best for her. Showing her love, giving her respect and treating her cherishing her while holding fast to his position of authority.

"Have I told you that you're beautiful?"

"I believe you spoke of my attributes while pleasuring yourself with my body." Claudia didn't speak the words harshly, yet Nathaniel winced.

"Honest and beautiful."

"Do you wish for me to pretend my time with you has been blissful?"

"No. Ignoring the hurts will not help anything. To pretend I treated well you would only add to my wrongdoings. I held so fast to the ways of the Order that I failed to see you were different."

"Nathaniel, it isn't right to believe I am so different from any other woman. Perhaps some wives do come to embrace their lives, but I honestly think many more simply give up and realize they must do as bid because there is no escape."

"While I understand your view Claudia, dwelling on the way of the Order and the other women married to its members makes no difference in our lives."

"But it does. Believing I am the only one who failed to find my new life tolerable means you still think the training and humiliation each woman receives is acceptable. Do you imagine you are the only man who would find crawling objectionable? And please don't tell me women are naturally submissive. We are submissive to men because we are weaker, and society has forced us to be."

"While I am glad to see the flush upon your pale cheeks and am certain of there will be a time in the near future when you and I will discuss philosophy, I wish to end this discussion for now."

This time when his hand tilted her chin back, he did kiss her. It was a soft, but sensuous one that spoke of a tenderness he had yet to show her in their lovemaking. His lips moved upon hers, and the tip of his tongue took a sampling of her sweetness, but sought no more. It was the complete opposite of the demanding and often punishing kisses that they usually shared, and it left Claudia both surprised and charmed. It wasn't that she hated the forceful kisses she was used to, but Nathaniel's chaste kiss spoke of the change in his demeanor despite the fact he wished for her to be silent.

Just as Claudia began to return his kiss with fervor, Nathaniel broke away and kissed the tip of her nose in yet another small act of affection, all of which Claudia found lovable, but somewhat maddening.

"While I find your tender acts enjoyable, Nathaniel, I don't wish to be treated as if I am made of porcelain."

"You've been ill Claudia."

"I took a bump to the head but am fine now. I do not wish to be treated as if I may break. There is a difference between forced submission and the forceful way you take me when we are in bed. The first will break my heart, but the second is something I have come to crave. Your kisses are sweet, but they aren't what I desire."

"I am well aware of what you need and crave, that however will not be swayed by what I think is best for you. Do not be fooled into thinking I will spare your lovely bottom from a sound spanking if you argue with me. Though you have the right to protest unjust treatment, it would be wise to refrain from attempts to manipulate me."

"I was not trying to manipulate you."

The crestfallen look that cast a shadow on his wife's face convinced Nathaniel she spoke the truth. There were no tears or attempts to use her womanly wiles after he had told her no. The fact that she had spoken honestly and from the heart helped to nourish the newfound respect he had for Claudia.

"I know just the thing to chase away that sadness. Come Claudia, I've something to show you." Nathaniel took her hand and headed towards the door that led to the small room where he'd taken her to play his special games.

"If I'm too fragile for arduous passion then surely I'm too delicate for other games."

"It's not what you think. Just trust me."

Claudia stopped in her tracks and Nathaniel stopped as well when a tug on her hand failed to move her. He turned, and the expression on his wife's face made his heart ache. The fear was back.

"Claudia you've nothing to fear. Why are you so distressed?"

"You told me to trust you, but I don't know if that's possible."

Nathaniel knew better than to try to persuade her. Time, respect, and giving her good cause to have faith in him were the only things that would allow the trust to grow inside her.

"You will struggle to believe me, and I will battle my past and my upbringing to afford you the dignity you deserve. I believe both of us will find what we seek in time. Come now, I promise you will be delighted."

The smile returned to Claudia's face as she followed Nathaniel through the play room and yet another door that concealed steps that led upward. They climbed past the point where the attic should have been, and continued upward. Just as Claudia was about to ask where they were going, they came to the door at the top of the stairs. Nathaniel opened it, then stood aside so she could pass, gesturing with a grand sweep of his arm.

Claudia paused just a few steps in, her mouth open in astonishment as she looked all around at the lush plants that grew everywhere. Some were flowering; some were as tall as the rooftop greenhouse that held them, and many were plants she had never seen. They filled the warm moist air with a heady perfume and beckoned Claudia forward, into their midst. She began down the path that cut through the dense foliage, hands touching a leaf here and there, stopping to smell flowers that were close to the pathway.

As Claudia paused to cup a white flower in both hand to breath in its heady scent, she remembered Nathaniel was behind her. She'd forgotten him in the magic that surrounded her.

"This is lovely. I have been in greenhouses before but never one like this. I can't even see the other side. It's as though I were in the jungle."

"My grandfather had it made for my grandmother. She became ill and painfully crippled as she grew older. The doctors said warmth and sunshine would help her be comfortable. Leaving England for good wasn't an option, so he had this built. It isn't always sunny in here of course, but it has the feeling of some tropical place. There are hidden woodstoves to supply balmy temperature on our cloudy and damp English days. It's a marvelous place, even when it's dreary outside."

"It's magical. He must have loved her." Claudia said the words without thinking about them, but even when she took time to consider them, she knew they had to ring true. What man would build something so grand for his ailing wife if he didn't wish to ease her suffering and see her happy? Though generations of men in the secret Order treating their women so callously, Claudia was being faced with the fact that love could still flourish.

"I imagine he did love her. Perhaps that means there is hope for us."

Claudia remained mum; she wasn't about to commit her heart. Nathaniel's tender words and gallant behavior was still too new. She stepped away to cup another flower, not wishing to meet his eyes until the awkward moment could pass.

"Come, there's more to see." Nathaniel led her down the path, pausing as Claudia stopped to run her fingers through the fronds of the ferns and gasped in astonishment as a beautiful butterfly took flight from a nearby flower and fluttered away. The trail ended in a small clearing carpeted with lush emerald grass. It looked so soft and inviting that Claudia kicked off the slippers she wore and walked about barefoot before falling to her knees with a smile that lit her eyes.

Nathaniel saw the sparkle of delight and smiled as well. His mission was successful. He'd wished to bring happiness into Claudia's life once more, and the trip to the magical greenhouse was working. When Claudia lay on her back and moved her arms up and down like a child making a snow angel so she could run her fingers in the plush grass. Nathaniel almost succumbed to his desire to lay with her and take her in his arms. Though tempted, he had something he wanted her to see.

"Come wife. As much as I'd love to lay beside you and kiss you breathless, there are more wonders to behold here." Claudia rose without complaint and took his offered hand, eager to explore the enchanting greenhouse.

"This place is incredible. I've never seen anything quite like it." They traveled down another path, Claudia gazing up at the tops of the trees and down at the polished stepping stones under her bare toes. When Nathaniel stepped out into the center of the greenhouse, Claudia gasped, and then slowly turned, her head back, eyes looking upward, wide as saucers.

The center of the glass building held a dome made of stained glass. The pattern held hues of every color that glittered like jewels. Claudia clapped her hands then flung her arms wide as she spun around. At that moment, Nathaniel saw the carefree girl his wife had been once upon a time before she arrived in Brighton.

"There are wondrous things around each bend, but this is the most magical. The clouds don't do the stained glass justice, but somehow they manage to be beautiful just the same. I imagine my grandmother spent many days here before her death."

Claudia had stopped spinning and was now taking stock of everything in the center clearing. There was a huge bed heaped with pillows, a table that held a chess set with two chairs, and a small pool edged with moss on the side that met the overhanging trees. There was even a swing hanging from a branch above, and the same lush carpet of grass that had beckoned Claudia's bare toes in the last clearing.

"I don't know if I should jump on the bed and mess up all the pillows, swing up high so I can take wing like the butterflies, or strip and splash into the pool."

"Any or all, we have the whole day, or at least until I see you tiring."

"I feel fine. Please stop worrying."

"I shall be the judge of your health. I believe you do feel well. Your cheeks are nice and rosy, but I'll put a stop to any antics if they turn pale. You've no idea how I felt when you were lying in bed limp and still as a ragdoll. I never want to see you like that again."

"I promise I will lay down in that scrumptious bed the moment I feel tired." The mischievous twinkle in her eye that was impossible to miss as she smiled up at him and Nathaniel thought she was quite the little minx. The presence of her desire after all that had happened elated him and sparked his yearning for her.

"Come push me." Claudia spun and ran to the swing, sitting down and leaning back so far her hair swept the grass beneath her. Nathaniel complied, marveling again, at how her youth was so very apparent when she was carefree and happy.

He complied, standing behind her and bending low to kiss her before putting his hands around her waist and pulling back to set the swing in motion.

"Higher. I want to fly like a bird in the tops of the trees."

"Hold tight." He pushed her as the swing swung back towards him, sending her higher and then higher still with the next swing of momentum.

"I want to touch the jewels in the glass. I shall steal them and wear them as a tiara so all will know I am the queen."

"All will know Claudia. I will set about a change in my household. While I can't crown you queen, I can make you mistress of the manor."

"Wheeeeeeeeeeee!" Her squeal of delight made Nathaniel laugh out loud. Why had he ever thought breaking her will was a thing that would create happiness in his life? He would, of course, still rule their marriage and play the special games, but he knew now he needn't tame her. Crushing her would turn the passionate and spirited woman before him into a somber and browbeaten shell. True she would obey his every command, but it wasn't worth the loss.

"Oh,,, Nathaniel I feel dizzy."

"Hold on, I've got you." He slowed her at once by wrapping her in his strong arm as the swing came within his reach. He walked forward with it, his other hand on one of the ropes, until it was at a standstill. Once he stopped her; Nathaniel went around to the front and gathered her close.

"Come now; let me lay you on the bed."

"It's better now." She pressed her forehead against his chest; eyes closed, breathing in the scent of him and loving the feel of his arms.

"Oh no, you don't. I think your flight was enough excitement."

"I want to go into the pond."

"In a bit. You need to rest now."

"Please." She picked up her head, giving him a look that employed all her womanly wiles as she glanced up at him through a fan of dark lashes.

"Do not think to use your charms with me wife. Though you look enchanting, I will still put you over my knee in a flash for trying to manipulate me. While you have convinced me on the subject of crawling and humiliation, you've gained no ground when it comes to decision making. You are going to rest. The bump to your head is still causing distress."

"I shall not argue as long as you lie with me."

"You're not to argue at all." He gave her a stern look that melted away when the shimmer of tears filled her eyes. "Why this distress? I'm not planning on beating you Claudia, I simply won't take sass when it comes to doing what I feel is best. I'm doing my best to take care of you."

"I don't mean to anger you. This truce between us is so fragile for ire. I fear it will be easily broken, and this day of magic will be the only one you give me."

"Would promising help? I don't imagine it will ease your fears until I've gained your trust." Claudia nuzzled into his chest again and nodded, suddenly feeling shy with this new man who was her husband. "Alright then, I promise this won't be your only day filled with magic. Better?"

"Yes." The smile returned though it wasn't as bright, and the mischievous glint was gone, as was the rosy color in her cheeks. In truth, she looked fatigued.

"Good, now it's time for a nap. The pond will be here when you wake up."

They walked arm and arm to the welcoming bed where he pulled her close for a kiss that was far from chaste. Nathaniel's hands pulled the dressing gown off her shoulders and his lips traveled along her jawline to the shell of her ear where he whispered sweet words.

"You're my darling now, and no harm will come to you, by my hand or another's. I won't lose you Claudia for I don't think I could bear it."

His words held no vows of love, but they were full of emotion all the same, and Claudia felt her own heart respond, and pulled his mouth to hers. It was a kiss that spoke of longing and need as her lips parted and moved over his, but Nathaniel pulled back. His action caused Claudia to try and twist away, but he held her fast.

"It's not for lack of want Claudia. My desire for you hasn't ebbed. I wish for you to rest now. Perhaps later we can swim in the pool, and you can discover the delights of making love in the water. It's nearly as warm as a bath. My grandfather was an ingenious man. Now up you go sweet.'

He lifted her up, the dressing gown falling away, and made quick work of her nightgown. He pulled it up and over her head, leaving her naked as he held her in one arm and tossed back the bedcovers so he could lay her down. Once he did, Nathaniel pulled the sheet up to her chin and stroked her hair.

"Close your eyes."

"Don't go."

"I've no intention of leaving but I'm overdressed for a nap." Nathaniel stripped off his clothes and went to the other side of the bed, climbing in and then gathering Claudia in his arms, spooning her as he kissed her neck and cheek. "Sleep now. Our adventures will continue after you rest."

They lay together under the canopy of glitter jewels made of stained glass, the sweet smell of flowers filling the air. Claudia was sleeping before long, her quiet snores the only noise breaking the silence of the tropical greenhouse.

Nathaniel propped himself up on one elbow so he could watch her sleep for a few minutes, and then lay back down, snuggling up behind Claudia, and slipping and arm around her waist to hold her tight as he drifted off as well.

Chapter Thirty-Six

When she awoke, Claudia was surprised by the feel of Nathaniel's hard warm body pressed against hers. The feeling was both foreign and pleasurable. In the moments as she surfaced from sleep, it had caused confusion, but as memories of the time spent with Nathaniel since her accident came back, the sensation became comforting and desired. Her husband's views seemed to have changed, but only time could tell if the transformation was permanent.

The slight headache and dizziness had fled during her nap, and Claudia now hungered for something else. Even in the times of turmoil, Claudia had never denied how she responded to Nathaniel's practiced touch. His skill as a lover had never been in question; it was his treatment of her that had caused her heart to rebel, and had driven her to flee. The need for escape had left her entirely, and all she desired at that moment was to feel her husband's hands upon her fevered skin, stroking her until she was out of her mind.

The sound of Nathaniel's steady breathing let her know he was asleep; the question now was whether or not to wake him. Leaning in favor of her body's demands, Claudia pushed her bottom back and wiggled. A hitch in her Nathaniel's breath and the feel of his cock stirring against the soft mounds of her bottom let Claudia know the he felt the movement even in sleep. Another wiggle caused the arm around her to tighten and sharp teeth to nip her neck, followed by a kiss.

"Is there something you need my sweet wife?" Claudia nodded and pressed back into Nathaniel's growing erection. "Never be embarrassed to speak of your passion. It is something I desired."

"Then yes Nathaniel. There is something I need. I wish for you to take me now. I want to feel your hands, hard and demanding, and oh so tantalizing."

"A soft touch can bring just as much pleasure. Your head..."

Claudia turned in his arms, eyes flashing. "My head and all the rest of me is fine. You taught me to crave your forceful ways, don't deny me now." Her arm wound around his neck, and she shimmied even closer, loving the feel of his hard member pressed into her soft stomach.

"Hush woman. Do not disparage something you haven't experienced. I will take you as I see fit. Now don't be so brazen. I enjoy your wild and wanton ways, but what pleasure you feel is up to me. You are mine Claudia. No matter the fact that you will receive more respect, the pleasure you find will be my decision alone. Behave, or you will find yourself over my lap. I will not issue that threat again. If you continue to try my patience, your bottom will receive my attentions instead of the sweet place between your legs."

"First you call me your whore and revel in the fact that I respond to each and every thing you do to me, and now I am to act like a nun. Please make up your mind. I have no idea how to please you when what you want changes continuously."

"Claudia, we've had this discussion. The fire that smolders in you is something I cherish, I simply don't wish for you to try and manipulate me."

Nathaniel silenced any further argument by rolling Claudia onto her back, so his body pinned her to the bed as his lips stole any further protests. His kiss was demanding, like his kisses always were, moving upon her mouth, urging her to open her lips so his tongue could sweep over hers. It swirled and danced about in her mouth; bringing forth an answering passion. Nathaniel's arm slipped around her waist as his hips pressed down upon her. The action caused Claudia to open her legs to allow his cock access as the base of his hard shaft met soft thigh, a mere inch away from being nestled between her slick folds.

As his hand tangled in her hair, he pulled back, nipping her lower lips as she gasped.
"We're going to get up and I don't want a word of sass. Your loving isn't being denied you, so there's no reason for the pout I see forming on your lips."

He rolled to the edge of the bed and then rose, gathering Claudia up before her feet could touch the ground. He swung her high, and she let out a shriek that made Nathaniel laugh, her own laughter joining his to break the silence of the greenhouse. Their combined mirth was a sound never heard before in all the days of their marriage. As Nathaniel realized the fact, he vowed that there would be a thousand times for her joyfulness to fill the room from this day forward. Remember how fragile she was, he tightened his hold on her, carrying his precious bundle close to his heart as he walked to the small pool half hidden among the ferns.

When he set her down, Claudia wiggled her toes in the soft moss, and then dared to give him a quick kiss. "Are we bathing Lord Tarrington?"

"We most certainly are Lady Tarrington. The water is warm so you won't catch cold, and we've yet to make love in the water."

Claudia took Nathaniel's hand and dipped her toes, testing the water. It was indeed warm. Not hot like a bath, but certainly warm enough to sink into without a bit of hesitation. She noticed that while surrounded by plants and moss, the actual pool was lined with small tiles the color of silt and rocks. Its creator did an excellent job of creating the illusion of a tropical glade complete with a pond.

She walked forward into the pool, surprised at its depth when she stood in the middle with the water lapping at the underside of her breasts. She turned slowly, taking in the canopy of palm fronds and leaves above her and then splashed her hands forward, sending water droplets flying toward Nathaniel. Claudia did it once more as Nathaniel took her up on her offer to play in the water, and came forward fast, under the pools' surface to wrap her in his arms and pull her down. Claudia let out another playful shriek as she was propelled downward, by strong arms. He guided her body closer to the far edge, so she was sitting upon the floor, water lapping at her ears as her hair floated about her like a fan made of sable silk.

Nathaniel surfaced as he set her down on her bottom, arms still around her, smiling as droplets shimmered on his lashes and dripped from the tip of his nose. "My beautiful water nymph could tempt any man, but she belongs only to me." He lifted her quickly from under the arms and turned her, so she was straddling his waist in the water. "Does my nymph wish to play or is she simply being a tease."

Claudia tightened her legs around his waist, effectively pressing her sex upon his hard shaft that was standing tall and ready. He could feel the slickness of her even in the water and knew she was more than ready. Good things may come to those who wait, but even better things come to those who must dance on the precipice of ecstasy before finding their bliss.

Nathaniel dropped his hands from her hips and cupped the soft cheeks of her bottom as he rocked his hips and jiggled her, so her clit was rubbing his shaft. Claudia cooed as the sensation sent ripples of pleasure through her. The coo turned into a cry of desire as Nathaniel lowered his head and caught one of her nipples in his mouth. He sucked the tender bud, drawing upon it, adding to the sensations coursing through her and centering in her core.

"Nathaniel, please. I've waited so long, please."

He chuckled as he laved her nipple with his tongue before drawing it between his lips and into his mouth one more time; the suckling of it even more intense. Claudia responded by wiggling against his cock, tightening her legs, so her sex pressed harder, the heat of her need blazing his shaft. He was rock hard and as ready as she was, sharing her powerful need.

"You are a wicked girl Claudia. What have you done to me?"

Claudia looked up at him through her lashes, a coy smile upon her face. "It feels as though I've made you ready to fuck me."

"Such dirty language from the wife of the Earl."

Claudia bit her lower lip and began a rhythm of quick little rocks, her hips tilting up and down so his cock felt her slick heat upon the length of it. "It was you who taught me such nasty words husband."

"So I did. It seems as though I've taught you many things, one of which is being a temptress. Are you trying to provoke me into fucking you?"

"I am. Perhaps I need a spanking for being such a strumpet."

"While I'm confident there will be many spankings in your future, you won't be receiving one now. I have other plans for you." That said, Nathaniel lifted Claudia up and moved her, so his cock was at the opening of her sex. He held her there, making her wait, smiling when she pursed her lips and tried to push down onto his shaft.

"Does my sweet wife want something?"

"Nathaniel."

"Tell me Claudia. Tell me what you want." He lowered her, so the head of his cock slipped inside her entrance, stretching her open, making her need him all the more.

"You. I want you. Please Nathaniel. No more teasing."

"Ah, the temptress seems to have fled. It was you who rubbed your clit upon my cock in an effort to tease me. Now you've been left all needy and impatient. Poor thing."

Nathaniel squeezed her bottom cheeks and chuckled as Claudia made a face of irritation. "Ah, ah, ah. No pouting Claudia." He lowered her another inch and kissed her pouting lips before leaving a trail of kisses from her mouth to her ear. "There are ways to take you that will make you crazed with need without being rough. I dare say you are as ready for me to fuck you as you are when I put you on your hands and knees and spank your sweet cunt before fucking you until your legs give out."

"Oh God, Nathaniel."

"Am I wrong Claudia?"

"No. Please."

"Ask me Claudia. Ask me to fuck you soft and sweet."

"Please. I don't care how you take me Nathaniel, as long as you do."

Another inch slipped inside her as Nathaniel suckled on her earlobe and the warm water caressed her sensitive nipples. The truth was; Nathaniel couldn't hold out much longer, but he was determined to take Claudia gently. It would show her their lovemaking didn't have to be hard and nasty, and it would allow him to use the caution he felt was necessary because of her injury.

"That sounded more like a demand than a sweet plea."

"Please Nathaniel. I need you inside me. Please."

Nathaniel moved his hips forward and lowered Claudia onto his cock at the same time, sheathing himself in her scorching depths. He was ready for the ghost of his guilt to retreat, at least for now, and to make sweet love to his wife. Nathaniel lifted Claudia up again, and then brought her down as he squeezed the cheeks of her bottom pushing forward into her deeply and fully yet again, causing them both to cry out in pleasure. She pulled Nathaniel to her and pressed his lips on hers, completing the joining of their bodies.

Slowly, Nathaniel began to move inside her, lifting her up and down as he pressed forward, fitting himself in her just so. Claudia moaned and moved with Nathaniel, matching his rocking rhythm with her own. It was gentle and fluid, small movements that aroused deep pleasure and prolonged the moment. Tongues entwined, arms wrapped lovingly, securely; they gradually built up the passions between them. Moving in the timeless dance, they had choreographed so well.

Tonight it was this simple joining and smooth movements that ignited them. Everything was tender and loving. Hip to hip. Mouth to mouth. Their hearts finally joined. Nathaniel pressed into Claudia over and over as she held him tight with her arms around his neck and her legs entwined around his waist, slowly squeezing her muscles, gripping him in velvet smoothness. He groaned and surged forward even deeper, filling her completely, pulling back, filling her again. His hands left her bottom so one arm could hold her close as the other reached around her shoulders, so his hand was at the back of her head.

Moving slowly, keeping the gentle rhythm, moving his hips to fill her completely, Nathaniel walked to the edge of the pool and lay her down upon the gentle slope. The soft moss cradled her upper body as her bottom lay upon the tiles, still in the warm water. Nathaniel never ceasing the kiss that joined them or the rocking of his hips to enter her fully and then slide back within her depths. His thrusts were fluid and smooth as they clung to each other, Claudia crying out as his lips left hers so he could whisper sweet words in her ear.

"You are my darling wife, and I vow this will be the start of a happy life. Can you feel how much you mean to me? Can you feel my heart?" There were no words of love. It was too soon. The changes in their relationship too new and fragile, but Claudia could indeed feel the sweet emotion that came from his heart. She nodded and nuzzled into his neck, her arms holding tighter, clinging to the man who was her husband, joy filling her at how right it all felt after such heartache.

Their passions and movement finally became faster. Beat to beat, matched perfectly, yet still it was not frenzied. Claudia and Nathaniel rocked and held each other, bodies moving in time until Claudia brought her hips up and cried out, heat exploding through her. Claudia held onto Nathaniel and buried her face in his shoulder. As she came, the pain, anger, and fear of the past rushed out of her heart, as joy and hope replaced it as the pleasure coursed through her. All at once, tears came as a rush of fire surged through Claudia igniting every nerve and emotion in her core. The pain she'd denied in an effort to be strong overcame her, and she clung to Nathaniel like a drowning man to a piece of wood in turbulent seas.

"Claudia, why the tears, are you hurting? Tell me what's wrong." He was new at reading women's emotions and more so at caring how any woman felt. She shook her head, unable to speak, the pain flowing out of her, nearly choking her as the dizzying pleasure rushed through every nerve. She lifted her hips and held him as tight as she could, her body conveying the words she couldn't speak. She would be all right as long as he never let her go.

Nathaniel continued to move within her as her orgasm peaked, then gently kissed her tear stained face as her sobs quieted, and her body ceased to tremble. He rocked his hips against hers until her breath began to quicken again, her body responding to his urgent need as the flames of passion rekindled in her belly. Nathaniel moved deeply, fighting his urgency, into his wife's searing heat as slowly as he could, swearing he would never cause her tears again, telling her he was falling in love. As one orgasm waned, a new one followed at its heels. Nathaniel struggled to control his hunger until he felt the walls of her sex flutter around his cock, signaling that she was ready to come again.

His movements became quicker, still gentle but now more insistent as his need overcame him, and he climaxed within her hot velvet depths. Nathaniel tossed his head back to cry out at the wave of sensation as Claudia rocked her hips and tightened her legs, squeezing him within her body, rocking with the rhythm he'd begun. She crested and then fell over the precipice, intense feelings rushing from her core to every nerve in her body.

Nathaniel's body arched as he called out his pleasure. His cock pulsed inside Claudia, and then he drove his hips forward, surging within her as deeply as he could, his orgasm so intense it stole his breath and made him weak as it ebbed. The strength left him, and he lay on her fully, pinning her beneath him, arms holding her close. They rocked together, Claudia loving the feel of his body pressing down on hers, knowing this was where she belonged. Nathaniel planted sweet kisses upon her face to whisk away the evidence of her tears, vowing as he did that she would shed no more.

Before the last remaining energy left him, and the feeling of satiated passion made his limbs and eyelids heavy, Nathaniel rolled onto his side pulling Claudia with him. He moved them so their bodies lay entirely on the soft moss, knowing that he would soon need to towel Claudia off and take her downstairs so her hair could dry before the fire. That could wait for a few precious minutes. Their hearts were building a bridge now as surely as the joining of their bodies had created a bond. The tender feelings that were taking hold of Nathaniel's heart were new and fragile, and he wanted to embrace Claudia as they flourished inside him, in hopes she was feeling the same.

Chapter Thirty-Seven

It had been two weeks since they had made love for the first time in the magic of the greenhouse. Though they had had sex before then, both Nathaniel and Claudia considered the time spent there the real beginning of their marriage. They had revisited the greenhouse a number of times, and Nathaniel took Claudia to the special room that adjoined his chambers as well. One place they did not visit was the attic. Claudia still associated the chamber with emotional pain and told Nathaniel she refused to go back. Though he'd spanked her a number of times in the past couple of weeks to adjust her attitude, he accepted her decision about the attic.

Life hadn't been all roses as the two struggled to come to terms with each other and the roles expected of them. Nathaniel fought the conditioning he'd received his entire life when it came to his ideals regarding wives and women in general. He also tempered his habitual responses to Claudia's strong-willed nature and sass. In turn, Claudia did her best to abide by her husband's wishes. As long as he was willing to listen to her objections, she was willing to concede without impertinence. Their relationship and their emotions still had thorns that could draw blood, but the fact that they had no desire to shame or hurt the other was what made the turbulent journey worth taking. Sometimes you just had to fight for the good things in life.

On three occasions, Nathaniel had put Claudia over his knee for a well-deserved spanking. These spankings consisted of mostly his hand, which Claudia would say was quite enough, and once her hairbrush. Corner time accompanied these spankings as well much to Claudia's mortification. Though Claudia had protested, arguing that standing in the corner was demeaning, Nathaniel had responded that it was not meant to be pleasant and that it gave her ample time to reflect on her discretion. In hindsight, Claudia gave her husband a sincere apology for her behavior each time he had resorted to spanking her. Some actions were meant to have consequences, and doing something that could have caused bodily harm or being outright nasty and rude were things couldn't be tolerated in a relationship that hoped to blossom into love.

Nathaniel had not set aside all of the games he loved to play, and Claudia was glad of it. There were times though few, when sweet lovemaking was what she wanted. Nathaniel had proven to her that soft and gentle touches could enflame just as well as those that were turbulent and tinted with pain. Claudia was a tempestuous hellion in bed. She responded with wild abandon to all of Nathaniel's touches. He often bound her to limit her movements and force her to retract her claws. Bondage was a thing that inflamed her passion and infuriated her at the same time. It was a double-edged sword that she both hated and loved. The ropes or cuffs took away all her control, but being completely at the mercy of the man she was growing to love and now trusted was also sheer bliss.

At the present time she was riding beside that very man on a gentle mare. They were enjoying an afternoon of fresh air and sunshine, and were now out of sight of the manor and all its inhabitants. Claudia slowed her horse and then turned its head away from the path that would lead them home, and Nathaniel followed without question. He'd learned that sometimes it was easier for Claudia to ask him about things that troubled her when they weren't touching. The intimacy of an embrace could change the nature of the conversation. Not intentionally, but when they held each other, the physical closeness sometimes kept Claudia from opening the deepest of wounds. When one was held within the circle of nurturing arms, the pain of the past was kept far at bay. On the other hand, when they were side by side on their horses, Claudia was more apt to open the cask that held memories of the days when she was first brought to Brighton.

"What's troubling you sweet?"

"The day I was punished you showed me mercy. You whipped me but with restraint. You made sure I could endure instead of causing me suffering."

"Yes."

"Why? By doing so, you risked the wrath of your Order, yet you made certain the pain built slowly, so it wasn't raw and horrid. You barely knew me then, so why?"

"You came here spoiled and full of meanness, but learned not only humility but compassion. You risked a very brutal punishment just to save someone else who you hardly knew. It showed courage. I wanted to leave you with your share of a hero's dignity."

"And Helena?"

"You hated me then. You would have met any attempts to give you affection and ease your suffering with a wall of defiance. You and Helena had a bond. She was the only one in Brighton you trusted. I knew you would accept from her the tenderness I wasn't able to give you."

"You cared for me?" Claudia's face registered doubt, and Nathaniel could fully understand her hesitation to embrace his words.

"I admired you. I won't pretend there were emotions that in truth didn't exist. The honesty between us is too important for me to create pretty lies."

"Nathaniel, your feelings or lack of them then don't matter. That is in our past. I needed to know why you acted that way. I hated everyone and everything around me, and I wanted to hate you too, but what you did made me think of you as a man, not a monster. The idea didn't sit well at first."

"And now?"

"Now I know that you are evil, but deliciously so. I know you are a man who is powerful and can use that power to make me crave wicked things, but who also can love and be the most tender man in the world."

Claudia moved her mare, so she was close to Nathaniel and then leaned in to kiss him. It was a kiss that spoke of her hunger, and held no hint of a woman who wished for a sweet lover. Claudia swept her tongue across Nathaniel's leaving behind the taste of honey, then pulled back and nipped his lip hard enough to draw blood. He jerked back in surprise then reached for her, but Claudia evaded his grasp. She kicked her horse into a canter as she looked back at a very startled Nathaniel, trailing laughter that was music to his ears.

Nathaniel spurred his horse on, racing to catch Claudia, evil plans of torment filling his head. If she wanted to play their rough and wonton games, he would not deny her. The two crested a hill and sped towards the manor, the fire of desire running through their veins as they raced towards the place where all of Nathaniel wicked wantings could come to fruition.

***

Nathaniel led Claudia through the door of the playroom that adjoined his master suite, blindfold like always. It was something he had done the first time he'd brought her there to play his wicked games in order to build a bond of trust between them. The ritual had taken root and turned into something they both enjoyed. For Claudia, it added an element of nervous uncertainty that put her in the right frame of mind for seeking comfort and instructions only from Nathaniel as well as heightening the excitement factor. Nathaniel, on the other hand, loved the way the blindfold made Claudia dependent on him for everything. It showed great assurance that her steps never faltered as he led her about, with only him to lead her safely through the blackness.

They came through the adjoining door, and Claudia paused in response to a quick squeeze upon her shoulder. "Don't move."

"Not even an inch?"

"Imp." He swatted her bottom, which bought him a smile, and the sight of her eyebrows raising over the top of the blindfold, making him laugh. In a bit, they would be ever so serious, but for now, they were two people on the brink of delicious satisfaction, sharing their happy anticipation.

Claudia remained glued to the spot as Nathaniel went about collecting what he would need to carry out his evil plan. Claudia's head turned towards each noise, but she didn't speak, though his preparations took a long time. It wasn't that he needed such a drawn out period to arrange the toys that would suit his needs. It was merely the second act in a series of many that would put Claudia in the proper mindset for what was about to occur. His goal was not to punish. It was to mix exquisite pleasure with the pain and to take Claudia to a place where her mind, body, and heart could soar without fear of ever being set adrift alone or crashing to the ground.

When he finished, Nathaniel stood before his wife and guided her across the room as she wondered just what piece of furniture he would tether her to today. He'd started to move the pieces around in the early days of their play, so she was always unaware until he was binding her to it.

"Turn." She obeyed, and they switched places.

"Good girl now step back." Claudia waited to feel the edge of the long table he bound her to when he was in the mood for agonizingly sweet sensual play, but she found herself with her back against the cross instead.

"Hands up." He fastened leather cuffs that hung from the top piece of the cross around her wrists.

"Spread those legs girl!" The order carried an edge; her sweet husband had fled, replaced by a man who was her master and guide into the realm of dark desires.

"Wider girl! You know what I expect." The sharp tone cracked through the air like a whip and his foot kicked her ankles wide. The game had most assuredly begun.

Claudia complied, parting her legs and backing her heels up until they touched the bottom wood pieces that made up the cross. Nathaniel bound her ankles with practiced fingers and then stepped back to admire what belonged to only him.

"Lovely, but these will never do." In a flash, Claudia felt the cold flat of a steel dagger and knew not to move a muscle. In the back of her mind she knew Nathaniel would never harm her, but blindfolded and tied, with a knife flat against the top of one creamy breast, made assurances flee from her brain.

He tugged on a shoulder strap of her chemise and sliced through the fabric, making it drop on one side to bare her breast. His hand cupped the soft mound as he rubbed the pad of his thumb over the nipple, teasing it to a peak before moving on. Nathaniel repeated the action with the other shoulder strap, breast, and nipple, leaving the chemise bunched at her waist. Nathaniel then made quick work of it, rending it down the middle with a savage jerk.

Claudia's breath caught, and her heart beat faster as the flat of the dagger pressed to her belly, just above the drawstring that held her petticoat together. The hand not holding the knife suddenly gripped her sex through the thin cotton, making her gasp as rough fingers sought entrance to her sex. The material barred the way but did nothing to diminish the pleasure of his hand tight against her opening or trapping her exposed clit under his groping fingers. He toyed with her until he was rewarded with a rush of her juices soaking the cotton fabric, then tsked at her.

"My sweet wife has left and my whore has taken her place. Naughty, naughty Claudia. I might have to punish you."

"Yes please."

"Silence, you do not have permission to speak." It appears you will be learning more than one lesson today." Nathaniel cut the drawstring that held her petticoat up and caught the material before it fell to the ground, then ruined it completely by cutting a strip of the fabric, which he then used to gag her.

"That will quiet that insolent tongue." He stepped back to admire his handiwork, his heart racing and his cock beginning a near painful throb of need as he gazed at Claudia. She was nude, blindfolded, gagged, and bound, all for his pleasure. Gooseflesh broke out on Claudia's arms, and she trembled, almost as if she could feel his eyes running lightly up and down her body.

"Perfect. All wrapped up and ready for my pleasure." Nathaniel came to her then and pressed his hard body to hers, his well-muscled thighs and chest crushing her to the cross. One hand snaked around back to fist in her hair and pull hard, making her neck arch back, as he gave her little nips from the sensitive spot behind her ears all the way down to her navel.

She squeaked behind the gag but showed no other protest. They weren't hers to make. Nathaniel was in control. Two fingers found her exposed clit and toyed with it until it was a firm little nub, just like her nipples. Nathaniel had a reason for wanting it swollen with need. This game would be much more fun if her most sensitive part stood hard and ready, crowning the slit of her sex.

He moved off her and Claudia sighed, wanting more contact. "Patience my sweet whore. There is much to come." That said, Nathaniel picked up the single tail whip he had readied, and stepped into position. He knew Claudia was accustomed to him using the flogger to stimulate her body when he put her on the St. Andrew's Cross, but he had something else in mind today. She had asked him about the day he was made to whip her in public, and why he had gone easy on her. What she didn't know was what he'd done could be taken into a whole other realm of pleasure. That was the lesson she would learn today.

Nathaniel took his place before Claudia and began swing the whip from side to side in a fluid motion. Claudia could hear the sound of it softly swishing in the air, and her senses could pick up its movement, making her skin goosebump again even though the tip wasn't touching her. He step just a hair closer, and the movement of the air displaced by the single tail tickled her nipples, but there was still no contact. Nathaniel moved up and down her body this way, his precision with the whip swinging through the air creating a soft breeze that kissed her with its gentle breath, but did nothing more.

She groaned behind the gag, needing him to stop teasing her, but Nathaniel took his time. He wanted all of her to yearn for the whip before he would grant her its caress. Finally, after many moans, pulling on her bonds and a tossing of her head. Nathaniel moved just a bit closer, so the tip of the whip made contact. He still limited the swing from side to side, the tail brushing her nipples now with just a hint of the fire that would come. Agonizingly slow he progressed over her body, moving back to her nipples with a soft tap, tap, tap, and down her belly to her sex, stimulating in the gentlest of ways.

He moved closer still, and the lashing became harder. Tiny fires were lit as the whip swung side to side over her skin, leaving faint trails of pink in its wake. Claudia cried out when he centered in on her breasts and nipples, and then moaned with a guttural gasp as Nathaniel moved the lash, so the fire was being ignited in her clit and mound. Slowly, ever so slowly he decorated her thighs, inner legs, her pelvis and most assuredly her sex and clit with a pretty pink hue that was now taking on the first tinges of red.

Again Claudia tossed her head, the sensation the whip was causing making her blood boil. The line between pain and pleasure had blurred, and when he changed his strokes to begin flicking all over her body with an overhand swing, Claudia was ready and wanting. Yes, the pain flashed bright as the tip of the whip bit into her sex. Her exposed clit had nowhere to hide, but Claudia also knew she would be able to cum, in fact, was in danger of doing so without much more stimulation if Nathaniel didn't stop.

He, of course, didn't have the slightest notion that stopping was a good idea. Nathaniel chose a different way to bank the fire, keeping it ready to blaze, but not so near boiling that Claudia couldn't maintain control.

"There is to be no pleasure yet Claudia. I would be ever so disappointed in you if you orgasmed before I allowed it."

She shook her head in reply then shot up her eyebrows again when the whip took on a sharper bite. There was no mistaking the lashes for sweet kisses anymore. They bit sharp and hot, leaving crimson marks wherever it touched. Swing after swing, Nathaniel threw the whip with precision, tormenting Claudia's body, making her cry out from deep in her throat when a particularly hard lash snapped upon her nipples or even worse, her clit.

"Aaaaaaaagggggggggggggggggg!"

""Breathe Claudia; let the pain take you away. You feel the pleasure it gives building in your belly. I know you do, I can see how wet your thighs are. The whip is cruel but its torment ever so sweet. Breathe deep and take what I wish to give, and my good girl will find bliss."

Claudia's mind was in a whirl, the darkness, her inability to speak, everything was taken away, all but the insistent fire of the whip cracking upon her tender skin. Over and over, belly, breasts, thighs, and clit it drove her onward into the darkness so there was nothing else in her world, but this man and the fiery sensation he brought.

Tossing her head, Claudia had no sense if she were still up and down. She was floating in the sea of exquisite pain, one, two, three, in succession on her clit, driving her need before its bite. Making her need to orgasm build higher and higher, but denying the final push that would send her over the edge.

A wail from deep inside her, primitive and raw came from behind her gag, and Nathaniel knew she'd had enough. Tossing the whip aside, he stripped off his trousers and went to her nude as the day he was born. Hot flesh pushed her up against the cross, its hard wood trapping her between Nathaniel's body and it. All of the harshest of whip marks singing as he ground his hips and his hard cock against her hips and cleft. Her clit was screaming from pain and need, and the only anchor she had in her dizzying blackness was him. He was her rock, her port in the stormy sea of warring sensations.

Nathaniel ground hard, his cock needing contact as it throbbed, ready to take the woman bound before him. He kissed her lips as he held her face, never minding the strip of cloth serving as a gag. He pinned her bound wrists with his hand to the unyielding wood and made the sound of a low growl in her ear, sending shivers down her spine and molten need running through every inch of her. Bending his knees and moving just right so the head of his cock nudged the folds of her sex apart, he let out a roar pleasure as he straightened his knees and surged upward to thrust his shaft forcefully within her scorching depths.

Claudia let out a muted wail, her engorged and painful clit protesting the harsh contact where the base of Nathaniel's shaft rammed against it. They were joined as one, Claudia utterly helpless as Nathaniel's hands held her wrists over the cuffs of leather, and the bindings at her ankles kept her legs spread wide. She was crushed between her husband and the cross and had to take the forceful fucking he was determined to give her.

"You are mine; you will always be mine." The words rasped into her ear, his lips so close she could feel his hot breath. He bent his knees, pulling out nearly all the way, and then thrust upward again. "You will stand and be fucked because it is my wish to do so." He pulled out again then drove up hard. Claudia's swollen clit again received the harsh contact, and though it was ever so sore, she was at the breaking point, unable to hold back her orgasm much longer.

"I will take what is mine." He ground his hips, and the need to orgasm made her shake her head, her eyes wide, her entire body shaking. He always made her beg permission to cum, but she was gagged, and he wasn't looking her in the eyes. Desperate, Claudia made a muffled wail and tossed her head. Nathaniel pulled the blindfold off, wanting to watch her every expression as he fucked her without mercy. He knew what she needed; he could feel her trembling, could see the desperation when he moved his head to meet her eyes that were full of pleading.

He pulled his cock out nearly all the way, so just the head was inside his wife and then remained motionless, loving the sensation of her inner walls fluttering. She was ever so close. The rush of power he felt when he had he on the brink, so frantic to orgasm, knowing one last thrust would send her spiraling in ecstasy was heady. He controlled all she felt. The only thing in Claudia's world was him, and how he could end her primal need.

"Do you need my cock sweet wife?"

"Aaaggggggggggggghhhhhhhhh." Claudia nodded her head, her fingers bending in an effort to grip the hands pinning her wrists.

"I wouldn't want to add more agony to your clit." Again, a sound arose from deep inside, born of the need that had her half-crazed.

"Shall I fuck you anyhow? Shall I ram your clit over and over so that when you cum it will hurt so very badly? Do you want to cum and cry for me?" He moved just a little, measured thrusts that filled her only half way. She was so close, but it wasn't enough. "Do you want to cum and cry for me?"

Her lips moved around the cloth, the word yes repeated over and over though the sound that came out was far different. Nathaniel paused to feast his eyes on her crazed desperation. Her eyes were open wide, pleading with him, her hair was a mass of sable tangles, her brow damp with sweat. It was this was that he loved to see her. Helpless. Her need overwhelming her, and the only one who could save her was him.

"Cum for me then sweet wife. Cum and cry for me." Nathaniel surged upward and began to fuck Claudia hard and fast. Though her clit was swollen and sore, the rough rubbing of his body against the nub as he thrust his cock deep within her sent her over the edge.

Claudia screamed behind the gag, every inch of her burning, molten pleasure racing upon every nerve in her body along with the pain of his brutal pounding against her clit. Her body was in a tailspin; her senses overloaded. She wailed a long unending sound as she indeed came for Nathaniel. He thrust into her sizzling depths hard and fast, fucking her, taking what was his, pinning her with his body, the force of his own need, taking and taking, the wooden cross creaking under the onslaught of his power.

Scorching pleasure combined with the agony of her tortured clit had Claudia's world turned upside-down. Tears did indeed fall from her eyes, and Nathaniel ran his tongue up her cheek, tasting her pain, savoring it. The power of his thighs thrust his cock in over and over, her slippery molten depths squeezing his cock in an iron grip as she came over and over. There was no beginning or end, nothing but intense mind numbing sensation that left her mad from its fevered heat.

The force of his taking of her, the ferocity and dominance, the male claiming his female filled Nathaniel's senses. He could feel her tumbling over the peak of pleasure as he fucked her relentlessly, could smell the musk of her and taste the salty traces of her tears. His need roared from him as he growled out her name, the hot ball of yearning growing and then exploding in his core. He thrust up and into her as he spilled his seed deep inside Claudia, pumping, crushing her beneath him. Savage sounds came from his lips as his primal beast found satisfaction in the sweltering depths of the woman who was his and his alone.

Nathaniel threw back his head and pumped once, twice, three times more, burying himself to the hilt of his shaft and then holding it there as the last of his orgasm coursed through him. Claudia could feel him spasming, his cock throbbing with the strength of his release until he slumped against her, his lips moving upon the shell of her ear, murmuring nonsensical words. A hand came down and tugged the gag free from her lips and then held Claudia's head as he kissed her over and over. Lips soft and tender upon her eyes, cheek, forehead, and mouth. Kisses sweet and gentle, whispering words of love.

When his senses calmed, and his breathing steadied, Nathaniel bent to unbind Claudia's ankles, leaving a trail of kisses as he did so. One of them lingering on his wife's clit that was indeed red from both the flicks of the whip and his rutting. He swirled his tongue around the bud making her entire body tremble, the nub still too sensitive to take anything more. Once her ankles were free Nathaniel pressed his body to his wife's once more as he unfastened the wrist cuffs, knowing she would slump down upon him when free. Claudia did indeed, her legs having no strength, her body languid, and her eyes heavy.

He caught her and scooped her up into his arms, walking into and through the sitting room and to the bedchamber where he lay her down, their nest of quilts made ready beforehand, the embers of the fire still giving off heat. He gave her small sips of water as he held her up in a sitting position, Claudia barely conscious of the action, Nathaniel careful not to give her too much water too fast. When her thirst was quenched, he crawled in beside Claudia, pulling her into his arms once again, legs wrapping around hers, arms holding tight, moving her head to his chest so she could nuzzle into him.

Words of love were whispered again for he did indeed love her though their path to happiness had been fraught with thorns. Claudia looked up to meet his eyes, whispering that she loved him too. Smiling as she said the words that tumbled easily from her lips. They had battled each other sometimes without mercy to find the love that lay deep inside them both, and now they were content just to be. The world fell away as they cuddled and kissed, saying the words that now felt so right, deeply content and gloriously happy, Claudia knowing she would indeed belong to Nathaniel for the rest of their lives.

Chapter Thirty-Eight

The household had adjusted well to the wave of change, even though it was a thing that was fluid and evolving. There was not always a set rule that was passed down from generation to generation to govern their often more progressive and permissive way of life. Both Nathaniel and Claudia found themselves learning to accept the other's needs. Most things were not set in stone any longer. Claudia did indeed have to accept that Nathaniel ruled at times with an iron fist, but Nathaniel also learned to listen to Claudia's way of thinking before making a final decision. Accepting that his wife's opinion made more sense than his own, while not a bitter pill to swallow, was nevertheless difficult at times. He was and raised under the principles of the Order. Those beliefs had shaped the very core of him. Opening them up for scrutiny didn't come easy.

Miss Reagan had been let go with a good reference and sent to a less enlightened home within their secret circle. Her behavior was normal and desired by those of the Order; therefore, she found a new placement at once. A gathering of the Order of the Blackguard had been brought together to discuss the radical change taking place in the Tarrington manor. The meeting was instigated by Lady Ellingsworth, who still had her sights set on finding a way to expose and therefore penalize those who denied her what she coveted.

Amid much cigar smoke and nude submissive wives, the men had argued about the damage Nathaniel's broadmindedness would have on their stronghold. Only one other man in the Order spoke of wanting to give his wife the respect he felt was her due. The rest shouted that perhaps in private the wives could be coddled and petted if they earned a reward, but to do so on a regular basis was ludicrous. In the home or at dinners and events held by others in the Order, the women should be made to kneel, nude and ready to fuck, suck or serve in any way ordered. The women in question remained mute as the discussion raged on. Even if they wished for a more progressive husband, their desire would never be known.

Nathaniel had refused to take Claudia, knowing even beforehand how things would go. In his eyes, she did not belong nude and on a leash, nor was her tendency to speak her mind something that would have swayed the opinion in their favor. In the end, the vote was cast to allow each man his beliefs, as long as he didn't flaunt the questionable behavior, and their surreptitious Order remained a secret.

Now the wave of change that began a few months ago was quickly becoming the regular way of life for Claudia and Nathaniel. Both business and societal gatherings with the other families of the Order had dwindled to near nil, but that night would be different. Both Helena and Claudia were abuzz with excitement over the small dinner party happening that evening. It wasn't that they didn't go out upon their husband's arms to the occasional opera or dinner in London; it was because they were welcoming a new woman into their unique guild. The man with the courage to vote in favor of Nathaniel and Bryce had recently married, and they were coming to dinner. Charles was attempting to use restraint with the girl who was now his wife, and was having a difficult time of it.

In the parlor, awaiting the arrival of the women, Nathaniel and Bryce listened with sympathy as Charles recited the struggles with his once rock solid principles. Though he knew the more progressive way of thought was what he meant to instill, he had as yet been able to find a balance.

"It isn't that I don't know what I desire for Nettie; it's that I don't know how to use both respect and absolute authority. Before I married, the women I dallied with were as the Order believes they should be. Silent, subservient, and meek. That may work for some, and of course having a woman as a sexual slave has its merits, but I desire some sort of companionship outside the erotic endeavors. I wish for a woman who has a mind and can say more than yes. From what I've heard and gather, your wives are allowed to think for themselves and share opinions. They actually converse with you do they not? You allow them to think independently and give voice to their notions?"

"Absolutely. Claudia and Helena have opinions that often differ from ours. The debate can actually create lively conversation. While there was a risk in the beginning that they would try to overstep our marital authority, firm and consistent discipline does away with that."

"I was under the impression that you spared the rod, so to speak."

"Good heavens no." Nathaniel looked astounded and Bryce, while not contributing his thoughts gave a hearty chuckle in reply. "It's when you allow them to think for themselves that you must keep a tight hold on the reins at all times."

"I don't understand. The morals of the Blackguards are plain though troubling. A wife is nothing but a thing of use. She is to be mute, docile, and subservient in every way. Move when I say move, speak when I allow it, crawl and kiss my feet begging for correction if she displeases me. Never grant her privileges or tenderness unless she performs in a way that merits it. Her body is mine. Nothing belongs to her, not her thoughts, feelings, needs, and most certainly not her wants.

"My father always made it seem as if wives were mere lumps of flesh, only animated when you pull their strings. Growing up, I often thought the Order made women sound akin to dolls or puppets, and yet here you sit and tell me I can rule with authority, punish when needed. How do I then show the respect I feel is due? Where does one draw the line between a puppet and a person with the right to love and respect?"

As Nathaniel and Bryce filled Charles in on what they had learned regarding the handling of their women, the ladies in question were upstairs in Claudia's sitting room. Helena was dabbing the tears from Nettie's face with a cold, wet cloth, trying to minimize the redness while Nettie wailed of her marriage woes.

"But I don't understand. He told me I could tell him my opinions. He said he wished for me to speak, but then he became furious and paddled my bottom in the carriage."

"Come now Nettie, you seem like a bright girl. You must know the difference between voicing your thoughts and telling him his father is a dense and pretentious buffoon." The girl looked at Claudia in the mirror with huge blue eyes and set a pout upon her face. It was a look Claudia suspected won Nettie many battles of will as she was growing up.

"No one in this household will be swayed by your look of misery."

Nettie stood and whirled around, confronting Claudia, hands fisting at her hips, bare red bottom surrounded by white petticoats now reflecting in the mirror. "You're just like them. You don't give a wit about my feelings."

"That isn't true. Of course, I care. We are both excited to welcome you here. Our husbands often receive the disdain of the other Blackguards because of how they choose to treat us. It's wonderful to have another man on their side. What I cannot stomach is your ridiculous attempt to sway my response by sulking. You are a married woman, and it's time to think about someone other than yourself. You can't behave like a spoiled little girl."

Nettie burst into a round of fresh tears and threw herself on the bed.

"Oh honestly! Get up, or I will paddle you myself. It's clear your husband didn't finish as he should." Claudia opened her mouth to say more but Helena held up her hand.

"Nettie, I think what Claudia wants you to do is act as if you care for someone other than yourself." The girl let out another wail of misery and both Claudia and Helena looked heavenward.

"Stop that!" Both women made the demand simultaneously, but it was Helena who continued. "When Claudia was brought to the school here in Brighton, she still put on airs. She was more girl than she was a woman and didn't give a care for anyone but herself. That isn't how anyone should behave, not those who are wealthy, and not our husbands or the men of the Order.

"Claudia learned the hard way that her life was changing, and though she fought against Lord Tarrington's cruel ways, she lost her superior attitude. No one is going to give you a thimbleful of sympathy if you carry on like a spoilt child."

"But Charles spanked me. He spanked me right there in the coach!"

"Rude little girls should be paddled. Ladies, on the other hand, who engage in conversation that states their reasons for disagreeing should not. Your words were a self-indulgent tantrum. You attacked his father. Even if your father in law is a pretentious buffoon, you keep the thought to yourself. If you have a valid reason to disagree with your husband and his father, say so. Do not resort to insults. It's childish."

"She's right. One thing you must do is learn to be gracious. Nathaniel spanks me, but not often. That is because I have learned how and when to state my objections. If I still acted the spoilt girl I was when I arrived, he would have cause to redden my bottom on a regular basis. Tears and tantrums will make him think he was wrong to have beliefs that go against the Order. Intelligence and deference will show Charles you deserve admiration. Do you understand?"

Nettie had pulled herself up and was sitting on the edge of the bed. She nodded and rose so she could wash her face for dinner. After splashing water on her red eyes, she sat in the vanity chair, looking at the two women behind her.

"I am to remain in the corner of the dining room with my bottom bared throughout dinner."

"It will be embarrassing but you will endure." Claudia met Nettie's eyes, looking for honesty and understanding.

"Yes, I suppose I will. It's better than other things I have seen. He allows me clothing and never insist I do my wifely duty in front of others. They are like trained dogs, the other women I mean."

"Don't judge them. You haven't endured what they have, and you are being offered a fate they have not. Do not squander it. Nathaniel and I still struggle. He listens to me, and I obey his decisions. Believe me when I say that isn't an easy task. Easy or not though, my life here with him is far better than I could have ever hoped it would be. Do not make Charles questions his ideals. Behave like a woman who deserves admiration, and he will know he has chosen the right path."

The clock on the mantle struck the dinner hour silencing anything else Claudia had to say. It was time to go downstairs. Claudia knew she'd done all she could at any rate. Nettie had her fate in her hands.

Helena adjusted Nettie's skirts to best display her well-spanked bottom before they left the room, and the girl didn't protest. Perhaps she was beginning to understand that if Charles wished to feed her a bit of humility for dinner, the choice was his. The punishment was fair. Only time would tell if Nettie could silence the spoilt child inside and become the mature lady Charles wanted her to be.

Nathaniel and the others were waiting at the bottom of the staircase to escort their wives into the dining room. Claudia smiled when she caught his eyes, joy filling her heart just to see him there waiting, unspoken words of love passing between them as Claudia jumped off the final step and into his arms, full of joy and quite content to be her Lordship's devoted wife.